A DEVIL FOR O'SHAUGNESSY

Tolbert O'Shaughnessy has been working the short con for years. He's not very good at it—he's a grifter with a conscience, a terrible combination. Just the thought of bilking old ladies out of their life savings sends him to the brandy bottle to ease his pain. But Miriam has a con that's worth too much money to ignore. Her cousin, Joseph Lancaster, has been away for years, and she has found out that he died in England. Their rich grandmother doted on Joseph, but doesn't know about his death. All Tolbert has to do is convince Grandma that he's Joseph returned, quietly smother her in her sleep, and the inheritance will be theirs. A fine plan—if Tolbert can keep his conscience from getting in the way!

THE THREE-WAY SPLIT

Jack Holland needs a break. His girl Sally is pressuring him to get a real job. His freeloading old man, Sam, is coming to visit—indefinitely. He needs dough. While taking some obnoxious tourists out in his boat one afternoon, he has to dive overboard to retrieve a tossed necklace, and discovers an old sunken ship instead. Could there be treasure inside? This could be the chance he's been looking for. But then some killers come to town looking to settle a debt with Sam, and things get complicated. And soon it's a race against time to see who gets the treasure first.

GIL BREWER BIBLIOGRAPHY

Love Me and Die (1951;
  w/Day Keene, published as by
  Day Keene)
Satan is a Woman (1951)
So Rich, So Dead (1951)
13 French Street (1951)
Flight to Darkness (1952)
Hell's Our Destination (1953)
A Killer is Loose (1954)
Some Must Die (1954)
77 Rue Paradis (1954)
The Squeeze (1955)
The Red Scarf (1955)
—And the Girl Screamed (1956)
The Angry Dream (1957;
  reprinted in pb as
  The Girl from Hateville)
The Brat (1957)
Little Tramp (1958)
The Bitch (1958)
Wild (1958)
The Vengeful Virgin (1958)
Sugar (1959)
Wild to Possess (1959)
Angel (1960)
Nude on Thin Ice (1960)
Backwoods Teaser (1960)
The Three-Way Split (1960)
Play it Hard (1960)
Appointment in Hell (1961)
A Taste for Sin (1961)
Memory of Passion (1962)
The Hungry One (1966)
The Tease (1967)
Sin for Me (1967)
It Takes a Thief #1:
  The Devil in Davos (1969)
It Takes a Thief #2:
  Mediterranean Caper (1969)

It Takes a Thief #3:
  Appointment in Cairo (1970)
A Devil for O'Shaugnessy (2008)

As Harry Arvay
Eleven Bullets for Mohammed
  (1975)
Operation Kuwait (1975)
The Piraeus Plot (1975)
Togo Commando (1976)

As Mark Bailey
Mouth Magic (1972)

As Al Conroy
Soldato #3: Strangle Hold! (1973)
Soldato #4: Murder Mission!
  (1973)

As Hal Ellson
Blood on the Ivy (1970)

As Elaine Evans
Shadowland (1970)
A Dark and Deadly Love (1972)
Black Autumn (1973)
Wintershade (1974)

As Luke Morgann
More Than a Handful (1972)
Ladies in Heat (1972)
Gamecock (1972)
Tongue Tricks! (1972)

As Ellery Queen
The Campus Murders (1969)
The Japanese Golden Dozen (1978;
  rewrites by Brewer)

A Devil for O'Shaugnessy
....
The Three-Way Split

TWO MYSTERIES BY
Gil Brewer

STARK
HOUSE

Stark House Press • Eureka California
www.StarkHousePress.com

A DEVIL FOR O'SHAUGNESSY / THE THREE-WAY SPLIT

Published by Stark House Press
2200 O Street
Eureka, CA 95501, USA
griffinskye3@sbcglobal.net
www.starkhousepress.com

Exclusive trade distribution by SCB Distributors, Gardena, CA.

A DEVIL FOR O'SHAUGNESSY
copyright © 2006 by Marvin N. Lee & Mary V. Rhodes

THE THREE-WAY SPLIT
Originally published and copyright © 1960 by Fawcett Publications, Inc.
Copyright © renewed January 4, 1988 by Verlaine Brewer

"Dig That Crazy Corpse" originally published by *Pursuit*, March 1955,
as by "Bailey Morgan"

"Indiscretion" originally published by *Swank*, March 1966

"Love... and Luck" originally published by *Cavalier*, July 1971

All stories reprinted with permission by the Gil Brewer Estate.

"The Novel That Had to Wait" copyright © 2007 by David Laurence Wilson.

"If I Can Tell All of This Straight and True" copyright © 2007 by George Tuttle

ISBN: 1-933586-20-6

Text set in Figural and Dogma. Heads set in Reporter Two.
Cover design and layout by Mark Shepard, shepdesign.home.comcast.net
Proofreading by David Laurence Wilson

*The publishers would like to thank Dorrie and Ted Lee, David Wilson and
George Tuttle for all their help on this project.*
Cover photo from the model collection of Robert A. Maguire.

First Stark House Press Edition: January 2008

0 9 8 7 6 5 4 3 2 1

Contents

The Novel That Had to Wait

BY DAVID LAURENCE WILSON

"She seemed greatly interested in art, but had the idea people would kill art. They would kill the artist and he didn't have a chance.... 'I don't like persons like you,' she said. 'Because I saw it happen to father. All the fine things he did went into the furnace. They heated the front parlor.'"
...From *Flight To Darkness*, by Gil Brewer, 1952

It sat on the table, 296 pages of unfinished business. Prepositions and verbs. A thriller. *A Devil For O'Shaugnessey* should have been printed thirty-five years ago, when it might have done its author some good.

Gil Brewer wrote crime stories with con-men heroes and the easily deceived. His loners inhabit the shady side of the street, the crossroads where the rich and the poor meet. He didn't write mysteries, he wrote crime adventure. He was a deft and calculating writer and sometimes he laughed while he worked on his pages.

Brewer liked to drop his readers in the deep end, to bring the water to a boil while his characters kissed, tense and rough. This was the stuff he could write and sell. He was the right guy in the right place at the right time.

He had a meteoric rise and a too familiar fall. His was a career that began with a thoughtful reflection, the first line in his first book, a classic: "It would have been far simpler for her just to kill me. Sometimes I wished she had."

Brewer was a second generation pulp writer who was younger and hipper than most of his paperback contemporaries. There was a twisted sense of both freedom and fatalism in his stories — and they oozed sex. He didn't have any big causes or a solution he wanted to push. He didn't have much time for religion. His subject was the human condition, sweaty and lustful. And don't forget the greed!

No one wrote more intensely of male and female relationships: "All right. I loved her," he wrote. "If you've never felt the way I felt, O.K. It's like nothing in the world. If you've never had it like that, then you haven't. When she looked at me, it was like hitting me over the head with a baseball bat.

Like an ice cube on a hot stove. When we touched I felt as if my fingernails were going to curl up and drop off. All right. If you don't know what I mean, then you're lucky, or unlucky. I don't know. But that's how it was with me."

That was Brewer in 1951, poetic as hell. That was the boiling point in books like *The Brat* (1957), *Little Tramp* (1958), *Nude on Thin Ice* (1960) and *The Tease* (1967).

Brewer was a big fan of jazz: Bix Beiderbecke, Louis Armstrong and Eddie Condon. He adopted the spirit and the vernacular of the beat generation. His was a different kind of crime-writing. Sometimes he wrote directly to the reader, dividing his words between action and explanation. The references in his books included Margaret Keene, Ernest Hemingway, Jackson Pollack and Edgar Varese. The word "groovy" didn't pop up in many crime stories in 1955 but it did in Brewer's story "Dig That Crazy Corpse", a rare detour into the "screwball" private eye category, reprinted in this volume.

It was a productive career but also a short one. He never promoted the books. He sold the rights for a couple films but he never came to the west coast. He never hit it big in Hollywood.

Between 1951 and 1959 he published 20 novels, all of them suspenseful noir thrillers, most of them first person and most of them set along the cities and barrier islands of Florida's gulf coast: St. Petersburg, Tampa, Y'Bor City, Pass-a-Grille and Indian Rocks Beach.

Between 1960 and 1967 Brewer published another eleven novels. After that it was all ambitious but unsold or unfinished projects and compromises, work for hire under a handful of different names. He was a hired gun with a typewriter.

He knew no other trade or lifestyle. In the beginning it had meant living cheaply. In his later years it meant that he took on a steady stream of assignments procured by the Scott Meredith Literary Agency. He was versatile but unsatisfied. He wrote three espionage novels based on the ABC television series, *It Takes a Thief*, starring Robert Wagner. He wrote erotic novels and gothics. In an age of protests and conflict, he wrote a first person college story, a trick that few of his contemporaries could pull off convincingly.

The last of his published efforts required more copy editing than original writing. In the mid seventies he rewrote the stories of an Israeli soldier and twelve Japanese mystery stories for Ellery Queen's *Japanese Golden Dozen* (1978).

His short stories, little tales of sex and betrayal, still appeared in the crime fiction digests, and sometimes in the second tier of men's magazines, like *Swank* and *Male*. Two of these short stories from the nineteen-sixties, "Indiscretion" and "Love... And Luck", are also included in this collection. But no new novels. It appeared that Brewer was through with the longer pieces of work.

Though the most productive period of Brewer's career was over, it didn't mean he had stopped writing longer works, descendants of the best-selling noir masterworks which had once been so routine for him. The novels he was writing weren't being published. Among them was *A Devil For O'Shaugnessey.*

The fate of unpublished novels is seldom a happy one. Unpublished novels tend to have short, unhappy lives. Novels are designed for a moment that passes with alarming speed. Style ages and paper crumbles.

If you knew any of the writers of that last century — the paper-based generation — you'd probably also hear stories of the books that got away — or the books that were salvaged.

W.R. Burnett (*Little Caesar*, 1929) had twenty-five copies of a manuscript that burned in the Bel Air fire of 1961. Niven Busch (*Duel In The Sun*, 1944) had a case stolen from his car and inside it was his only attempt at a mystery novel.

Harry Whittington threw out a legendary cache of stories — and his daughter saved his last novel, drying out pages after a plumbing disaster.

In the early nineteen twenties Harold H. Armstrong's short stories appeared in *Smart Set* magazine. His three novels were published by Knopf and Harper's. According to *Time* magazine, his 1923 novel, *The Red Blood*, was a "sound, capable novel".

Twenty-five years ago I awoke to find at least a dozen unexpected manuscripts littering my yard, multiple drafts and copies, corrections and rejection slips, the production of a lifetime. It was the essence of Harold H. Armstrong, piled into the gray plastic trash containers in my front yard, short stories and novels on ruffled, crinkling paper. To look at his journals and pages you had to brush away eucalyptus leaves.

While Armstrong sat and baked in the Southern California sun, Brewer's books, his magazines and manuscripts were being delivered to a concrete pyramid in Wyoming. All those old pulp manuscripts were being treated with the kind of respect due mummies.

After Brewer's death in 1983 his stepson Marvin Lee Jr. cleared out his apartment. He threw out the gin bottles and the jazz records that were scratched beyond listening. He boxed up the manuscripts and they were sent to the University of Wyoming's American Heritage Center, an archive which was aggressively recruiting from western writers and their estates. Lee kept Brewer's typewriter, a few of his jazz lps, and a ragged, one-sheet poster for THE LURE OF THE SWAMP, adapted from Brewer's novel *Hell's Our Destination* (1953).

To look at Brewer's notes in the archive you had to wear tight white gloves. Then you could read the only copy of the novel *The House of the Potato*, unpublished, begun in 1946, spattered with what looked like the stain of red wine, the same manuscript that was sitting on Brewer's desk the day he died.

So what is it that makes for value and longtime staying power? What would it have meant if Brewer had received the kinds of reviews that Harold Armstrong received thirty years earlier? If he could have worked on the big novels that eluded him? Unfortunately, it might have meant a lot more than the white glove treatment his manuscripts received after his death.

Without the gloves, who knows...? It is an unknown but dismal future after a page leaves a typewriter. It's a rough world out there for pieces of paper. Things — especially things made of paper, don't last forever, even under the best of times and conditions.

I took those Harold Armstrong manuscripts to my parents' house, put them in the bookcase of my old room. At least I'd saved them from a landfill.... Years later I opened one of the boxes and less than half of the novel remained. No page was intact.... Generations of silverfish had feasted.

Maybe some things just aren't meant to survive.

The only way the words and the stories really stay alive is to keep them in print. For a long time Brewer was so far out that you couldn't buy his books. There was a flicker in the 'eighties. He was almost one of the writers who was reprinted by Black Lizard. Almost. The manuscripts waited. The pyramid remained above the snowline in Laramie, Wyoming.

The curriculum vitae of Brewer's life is known, as are some of the legends. He was born in 1922, wrote a story a day in high school, and he began writing professionally in St. Petersburg after returning from World War II. When he refused to seek a "real" job his mother asked him to leave his parents' home. His next stop was a screened-in porch, for $5 a week, where he worked on his serious novels.

In 1951 he broke into print with two sales at *Detective Tales*, one of the best paying pulp magazines. "With This Gun" was rewritten as his first novel, *Satan Is A Woman*, (1951). Joe Shaw, the legendary editor of *Black Mask* magazine, became his agent.

Gil lived just a few miles from Harry Whittington, who would ultimately become known as Florida's "King of the Paperbacks". Harry's daughter Harriet recalled her introduction to Brewer, seven years younger than her father. She saw a man walking down the street, wearing shabby clothes, his pants ripped at the knees. He asked her if she could tell him where Harry Whittington lived, and she walked him home.

"From that first moment, when he showed up at my home, he had one obsession," Harry Whittington wrote. "He wanted to write fiction. He was convinced of his great natural talent and he refused to take any kind of job, even to keep himself in cigarettes, until that great day of editorial acceptance came.

"He came to visit me because I'd sold some short stories and a couple of novels. Plainly, he wasn't very impressed by my achievements, but until we met Day Keene, Talmage Powell and other published writers, I was the one role model he had, though he would have insisted he learned nothing from me. About this, he was probably right.

"But Gil and I sat up until midnight and after, night after night, and talked writing and plotting. I had a government job, but he always slept past noon."

Brewer became a frequent guest at the Whittington household. He would tease Harriet, telling her that she spent too much time looking at herself in the mirror. During a subsequent visit he brought black fabric, and he hung it over the mirrors in the house.

Whittington's son Howard called Brewer an "Ernie Kovacs" type, with clever, sarcastic wisecracks. They had something in common. They both played the trumpet. Brewer urged Howard to loosen up, to "feel" the music. On a fishing trip with Whittington and Day Keene, Gil suggested that his companions throw the boy overboard.

Keene and Whittington were selling short novels to the paperback publishers. Keene gave Brewer one of his short stories with the instructions to extend it to novel length. The result was *So Dead My Love*, published as a Day Keene novel.

In 1950 Brewer married Verlaine Lee, an artist and musician who would later sell her own stories to the true confession magazines. Now he had a family, including Verlaine's daughter Mary Verlaine and her son, Marvin.

Both of the teenagers would assist Gil and enrich his rather reclusive life during the next thirty years. Marvin lived with the couple during intervals between 1950 and 1954, when Brewer was writing the books that remain the bulk of his legacy today: When a new novel came out Verlaine would read it before passing it on to her son. Ultimately those were among the books that winded up at the University of Wyoming.

Lee described Gil's working process: "If he had an idea, and it couldn't wait, he might work steadily for 24 or 36 hours. Other times, when things weren't clicking, he might go three weeks and only get a few pages out.

"Most of his work started around noon or one o'clock and he would work into the night, through the night. When he was working everybody had to be quiet."

Brewer had books all over the place. There are not many pictures of him, and no film or videotape. It's even harder to find a picture of him without books in the background, everything from David Goodis' *Nightfall* (1947) to *The Electric Kool-Aid Acid Test* (1968) by Tom Wolfe. Brewer hired a carpenter to cover all his walls with bookcases. He worked in cramped quarters, like the driver in a race car.

He always seemed to have trouble sleeping. At two a.m. he'd be reading or he'd be sitting on his sofa, drinking and playing the trumpet. Sometimes he'd begin making phone calls. If you were a friend you might get a trumpet recital.

Later he had his whole home wired for sound. He'd put on a four to five hour reel to reel tape of soothing, relaxing jazz and he'd go to work. There was a sign above his typewriter: "Work, You Bastard!"

What class would you place him in? What was his station in society? For the most part, he didn't seem to care. He was poor, often enough. In the early days he'd make the rounds of the ash trays, after a party, and he'd collect the cigarette butts that looked promising. He bought a 1939 Convertible without an engine, hoping to turn it into a hot rode. The car sat,... and waited.

The legends are about what he did when he wasn't poor, when he had a bankroll. He'd buy a Porsche or he'd invite a barroom of drinkers to Cuba and leave them stranded on the island. He'd bring a case of beer to a party and he wouldn't leave until the last can was empty.

Brewer's social circle was small, though he loved music, he loved to write and to talk about writing. Sometimes Al James would visit. James was Day Keene's son, who wrote magazine nonfiction and novels like *Born For Sin* (1960) and *Captive Wanton* (1962).

In the late sixties Brewer met and befriended Richard Hill, a young writer who also played the saxophone. Depending upon your perspective, Hill was a confidante or a hanger-on during Jack Kerouac's declining years in St. Petersburg. Brewer introduced him to Alcoholics Anonymous.

Brewer wanted to stay in the background but he made an exception for his friend, in a 1969 story in the *Tallahassee Floridian*. "There's an element of crime and sex in every piece of writing, from Mother Goose to the Bible," he told Hill. "There's also the necessity to entertain the reader. Books with messages leave me cold, if the writer doesn't understand that he can deliver his message as well while he's entertaining." Hill's first novel, *Ghost Story* (1971), was dedicated to Gil and Verlaine.

In 1978 Brewer sounded cordial and enthusiastic when he responded to a four year old inquiry from *Contemporary Authors*. It had been addressed to Elaine Evans, the name he used for four gothic novels. Under the description of his work in progress he offered the titles of eight novels, including *Sleep With Satan* and *The Man Who Collected Dolls*. He asked that his home address be omitted from his biographical entry.

Thirteen years later the pop culture essayist Mike Barson tracked Brewer down for an interview in *Paperback Quarterly*. Adversity had not made the process of publicity any more comfortable for the fifty-eight year old writer. The interview was published as three pages, just six hundred words, including these: "Critics. Blast. They didn't read the books. They had some silly preconceived notion as to what they were and they demolished many a fine author because of their gross carelessness. They missed out on a lot of fine writing by behaving in such a negative fashion."

Finally it all washed together, years measured by vacations with the bottle. There was a big accident and chronic pain. He felt he was losing his ambition and his confidence. A lifestyle had caught up with him.

It was slow death by an affable poison, his companion for nearly forty years. Sometimes the liquor seemed like a character in his stories. Sometimes it was a vital part of the plot.

He died in 1983 at the age of sixty, a splendid writer who had lost years to alcoholism.

"I didn't say anything. Outside I could hear the surf piling up on the beach. It was a lazy surf. Somewhere out there a dead man sat on the bottom of the Gulf and pondered."   *... Satan Is A Woman*

After Verlaine Brewer's death in 1992 a cardboard box showed up at her son's home. Inside was a manuscript on onionskin paper, *A Devil For O'Shaugnessey*. The novel had been sent to the Meredith Agency but there was no record that it had ever been submitted to publishers.

There seemed to be little interest and no immediate value in his stepfather's career so Lee put the box on a shelf in his closet. The manuscript remained on the shelf until 2006, after Brewer's novels *Wild To Possess* (1959) and *A Taste For Sin* (1961) were reprinted by Stark House.

Lee decided to send the *O'Shaugnessey* manuscript to Stark House, to see if the publisher had any interest in the rejected novel. As he photocopied the pages at a St. Petersburg Office Depot, he discovered that there was another novel, *The Erotics*, sharing the box with *O'Shaugnessey.*

A Devil For O'Shaugnessey did not spring up as an isolated, unique product from Brewer's imagination. It wasn't a new direction but an old trail done well. In many ways it is still a reflection of *Satan Is A Woman* and all the novels that followed. The titles are very nearly synonyms. There always seemed to be the same sort of characters, like a big extended family with bad breaks and bad choices. Imagine the wedding ceremonies.

O'Shaugnessey is denser, by the word, the writing exaggerated. But in spirit it is lighter, not quite as grim, with a hint of supernatural and the absurd.

One of the responsibilities of a publisher should be to know when a book was written. This time it's tough. There's no serial number with *O'Shaugnessey,* no cover letter. No date, only guesses. The best clue is in chapter two, when O'Shaugnessey purchases a used 1968 car. That would set the date for the manuscript in 1970 or 1971.

Another clue is Richard Hill's 1971 *Ghost Story*, the tale of a rootless man who assumes another fellow's identity in an old Gulf Coast mansion. Sound familiar? It should, after you've finished *A Devil For O'Shaugnessey*.

Like jazz musicians, both Brewer and Hill seem to have been soloing from the same melodic structure. Two interpretations of the same song and two grinning writers, both of them improvising on their keyboards. The similarities between the two novels may be the best way to date *A Devil For O'Shaunessey*. My guess is that they both could have been published in 1971.

O'Shaugnessey's companion in this volume, *The Three-Way Split* (1960), was Brewer's twenty-fourth novel, and really, you can't do better. This is essential Brewer suspense, lean and direct, with a first person narrator whose frustrated, morally challenged voice has become familiar: "It was like being in a room with no windows or doors. You kept running against the walls, slamming into them. You knew there was no way out. So you rammed, and rammed, smashing against those walls. You'd feel around and try again. Something had to give — either one of the walls, or you."

This is another crime novel, but it's actually in its adventure elements that the story is at its most suspenseful, and when the first-person narrator, that familiar voice, is closest to his own death.

What made Brewer unique was not the stories he told but the way he wrote them. It was important to him to be the very best writer he could be. He read Tolstoy, Proust, Turgenev and Stephen Crane. He yearned to break out of the category of pulp suspense.

Brewer claimed that he had never been satisfied with his novels. In 1977 he wrote in his journal: "I'm 54 and I haven't even started. Drank too much and was always in a rush to make enough $ to get by. Now I'd like to try my hand at writing well.... If I was well I might stand a chance."

Gil Brewer has been gone almost twenty-five years but his passion remains. Sometimes you can still see traces of the fifties and sixties on those Gulf Coast towns, where Brewer wrote and played his jazz for Death. There are still beaches on the Gulf Coast of Florida. There's still a big Bay and sunsets that make you feel sad and glorious.

What you have in your hands right now is just one step away from Brewer's original manuscript, no compromises or updating, an entertaining read that spent thirty years in exile. It's a pleasure I'm keen to share.

Turn on the jazz, the "cool blue" jazz.

Downieville, CA
September, 2007

A Devil for O'Shaugnessy

by Gil Brewer

•••ONE

Caveat, emptor. This was the definition of my lovely con, only at the moment there was little to sell; and, as a certain infamous writer-wag might have put it, I felt lackadaisical as a side-hill phimph.

The business in Denver had turned out well, with a buttery stop-off in Atlanta that netted $5,000. This added to what I already possessed—may that sweet little lady find a house *somewhere*—summed out as a pleasant $12,000, with some odd change. I had this much even though I had purchased the bronze Porsche, was living in a succulent enough dwelling on the Gulf Coast of Florida, and had learned to play rather more than footsie with Miriam Kindott, of the acceptable Kindotts, who had a grandmother.

I had not met the grandmother.

They were not socially minded.

I was located on Indian-Rocks Beach, thus situated in a central fortress where I could, if inwardly urged, easily bombard Tampa, St. Pete, Clearwater, or, across the Sunshine Skyway, Sarasota, and points between. Also, this was a luscious September; tourists swimming down Route 19, posing as marks just about like 12 lb snook. Some even had their mouths open for the hook; as finned up and ready.

I had been here a touch over one month.

$12,000.00 was indigestion and the only antidote was the Big Con, as they say. But I had some thinking to do.

Wheeling along Gulf Boulevard behind a gleaming fat black Lincoln Continental with a white cap and cigar at the wheel, I prodded the last of the steak from between recalcitrant teeth, and tossed the toothpick out the window. I was on Redington Shores now, just passing 160th Street. The two double brandies definitely needed immediate topping. Speeding up, I passed the Lincoln, smiled at the white cap, and drifted onward. Without the brandy and the wine, the occasional beer, even, I would have been emotionally sick. As it was, I was only intellectually sick. This was a kindness, of course. I could dwell on my problems from a height, so to speak. Doctors had told me this.

I was loot minded. Still, there was anticipation over meeting Miriam at two o'clock. Sex, in its place, or even out of its place, was always conducive to a kind of urgent eagerness. But it was one o'clock now, and lunch was digesting, and I knew very well that the anxious sensation was very present in my chest. I should have known better than to have had only two doubles.

Turning in at *La Playa Cocktail Lounge,* I parked the car, and left it without even securely closing the door. After drinking half the double brandy, I looked around the dim room, and stared at the desolate looking dais with the lonely drum set, the piano, the battered chairs that would gleam later tonight. The barman was doing something with ice cubes.

I finished the brandy, rapped the glass, and soon sipped at a fresh one.

Some of the feeling vanished. I took a deep breath. Perhaps it was my heart. At thirty-one, it could be anything.

I mused on the girl...

Miriam was peculiar. She did not want me to be *seen* anywhere. One learns to spot hidden meanings. It was part of my trade. Just because I had been working the short con with satisfaction for a long time, did not mean I was dim.

"But, Tolbert, I don't want to go anywhere. Let's just stay here like this. We can send out—"

Or:

"Where d'you go when I'm not with you?"

And:

"Tell you what, darling. I'll cook up everything in the evening, then we won't have to run out at all."

We ate in shanties on scruffy bayous. *Jack's Fish Foods. The Crystal Palace Lobster Room.* Or just plain *Sea Food.* Even hamburger joints were out. She would regard them coolly as we rode past, and sometimes glance at me with a nervous smile. I took it all as it came, and said nothing. But it did occur to me that something was up. I had no idea what it was, and I waited an answer patiently.

Now the lounge was empty. This was a pleasant factor.

I watched my emotions from afar. I checked my pulse. It was my heart, of course. It felt rather rapid. Tachycardia, they called it. But then I had always had a speedy pulse.

My glass was empty and it was one-twenty.

...Modus Operandi, of Tolbert O'Shaugnessy.

Actually, this reticent attitude of Miriam's about my being seen anywhere hadn't developed until some three weeks ago. I had met her the first night in the new place, *Food & Booze Till Two—Come as You Are,* where I'd had a particularly spectacular rush for liquidity, what with my chest acting up. We hit it off from three stools apart, and roamed the beaches that night together. At the time, and for some days thereafter, she did not care where I went, or who saw me.

But now that had all changed.

I sipped the fresh one. It is said that there are now six born every minute. In Barnum's day it was only one.

My mind wandered with my mood, but never outdistanced the hollow feeling in my chest, even though at this point it was purely intellectual. I was satisfied. I would not even finish my drink.

"You have a nice tie," I told the barman, "I like that red design."

"Pueblo village," he said.

So he was in New Mexico. I was still in Florida.

I went out and sat in the Porsche. I stared at the tachometer, then at my hands, gripping the wheel. Indianapolis. But don't be reckless, O'Shaughnessy, you have to meet the plum in a few minutes, and you should play at least par for the course, even though it turns out to be miniature golf.

It wouldn't be anything small, though—there was nothing middling about Miriam. And this, too, in its way, had me puzzled.

I wore a bloodstone on my left pinky. The setting was silver. A bloodstone was supposed to be good for the heart, and I was a Scorpio, too, only it would not work... I mean, sometimes I was the entire Zodiac.

I waited another ten minutes, then drove to our place of assignation, in front of the *First Federal Savings & Loan*. Actually, it was the stepping-off point, as it were.

Then I saw her coming.

She ran through the sunlight. For a moment I thought she had an aura, but I immediately put it down to the brandy. The long pale blonde hair pleased me—the pale oval face with enormous brown eyes, the mouth, teeth, breasts, hips, arms and legs. She wore short flowery green tucked in at the waist, and was swinging an alligator purse.

"Hi."

She slammed the door.

"Can't you say anything?"

"I'm saving it, Miriam, I have a great deal to say, rather to ask. But you'll have to wait till we get there."

I had come to a decision, I had to know what was going on.

"So you'll be mystifying?"

I did not reply. We drove for a time in heavy silence. She was thinking, I knew. Her tone had been just the least bit querulous, and she had lost a trace of her normal cool. Yes. Miriam was a cool one. Matters deep and dark progressed in that pretty blonde head, and this was troublesome. Sometimes you thought it might be completely sex she was thinking about. There was that faint strain of concentration. You see it to a considerably stronger degree in the retarded; they stare at you with an intense frown, mouths quite grim.

But Miriam Kindott was not retarded. If anything, she was too bright. She did not reveal this ostentatiously, but after about an hour you knew full well that she was some sort of computer, with lots of tiny lights flicking on and off, wheels spinning.

I glanced at her crossed legs, her silken round knee. This did not pay. Slim, lovely, it was only when she was quite close that her full impact registered. It was not a glancing blow, either. My libido dug its feet in the sand and growled throatily. She exuded a personification of promise, and she did this merely by being present, without movement, without word.

There was this about her, too; she would not give the edge to you. The instant she realized something was stirring, she grabbed the edge. She would not ask questions, as a normal person might. If you were on the offensive, she immediately recognized it, and subtly put you in defense of your position, without even knowing what your position was. She was very subtle; a delicate nuance that left you groping.

I patted her knee. See what I mean?

She put her hand over mine and held it on her knee. I turned the Porsche in the drive at my place on Indian Rocks, released my hand, and switched off the ignition.

She smiled at me, but said nothing. She possessed the patience of a Hindu.

And all the time her eyes were eager. Those big brown liquid eyes that somehow reminded you of Keane.

Still not speaking, we walked to the door of the house.

The place was two and a half stories, but with only one central room. It was surrounded by tall, thin, bent palms, Washingtonians, enormous queen sagos, with a hedge of oleander. I was frightened of the oleander because I had read somewhere that if they burned, the smoke was toxic and could kill you.

We went inside.

I could not stand it this way. I drew her clumsily into my arms and we kissed. Now she altered; she did not hold back, and our increased breathing mingled. Her lips were the tenderest, and she was very strong in the hips, with urgent rhythm.

The house had been an artist's studio. Gray rafters shadowed high overhead. The monk's cloth draperies were mostly drawn across the enormous window on the north side. This window was nearly two stories high.

"Undress," I said.

There was a sly look to her eyes now; sinful secrets that she would reveal lewdly, one by one.

By the time we reached the broad studio couch which was my bed, she was nude, and I was down to my shorts, and boots.

"You look so funny!" she said

"I'll have you know—"

Then she was on the bed with her knees up. Her breasts always startled me. They were huge, but you never realized this until she was nude. She was extremely pale, which always made me think of the French. I did not know why this was.

"You are now straddling the generation gap," I told her.

"That's no gap, darling,"

There was much groping and lots of smoothness, with her head thrown back, eyes tightly clenched, and we peaked twice, then lingered on a slow grade, after which she exclaimed something that sounded like, "Griddle cakes, griddle cakes!" with great urgency, and with some violent heaving, we topped the rise.

We lay there. She lit a cigarette.

I got up and fixed two drinks, mine a healthy three quarters, then lay beside her again. We sipped.

"The fact is, Miriam—you don't want me to be seen by anyone, and I have to know why. There's no point denying it. I know it's true."

She set her glass on my bare chest, holding it steady, "I was pretty certain you'd caught on."

"Then it is true."

She gave a great sigh.

"Yes."

"Why?"

"I've wanted to tell you. But I couldn't before everything was straightened out."

"Why, Miriam?"

"Because I have a plan. Oh, damnit!" She sat up and butted the cigarette, leaned over away from me and put the ash tray on a shelf. "I don't know how to approach you, Tolbert. I'm going to approach you, but you're so broody." She sipped quickly from her glass, then said with what I knew was mock petulance, "You keep it so damned cold in here. Like ice. D'you have a robe?"

"I like it cold. Over on that chair back."

She climbed across me, unsmiling, moved with stiff grace to the chair, picked up the blue terry cloth robe, and slipped it on. She freed her hair, belted the robe, thrust her hands in deep pockets, and came back to stand beside the studio couch, looking down at me; regarding me with more hesitation.

"Please, Miriam. Get on with it."

"If you must know, I planned to tell you today."

"Marvelous."

"All I ask is that you stay quiet, don't say a word till I finish."

"Agreed."

She took a deep breath. "I know all about you, Tolbert. You're an ex-convict. You did somewhere between two to five years in the Colorado State

Pen, at Canyon City. You're what they call a con man. You take other people's money, by ruse—that way. You even take advantage of little old ladies,
and everything. But you slipped up on something big, some sort of housing development thing, in Colorado Springs, and you were caught—"

She must have seen something in my eyes. She pressed her lips together, then said quickly, "Don't talk, now. You're wondering how I know, how
I caught on?"

I nodded. She turned and moved toward the far side of the room. I got
up, hurried to the small mobile bar, poured my glass nearly full, and
returned to the studio couch. I had mixed feelings. I slipped my shorts back
on, and lay down again. I closed my eyes, gripping the glass tightly. I knew
she was a computer. The lights had flashed and warned me. It was a killing
game and there was always retribution. I opened my eyes and watched my
chest move with rapid heartbeats.

"This," she said, beside me once more, "I found it in your suitcase."

"You broke—?"

"Don't talk, Tolbert. No, I did not break in. You gave me a key, remember.
To the house, I mean. I simply came here and looked around. I have a reason, Tolbert. Will you please give me credit?"

She was holding the old newspaper clipping that I'd had laminated and
had kept as a reminder to watch out. There was a news photo of me trying to hide behind a policeman's cap, not succeeding, and the story below.
It came back to me how I'd felt at the time. I felt worse now.

"It tells a lot about you," she said. She tossed the clipping on the couch,
and sighed again. Then something schemy came into those big brown
eyes; they hardened. "Look, I found a gun, too. I think it's what they call a
German Luger—"

"That's only something I—"

"No talking, please, You promised."

I had not promised. I stared at her. Why had I kept the damned gun? I
did not know. Actually, I was afraid of the thing. It kept reminding me of
some horrible future, like scrying to ink and water. I was very emotional
about my future. I couldn't think, just then. More to the point, I could not
control the flood of thoughts. Maybe this was how a pigeon felt at the
moment of awakening, his roll vanished.

"You know I live with my grandmother in Belleair," she said. "I suppose
you have plans about her, right?"

"Miriam, for God's sake!"

"*Quiet*. Well, it doesn't matter, really. But I will say, now, that my grandmother, Loretta Kindott, is worth a million and a quarter. Does that tickle
your gizzard?"

I watched her, I did not speak. I was at a disadvantage, lying down, with her standing beside the couch, looking at me with that smug grimness. But I did not have the strength, or inclination, to sit up, to do anything. I took a long swallow of brandy.

"Frankly, Tolbert —it tickles *my* gizzard."

I tried to see inside her head, attempting to read those limpid brown eyes. It can be done. I found nothing. The pale face hovered there, and all I could see was a prominent inner satisfaction.

She went on, "Did you plan to work it through me? Have you cased the joint?"

"I don't even know where you live, Miriam." My voice cracked as I spoke.

"I'll bet." She gave a short laugh. "Well, don't bother your poor head. Now, as to the reason I didn't want you to be seen too much. I don't suppose it would've mattered, but why take the chance? You're going to be living right there at that house before long, Tolbert."

I was calm now. It was a bitter calm. I listened, but there was a certain control now. She was a bit mad, I knew, though it had not revealed itself until this moment. I knew she had a scheme, and I could not wait to hear all of it—especially my place in it.

"My grandmother is leaving all her money to my cousin, Joseph Lancaster. Oh, I get a pittance, but that's all. I'm supposed to get married, all that, with a husband to give me mine. That's how she thinks, see? The romance of romance. She adores Joseph. But, get this, she hasn't seen him since he was eight years old."

If I reacted in any way, Miriam did not see it. There was a kind of satisfied nonchalance in the way I took another drink.

"The trick is, Tolbert—you're going to pose as my cousin, Joseph Lancaster."

I put the glass on a shelf, got up and went over to the stereo. Some subdued jazz was on the tape deck, so I turned that on. I stood there, listening. The volume was low, but because of the room's height, and because of the furnishings, there was real presence.

Miriam was running across the room. She leaned down and flipped back the edge of the rug, picked up a manila folder that I had not known was there, and trotted over to where I was standing.

I turned the music up slightly.

"This is a dossier on Joseph Lancaster. Everything about him."

"Peachy."

She plucked a small news clipping from atop white typewritten sheets. "He's dead, Tolbert. This is his obituary, for God's sake. He lived in England."

I turned the volume up very loud. Music pulsated in the room with explosive throbbings. A muted horn that sounded like an elephant's trumpeting swung into *Raindrops Keep Falling on My Head*... She began to speak and I turned it up still louder. The huge north window commenced rattling.

She ran to me, put her lips close to my ear. "He's dead, don't you understand? She doesn't *know* he's dead. She'll never know. You'll be him and come live right there, and I'll be there—we can do it anytime. Grandma will accept you. She'll adore you. You even look like Joseph." She backed away. "*Will* you turn that goddamn thing down!"

She thrust a shaking hand gripping the obituary news photo in front of my eyes. It was gray and blurred. There was a bleak resemblance. She tried to get to the stereo volume. I protected it from her invasion.

I stared at her. The music slammed.

Suddenly she was like a wildcat. She got past me, somehow, and turned the music soft, then whirled. "And we take care of Grandma, see? It should look like an accident." She was whispering harshly. "*Will* you listen? We'll have everything." Her face was pink with effort, angry-eyed now, as she leaned forward, brandishing the manila folder. "I've planned it all the way. I hired an investigator to check things out. All you've got to do is do it—"

I reached around for the volume knob on the stereo and turned the music up even louder than before.

Do *it,* I thought.

She was shouting now.

I went over to the studio couch and buried my head under a pillow. It did no good.

...TWO

What a trick! I kept thinking that.

But I was quite drunk by the time I came back to my place at Indian Rocks, because Miriam was taking quick steps, and I'd been playing pawn. First we went to the Highway Patrol Offices on 19, and I took a driver's test in the name of Joseph Lancaster. I was still dazed, running ahead of the machinery, like a loose ball-bearing. The next thing I knew, I had a temporary driver's permit, and we were parked at *Al's Tru-Blue* second hand car lot. We ended up with a yellow two-door '68 Chevelle in fair knock-about condition—all in Joseph Lancaster's name.

"Isn't it nice?" Miriam commented. "You see, Tolbert, darling, it simply wouldn't do to come to Grandma's with that brassy thing you drive. That's O'Shaugnessy's car, anyway."

I said nothing. We stopped for drinks, and she sipped a quarter of a beer, while I drank three or four brandies.

Then, with Miriam driving the Chevelle, and me in the Porsche, we headed for my place. She parked the Chevelle down the road, under a palm, and walked back to the Porsche.

"Now you can take me to my car."

I drove that way, rather giddy, and dropped her off in front of *The First Federal, Savings & Loan.*

Now I was home. Home, dear home. I was beginning to realize why she had never driven directly to where I lived, but always insisted I pick her up. We had discussed everything at length. She insisted vehemently that we act immediately, and though I still had given her neither yes nor no, she would leave details to me. I parked the car rather haphazardly, bumbled into the house. I kept thinking of that Chevelle down the street. Music still pounded wildly from the stereo. I tuned it to a whisper, moved blindly to the studio couch, and sprawled on my face. Snatches of her loud talk wafted through my head. I could hear her plainly. I tried to escape her by burrowing into the couch, but it did not work. One arm drooped from the couch to the floor, and my fingers fiddled with something. It was the manilla folder with Joseph Lancaster's history. I retracted my hand—as if I'd touched fire.

My heart was outdoing itself; almost a painful striking in my chest. I couldn't get enough air. This was the first sign, of course, and I waited for pain to begin in my left arm. Then I knew it could not possibly be a heart attack, not with all the booze I'd put away. But I immediately recalled someone telling me you could overdo the drinking, as regards the heart.

I lurched up, and headed for the shower, stripping off my clothes as I went. Beneath needles of hot water, I refused myself the pleasure of thought, humming, and otherwise digressing. I turned on bright cold water. After that, I dried briskly, feeling somewhat enlarged, put on shorts, and made coffee in the kitchenette.

Seated on the couch with a mug of coffee, I sipped, and tried to ignore the fact that Miriam had been here at all. It did not work.

I was supposed to call her at seven. *"And, please, Tolbert—for God's sake, be precise. I'll stand by the phone."*

She wasn't mad, she was insane. She was raving.

She had checked off every item with a meticulousness that approached paranoia. She was obviously tropistic, like primordial one-celled creatures with built in antennae, because every time I tried to say something negative, she smoothly moved in to debunk, and it was more than mere instinct, or intelligence. Talking a blue streak, never faltering, she parried each of my attempts at counterthrust with oiled aplomb.

Oye. Bananas.

My tongue was scalded neatly. I set the accursed coffee mug on the floor—horribly beside that manilla folder—and stalked the refrigerator. With a can of Bud, I sat on the couch again. I drank the entire can at one swill. I hated canned beer. Returning to the fridge, I discovered a bottle of Dutch beer, uncapped it, and went back to the couch.

The music pulsed gently.

All I had to do, Charley—

...like an accident, I could take my time, there was no rush, she would help. She had no feelings about her grandmother, none at all. This bothered me. The old dear was simply up to her neck in moo. It amounted to a million and a quarter.

I tried to ignore the dragon's *chomp* of this fact.

And grandma loved Joseph Lancaster to the core, and she had not seen him since he was eight, and yes, *"She is slightly batty, you could say."*

Oh, Miriam. I groaned it aloud, actually, and nuzzled the beer bottle.

All the time, I was considering, devilishly, *I can go there, maybe work something: I don't have to hurt anybody.* I was thinking this at sub-level, while the rest of my mind fluctuated around the horror of the actuality.

The hell of it was, I knew I was not going to work anything. Miriam was entirely too perspicacious. She had frightened me. I did not like to admit this.

Joseph Lancaster had been dished, as it were.

I set the bottle down and picked up the manilla folder. I held it on my knee, remembering that Miriam had said something about an "investigator." She had hired somebody to probe Lancaster's death, and situation. This was a gaping wound in the body of her scheme. I did not like it, and with this thought realized I was visualizing the whole thing. Sick, I threw the manilla folder on the floor, and stared at it.

I picked it up again. It was a tiny obituary, befitting the death of someone destitute and insignificant, without antecedents. Apparently he had been an alcoholic, a London stray, who had begged around the edges of lesser pubs in a place called Hedgeton, Southern England. He died of D.T.s and exposure in an alleyway between *Bromley & Betts Dustbin Mfgrs.,* and a chemist's shop. Obviously already overripe, rotting on his feet, more or less, he had been buried forthwith, and this had happened three years ago.

I riffled the typed sheets, muttering to myself. "Joseph Algood Lancaster. Who the hell compiled this? Miriam? Probably."

He'd been thirty-one. The same as O'Shaugnessy. He loved Grandma Kindott, and was loved in return. She sang to him, *"Oh, I went to the Animal fair, the Birds and the Beasts were there, the Big Baboon,* etc." Lancaster always laughed and leaped over this one, and therefore would probably recall it. His mother, Lucille, had died when he was born, which brought him closer to Grandma. His father, Keith Lancaster, a wastrel, vanished soon after, and supposedly met a sordid death, trapped in a coal mine cave-in disaster, in Pennsylvania. Joseph lived on with Grandmother Kindott, worming deeply into her affections. Grandfather Desmond Kindott also admired the boy, but without the fervent antics of Loretta, who showered Joseph with presents and extreme devotion. It was heavy; she spent every minute with the boy. Then, abruptly, Keith Lancaster, the wastrel father, showed. He had not croaked in the cave-in, after all. He demanded custody of his son, and though Grandma Kindott fought it, the law was on his side. He whisked Joseph off to Vancouver, where he went to school. Grandma Kindott grieved, but never saw him again. She had a letter from Melbourne, Australia, demanding money to help the boy.

There was a photostat of that letter.

It still held a kind of immediacy.

"Dear Loretta, I find myself in a predicament, and reach out to your for help, but at the same time I cannot forestall hints and feelings of bitterness, because you spoilt my son rotten—I can never forgive you for this, either, and though I experience shame and deep embarrassment in writing to you like this, I'm beseeching you to send some money for the boy's welfare, and his alone, in case you have your signals crossed already, reading into this letter all sorts of things not meant. I mean to give my son every advantage. I call upon you because I'm in bad and evil straits, and expect you to send along a tidy amount the moment you receive this epistle, to Gen. Delivery, Melbourne. I have nothing further to say, excepting that you had damned well better come across, Loretta, for Joseph's sake, and his alone. I might

add, if you think of him what and how you pretend to think. As for me, I want nothing from you except for your usual spite, I suppose, and you can damned well consider this a demand, Loretta. Yours in the world, Keith Lancaster."

Whether or not Loretta Kindott sent along the money was not disclosed. And there was a vacant period during which there was no further word from Joseph or his father until years later, a letter from Joseph himself, posted in Capetown, South Africa.

There was a photostat of this one, too:

"Dearest Grandma: I'll bet you thought I was dead. No such luck. But Dad passed away unexpectedly and I miss him. I know you never had many good thoughts about him. He told me. But perhaps you didn't really know him. Anyway, this is just to tell you I remember you so clearly, and think of you ever so fondly, Grandma. They were precious days I spent with you, and I shall never forget them, never. I wish I could explain how much they mean to me. And you, dearest Grandma—how very much you mean to me. My fondest wish is to return to you, live with you—but not until my fortune is made. I know that sounds silly, Grandma, but it's the truth."

The letter went on in this vein, larded with love until it was faintly suspect, pressing the fact that he would return like some king from the Orient, laden with precious jewels.

Grandma Kindott received five letters in all, over the years, She had preserved them carefully, and they were filled with boyish enthusiasm and earnest promises, but all echoed faintly of defeat and of the General who climbed on his horse and rode off in every direction. There was the African letter, two from Glasgow, and two from London. The London letters, if anything, sounded a touch desperate:

"...I love you so much and my only desire is to return to you as a success. I have marvelous prospects, and hardly know which to pursue. If I could only have you hold me in your arms, I would know everything. I know I don't write often, but it's because I'm so busy—you just can't possibly imagine..."

Meanwhile, with Grandma Kindott, memories of Joseph never dimmed. His room at the Kindott home was a shrine. Nothing in the room had been altered since he went away. It was dusted daily, and all was exactly as he had left it. Every toy was kept intact.

There was a list of toys he might recall. A dump truck, a Teddy-Bear, a clown doll with one leg whom he called "Gimp." There were many things listed, along with poems and songs. Joseph had been able to stand on his head, walk on his hands.

This jarred me, because it said that Grandma Kindott's devotion was a sickness. Perhaps I could pass it off, saying I'd forgotten how.

I mused on that thought for a time, then read further. On his first day at school, Joseph cried and they sent for Grandma to come and sit with him.

He loved to swim, and built sand castles. They were to be the only castles he ever laid eyes on, apparently.

Then there was a listing of jobs he had had while in London:

Waiter, plumber's helper, newspaper-boy, gardener to several different families, chauffeur, cab driver, gasoline station attendant, worker in warehouses, and also on the docks, boat painter and scraper, garbage man, street cleaner. The jobs all tended to be on a descending scale, until he was janitor in a warehouse, and then—nothing.

He had been mixed up in a killing which ensued after a fight at a pub called the *Fox & Hounds* in Caddistock. He went to trial, but was acquitted because of small evidence and because of the fact that the victim had been a drunkard and roisterer and had been in many fights throughout the area.

He apparently grew more and more despondent after the above occurrence, and took to drinking heavily. His history became dimmer and dimmer. I supposed the investigator Miriam had employed had done as much as he could with this. If she hadn't had someone search out these facts, then how had she come by them?

Grandfather Kindott, whose avid interest was the study of ESP, died. Grandma Kindott made her will, leaving the entire estate to Joseph Lancaster, and then she settled down to await his return. She never seemed to lose faith that he would return:

A place at table was always set for Lancaster.

This was a macabre touch.

Further note, insert: Grandma Kindott was deeply involved with her husband, whatever that meant.

From an intermittent diary that Joseph Lancaster kept, it was discovered that he had been trying to save money over the years—save enough to return to the United States. Apparently that dream was never realized. There was little else of interest in the diary; it was a spotty collection of the miseries of a small, desperate man who had entirely lost himself along the way. He liked street girls, and apologized for the fact repeatedly, building the breed. There were two pages devoted to the diary, but I came up with nothing of interest.

"Dotty is sweet and I love her much. I know she is a prostitute, but this does not affect me, except perhaps that I love and care for her all the more. Dotty is a dream. She's tender, and she has good things to say bout everyone."

This was all very well, but the next entry voided it all with a brush of the hand:

"I have met Lucy. She is a girl of the streets, I realize, but so different from that horrible cat, Dotty. We were having fish & chips the other night, and Dotty came into the place and ordered, then threw the entire contents in Lucy's face. Lucy was so surprised. But she came back and squirted vinegar all over Dotty. She ran from the place yelling, 'Stink, stink!' It was very funny, in a way."

There were other girls, all of the same caliber and content. Maybe there was even a streak of sadness through it all. He mentioned Grandma Kindott a few times:

"Will go back, I will return, after I've made mine."

"When I think of my room and remember, it makes me weep. And to think Grandma is waiting. I know she is waiting."

There was a page devoted to his peregrinations. Apparently he had wandered all over England, Scotland and Wales, only to end up in London again, and then Southern England, where he died.

It was a rotten shame, really.

And she was a poor old bat, chewing on a dream.

I dropped the manilla folder to the floor.

I sat there, staring hazily at the wall. There was a certain numbness. I stood up, moved slowly to the mobile bar, poured a small brandy, drank it neat.

It was the Big Con, for real—and beautiful. All but the accident, which left me feeling rather faint.

Still, I was beyond the first shock. It was like syrup now, with me standing knee deep.

I found myself checking my watch, thinking, Seven o'clock, seven o'clock. Like that. It was sickening, really, the way it gnawed at me. My nerves were jumpy, the hollow, tingling feeling of anxiety in my chest quite pronounced and developing with promise. I began cracking my knuckles, an old habit that sent Miriam up the wall. If I had a headache, I could crack my neck, too, the cervical vertebrae, thus relieving tension. The headache vanished. I had picked this trick up from a chiropractor friend in Des Moines.

Suddenly I realized everything was static; a breathless quality to the very air. Was Miriam really a silly monster?

I sat on the couch again, hands clasped in my lap. I took one hand and put it over my mouth, sitting there, knowing what it was. My watch read five-fifteen. How could I wait till seven o'clock?

I began to muse—searching for the wonder, finding a smoky trace, trying to hold smoke in my hands, watching it fade between clutching fingers...

And I began to know I would do it.

Here was decision amid a thousand arguments. Action, immediate, while you ignored all the bites and chews and tiny shouts and nays and prods and exclamatory visions.

I almost ran into the kitchenette. I made fresh coffee, and fried three eggs, musing about cholesterol as a panacea to urgent doubt. I dropped bread into the toaster.

I would do it.

One had to take the chance, or drown.

I kept moving. First I got the milk, then the butter, then blackberry jam for the toast.

"Bye-Bye Blues" was on the stereo.

I put cheese atop the eggs. It was cheddar, and very sharp.

I was shaking inside. It had to stop. I had made up my mind, damn it.

The thought of a million and a quarter was like a squeezing around the heart.

Miriam had known how I wanted money. It was my precious infirmity, the ache of my life, the wound that sought not a laying-on of hands, but a Swiss bank account.

I ate standing up with a feverish indifference to the food, my mind caterwauling, nibbling, galloping. This was the big thing and I planned to do it. But there was a blind pulled down over the vital part of the picture. I opened a bottle of port, went in and on the couch, sipping, feeling like a shadow on the wall, a shadow with eyes that watched what I was doing.

The principal thought now was seven o'clock.

I sat there, sipping and sipping, tipping the bottle for what seemed hours, and suddenly it was seven o'clock. A gentle shock.

Approaching the phone was like stalking an enemy sentry in an open area. It stood on a table beside a huge red leather Streit lounge chair. The receiver felt unnaturally smooth and cold as I dialed.

Half a ring. "Yes?" It was Miriam.

"Your whim is my command." It took a lot of guts to say it, but I managed.

"All right." She had known I would. "Now, have you read that stuff in the folder?"

"Yes."

"You'd better destroy it, then—if it's well memorized. You won't really need to know much, just the high points. You can make it up as you go along, see?"

She was excited. I could tell by the sound of her breathing. But that was the only way she would reveal how she felt. Now that I had committed myself, there was a sickening surge of anxiety mingled with wild urgency. I could never get used to this. It always happened, but never quite this powerfully.

"Miriam."

"Yes?"

"About this investigator you hired. I don't think that was quite—"

"I'll take care of it."

"But, really, Miriam."

"We'll discuss it later. It's perfectly all right, will you believe? I can't talk now. Just get over here I'll be here—"

I broke in, "Tomorrow morning."

"Tonight."

I had already fixed my sights. They could not be changed now. "In the morning. Now, how do I find this joint?" I had the address, but that wasn't enough.

She told me. I sat down in the red leather chair. My entire horizon was paranoid schizophrenic. My palm was damp, even though I knew the fear, and could at least try to combat it. But speaking to Miriam was somehow like talking to a detached voice that you were certain had no body. This frightened me, too. But I held on grimly.

"Tolbert!" She was whispering hoarsely.

"Yes?"

"Are you there?"

"Certainly."

"You sound funny."

"I do?"

"Yes."

I laughed gently. "I feel fine."

Her whisper was fast. "You think it'll work, don't you?"

I sat there holding the phone, staring at the bottle of port over beside the couch on the floor.

"I mean," she said, "you agree, don't you?"

"Perfectly."

"Oh, God," she said. "Damnit!"

"What's the matter?"

"Nothing. *Damn you!*"

"Me?"

"No. It's just—never mind."

There was a long pause. She gasped something I could not make out and cursed again.

"Miriam?"

"Yes?"

"What the devil are you doing?"

"Nothing. I can't see you there tonight. You'll be here in the morning, then. Just walk in unannounced. Give the old girl a real surprise. And bring plenty of clothes, because you'll be staying. Remember, you're Joseph Lancaster, now. But I'll leave all the details to you—you're the con man." She gave a little laugh. "Are you nervous?"

"Of course not."

"Hm. Well, naturally, you're used to things like this."

I did not answer that.

"I've got to hang up," she said. "I'll try—"

She hung up.

"*Try to—*" what?

I sat there, musing. It had always been like this when planning something. Little things left unanswered. But that wasn't it. During my peregrinations, I had sometimes considered what it would be like if I had, necessarily, the problem of killing somebody. Yes. Why not say it straight out? Every time I thought about it, I knew there would be more little things even than with an ordinary job.

I had been correct. It had begun. I could sense it. Multitudes of details that twisted themselves out of their normal shapes, like tiny, writhing snakes. Then I told myself that this was not so. Nothing had happened. All right. Why had Miriam hung up like that? What had she been whispering about? Could I trust her?

Certainly I could trust her. I had to trust her.

Someone came into the room, that's all.

This was another thing. First there was the action, then my immediate reaction, supplemented with vivid imaginings, all of a detrimental type—detrimental to me, understand. Then I had to fight back, searching for the normal conclusions. Stratagems that sometimes gave as the worst kind of headache, so that I had to crack my cervical vertebrae.

It was now seven-ten.

There would be a long, horrible night. Doubting Castle, with the Giant Despair custodian. I could not face it. I knew myself too well.

I took a long slug of brandy, said, "Oh, shit!", very loudly, and selected two cowhide bags and began packing them carefully. I had a two-suiter in which I could easily stuff four suits. I packed that, too. I went and picked up the manilla folder, glanced at it, laid it atop some shirts in one of the bags. I closed and locked the bags.

I stood there, alone. I turned the stereo to FM, and music smoked softly into the room. I went to the shelf above the couch, opened the white-capped bottle, and swallowed five seconal caps. Lying down, fully clothed, I grimly closed my eyes. Boarding my tiny submarine, I drifted off through the green, icy waters, and so to sleep.

•••THREE

By ten-thirty in the morning, I was on my way, but just as I reached the approach to Belleair on Gulf Boulevard, a burning commenced in my stomach. I had breakfasted on rum and fried eggs and as this was fairly normal, the pain was out of the ordinary. I had mixed the rum with coffee. Taking out three Tums, I popped them into my mouth, chewed rapidly, swallowed, slowed the Chevelle, and waited.

The pain eased somewhat, but I knew I walked a wire regarding ulcers, or worse. It was tension, the necessity of facing the unknown. I would never become used to it, but knowing this was no nepenthé. However, I drove on.

Moments after entering Belleair, I began searching for the sign Miriam had mentioned. I glimpsed it beneath a towering dark cedar; varnished wood with brass lettering: *Kindott.* They were elegant numerals.

A blue gravel drive led from Gulf Boulevard toward the Gulf. I took this, listening to the sound of purring tires, moving between more tall cedars on either side.

I drew a deep breath and stopped the car. Twisting in the seat, I opened the smaller cowhide bag, brought out one of the three bottles of *Martell's* I had judiciously packed, having no notion as to whether or not Loretta Kindott kept a stock. I took a long refreshing pull at the bottle, then another, and a final heavy swallow. The volatile warmth was encouraging, and there was no ensuing pain. The morning brightened inwardly.

Driving on, the road circled to the right, and I approached a weathered brick wall filigreed with elephant vine. Tall obscene looking white punk trees, their leaves pea soup green, were lined behind the wall. An open latticework wrought-iron gate presented itself. I drove through, trying to ignore the thin touch of anxiety, gripping the wheel rather tightly.

The huge vine-covered brick house loomed, with gleaming, sun-touched vertical strip windows, narrower than average, the entire scene touched with an air of gloom in the morning dazzle. I wondered if that gloom were only mine. So far nearly everything had been as Miriam related on the phone. I slowed the Chevelle, though, crawling along, knowing I was entering upon something that gouged the grain of my being.

I gave a nervous yank at my boot straps.

The house looked still, deserted.

To the right, beyond a parking area, manicured blue-green lawn sloped turfily to water; a bayou. Offing was more water, interspersed with tiny jungled islands, revealing white beaches among snarled mangrove. At the edge of the lawn was a small red-painted structure, a boat-house probably, a short rustic pier. A-good-sized Chris-Craft swung in the tannic water, tight brown canvas tarp laced down over the stern. Two or three smaller boats were also moored nearby.

The stillness touched me. There was no whisper anywhere. I stopped the car, rolled down the window, listened. Nothing. Then, faintly, the rusty shriek of a single jay knifed the air. One cry, there was, then silence.

Beyond the house, connecting the Gulf of Mexico with the bayou, was a narrow channel. This, too, was lined with interspersed cedar and punk trees. Here, at the rear, several large dense-leaved oaks shaded the remainder of the lawn. Perfectly shaped bushes stood about. I glimpsed a waist-high sundial with molded concrete pedestal and copper face.

Had Miriam spotted me, white face pressed against a window? Oddly, there was a feeling of finality here. I did not like it.

In the four car garage, the rear ends of three vehicles shot off metallic glints. Between trees and garage, I could see a broad, long spreading lawn, a wind-shaped Australian pine and, beyond, the Gulf itself—slick as mint syrup this morning, blue-green, pale, still.

Too aware, I found my pipe, filled it, lit up. Then I drove into the parking area, got out, and stood there.

The stillness was even more intense outside the car. Warm, unmoving air. The jay screamed again. He was in one of the punk trees beside the channel; I caught a flit of blue. The witch's cry of the bird only made things more unrealistic.

Right then I nearly quit cold. The temptation was unnerving. But I had felt this way before, pressed on to success. Instead, I sat in the car again, had another long snort of the brandy.

This joint was nothing more than a house, and that was all it was. It had trees and a bloody bird screaming its head off, and some boats, and water. It was a house, and nothing more.

Outside again, I looked at the entrance to the house. This was the rear, but imposing. Large paneled doors, with immense knobs, set with flanged hinges, stood above white steps. There was a short blue glass entrance areaway, bordered with boxed red roses.

So this was where Joseph Lancaster had lived.

Was it where he would live again?

I was wet-nursing the whole damned excursion.

I walked briskly across gravel, lawn, then stepping stones between the glass walls, up the porch steps. I stood at the door, pressed the white pill encircled with brass.

I hadn't drunk enough brandy. My head was beginning to throb. I could run for the car, desperately—but the door opened.

"Yes?"

Her voice was musical, soft-throated, contralto. She had a slight lisp, with a startling, but extremely sexy revelation of tongue-tip, and I had never seen her before.

I wanted to escape. Miriam had said nothing of anyone else. The quick shot of mahoganied hall behind the girl, immense, gleaming, silent, museum-like, only agitated blooming anxiety.

"Hi," I said. Training abruptly asserted itself; I felt a rush of well-being. I grinned at her. "Certainly don't remember you."

This puzzled her. She frowned faintly, looked me over with quick care, and some concern. I had on pale gray slacks, a powder blue pullover. I took off my sunglasses, held them in a damp hand with my pipe.

"I'm Joseph Lancaster," I said as brightly as I could. "Came to see my grandmother, Loretta Kindott. Really didn't mean to shake you up."

Momentarily she did not speak, transfixed, sort of. Dark spills of shining black hair brushed her shoulders. The hesitant face was heart-shaped, rather, with a broad, almost over-lush mouth, full and pink-lipped. But the eyes were what stopped me, had me in a kind of vise, where my mind would not function at par. They were dark, impressive blue—the darkest I had ever seen, with whites as healthy and clear as paper; intelligent eyes, kind, and very sexy—almost shady. They were wise eyes. They might judge too correctly. It was a bit frightening, She wore something saffron and gold, medium short—with large, perked breasts.

"Joseph Lancaster?" She did that with her pink tongue again. It just slipped out between her lips when she spoke certain words. It was exciting as hell.

"Yes. The prodigal, sort of." I gave a short laugh. She kept on staring. "Perhaps you don't know of me?"

It came in a sudden burst. "But, I do!" She was eager, "Why, it's all she—but, please, come in—don't stand there."

She moved. aside, her body twisting delightfully, and I entered the hall. I smelled lemon oil. But through this, her perfume was allusive and elusive. She was excited.

The stillness was everywhere.

"You're really *you?*" The eyes were impatient now.

"I think so."

"I'm sorry, really. I'm Ann Elliot, Mr. Lancaster. It's Just that—" She ceased, closed the door, leaned against it, still staring at me with disbelief. "I'm a sort of companion-secretary, Mr. Lancaster—to your grandmother, that is." She paused. "And you've come!"

I looked around uneasily. The hall was extremely broad, shining floor revealed around rich looking Orientals. Sloping stairs flanked the left wall, polished banisters gleaming. The stairs peaked on a small landing, then descended again to the front entrance.

"Loretta will simply—"

Violent chattering and oinking sounds that sounded like a wild pig stopped her. The sounds were emanating from somewhere at the top of the stairs.

"Oh," she said. "That's Gargantua."

I watched as a furry form sprang savagely into view on the stairs. It swung against the banister, chattering and yelping, flew down the stairs with a crazed rush of arms and legs and balancing tail. It was a monkey, glint-eyed, yellow teeth bared, the onward run tumultuous and disorganized. An ape? I took a step backward as it reached the foot of the stairs. It stared at me viciously, blinking, mouth wide, a string of slaver hanging from wet teeth. Then it sprang violently at me in a running, bounding, leap.

"Gargantua!" She was sharp.

The whatever-it-was veered to one side, but reached out deliberately and struck me in the thigh with one fist in passing. It chattered more wildly than before, stared at me, head cocked, oinking, making a shrill sound that was like "Eyolp!" It jumped up and down, brandishing semi-fisted hands overhead. The body was thicker than monkeys I had seen, the head peculiarly shaped, a kind of distorted human-type.

"Please," Ann Elliot said. "Don't let him frighten you. That's what he's trying to do. He won't hurt you, I'm sure."

The way she spoke alleviated nothing.

The damned thing abruptly hurtled at me, seemed to stop in mid-air, and began leaping up and down again, its feet thumping the floor like a drum.

"He's irritated about something," she said.

Miriam's voice reached me from the stairway. "Hello? I'm sure, Ann—it's—who is this?"

The thing called Gargantua continued to leap and pummel the floor, glaring at me with a maliciousness that disturbed my thought.

I watched Miriam. She attained the foot of the stairs with hardly a glance at me, her gaze on Ann Elliot.

A short red silk dress snicked at her thighs, enormous pearls swung to her midriff, and she looked paler than ever. The tone of her voice was tinged with superciliousness, and I wondered if this could be the same Miriam.

She closed the distance between us, halted, blinked at the other girl.

Gargantua leaped at her, clutched her knees, staring at me all the while.

Ann Elliot's revelatory introduction, stating that I was Joseph Lancaster, became a fumble of words, while Miriam made tiny exclamations of what

I supposed must be delight. She daintily took my hand, and Gargantua took another swipe at me, but missed, which disturbed him. He made guttural throat noises.

"This is indeed a surprise," Miriam said. "Grandma will positively go through the turret."

I grinned haphazardly. "How is she?"

Miriam turned to Ann Elliot. "Would you mind taking Gargantua to his cage? I'll attend to Mr. Lancaster."

There was the slightest trace of the knife in her words, and for a moment the two girls' glances sparred.

"Certainly," Ann Elliot said. "Here, now—come, baby." She took the big monkey's hand, and tugged. The animal was taken with me, however, and did not want to move. Finally, with brute strength, she managed to pull him away from Miriam. They moved off down the hall together. The monkey kept looking back at me, with glinting eyes. Ann Elliot had disturbingly marvelous legs.

"Well," Miriam said in something close to a whisper. "You made it, didn't you."

"We'd better go see Grandma."

"Are you sober?"

"Reasonably so. Listen, you didn't tell me anything about this place. Her—and that damned thing, that—"

"I didn't want to trouble you. Haven't you a mint or something? You smell like a varnish factory."

"He doesn't like me."

"Don't worry about him. He doesn't take to me, either. But he's a sneaky bastard, Tolbert—I mean, Joseph!" She winked. "You saw how he hugged me? It's all an act. Actually, he's apt to do anything. But we have to put up with it. There's a story behind—but, never mind. Come. You'll meet Grandma, darling."

It had been a garble of words, and I knew she was hiding something. Ann Elliot had vanished through a large archway down the hall, to the right. Now she reappeared, moving toward us.

"Come along," Miriam said quickly.

We went up the stairs, mahogany gleaming around a tufty sand-colored runner.

"She's up here mostly," Miriam said, "But you can't depend on that, either. You may as well know, Joseph—" she gave me another brittle wink—"you can depend on very little in this house."

"I see."

So far, in the back of my mind, I still knew it was only a house with a damned ape in it. But the events had me a touch rocky.

Ann Elliot called up from the hall. "He won't stay there, you know."

"Yes, dear," Miriam said. "But one must try, mustn't one?"

"Can't you lock him up?" I asked.

"Grandma would never hear of such a thing."

The atmosphere of the house was foreign, and quiet, Always sensitive to interior currents, I did not like it. I took a deep breath, which only served to increase the hollow feeling in my chest. It was all rather disturbing. Miriam was not exactly Miriam. I could not put my finger on what it was. I felt awfully fallible. I decided Miriam was nervous, but received no satisfaction from the thought.

We reached the landing, ascended three more broad steps, and I realized the second story landing itself stretched completely around the stair-well. It was banistered glisteningly. We circled to the left, moving on thick, silent cerulean blue carpet. An enormous filigreed gold-framed mirror stood against the wall; angels and cherubim. There were oil paintings of summery scenes, hedges, gates, smoky sun-touched clouds, English gardens with plump girls carrying baskets. Sunlight scattered multi-hued through an immense church-like stained glass window at the front of the house, the end of the landing.

"Here," Miriam said. She placed a slim white hand on a large glass knob, and whispered, "Good luck."

She opened the door. I entered carefully.

"Ah! I heard something—" a tall, goggled wraith said. "Oh! I'm sorry." She clutched at a sagging blue- and yellow-flowered silk dress. "You've brought company? You should have called, my dear. I'd have come down. Well, well."

Thin as a stick, she stood there staring at us. The dress drooped and clung to bony protuberances, was dominated by an enormous, foggy mass of curled bright pink hair. It took your eye. The hair was thin, yet like a balloon around the boniest, starved face I had ever seen. A crimson mouth had been indelicately painted, the lips broad and curling up at the corners, marked with deep vertical grooves. The nose was a white blade. But she was not actually goggled. They were merely surprisingly thick tortoise-shell glasses, and the jet eyes behind them were intense with energy.

"Now, Grandma—I've got a surprise."

"Surprise? Surprise?"

"Yes."

The room was large, cluttered with furniture of every description. Tall windows were heavily draped, but the drapes were open, the room inordinately bright. Dust motes swam in the lemon yellow light. A tall secretary stood to the left, open, tumbled with papers. An archway led to another room.

"Miriam! Will you get on with it?"

Loretta Kindott's voice dripped with intelligence and breeding, but she was obviously one who might say anything at all. The sound was throaty and dry.

"Grandma, this is Joseph, Joseph Lancaster."

The woman stared. Large, ring-bedecked hands clutched at each other along her waist front. She leaned slightly forward, brought her hands up, stretching them toward me, and began to weep. "No, no," she said. "Joseph. It is, it is." Tears wormed fatly from beneath the thick-framed glasses, trickling down her cheeks.

"Grandma," I said, feeling suddenly worse than ever about the entire thing.

She moved toward me, hands still out, beginning to snuffle now. Then she ran to me, flung her arms around my shoulders, sobbing. The sobbing began to alter, changing into laughter, and I could smell lavender perfume. Pressed against me, I could feel her bones; she was like loosely stretched cloth strung over sticks. It was as if I could feel the sticks, her bones, move brokenly about.

"Joseph, Joseph," she said, laughing around the words. "I knew you'd come home, I knew it. Desmond tells me it's only a question of time, and here you are." She gagged a little, snuffling, and turned her face up to me, smiling. She was feeling my arms now, pressing, grabbing with her fingers, checking to make sure I wasn't a mirage. "My little boy," she said, "My boy's come home."

"Yes, Grandma."

"Isn't it wonderful?" Miriam said absently.

Someone knocked on the door, and I heard it open. Looking around, I saw Ann Elliot enter the room. She seemed about to speak, but cleared her throat instead. I wondered what Loretta Kindott had meant with those words about her husband, and at the same time waited, watching for the appearance of Ann Elliot's tongue.

The older woman, still gripping my upper arms, stepped slightly away and looked at the girl.

"Ann," she said, swallowing excitement, "it's Joseph. He's come home."

"Yes." Ann smiled, looked rather worried, and said quickly, "I hate to interrupt, but—"

"What is it?" Miriam asked in her own special way.

"There's a man downstairs. A police sergeant. He wants to speak to someone in charge." She paused. "He asked for you, Mrs. Kindott."

"A policeman?" Loretta Kindott's eyebrows arched above her glasses. She released my arms, wiped her nose.

"I'll go down," Miriam said, shooting me a quick glance.

"No," Loretta Kindott said. "Wait. Joseph, you go with her. You're the man around here, now. You see what he wants. It can't be anything surely. But I'd rather you took care of it. Explain that I'm busy and cannot be disturbed." She leaned quickly toward me, gave me a quick peck on the jaw. "Run along, Joseph—we'll have all the time in the world now."

I said, "He did ask for you, Grandma."

"Please, Joseph..."

I looked at Miriam. Her face was utterly expressionless.

"He say what he wanted?" she asked Ann Elliot.

The girl shook her head. The tip of her pink tongue had revealed itself wonderfully, but I hadn't been in a position to enjoy it.

"Okay," I said. "I'll go down."

Miriam's words were clipped. "You think you should?"

"Why not?" I patted her arm, and started from the room. She moved quickly to my side just as Grandma Kindott said, "You stay with me, Ann. You can get me one of those Equanils, I'm so excited I could fly."

I envied her the Equanil, and took a Tum instead.

"What could he want?" I asked Miriam.

She was quick. "I don't know."

We came silently down the stairs. I did not like the stiff set of Miriam's jaw. A cop, I thought. But I wasn't really worried.

I was thinking of what Loretta Kindott had said. "Desmond *tells* me it's only a question of time—" What had she meant? Desmond Kindott was long in his grave.

...FOUR

The big furry monkey ran past us just as we reached the foot of the front stairs. He took a swipe at my leg, snagging the cloth of my pants and, with a quick, beady-eyed stare of vehemence, scampered upstairs.

A man stood in the hall by the front door.

Miriam said, "Hello."

Across the hall, by the entrance to an archway, stood a mellow mahogany waist high chest, topped with two weightly looking brass candlesticks. I stepped over there and deposited my pipe and sunglasses on top of the chest. Then I turned toward the waiting man.

Miriam was already shaking his hand. He regarded me past her shoulder with a sober face. As I walked over to him, this was the thing that struck me most about him—his rather affected sobriety.

I nodded.

He said, "I'm Sergeant Martin Brundell." Then he waited a second. It was as if he expected some sort of sudden recognition, a slap on the shoulder perhaps, an *"Oh, yes, good old Marty."* Something of the kind.

I could tell Miriam was under a strain.

Another thing that troubled me during this quick passing moment, was that he'd had nothing whatever to say about the monkey, Gargantua. He did not mention the beast.

"It might be best if we were comfortable," he said. "I'm afraid this might take a while." He spoke with a soft, cottony voice; there was no vibrance to the tone.

"Surely," Miriam said, "Come, we'll go in here."

She led the way through an archway at the left of the hall. It was a large front room sitting room, dominated by an immense flat-stoned fireplace, the stone reaching to the ceiling. The dark blue carpet gave the room an air of coolness, a quiet sedate quality that was enhanced by big comfortable leather chairs, glistening tables.

To the right of the fireplace, facing two chairs, was a tan sofa. Brundell immediately went to this, and sat directly in the center. He glanced up at us, and his mouth jerked in what probably was a smile.

Miriam sat in the left chair, I to the right.

Brundell cleared his throat, but said nothing. He glanced around the room, pale blue eyes checking things from behind glinting square-framed glasses. The frames were silver and very thin. It was difficult to see his eyes, really. Sunlight paled the area, entering at tall front windows, gleaming and glinting on the lenses of his glasses. I began not to like the fellow. There was something about him.

He was in plain clothes, dark blue pants, a lighter blue jacket, white shirt, dull maroon tie, a broad tie, with a fat knot, his collar immaculate. Not a large man, by any means, but extremely neat. His creases were in mint condition.

"You are—?" he said abruptly, blinking behind those damned glasses.

"I'm Miriam Kindott," she said. "And this is Joseph Lancaster."

"Ah," he said softly. "I take it, then, you're—?"

He took nothing, actually. He wanted explanations.

"Grandson and granddaughter," Miriam said. "Our grandmother isn't too well, you understand? She sends her apologies."

"I see," he said.

He sat quite straight on the sofa, not leaning against the back. One hand on either knee, he regarded us soberly.

I liked none of this. Too much bloody ceremony.

"What brings you, Sergeant?" I asked.

"Yes," he said. "Sesto Vecchi has disappeared."

I sat there, looking pleasant, I hoped. Who the hell was Sesto Vecchi? I watched Brundell and wished I had my pipe with me, so I could fool with it. I sorely needed a drink.

"I hadn't noticed," Miriam said.

"You mean you didn't realize he was missing?"

"No. Should I?"

"You certainly should, yes." Brundell gave a tiny little laugh, and frowned.

I looked at Miriam and smiled.

"Sesto is our gardener," she said to Brundell. "Really, I don't understand—"

"And Maria Vecchi, Sesto's mother, is your cook," Brundell said.

It was becoming involved. I liked less of it.

"Oh, yes," Miriam was abrupt, "Now that you mention it, I recall Maria saying something about Sesto gallivanting off—"

"Gallivanting. That's it." Brundell leaned slightly forward. "What else?"

"That's all."

"Did she say the word, 'gallivanting?'"

"Well, no, Not actually. I think she said he must have 'run off,' something like that."

"Exactly when did she say this?"

"Yesterday, I think. Yes. Yesterday morning."

Brundell shrugged. "He's been gone four days."

"You're from Missing Persons, then?" I said, to be saying something.

"No," Brundell said. He sighed, scratched his knee, his right knee, "You see, Angela Vecchi is concerned. Quite concerned." He turned his head so he was looking straight at me, and said, "Angela is Sesto's wife, Mr. Lancaster."

"Yes. I'm aware of that."

He continued staring at me. I knew it meant nothing. It was purely habitual, you could tell. He stared at everybody. Nevertheless, I felt uncomfortable.

Miriam said. "I should think you'd discuss this with Maria. Certainly she'd be in more of a position—"

"I have," Brundell said breaking in softly, with that airy, throatless voice. "I've spoken with Angela Vecchi, too. Last night. They thought perhaps Sesto might have said something to you, that you might help in some way."

"Maria hasn't shown this much concern," Miriam said. "She only mentioned she was worried about her son. Otherwise, hardly a word."

Brundell ran one hand carefully across his hair, as though he might get a shock if he touched it. It was meticulously immaculate straw-colored hair, with a gentle wave, combed with the exactitude one used to see in high school sophomores. Conservative mid-ear sideburns carried knife-edges. Gently, he said, "Oh." Then he said, "I'm afraid she's very frightened."

"Goodness," Miriam said. "What can there be to be frightened about? Sesto is a handsome boy, and he probably just—"

Brundell was abrupt. "I don't think so." He turned to me and said, "You live here, Mr. Lancaster?"

"Yes."

"You've always lived here, then?" He raised one hand, and a right eyebrow. "No. Of course not."

I experienced a tricky impact in my mid-region. I was in a corner and did not like it..

I said, "My grandmother's been at me to come and stay for a time." Always stick as close to the truth as possible. I forced a smile. "Finally decided to accommodate her wishes." I hesitated, went the whole way. "As a matter of fact, I just arrived this morning."

"Oh." That again. "From the west?"

He was right, of course, like radar, but I said, "No. As a matter-of-fact, New York." He had me rattled, and I cursed myself for this.

"Wife with you?"

"Not that lucky, Sergeant."

"Not married?" he frowned.

"No."

He leaned slightly forward, revealing faint traces of interest I knew were feigned. I had used the same actions many times. He was an actor, the son-of-a-bitch. "What's your line of work, Mr. Lancaster?"

"I'm in real estate." Then, as smoothly as I could, "You say Maria is frightened? What reasons does she give?"

He sighed and blinked behind the square-framed glasses. "Well, actually, it seems that on Saturday afternoon, four days ago, Sesto phoned his wife, Angela, from someplace, and he was wrought up. Excited. He indicated he had some rather terrible news to tell her, but didn't want to say it over the phone. He said he had to tell her immediately, and she should meet him out here on the beaches. He chose a small Italian restaurant, *Mama Mia's*, on Redington. They were to have dinner there. He said she had to help him decide something. She said he was in a provoking state." Brundell hesitated, scratched his chin, shook his head. "Angela waited till nine-thirty at *Mama Mia's*. Her husband never showed up. He hasn't been home since."

Miriam said, "Sesto was very excitable. Really. Discovering a strange seashell, a fossil, it would set him to waving his arms, shouting. The slightest thing, really."

"I see. Then he said nothing to you about going anywhere?"

"No."

"Well!" Brundell put both hands on his knees, pressed, and stood up. He gave a tiny laugh. It was like spitting a beebee. "I think that covers it, and I thank you both. Terribly sorry to have taken up your time, especially—" he smiled at me—"since you've just arrived, Mr. Lancaster."

"That's perfectly all right. Glad to help. If we hear anything, of course we'll contact you, Sergeant."

"That certainly would help."

He looked at Miriam as she stood up, rocked slightly on his heels with very faint appreciation, shook his head again.

I looked at Miriam. She looked at me, and her eyes were veiled.

Brundell said, "Well, then," turned and began walking from the room. He was a beauty, and I could not figure him. His walk was stiff in the shoulders. We came along the hall toward the rear entrance.

At the door, he said, "Thanks again." Then, "By the way, what was that strange beast I noticed earlier?"

"Oh," Miriam said, "that's Gargantua. A monkey."

"I see." He gave that tiny laugh again. Another beebee hit the floor about six feet away. He gave me a long, lingering look, and left.

Miriam closed the door, and immediately began walking off along the hall.

"Wait a minute," I said.

"What?" She paused, half turned.

"You didn't tell me anything about Sesto, either."

"I did not want you worrying, Tol—Joseph." She quickly whispered, "I've got to remember that."

"Please don't change the subject. Do you know anything about the gardener's disappearance?"

"Of course not."

I came up to her, my chest tingling. That pale face with the enormous, child-like brown eyes inclined toward me. The mouth was expressionless.

We stood that way for a long moment, not moving, my examining, Miriam unchanging. I was trying to see into her goddamn head again, "Damn it, Miriam, you're holding something back."

"You *are* a fool."

"You know better than that, too."

"Don't talk so loud."

"Why?"

She ignored this, "I don't know a *thing,* Joseph. Sesto was nothing to me."

"Handsome? 'Was?'"

"Is. *Is,* for God's sake. Well, something like Rory Calhoun. A very thin, exciteable, big-eyed Rory Calhoun. Only curly haired. But he had the white lock. What *are* you getting at, anyway?"

"Nothing, Absolutely nothing."

She sighed.

I said, "'Had the white lock?'"

"Oh, Jesus, Joseph." She turned quickly and began walking again, fast.

I jumped after her, grabbed her arm, wheeled her around, and took her by the shoulders. "You're growing away from me already, my child."

"You are *absolutely* stupid!"

"Yes. Sure."

"Oh, Joseph." She was calling me by that name, now, as if it were actually me. "It's that damned, that icky Brundell. He frightened me. He was so pompous, so superior."

I winked at her.

"Well, he was."

"Why should he frighten you?"

"I just don't like people like that."

"Neither do I. Miriam, honey."

"Do not *call* me that."

I took her by the hips, pulled her close. "Let's knock off a quick one in the broom closet."

She banged me with her pelvis. "That'll have to hold you, buster."

We stood there, locked.

Her whisper was tense. "What d'you think of Ann?"

"Cute as a bunny."

I placed both hands on her tight behind.

"You are remarkable," she said. "What if someone sees us?"

I released her. She stepped away. "You'd better run up and see Grandma, now." She took on a sly look. The big brown eyes were open wide, but you could see the veil come over them. Evil little things were going on in her head. "We should start planning."

Just the same, she awed me. "Miriam, last night when we were on the phone, you acted disturbed. You rang off before we finished. Why?"

"I *was* disturbed, that's why. That idiotic Gargantua. I told you he doesn't like me. It's as if he suspects. Really. He was all over me, and he had hold of the telephone wire. He tried to pull it out of the wall. Then Jinny came in, and—"

"Jinny—?"

"The maid. Before she left for the night. Jinny Kirkus. You'll meet her."

"The place is overrun."

"Have you figured a way?" She whispered it.

Her attitude stopped me for a second. I was beginning to see clearly what I dealt with. I needed a drink, and my heart gave a curious lurch. "You may as well get it through your head, Miriam. I've come to no decision, I don't work that fast. I'm here, and that's enough. As for the other, it's a big risk, and there's a moral quotient involved. I'm Joseph Lancaster now, and I'm here. We're together in the same house. It'll have to do for a time. Putting it bluntly, you surprise the hell out of me. It's difficult believing you mean what you say."

I knew she meant it. I had dallied with the problem. But my own words encouraged a relieved feeling in my chest. It was a brink, rather.

She stared. It was as if I'd punched her in the belly. A wicked crimson flush colored her neck, and rose into her face, blooming. I'd never seen her this way. I had struck home. The normal paper pale quality of her skin altered to tomato, her cheeks flamed, her eyes glistened with abrupt anger.

Somebody spoke from upstairs, a woman's voice. I heard footsteps on the stairs.

"That's Jinny," Miriam Said. "You come with me!"

She grabbed my hand and yanked. We stumbled stiffly across the hall, through an inner hall, and on into a large dining room. It was dim in here, but stray sunlight flickered on cut glass, more mahogany, bits of silver. A long polished table, covered with creamy lace stood in the center of the room, and there was a rather dazzling chandelier with tear drops of glinting crystal.

I glimpsed some bottles on a gigantic sideboard.

"Damn you!"

"Now, wait a minute, Miriam. I came, didn't I?"

We were both hissing at each other like two snakes on a rock. I had the impression that she was insane, the way her eyes looked. She had one hand up in a kind of claw.

I said, "Calm down, will you?"

"You agreed." Flatly.

"I agreed to nothing. What the hell do you think I am?"

"You agreed."

"You're in a rut."

Her hand flashed out and smacked my jaw. I grabbed her shoulders. She struggled, then went limp. I let her go, She stood there staring at the floor. Then she looked up at me again.

"I'm sorry," she said. "I've been on a kind of peak. It was as if you knocked the peak off— never mind. Listen, you've got to go through with it."

"That's better," I said. "At least, you're giving me a chance to decide. Christ, woman."

"I said I was sorry."

"Forget it." I went over to the sideboard. There were some beautiful cut glass tumblers on top. I hefted one, feeling the smooth solidity. I uncapped the closest decanter, poured. It was sherry. I filled the glass and, watching Miriam over the rim, drained it. I set it down. She kept staring at me with a kind of helpless, little girl air about her. In that red silk dress, with the pearls, the terrific legs, that face, she was anything but a little girl. Christ. She was a monster, after all.

I checked the next decanter. Whisky. I poured out two fingers. It was an excellent sour mash bourbon, and delectable. The picture began to change.

I sighed, "Miriam, you've got to understand about me. I'm all you said I was, and more. But, for goodness' sake, I'm not the other, either."

"But—you will?—us, together?"

I sipped again. It was pleasant on my tongue. She said, "you've *got* to, Tol—Joseph. I need your help."

I still said nothing.

She came over by me, and looked up at me and took a deep breath. She spoke very slowly, in that flat whisper. "I want her dead."

I expelled air through my teeth.

"I mean it," she said. "She's eighty. She's lived her life. I'm sick of it all— of everything. I can't stand it, don't you see? I want things, too. I don't want to stay here forever."

"When you're eighty, you want somebody saying you've lived your life?"

"You know what I mean!"

"Relax. No more of that." I finished the whisky. "Now, look. I'm considering angles, Miriam. I'm toying with the whole thing. But give me time, will you?"

She chewed her lip. She was the reproached maiden in a silent movie.

I reached out and slipped my hand inside her arm, so I could feel the side of her breast. "Miriam, if it'll make you happy, I'm inclined to lean in your direction." I paused. "Much as I hate myself."

"You're so—so damned—"

"That's a fact, my dear."

She looked up at me, her face pale again, smooth. "All right. But you will, won't you? If you'd only say you will."

I pursed my lips. "This Brundell—he's a character, believe it."

She was quick. "He's just doing a job. It's nothing, nothing at all." She was no longer frightened, then. She was becoming hot again. Her voice softened, like a spiteful child's. "If you don't do it, you'll be sorry." She said it as if she had been holding that back for some time.

"Implications," I said. "For shame." I patted her arm. "I'll get my stuff out of the car now, bring my bags in."

She stared some more.

"And, Miriam. I don't think we should lurk in corners too much. There should be some degree of professionalism about this."

"Oh, cool. Cool."

"As to the other," I said. "I'll keep it at the front of my mind. Okay?"

"Go to hell."

I smiled, turned, and left the room.

...FIVE

"Lagothrix lagotricha," Grandma Kindott said, with an excited smile. She hesitated. "At least, I think that's it," She stopped scratching Gargantua's underchin, and patted her pink hair. "I never can get these Latin names straight. Anyway, he—" She paused and looked a touch mysterious. "Well, anyway, he's a South American woolly monkey, actually."

She was seated by one of the bright windows in her front room. I stood a careful five feet away. The monkey eyed me with human eyes. He crouched on her lap, his thick tail curled on the floor, one furry arm around her neck.

"He's very human," I said.

She released a slow breath and said in an undertone, "You noticed, then."

"Well, yes. I mean, the eyes. I guess that's it."

"It's much more than the eyes, my darling." Then she seemed to realize how she was speaking, and cleared her throat. "He's a male, of course. Ordinarily, it's extremely difficult to keep them in captivity, but Gargantua is different." Again, with the last word, she was mysterious. The jet eyes were veiled behind those thick tortoise shell glasses. She was almost sly. Then she began to laugh. A staccato expelling of tiny gasps, like a miniature steam engine. The eyes were wise and sly.

"I've heard a monkey can't be housebroken."

"Oh!" She flapped at the air with one hand. "It's utter nonsense—at least in this case. He returns to his cage when there's a call of nature. One might say he's diffident about it. Quite."

"I see. Well, perhaps I'd better unpack now. Where shall I put my things, Grandma?"

She stared at me for a long moment, as if debating. "Wait, Joseph. Then I'll show you your room. I'm bursting to tell you."

"Tell me what?"

The lowered voice again, the sly look. "This isn't just a monkey, Joseph. You must never think that. He's something else."

I agreed with that.

"Your grandfather Desmond died nearly ten years ago, my darling. He loved you very much, you know?"

"I loved him, too, Grandma."

"Certainly you did. Desmond made a deep study of things. ESP, you know. Things like reincarnation."

"Oh." I knew, then, but I would let her tell me.

Her voice was almost a whisper. "He promised to come back, Joseph." She
paused. "He has come back."

"I see."

"He's right here with us, Joseph. He's inside Gargantua, trying to make
us understand."

"You mean—?"

"Yes, in a million different ways, he shows me."

She bent her head and kissed Gargantua's brow. He rolled his eyes, the
whites alarming. He clutched her. He ran his lips across her face. Abruptly, she stood. Gargantua sprang to the floor. "Now, I've told you my secret.
What do you think of that?"

"Can you be certain?"

"Very certain."

"How long have you known?"

"Nearly a year, Desmond had great difficulty, you know. Such things are
not easy. It's the only way he could return to me. Oh, he's not always here,
Joseph. Sometimes he returns to wherever. But, most of the time, Desmond
is with me."

"Marvelous, Grandma."

"I knew it would please you to know."

"Do you converse with—with him?"

"Only to a small extent. He makes me know in little ways, you see?"

"Ah."

"Yes."

We regarded each other. She was sharp and determined. I had my mouth
slightly open.

"Now, we'll go to your room, Joseph."

"Yes. My bags are in the hall."

"Do you remember much about the house?"

"Well, it's rather dim, really."

"It's your home, Joseph. But it's been such a long time." She turned and
gazed at Gargantua. He stood like a stone, now, eyeing me, making almost
silent stuttering sounds. "He isn't restful with you as yet. I don't think
Desmond is here right now. Otherwise he would behave differently, you
see?"

"Could we leave him here, for the time being?"

She glanced at me and frowned. "Why, of course, Joseph—if that's what
you wish."

"I only—I can't wait to see... That is, am I to have my old room?"

"Yes!"

She opened the door and we stepped into the hall. My bags were on the
landing at the head of the stairs.

"Come..."

We walked around the banistered landing, and across to the left side of the house.

"You remember your room?"

"Only faintly."

"Of course, you know where it is."

"Of course."

She had hesitated before a door in a small alcove. I felt certain this was where the little Joseph had bided his time. She stepped to the door, so frail, so like a clothes tree topped by a pink cloud, and turned the black agate knob.

"It's precisely as you left it, Joseph. Of course, it's dusted daily."

There was a catch in her voice, and she watched me with an odd kindness, a tenderness. Then she took her hand from the doorknob.

"You open it Joseph." The dry, throaty tone was strained; she was close to tears.

I opened the door, stepped inside. She followed, plucking at my elbow. Sunlight swam in a large, colorful room. It was at the left front of the house. For an instant, I felt as if I were invading someone's privacy. A single maple bed stood to the left, against the wall, covered with a vari-hued patchwork quilt.

"I've had your bed made up fresh," Loretta Kindott said. "Everything else is as you left it, so long ago."

"But, why, Grandma?"

"Because you're special. Because you're mine."

I swallowed the proverbial lump.

Toys of all kinds were scattered about: a crimson rocking horse with Barney Google eyes, a flowing hempen mane, an electric train sitting yellowly amid a tangle of track, tiny tin cars, a huge dump truck, a basket of rubber balls, a sky-blue phonograph with a stack of records, a battered, one-eyed Teddy-bear. On the wall to the left was an enormous poster in blazing color of Long John Silver, with his crutch and parrot, palms and a pirate's chest in the background. An open green desk stood over by the front windows. A long bookcase gleamed by the wall, packed haphazardly with bright-backed books. Other paper cutouts of cartoon characters were pasted to the walls; Prince Valiant, Dick Tracy, The Dragon Lady, and more. I spotted a torn orange kite, marbles, a baseball bat, a dark oil-stained catcher's mitt. The floor was covered with a large circular hooked rug; olive and tan predominating.

She was speaking. "I would come here and sit, over there in that chair, and remember. The times when you were here, running through the house. We were so happy then." She paused. "And, now, Joseph, you've come home again."

"Yes."

Her light bony hands sought mine. Her grip was light, too, touched with energy, but without tension. She peered into my eyes and slowly moved her head from side to side. "You've made an old woman very, very happy, my darling."

I squeezed her hands.

"Now," she said briskly, withdrawing her hands. "I'll leave you to yourself. You'll want to examine the house, won't you? You must unpack. If you like, you may put your toys away, in that chest. Remember? And, Joseph, I do not eat lunch, but I'm sure you must be starved. Just ask Maria for something. Then you'd better take a nap. You do look rather peaked."

"I'll be fine, Grandma."

She turned in that droopy yellow- and blue-flowered silk dress, moved stiffly to the door, then glanced back at me, her head tilted. "Your grandfather is happy too," she said in a small, remote voice.

I tried to smile. She left the room, and I heard her moving slowly off along the hall. Christ.

To the left was a partly open door—the bathroom.

I stared at the door. For a long moment, everything was quite unreal, dreamlike. The feeling was intense, almost exotic with the brilliant sunlight. I felt as if I were living someone else's life, name; wearing his very shoes, you might say. Did the real Joseph Lancaster's ghost look on with disapproval? He could not have cared, really. But, then, too, who could say? Transmigration...

My stomach was burning. I took three Tums, left the room with deliberation, picked up my bags, and returned. I packed some clothes in the small maple bureau, left one bag open on the floor, put the other two bags in a deep cluttered closet, where I also hung my suits. I hid the Luger under some socks in a top bureau drawer, took two bottles of brandy into the closet, and sat on the edge of the bed with the other resting on my knee. I did not like the way my heart was beating. There was a certain frightening erratic tumble to it. I had a warming, hopeful swallow of brandy. It burned its way down, and settled unhappily. I took another in desperation. Gradually the aspect altered, became less knife-like. The edges softened.

Anxiety did not disperse. If anything, it increased, rather surprisingly, possibly because there was a looseness to my mind. My imagination took long black sweeps, Miriam centered there, a shrouded, argumentative figure, adamant, like a steel wedge.

The sunlight was too much. I set the bottle on the floor, went to each window, and drew the long flower-printed egg-shell drapes almost closed. From the front windows, you could see the long sweep of dream green lawn, motionless royal palms, the breadth of white beach, the minty Gulf.

What was I doing here? Miriam seemed so impossibly unreal.

I turned and John Silver glared at me with wild eyes. I looked back out at the Gulf again, and saw her run down between the royal palms, on to the beach.

It was Miriam, all right. She wore a white bikini, and she seemed tiny, doll-like, at this distance. I knew it was Miriam because of the pale blond hair, and the way she moved.

I watched her, feeling the quality of silence in this house that I had noticed before. It was intense now. There was no sound at all, just my rather rusty breathing.

I was supposed to help kill that old woman in the other room...

Miriam splashed in the Gulf now, the water to her knees. Suddenly a head popped up near her. She dove under the water, broke surface near the bobbing head. Two arms revealed themselves. Now there were two heads, one Miriam's. They faced each other. It was a man, but so distant I could detect nothing else. They remained in the same position for some seconds, then, abruptly, the man's head disappeared again. He surfaced and began swimming directly out into the Gulf. Miriam came on to the beach and stood there, looking at the house, maybe at me, who could tell?

A muted stuttering commenced behind me. I whirled. Gargantua was poised just inside the door, watching me, head cocked, eyes bright and inquisitive.

I stepped back to the bed, sat down, picked up my bottle and waited. The big monkey was silent now. He began prowling the room in quick lunges, the long thick furry tail curled out behind him. Every movement he made was followed by a fast, flashing glance at me from the corners of his strangely human eyes.

"How you doing, Grandpa?" I whispered.

He hissed, made a rattling sound in his throat, and continued prowling. He was stealthy. I took a pull at the bottle, then rested it on my knee. There was something at once savage, untame, about the beast. Tremendous energy of a wild kind revealed itself with every step he took. He was inspecting me with animalistic trepidation.

He spotted the open bag on the floor, and leaped toward it. He stood poised, staring at the packed clothes, chattering softly. He looked at me. Then, without the faintest hesitation, he began grabbing folded shirts, ties, shorts, hurling them into the air, chattering louder, shooting glances at me.

I just watched. I suspected what he could do to me, if I tangled with him. Then, even before he did it, I knew what might happen. I came to my feet, holding my breath.

He was quick. He spotted the manilla folder containing the typewritten history of Joseph Lancaster, the newspaper obituary, and he was going to do exactly what I figured. He went silent, grabbed the folder just as I took a step toward him. I cursed myself, because my lunge had alarmed him. He clutched the folder to his chest, and made a running leap for the bed. I rushed him. He went sailing over the top of my head and landed in a crouch, making no sounds at all.

I set the bottle on the floor.

"Here, Gargantua—here, boy!"

He held the manilla folder with both arms, pressed against his furry chest. He stared at me, mouth gaping, eyes darting wildly.

"There, now, there. Here, now." I took an inching step toward him.

He came to life with a sharp cry, turned and ran leaping from the room. At the back of my mind, I knew he was frightened, that he did not even realize he held the manilla folder. This changed nothing.

I went after him.

He scampered around the landing, heading for the far side and Grandma Kindott's rooms. I plunged after him, my throat burning, heart thundering painfully. He paused, turned and stared at me. I ran lightly toward him. He turned and leaped again. We were nearly to her door.

He reached the door. I gave a kind of moan in my throat, abandoning myself now, I had to get that manilla folder. If she saw it...

He reached up with a hind foot and scratched at the door, glinting eyes on me. I heard her voice just as I came up to him.

"Desmond? Is that you?"

The monkey hissed, gave a single bound and landed on the banister over the stair well, I heard her footsteps. I went for him.

He ran briskly along the banister, traveling like wind. I chased him. We came to the head of the stairs and he leaped racing down.

"Gargantua?" It was Grandma Kindott.

I did not look up, just went after him. But before I was halfway down the stairs, he was in the hall, crouched, staring up at me.

Luckily nobody was in the hall. The absolute silence of the house was awesome. I reached the foot of the stairs.

"Here, boy!"

"Eyolp!"

He ran, scampering, leaping. Along the hall toward the rear entrance, where he was heading, I saw a partially open door. He spotted it, opened it with a fling, and vanished.

I reached the door, stepped through... into blackness. The house was air-conditioned, but a light wave of cooler air swept over me. I smelled the unmistakable odors of a basement, dampness, winey odors, and saw a light switch on the wall. Desperately, I flicked the switch and closed the door. There was a small brass dead bolt. I shot the bolt.

I gave a tight sigh. Now, at least, we were together, separate from everyone, Gargantua and I.

There was no sign of him on the stairs, and there was absolutely no sound.

I stepped down slowly, feeling sick. Adrenalin was shooting into me until I was dizzy with it; tense and terrified to the point where I could hardly breathe. I took another step. The stairs broke in the middle, cut off at an angle. I reached the turning.

"Here, boy!"

Nothing.

I came down on to the cellar floor.

All I needed was for someone to begin pounding on the cellar door.

The lighting was dim. To the left was a raw boarded wall, with a large arched opening. In the dimness, I saw racked bottles and knew where the winey smell had come from.

To the right was a still dimmer hallway, ending in faded darkness. Straight ahead I saw what looked like a part of a workshop, the corner of a lathe.

I heard a rustling noise.

I stepped toward the lathe. It was some distance. The boarded wall to the left ended, meeting a cement block. The cement block wall made a turn.

I looked carefully around the corner.

Gargantua stood under a dim yellow light, beside a high work bench. There were tools of all kinds; saws, another lathe, smaller tools racked on a gigantic peg-board against the high wall.

I advanced on him. He moved to the end of the workbench, partly in shadow. He stood beside what looked, at first glance, like a rolled carpet, bound with cord.

I smelled something curiously sweet.

The monkey was sniffing, his eyes glinting toward me, lips curled. I kept coming toward him.

He did not move.

Then, suddenly, he turned to the rolled carpet and began plucking at it. I was closer now. It wasn't a carpet. It was a bound. rolled tarpaulin, red brown in color.

The odor was stronger.

The monkey stood transfixed, back toward me now. He still clutched the manilla folder to his chest. Then, suddenly, he leaped atop the rolled, bound tarpaulin, and began jumping up and down, emitting tiny, almost soundless screams.

I dove at him, snagged the manilla folder, and snatched it away from him. He gave a wild, "Eyolp!", and leaped past me, running across the cellar floor.

I stood there, feeling the stammering thud of my heart. I closed my eyes, trying to still the gasping. The burning was in my throat. Eyes still closed, I found the Tums, took three, crunching them rapidly, so they could do their blessed work. The pain began to ease.

I stared at the rolled tarpaulin.

At the right end was a slight jut. I knelt down, pulled back the carelessly tied flap at the edge, and saw a booted foot with dirt on it.

I stood up again. The odor was strong, and now it was an obvious odor. I did not think then. I simply stood there. I heard the cellar door open and close, but still did not move. There was no sound; just my breathing.

Kneeling at the left end of the bundle, I untied a piece of hemp twine, quickly yanked back the curl of treated canvas, and stared at the face. I had never seen him before. The mouth was in a kind of lip-drawn snarl, teeth bared. The rictus of death held him in alarm. Dark eyes were starting, the lids only slightly closed. Part of the tarp still covered the head. I pulled this away, and saw the curly black hair, and the white lock at the forepeak.

He had reminded her of Rory Calhoun.

Quickly, I closed the tarp over that face, and stood up again, my throat dry. There lay Sesto Vecchi, the missing gardener.

Oh, Miriam, I thought... Miriam... what have you gotten me into?

...SIX

It was a dark contamination. I had dreamed of things like this, dreamed of actually killing someone; then the long-drawn horror of knowing what I'd done, knowing there was no escape ever.

I walked softly through the cellar in a kind of trance, reached the stairs, started up. Devious, terrifying patterns filtered through my mind, setting off emotions that made me weak. I had not seen many dead persons. My father, my maternal grandfather and grandmother. I stopped at the turn in the stairs, remembering vividly how when my grandmother was in a casket in the front room, my mother, unknowing, helpless in the clutch of sudden lost love, had led me to the casket. I was six at the time. She held me up, so I could see the body. "Kiss her good-bye, Tolbert." I fought, unable to speak. "Kiss her, Tolbert." She held my head down over that white, wrinkled, sleeping horror, that stillness. "Kiss Grandmother!" My lips touched the chill parchment of the cheek. I screamed. I was ill in bed for a week, lost in a black tunnel of fear.

Now I came on up the cellar stairs.

What was the body of Sesto Vecchi doing down there, wrapped in a stiff tarpaulin?

Oh, Miriam...

I gave the monkey but a single thought. The bolt on the door was drawn. I knew he had done this, I opened the door, switched off the light, stepped into the hall. I was somnambulistic, aching and frozen inside, wanting to take action, not knowing what to do.

"Mr. Lancaster!"

It was Ann Elliot; she of the pink tongue.

"Please," I said off the top of my head, "call me Joseph."

"Then you'll call me Ann?"

"Fine."

"You were in the cellar?"

"Yes. Just—looking around the old house." I gave a little dry laugh that surprised me. I cleared my throat. I tried to look at her and actually see her. She still wore the saffron dress, rather short, and the gold was at her waist, a linked chain. The dark blue eyes seemed faintly puzzled.

"Did Gargantua bother you?"

"Not at all. Why d'you ask?"

"We thought, that is, Mrs. Kindott thought—but it's nothing." She smiled with that lush mouth, and the pink tongue had shown itself twice, with the slight lisp. It gave me heart, "I'll bet you've had no lunch," she said.

"As a matter-of-fact—"

"You come with me."

"Really, Ann—I'm not at all hungry right now."

I wondered, *Should I tell her...?*

I remembered Sergeant Brundell, and knew I was a touch aberrant.

The police would come. There would be questions. *"You're Joseph Lancaster, then?" "Yes." "Mind if we take your fingerprints? Perhaps you'd better come to headquarters with us. Purely routine, of course."*

Ann Elliot was speaking. I tried to catch what it was, but missed. The echo of her voice died in the hail. The silence moved in again. She was staring at me with those dark blue eyes.

"I'm sorry, Ann—I lost track."

"You sure you're all right? You're a bit pale."

"I'm fine. Just all the surprises, everything."

I gave that little self-conscious laugh again. It was something quite new.

Even so, now I was conscious of her body under that dress. She must have been wearing a silk slip. Her body seemed to slither under the cloth of the dress. There was quite a bit about this one. She emanated a sexuality that could not be denied. It was in her tone, in her pink tongue, in every movement she made. There was an impression of familiarity, of closeness. She generated need.

To our left, at the end of the hall, a short, broad-calved girl in a gray-blue dress, a sort of uniform, hurried across to an opposite door. She had bright flame-red hair. She carried a cloth, flipping it against her hip.

"That's Jinny," Ann told me.

"Ah. Jinny Kirkus."

"You've met her, then?"

"Miriam mentioned her. I think I'll just—" At that instant the front entrance door opened, and Miriam slipped quickly inside, with a stealthy hurriedness. She still wore the intricately minute white bikini, her slim paleness looking somehow over-lush, provocative. She did not see us, at first. Her expression was preoccupied. "Excuse me," I murmured to Ann, "there's a bit of business I've got to check with Miriam."

Ann Elliot smiled and winked. It was more a lowering of one lid, the left. It was startling, out of the ordinary. It was a lewd wink if I ever saw one. I had no time to consider its implications, or possible promise, but for a moment it dichotomized my emotions regarding Sesto Vecchi lying down there in the cellar. I gave Ann a long look, and she returned it almost boldly.

I headed for the front entrance. Miriam was moving toward the stairs, rapidly. She saw me.

"Miriam?"

"Oh?" Then she glimpsed Ann. "What is it, Joseph?" Then she noticed I carried the manilla folder, and put her hand to her mouth. At another time it might have been comical. Presently, it was nothing of the kind.

I walked quickly over to her.

"Could you please come up to my room, Miriam? There's something I'd like to run over with you."

"Sure. I'll just change this—"

"Now," I whispered. My back was to Ann, who still stood, down the hall. I made a berserk face, Miriam's composure did not alter. Turning quickly, she hurried up the stairs.

I was right behind her, watching the movements of her legs, her alert bottom. We reached the landing, made the circle around to Joseph Lancaster's room. I held the door and she entered.

Inside, she whirled, pointing at the manilla folder as I closed the door and locked it. "What's that?"

I said nothing. I went over and opened a bureau drawer, tucked the folder under some socks by the Luger, and turned to Miriam.

"The monkey stole it," I said.

"Gargantua?"

"Is there another monkey?" I paused, then said, "He took it, and I couldn't catch him to get it back."

She was sharp, paler than ever. "I told you to destroy that!"

"You'd better just take it easy, Miriam, baby, because it's actually unimportant, considering."

"Unimportant? Suppose somebody got hold of it? Suppose Grandma saw it? You're a fool. My God!"

"Sit down, please."

"I won't sit down." But nevertheless, she backed over against the rocking horse, and leaned on its glittering saddle. She held to the hempen mane with her right hand. She knew something was coming, you could see it in those big brown eyes.

"Who was that out there with you?" I made it light.

"Out where?"

"On the beach, Miriam. In the water. A man."

"You're out of your mind."

I drew a deep breath. "I *saw* you, Miriam, my child. From the window. A bobbing head, right beside you. Then he swam off toward Mexico. Who was it?"

"Oh." She made a face, wrinkling the corners of her eyes, "You mean Mr. Abercrombie. He lives down the beach. He's always swimming up here. He asks questions like, 'Shouldn't we do something about erosion? Are you going to get a sea wall?' Stuff like that. Really, he comes up to look at me."

"I see, Mr. Abercrombie."

"Yes."

"What was it today?"

"Well, did I think the Australian pines would ever really come back. After that horrible freeze we had, you know?"

She knew that wasn't it, too.

I moved over by the bed, picked up the brandy bottle, and sat down on the edge of the bed. I tipped the bottle up and took a short one. I needed it more than I had figured. I rested the bottle on my knee. She was watching me with something like veiled concern. There was a slight ache in the elbow of my left arm.

"I suppose I'll have to call the police," I said. "I hate doing it, being in the position I am, but it seems the only logical thing."

"The police?"

"Yeah," I stared at her stare. "I was going to do it before, but I thought I'd better wait and talk with you first."

She said nothing, just watched me.

I said, "Did you know Sesto Vecchi is in the cellar?"

Her mouth opened. She closed it.

"You *did* know, then?"

She still did not speak.

"I *know* now that you knew, Miriam. I can read your expression. I'm rather good at reading expressions, especially under pressing circumstances. If I know the circumstances, to some extent, then it's rather simple, really."

She moved over to me. She moved between my legs, and placed her hands on my head, and brought my face against her bare belly. It smelled faintly brackish.

"You can't contact the police," she said softly.

"Why not?" My mouth was against her soft skin, and it came out muffled. I moved my head slightly. "Why not?"

"Because, you can't."

"That's no good reason, Miriam. Sesto Vecchi's lying down there, quite dead, wrapped in a tarp."

"Don't keep talking about it."

"He can't possibly lie there much longer without everybody in the house knowing about it."

There was a long silence. Her stomach growled faintly. She kept her hands pressed tightly against my head, standing there like that.

"Tolbert? I mean, Joseph?"

"Yes?"

"If you told the police, they would come, and there would be questions. They would be nasty questions. I'm sure. I have that feeling. And they could very possibly find out about you. Everything. You know that. You know you're not Joseph Lancaster. That you're actually a con man named O'Shaugnessy—and they would find that out. No telling what they might uncover."

"You put it succinctly." I set the bottle on the floor.

"That isn't all." She hesitated, and I waited. I felt her hands becoming tense. I touched my tongue to her belly. It was definitely brackish. She said quietly, "You see, Joseph—*I did it.*"

"Did It?"

"Yes. I killed Sesto. Oh, God. I was going to tell you, because I've got a plan, and—"

She ceased talking as I slowly reached up and took her by the delicate hip-bones, pushed her slightly away. I looked up at her. The huge brown eyes stared down at me. She licked her lips. The mouth was faintly drawn. I said, "You killed him."

"Yes."

Maybe, at the back of my mind, I had known, all along. Maybe that was why I'd been in such a fog.

She tried to hold to my head, but I twisted away, stood up, and stepped over by the bureau. I leaned against it, staring at her. She was a monster, a damned monster, all the way. "And you have a plan."

"I *had* to, damn you!"

"Enchanting."

"I was going to tell you tonight."

I said nothing.

"You are a conceited ass," she said briskly. "You stand there with your stupid nose in the air, and you don't even know how it happened." Her chin began to tremble.

"That's it," I said. "Cry."

She gave a little sniff, wandered over by the rocking horse, and began tugging at the hempen mane again with her right hand. "He'd been acting funny."

"Sesto, you mean?"

"Who the bloody else?" She tore some of the mane loose and dropped it on the floor, began tugging again. "Anyway, I've been missing panties—for some time."

"You mean—"

"Jesus, you are stupid! Panties, for God's sake. Yes. Maybe twenty-five pair, that's all. Gone from my drawers. Now make a crack, huh? Yes. And they'd always vanish on a day when Ann and Grandma went into town, or somewhere. Ann goes with her. And four days ago, they went into town, and I decided I'd have a swim, and I went to my room, and there was Sesto, with—"

"In your room?"

"Standing there with my panties crammed under his arm, like that. Only he was reading that goddamn folder of stuff I gave you on my cousin. I'd left it in the drawer with my panties, and he found it. The obituary, everything."

I let out a slow breath. "I see."

She leaned toward me and said, "I'm so *happy* you do." She straightened, put one hand on her hip, and began tugging at the rocking-horse's mane again. Bits and pieces came away, fluttered to the floor. "He was caught red-handed, not only with the panties, but reading that—" She shook her head. "He tried to smooth it over. He was a mess. Then he told me he loved me. I knew I couldn't let him go. It was all planned for you to come here. I didn't know what to do. I was furious. He dropped the folder, and rushed for the door. He didn't drop the panties, and he ran downstairs with me after him."

"I can visualize this," I said.

"Sure. And the cellar door was open. He headed for that, trying to talk back at me over his shoulder. He was really shook, and there was this flat-iron, an old iron, painted red, used for a door-stop. I grabbed it up and caught him by the door and hit him with it. On the head."

"Hard."

"It cracked, and there was blood all over, and he fell down. He was dead, Tolbert! There was blood on my panties, too." She just stood there now, wide-eyed, unmoving. "It was hell. Believe it. Luckily nobody was here, not even Jinny. I dragged him down cellar, somehow, and wrapped him up. That's how it happened."

She stood there waiting for me to say something. I was waiting for the same thing.

Finally, I said, "And the plan?"

"What plan?"

"Something about the body in the cellar. You said you had a plan—something."

She came across the room, put both arms on my shoulders, and looked up at me. "You've got to help me."

I waited.

She said, "You will help me, won't you? Listen, we'll take it out in the Gulf and drop it. Tonight." She kept looking at me, and I did not speak, and she said, "You've got to, anyway. Because, if you don't then it's your neck as much as mine."

"How do you figure?"

"You want them to know?"

"No."

"Then, that's what we do. Listen," she said, lowering her voice, very conspiratorial. "I could not help doing what I did. He was sneaking my panties, don't you see? A real freak—he wouldn't even let them go when I caught him." She paused, then said, "I'd think you'd sympathize, for God's sake. You just stand there, staring at me. Damn you!" She gave a wild toss of her head, and started for the door. "I don't care *what* you think. You've got to help me."

"Wait. Miriam."

She unlocked the door and stepped outside. I followed her. She walked rapidly along the landing, and entered a room. I supposed it was here, and I went after her. I opened the door against her thrust.

"Miriam, can you blame me? Listen—" I closed the door. It was a large sunny room, all sky-blue frills and lace, with a large spool bed, and other comfortable furnishings. There was a small circular table at the foot of the bed, an immense chest of drawers beyond. She turned and looked at me, leaning with one hand on the table, fingers fiddling with the pages of a magazine. I said, "Miriam, you throw a mean curve."

"I should think you'd be used to that."

"No. I'm the one who throws the curves, remember?"

She just stood there, pouting. I knew now that she was dangerous. I had known this before, of course, but now it was real. My stomach and throat burned, so I got out the Tums and began chewing quickly. Just for something to say, I said, "Where was it Sesto found the folder?"

"In there." She pointed at the third drawer in the chest of drawers.

It was only something to do while I tried to think. Keep moving and you've got a chance. I went over and yanked the drawer open. She was standing with her back to me now, by the table, probably still pouting, The drawer was filled with vari-colored panties, red, yellow, orange, blue, pink, white, black. I plunged my hand into the piles of nylon, trying to think of something to say, trying to see beyond the film of gauze that shrouded my mind. I gave a little belch, and felt something strangely solid in the drawer. This happened just as I was about to withdraw my hand. I pushed panties aside, and came up with a nickel-plated .32 automatic. A pair of lace-trimmed scarlet panties dangled from the barrel. I threw the panties back into the drawer. I stared at the automatic and said, "What's this?" very stupidly.

She turned. "A gun, for God's sake."

"Beautiful. What for?"

"What do you mean 'what for?'"

She stepped quickly over to me, grabbed the gun, snatched it from my hand, and tossed it back into the drawer, "I've had it for a long time, just in case. Now, listen, you're avoiding everything." She thrust against the drawer with the backs of her legs, closing it. "Your job is to think about *her.*"

I knew whom she meant, but said nothing.

"And you've got to help me tonight. I'll come to your room, and now—you'd better go and see her. Make up to her."

I said nothing.

Her voice was pitched low. "Listen. It's a million and a quarter dollars, Sunshine. Will you please try to remember that?"

Nobody would ever think, to look at her...

There was a light rapping on the door. "Joseph?"

Somebody said, "Are you in there with Miriam?"

It was Grandma Kindott.

"Go out and soothe the old bitch," Miriam whispered. "I'll see you later."

"Joseph?" Grandma Kindott called again.

I headed for the door. My stomach still burned, and this frightened me, because the proper balance of body chemistry is a very important thing.

•••SEVEN

That afternoon, Grandma Kindott and I got drunk on sherry. We sat in her front room, with Gargantua perched on a studio couch, grunting softly to himself, and we tormented each other with memories. I managed to let her do most of the remembering. Old Pop Carmoody, my mentor from the early days, had taught me well how to prime the pump, and keep the water flowing, without allowing any disrupting doubt to enter the other person's mind. I smiled, nodded, demurred, and wiped away a stray tear at the early Joseph's shenanigans. And one thing for certain, Grandma Kindott loved Joseph Lancaster with an endurance that approached the psychotic.

But behind my facade of pleasantry was a warming hell. Sesto Vecchi lay dead in the cellar in his canvas winding sheet, skull crushed by a flat-iron. Sergeant Martin Brundell prowled at the back of my mind, with his too-neat hair, and square-framed glinting glasses, the epitome of patient police sleuth; and most of all Miriam hovered at the edges of my thought, once elf, but now truly approaching monster status.

Snatches of Grandma Kindott's monologue reached me, and I would smile and agree and finish another glass of the good wine.

"Of course, you were introverted," she said, "I had great difficulty getting you away from the books, and even just staying in your room. Remember how I'd make you bat the ball?" She gave a tiny snicker, and wiped her mouth with the back of her hand. The pink hair was wilder than ever. She sipped from her glass. "And the comic books. You couldn't get enough of them. Do you still read comic books?"

"No. Actually, I grew out of that."

"I'm so glad. I remember the time..." And she would remember, endlessly, while I became more and more conscious of the evil fact that stared me in the face.

We were supposed to kill this woman. I was supposed to "plan."

The dry, throaty, intelligent sound of her voice rippled on. She sat crookedly in a straight-backed chair against the sunlight from the western window, weaving about, describing intricacies with her wine glass, the jet eyes darting behind those tortoise shell glasses, first at me, then over toward the monkey on the studio couch.

She drank with finicky jerks of hand and head, and the more she drank, the more often her husband's, Desmond's, name was mentioned. "Desmond says—" "Desmond agrees with me—" "Desmond claims—" "Desmond told me to be patient."

The monkey seemed irritated. He nervously picked at his furry leg, ate what he discovered, and made small chattering bursts of sound.

A million and a quarter...

My elbow and shoulder ached. It was rheumatic, I felt certain. Then I recalled with a start that recently I'd taken to leaning on my left elbow, when in bed, thinking. That was it, of course. I'd actually brought on an attack of rheumatism. I'd heard of such cases in my readings, and once present, the sufferer never was able to rid himself of the debilitating disease. It spread rapidly to other joints in the body, slowly, but certainly incapacitating its victim.

I sneaked a quick glance at my knuckles, half expecting to see them protruding obnoxiously, I gripped my glass, but experienced no pain. Desperation began working inside me. I had a burning stomach. Rheumatoid arthritis, ulcers, or worse. Also there was a troublesome heart condition that every now and again signaled brief hints of future devastation.

I finished another glass, refilled it from the nearly empty bottle on the table between us.

A million and a quarter...

Thinking this brought conscious excitement.

You are Tolbert. I am Miriam. We will share it, my love, and quaff the wine of Life to the very dregs...

"What was that, Grandma?"

"You weren't even listening, Joseph." She leaned precariously to one side, shaking her finger. She hiccuped, the sharp white blade of her nose shining with perspiration.

"Certainly, I was listening."

"What d'you think of Miriam?"

"She's quite nice," I said.

The black eyes probed. She was no fool.

"Oh, Joseph. You haven't changed at all, really. You still say the first thing comes into your head."

"I mean it, Grandma. She's very nice. Of course, I hardly know her."

She hiccuped again, belched lightly, said, "Oh, my."

Then she said, "Miriam is mercenary. All she thinks about is money."

"Ah."

Miriam's voice echoed in the back of my mind. *"We'll take it out in the Gulf and drop it, see?"*

Grandma Kindott said, "It's true, Joseph. She doesn't fool me, Oh, she's *nice* enough, at least to one's face, she is. But what does she really think about?"

"Are you trying to tell me something, Grandma?"

For a long time she did not speak. I was paying attention now. Anything might jeopardize the scheme. Immediately, I realized what that thought contained and what it meant. It made me a touch ill to know how I was thinking.

Grandma Kindott was quite pie-eyed. Almost out of control, except for her speech. She held on like a trooper, and said, "No. Not trying to tell you anything, Joseph."

"You simply wondered what I thought of Miriam?"

"That's right. Desmond says Miriam tells lies."

"But why should she do that?"

Her expression was slyly drunken. "Why didn't you return home sooner?"

"I wanted to, desperately—but I was ashamed."

"Why? Tell me, for goodness' sake."

"I'm a failure, Grandma. I wanted to make some money, make you proud of me."

She gave a deep sigh. "Darling. Really. I have all kinds of money, you must know that. And I'll tell you something. It's all yours. All of it. And it's a great deal of money, Joseph. You must understand, I have no one but you. Yes—now, now. So many years have vanished. If only we could've—"

I broke in. "What about Miriam?"

"It isn't the same with Miriam, Joseph. She's a woman. She'll find her husband, love, and he'll take care of her. That's a woman's way. Of course, I'll help her. Now, have you considered what business you'll get into?"

"I've given it deep thought."

"Desmond says—" The wine glass fell from her hand, and she toppled. I lurched from my chair, caught her before she struck the floor.

"I don't do this often, Joseph," she muttered, slurring the words.

Gargantua bounded from the studio couch, alarmed. He eyed me fiercely, flapped his arms over his head, and began chattering.

I carried Grandma Kindott to the studio couch, and stretched her out. Her eyes were half open, like Sesto Vecchi's, staring. She breathed in short gasps. She was a rack of sticks under the silk dress.

All I had to do was drop a pillow on her face.

The monkey screamed horribly. It was as if he'd read my mind. I turned to him, and he made a savage leap at me, stopping a foot or two away, wildly brandishing his arms. He looked at Grandma Kindott, then at me. Thick lips rolled back from glistening teeth and frightening hoarse sounds burst from his throat.

He bounded between me and the door. I made a circle, moving around him, keeping a close eye on him, and managed to reach the door.

I quickly left the room, went downstairs, and found Ann Elliot in the hall. I told her what had happened; Grandma was crocked. She said, "I'll go right up," and ran for the stairs.

Gargantua was racing madly down. He barked softly at Ann, leaped into the hall, and just stood there staring at me, baring those yellow teeth, making sounds like groans.

My stomach was on fire, and I had no Tums. I hurried to the other stairs, went up to my room. Then I remembered. I'd left my cache of Tums at the Indian Rocks place. Nothing else would help. Sodium bicarbonate only aggravated the condition.

Swallowing fiery gall, I went back downstairs, and out the rear door to the Chevelle. I drove fast, hit Gulf Boulevard, and kept my eye out for a drug store. I could not recall one. Mixed up with the burning pain of indigestion, if that's what it was—ulcers, appendicitis, insipient coronary— the monkey, Gargantua, had his savage fingers dug into my brain, and I could actually hear the jungle-like screams. But I knew it was good for me to be away from the Kindott home, if even for a short time. Whenever I had this burning pain, all sorts of dreamlike thoughts railed in my mind. Sesto's dead staring face would not leave me. I couldn't help thinking, too, how his mother, his wife, would feel if they knew.

I came speeding into Indian Rocks, reached my place, and stopped. Relief was in sight. I already felt some better. I went to the door, opened it, and stepped inside.

The Tums, an entire carton of them, were on the shelf over the couch. I knelt quickly on the couch, fumbled them down, and crammed three or four into my mouth, chewing rapidly. Almost immediately the pain vanished, easing from my body. Shaken, I was nearly in a swoon with the sudden normalcy. I lay there, panting, knowing something had to be done about my condition. Would I have to consult a physician? I could never face that; he would discover too many horrible things. It was a disturbing thought.

I rolled over and sat on the edge of the couch, rattled and tense, but gulping in the shadowed peace of this sweet place, remembering the contentment before Miriam's crazy proposal.

Then I knew somebody had been here.

Someone had been on this very couch. I leaped up, staring at the couch. The covers were in disarray, not at all as I'd left them. I was never overly neat, but I always made an attempt. You knew when your private possessions had been touched by foreign hands. I looked quickly around the room. A stack of books I'd left on the floor beside the red lounge chair was tipped over. A small Numdah rug was displaced, curled upon itself. Cigarettes littered an ash tray.

Who?

I drew a deep breath and went for a bottle of brandy. It stood on the kitchenette bar, and I recalled it was three-quarters full. It was down to half. They had been at my precious booze, too.

Troubled, I poured some and sipped, making further inspections. I noticed nothing else out of place. But who had it been...?

The liquor soothed. My brain functioned well now, though overfast. My body was at rest. I slumped on the edge of the studio couch.

I thought of Grandma Kindott.

It was a mess. But the thing was, I could not back out of the situation. I had to return to that monstrosity of a house and carry on. If I walked away, I had the curious notion police would be on my tail before I'd gone ten miles. I put nothing past Miriam.

So far as working out the deal to precipitate the Kindott fortune into our laps, I trusted her. But I trusted her no further than that.

If I vanished, Grandma would hire detectives.

A thought flashed in my mind. Had the intruder here been Sergeant Brundell? I was immediately sick with such thinking.

I took another sip of brandy. Was Brundell on to anything? If he'd been here, he was. It scared me. Everything could go to hell in high rapid fashion, and right then I remembered clearly the mucky taste of prison food. This new fear kept eating at me.

I mused: Tolbert O'Shaugnessy-Joseph Lancaster.

And the more I considered, the worse it became.

The bad thing was that million and a quarter. It prodded at my mind like a silver chisel, a nightmare dream of money, a brimming bagful—something I had yearned for with every cell of my being for as long as I could recall. The opportunity revealed itself just once, I knew, all hokum to the contrary. And when it showed, you had to grab it, no matter who got hurt. I was trained for that. All my experience pointed to it.

My shady past was minor, compared to this.

Damn it all, I was hooked.

I was young in years, but ancient with trouble and ailments. I would need money to hie me to a sunny spot, where I could rest and try to discover peace of mind.

Dear, sweet, peace of mind—Jesus H. Christ on a mountain...

"Ain't it a bitch?" I whispered, sitting there on the edge of the couch.

Indeed, Life could become knotty.

Then I got to thinking again how somebody had been here, disturbing things. What *had* they wanted? Who the hell were they? I stood up slowly, thinking maybe it wasn't Brundell after all. Trying to convince myself it was merely the landlord making an inspection of the premises. One could not be too careful with unknown tenants, could one?

I took the carton of Tums and left the house. The drive back to the Kindott estate was fast, made in a hectic dream, without thought.

At the house, nobody was around. I went to my room, stared at the rocking horse, set the Tums on the bureau. Then I got to thinking about how anxiety could affect the physical body. This did not help. A friend of mine had wanted to be a great writer, but all he could sell was confession stories, written for the women's trade. He began to drink gin hugely, and the conflict was so strong he broke out in running sores. They covered his entire body. He would work wearing only a towel between his legs, drinking the gin, telling of love, sin and repentance. He had to make money because of heavy alimony. The sores grew worse, and so did the stories. He died like that.

I pulled up my sleeves, checked my arms.

Somebody knocked at the door. It was Jinny Kirkus, announcing dinner, with her flaming hair and crooked teeth.

"It's good having you here, Mr. Lancaster. Mrs. Kindott must be out of her skull."

"All of that, I'm sure."

"Mrs. Kindott's told me so awful much about you, y'know?" She rattled on as we moved side-by-side down the stairs. "And you lived in England, and all. What's it like, Mr. Lancaster? I never been there. I always wanted to get to London, you hear so much, but I s'pose I never will. It just eats at me. All them pea fogs and Big Ben and everything, y'know?"

At the foot of the stairs, she seemed to realize she was monopolizing the conversation.

"Sorry," she said quickly, and hurried away.

I stared along the hall at the closed basement door, and suddenly Ann Elliot appeared from another doorway. She stepped over to me. "Hi. Grandma's all right'" she said. "She won't be eating with us, and she sends her sorries. She'll have dinner in her room." She paused. "You've been out?"

Those eyes were on me. I sank into them.

"Had to buy some Tums. A touch of acid."

"We have Rolaids. You should've asked, Joseph." She cleared her throat. "Shall we?"

We strolled into the dining room. There was something about Ann Elliot now. Ever watchful O'Shaugnessy. It wasn't just the questive touch, either. It was more a hesitant frowning, mixed with fixed interest. It was difficult to define, really.

There was no sign of Miriam. Only two places were set at the long gleaming table, with a silver vase containing two red roses in the center.

"Where's Miriam?"

"She had to run into town. You and she seem pretty close."

I looked at her. "How d'you mean?"

"Oh, nothing, I guess. I just—say, I hope you don't mind eating with me. Actually, I've become sort of one of the family."

I focused on her tongue. One will cling to anything.

She leaned lightly against me, her breast thrusting upon my arm. She exuded sexuality. It seemed to burgeon in the thick black hair, in those strange blue eyes, in the way her mouth was shaped, in her movements. She wore a short black silk Jersey dress, with a low-slashed front that exposed swells of buttermilk breasts. Around her neck, across the obviously resilient flesh, dangled a strand of red beads. They lay on the skin like a nestled caress.

"You drink a lot, don't you," she told me, "I can tell. Your nostrils are all white. My daddy used to lush it up. He'd get the same way. They were like wax."

I forced a grin.

We took our places at the table. Her rather nervous long fingers fiddled with the red beads, touching them, moving them about, tucking, arranging.

"Isn't it strange about Sesto Vecchi?"

"He's probably around someplace," I said carefully and truthfully.

"Maria's beside herself. And Angela, Sesto's wife, is wild. He's never done anything like this. He's always been a real family man."

I thought of the panties, saw Sesto in my mind's eye, crouched over colorful piles of nylon, breathing hard.

"So I understand," I said.

"What did the policeman say?"

"Just routine checking, is all."

"Oh. What questions did he ask?"

"I don't remember."

"Does he suspect someone here?"

"Of what?"

"Oh, you know—just—"

"Not really."

"Then why did he come here?"

"Because he worked here, naturally. Sesto, I mean."

"Yes. But why should he be so inquisitive?"

"That's the man's job." I fussed with a fork.

"You have quite an interest. Is there something you didn't tell Brundell?"

"No," she said. "Of course not. It's just that I'm interested. I never came this close to a thing like this before. Policemen fascinate me."

"I thought maybe it was just me." I smiled.

She returned the smile, "You fascinate me, too."

A buzzer sounded distantly.

"I pressed it with my foot," she said.

I said, "Don't change the subject."

This time we both laughed.

"Will you be staying for a while, this time? Or are you going to disappear someplace?"

I kept looking at her. "I'm staying for good."

There was a long silence. It was a beautiful lie. If she only knew...

I had known many women, but never, somehow, one like Ann. She was a strange mixture.

Too, she hadn't actually said anything that should disturb me, but there was something about her attitude; a consequential sniffing around.

She leaned slightly forward, revealing more breast, elbow on the table, chin in palm. "You've been just everywhere, haven't you? Australia, England—where else?"

"Just those places." Then I remembered, but it was too late; she seemed to jump at it.

"I thought you were in Africa, too."

"Capetown. Only a short time. Yes."

"How in the world could you ever forget something like that? Especially Africa." She hesitated, frowned, then said, "Joseph. Were you around here long before you came to the house?"

I said quickly, "Nope. How do you mean, exactly?"

"Well, I swear I've seen you someplace." She gave a short laugh.

I was quick again. "Came direct from the airport. Except to buy a car."

"Oh."

"They say everybody has a double somewhere."

She said, "Perhaps that's it."

I held back a breath as the swinging door to my right opened, and a large, round, aproned woman entered, carrying a silver tray. My throat was tight and dry. There was a glass of water on the table in front of me. I drank some.

"Maria, this is Joseph."

Maria set the tray down, wiped large red hands on the white apron, and nodded, "Mr. Lancaster." She had a slight accent. Her face was obviously rather large and fattish to begin with; now it was swollen, with a narrow-lipped mouth, like a clamp. The dark eyes were inflamed, and I knew she had been weeping.

Sesto, I thought—her son, in the cellar. I remembered the booted foot, poking out through the tarpaulin, caked with dirt—Sesto; of the soil, dead.

I felt ill. There was no controlling it.

Maria seemed happy to see me, hoped everything would be all right, in reference to the food, and stumped away looking inordinately sad.

"She takes things so hard," Ann Elliot said. "Do you think anything serious has happened?"

I was already standing, "I'm afraid you'll have to excuse me."

Her forehead wrinkled. "What's the matter?"

"Nothing really. A touch of that damned malaria, I think. Picked it up in Australia, you know? Best thing is to lie down, cover up— quinine..."

She stared at me rather strangely, I thought.

I hurried to my room, flopped on the bed, with the door closed. It was not malaria, nor even the common cold. It was Maria Vecchi, and the knowledge of what had actually happened to Sesto, her son.

I eyed the brandy bottle.

...EIGHT

Face it, O'Shaugnessy—there's nothing you can do.

I could not run off, ducking Miriam and what she proposed. There was no escape now. And the brandy would not help much, either. If anything, it could only set my mind going in more vicious circles, increasing imagination and the general influx of disturbing notions.

I kept telling myself I'd had nothing to do with the death of Sesto Vecchi. It did not lessen how I felt, because at the back of my mind was the vision of what Miriam wanted me to do regarding Grandma Kindott. It was a sickness now, something I could not control. The hollow sensation of growing anxiety cramped my chest, made me still more worried.

Once again, I recalled the torturous nightmare dream of my killing someone, then, immediately after the deed, realizing I would never be the same again; no more O'Shaugnessy. *They* would always be searching for me. I had committed Number One, the Big Error. I knew, desperately, what it was like, was familiar with every deadly nudge of the fear that was beyond fear. Because when you had done that, there was never ever any turning back, no way to fix it. It was all over for you. The rest of your life would be spent with the sweating fear of that knowledge—and you would probably get caught.

It was sickening...

I sat up on the edge of the bed, and stared at my feet.

There was a scraping at the door, muffled chatter. It would be Gargantua, I knew. There was more scraping, followed by throaty grunts. He was inspecting the door.

The knob slowly began to turn.

I rose quickly, leaped across the room, and locked the door, then returned to the bed. The knob rattled.

She called him Desmond...

I remembered the scene in the dining room. Why had Ann Elliot been so probing? It was as if she were trying to catch me in something. At the same time, she had been making herself sexually inviting, and rather obviously, too.

Sesto Vecchi, I thought—out in the Gulf of Mexico...

Then I damned that monkey.

A thin trickle of desperation had begun working inside me. I did not want it to develop, but knew there was nothing I could do.

I lay back stiffly. Old Pop Carmoody had said it at the very beginning.

"You're not quite the type, lad. I hate to say it, but I been watching you, and you suffer—that's not good. You got a damned conscience, boy. How you going to con folks, you got a conscience? You feel too much. I never knew a man with a conscience made a good con man. And I never knew a conscience to quit, either. If anything, it grows on you, like some kind of Mesopotamian wart. Ever been to Mesopotamia, lad? They got warts there, let me tell you. But, take me now, I got no conscience. I just purely don't give a damn, but mostly it's intellectual. See?"

All my life had been spent in hopes that I could somehow develop that intellectuality of feeling. I had it sometimes when drinking. Maybe that was why I boozed as much as I did.

"You're emotional," Pop Carmoody said. "That's the absolute worst possible thing a con man can be, don't you see? Why you insist on learning all the tricks is beyond me. Take yesterday afternoon, when we tried that pigeon drop in front of the Union Trust. I could see your color, boy. You were pale, inside and out. Not frightened, I give you that. You're bold, at least I think so, But suffering—you got that damned haunt called a conscience." And I remembered at this late date, how he had paused, and sucked his pipe, and shook his hoary old head. "I'm afraid you'll never be really good. Not your fault, either. Your parents let you down, Tolbert. They done that. They messed you up. It's back in your subconscious mind, lad. You don't know why you suffer, but you always will."

I always had. He was right. But I was also persistent.

Old Professor Carmoody had said it. "You should get into another line of work, lad. A healthy kind of work. Hear me? Some day you'll run smack-dab into the hottest kind of con imaginable—one that'll net you a bag full. And you'll foul it, boy—you'll dog it to the ground."

I remembered, well.

I lay there, staring at the ceiling. The same ceiling Joseph Lancaster had looked at so long ago.

Old Pop Carmoody'd had asthma, very bad. It finally suffocated him to death in Newark. He would stand in the bathroom, with the door closed, inhaling this smoke from a medicated candle. I found him that way, the bathroom choked with fuming yellow smoke, the old man draped brokenly over the bathtub, dead.

Afterward, I read up on asthma, in case I was ever troubled, and discovered it could be psychological, induced by emotional disorder. So I wondered if all this time Old Pop had been hiding his conscience up his sleeve, where he had so many other fascinating gimmicks.

Then I remembered Miriam, again...

I got up, went over to the bureau, and took two Turns, crunching them down. For a brief instant, the anxiety melted away with the burning in my stomach. But it returned quickly enough, too.

I mused on my commitments. It was not likely that Grandma Kindott would want to see me this evening. I preferred to forget everything.

I took two seconals, and lay down again, knowing I was centered in a mix-up that could only become more foul. I started to close my eyes when something flashed across my mind. It was what that damned cop, Sergeant Brundell, had said. I sat up sharply, feeling intimidated.

Brundell mentioned that Sesto Vecchi had phoned his wife, Angela, and inferred something bad was happening. But Miriam told me she had caught him in her room, reading the information on Joseph Lancaster's life in the folder, with her panties under his arm.

How could he possibly have phoned Angela, his wife? Miriam had crowned the man with a flat-iron before he'd been able to do anything.

Lies... lies...

It was disturbing. The probing finger of trepidation I already felt about Miriam increased with provoking abruptness. I came fast off the bed, determined, moved across the room, out of the door into the hail. There was no sound anywhere. Ann Elliot had told me Miriam was in town. Perhaps she had returned.

I headed for the stairway, and coming down I felt as if someone had a pair of pliers, pinching, jabbing my middle. Then I heard her voice, unmistakable, muted, from somewhere toward the front of the house. It was Miriam, all right. I hurried along the hall, peering into empty rooms, reached a large, surprisingly bright room at the end on the right.

Spotlights glared down over a wild scene.

It was a jungle. Miriam stood in the middle of grotesque palms, leafy vines, and gnarled tree trunks mounted in metal containers, by an enormous black steel cage. Vines entwined between the bars of the cage. Artificial grass and moss covered the floor. There was a nose-flaring odor of mildew, dampness, and of wild animal.

Gargantua swung crazily back and forth on a small trapeze inside the cage. Miriam was baiting the monkey. She held a length of dowel, jabbing it between the bars of the cage.

"I won't let you out—there, you bastard! She doesn't know, you idiot. There! There!" Miriam poked savagely at the animal with the stick. The monkey chattered throatily, watching her with wild, violent eyes.

I reached her in three long strides, grabbed her arm, whirled her around, snatched the dowel from her hand and threw it to the floor.

The monkey screeched, bounded to the cage door, fumbled through with one hand and had the door open in seconds. He came out running, yelled, "Eyolp!" twice, and vanished into the hall.

"What the hell's the matter with you?" Miriam said. Her voice was nasty.

"Calm down, baby."

"I asked you what's the matter?"

"I'll tell you," I said. "Brundell told us Sesto Vecchi phoned his wife." I paused, feeling a tightness in my chest. "How could he have phoned his wife. Obviously, he *did* phone her—but how? If you—"

"Shut up!"

I stared at her. She wore flame-colored shorts that bit into her slimly plump thighs, high up, and a canary yellow jacket. Her face was flushed, the eyes very bright.

She spoke in a heavy whisper. "You're like a child. You want somebody to hear you?"

I took her by the shoulders and shook her. "I need to know, damn it."

She twisted free, still whispering. "I didn't tell you, because it'd only worry you more. Because we don't really know what he told Angela."

I drew a long breath. "Go on."

"He had apparently found the folder," she said, "and he went right off and phoned. Then he came back, got the panties, and was checking the folder again—reading it. See?"

"He said that?"

"Yes. He said he'd phoned her. He was very wise. He was a threat." She paused now, the brown eyes larger than ever, the face very pale. "If you must know, I had another sheet of paper with the other stuff, I'd sort of doodled on it—your name, and Joseph's—a lot of junk, I was planning. He read that, too."

"Beautiful."

She took a sharp breath, staring at me.

I turned and started to leave the room.

Her whisper was Barrymoresque. "Be ready!"

I kept going. Goddamn her. I traipsed up to my room, closed the door, I sighed. Actually, it was more of a gasp. I took the seconal bottle, popped one more, then stretched out, closed my eyes, and drifted away, trying to climb onto my little submarine that carried me to slumberland, and everything went black nicely until I saw a huge, hairy gorilla leering at me, slaver dripping.

"Joseph!" the gorilla yelled, screaming, frothing. "Joseph!"

"Joseph—"

I came awake, frightened, like a shot, with Miriam bending over me, her fingers digging into my shoulder.

I could still, in my mind's eye, see the gorilla, with clawed arms, reaching out...

"It's time," Miriam said, "What's the matter now?"

"Nothing. Sure. I see."

"Come on, then."

I swung my feet to the floor and groped for the brandy bottle. I took a short swallow, and waited patiently. It was gradual, but firm. I took two long ones.

"What time is it?" I asked.

"You've got a damned watch."

"Oh, she's very bright."

Miriam made a face. "Don't fool with me, damn you. We've got a job ahead of us. You'd better get with it."

I looked at her for a strained moment, knowing what she was here for, trying to still rising anxiety, and establish the fact in my giddy mind that she was real. I took another tentative swallow of brandy. Everything nearly bounced, while my throat worked, and for a minute my vision skidded alarmingly.

"What *is* the matter with you?" she said nastily.

I tried to say, "Nothing's the matter," but all that came out was a garbled gasp.

I sat there shivering on the bed, staring at her through watering eyes. I didn't want any part of her. The very hell with her. But there was no way out. She kept staring at me, bent slightly forward, pale washed blue jeans tight on her thighs, a small man's white shirt crisp across her breasts, the tails hanging out. Her long pale hair looked like dead fingers, and her face was like paper. She looked elfin. But it was a sly, scheming, murderous elf, with enormous eyes of mirrored evil. She resembled somebody's dream of the wrong kind of moon maiden. Concern frowned in those eyes, too, and in the line of her lips, but it was all tinged with a plotting, impatient wickedness.

I stood up, feeling rocky and half present, and went into the bathroom, holding the bottle. I switched on the light and stood in front of the medicine cabinet mirror. What regarded me with a strange type of awe, needed a shave, had a drawn mouth, and alarmed eyes. The hair was mussed and wild looking, and the face kept swallowing, the throat working. I set the bottle down, turned on a tap, and splashed water over the face, in the hair, then looked again. I was scared and wet. The skin was rather blotchy under the sprouting beard.

Miriam said, "Will you for Christ's sake hurry up?"

She stood in the doorway behind me.

I turned, thrust past her, found my shaving kit in the bureau drawer, and returned to the bathroom.

"What are you doing?" she said.

"I'm shaving." I lathered my face quickly, checked the razor, and began to shave.

"You know we've got to hurry."

I said nothing. I scraped my chin carefully, then rinsed my face. Having found my toothbrush, but no toothpaste, I used a fresh bar of soap from the sink, and scrubbed my molars. I spat neatly into the drain, feeling a touch better, then combed my hair. I turned to Miriam.

"Okay," I said. I reached for the brandy bottle, knowing it would taste better over clean teeth. It did.

Her lips were very tight, but she had obviously accommodated herself to the fact that I would not be rushed. Actually, the entire episode of shaving had been an attempt at escape, and to help in some way allay emotional disorder, namely anxiety. I knew this. But nothing had changed and there was no escape. My normal, ever-present burden of anxiety was now a Mount Everest, and it had me scared.

Sesto Vecchi waited patiently in the cellar.

"What about the monkey?" I asked.

"He's caged. Raising hell, too, because I locked the cage door, and that's never done. Grandma will flip out, but I don't give a damn. Gargantua's disturbed, too. She had to diaper him again. I mean, he's disturbed above and beyond—"

"Grandma's asleep?"

"Certainly. Will you please stop this goddamn nonsense?"

I shot her a look that would have dropped the ordinary bitch. It did not faze her in the least. She grabbed my arm with an eagerness that was straight out of hell, and nudged me with her hip.

"Won't be long now," she said. "You with it?"

I took another hopeful swallow of brandy, and set the bottle on the floor. "What about Ann Elliot?"

"Asleep too. Idiot."

"You have it all worked out, huh?"

"Perfectly. Now, let's go."

I knew I was being led by the nose, but felt utterly helpless.

Miriam switched off the bedroom light, and we slipped into the hall. Faintly, from downstairs, I could hear noises from Gargantua. It sounded much as if he were gargling rocks.

We came silently down the stairs, and into the lower hall, with Miriam gripping my forearm tightly.

"How about Maria?" I said.

"She goes home."

"And Jinny Kirkus?"

"The same. Will you *please* stop? Let's get this the hell overwith."

For all her nasty overtones, I knew she was uptight. But she was a brave one, and I had to hand that to her.

We reached the cellar door. There was a dim orange glow from an overhead light in the hall. Miriam opened the door, motioned to me, turned on the cellar light, and down we went.

I said quietly, "What about a boat?"

"It's all ready, you boob."

We drifted on down, across the cement floor, and stood by the cement block jut. Pale light washed over the workbench, the racked tools, and the shadowy tarpaulin. If anything, the sweet, cloying odor was more pronounced, now, which set off macabre visions in my mind. For some reason, I thought of Christy, the English murderer who had hidden so many slaughtered victims. How did he conceal the smell?

Just thinking that stopped me rigid.

"Now, what's the matter?" she said.

I stared at her, at those big eyes and that pale face.

Her voice rose. "We've got to hurry, Tolbert!"

What could I do? Nothing. It was actually happening. Never one to have any real success with viewing myself objectively, I was suddenly, now, floating overhead, among the cellar beams, watching the entire horror, while at the same time experiencing real fright. I moved in my sleep, with Miriam tugging at my arm, over to the tarpaulin.

"You'll have to carry it, somehow,"

Weeping inside, I reached down and hauled the wrapped body to a sitting position.

"That's it, that's it," Miriam said. "You can do it—I knew you could."

•••NINE

Miriam was right, as usual. Somehow I managed, with her mildly grunting help, to manipulate the burden till I had it draped over my left shoulder. I tried to keep from breathing, so I would not smell, but that didn't work. I staggered slightly under the weight, my cheek and chin forced tightly against the rough treated canvas tarp. Already, I was gasping, and I felt dizzy.

"Now hurry," Miriam said. "C'mon!"

We crossed the cellar, and started up the stairs. Gargantua was coming down, straight toward us. He had come silently until that instant, but suddenly his wild, vicious chattering and savage "Eyolps" sundered the whispered quiet. He jumped up and down, three steps above me, eyes glittering, arms arched over his furry, horrible head.

"My God," I said crazily. "He's loose."

Miriam said something obscene, worked past me on the stairs, and leaped at the monkey, shirt tails flying. Gargantua turned and sprawled headlong toward the top of the stairs. He would wake the entire house. Miriam whirled to me, lower lip trembling.

"Take it out to the boat. Hurry. I'll see to him."

She vanished into the hail.

The weeping went on inside me, and I had begun to sweat. I struggled up the stairs, with the feet part of the tarp dragging along the wall. If the monkey awakened Ann Elliot, and she appeared, I knew I would drop everything and run.

Then I thought, Run where? And I began to laugh in my throat, nervous laughter that tore at the back of my tongue, bursting from my mouth. This lasted for no more than three seconds.

In the hall, I hurried as fast as I could toward the front of the house, remembered, turned wildly, and stumbled in the other direction. There was no sign of Miriam or Gargantua, but I heard a barked "Eyolp" from the cage room.

I twisted the door open, and went on out, not closing it. I hurried, lurching, reeling, down the porch steps and over the stepping stones between the glass walls, out across the lawn and down toward the water.

It was quite bright out here. Spotlights were strategically placed, and my shadow flung itself along the turfy gray-green dewy grass.

I hesitated by the short pier, not knowing what to do. My head was a swarm of fear, and the anxiety in my chest had attained unmanageable proportions. Inside, I shook and trembled. I wanted to fling down the awful thing I carried, and just run—run anywhere. But somehow there remained a tiny star of sanity, glowing distant and dim at the back of my mind. And then I heard running feet. Miriam came up to me, gasping.

"Into the boat, you idiot!"

She led me on to the pier, and leaped off into a fair sized rowboat, with an outboard motor, and oars.

"Put it here, will you?" she said.

I stepped off the pier into the boat, and nearly fell as it rocked disconcertingly. Then I did sprawl down in the boat, letting go the body, falling directly across it. I sprang away, and sat on a wooden seat.

Miriam said, "You'll have to row out into the Gulf—then I'll start the motor. Not far, darling—it won't be bad."

The spotlights around the house glared on the building, glinting on windows. The house looked stark and cold, empty. Even where we were, light flickered on the black water, flashing, and I knew we could easily be seen.

"Tolbert—will you, for God's sake—!"

I took up the oars, my hands shaking, placed them in the locks, and Miriam unfastened the rope on the pier. We were adrift. We bobbed and twisted. I dipped the oars, and began rowing desperately toward the channel.

Night birds called lonesomely. There was a crescent moon, with sparse fluffs of cloud. A fishy smell pervaded the muggy air.

"What'd you do with the monkey?" I asked.

"Locked him up again. He lost his diaper. I don't know how he got loose, the bastard."

"What if they see us?"

She did not answer.

We reached the channel and I nosed toward the Gulf. The tall cedars and punk trees lining the channel helped shield us now. I hadn't rowed a boat since I was fourteen on a Wisconsin lake with a tongue-tripping Indian name, and I remembered how my father was counting worms into a tomato soup can, and my mother had left him two weeks before because he hit the juice too hard, and carried on with other women, and the next day after that fishing expedition he died of a stroke, and I remembered going to Madison, living in the first of the foster homes. Then they moved to Portland, Oregon, taking me along, and we lived in a big house and I hated everybody. The man had a wine cellar, and I raided it regularly until he caught on and beat me senseless.

Memories...

I was trying to avoid thinking about what was going on now. We were nearly to the mouth of the channel, and I could already feel the swell from the Gulf.

"Keep it up," Miriam said. "You're doing great."

I said nothing, just rowed. The body hulked in the bottom of the boat, a grotesque dark hump between us.

I looked back at the house and saw what seemed like the figure of a man, a tall black patch, detach itself from the bole of one of the royal palms, then mold back again.

I stared, a fresh jab of fright attacking my solar-plexus.

"I saw somebody—over there," I told her, and pointed with one of the oars. We had just left the channel, and were actually out in the Gulf of Mexico now.

"Don't be crazy," she said.

"I mean it. I tell you, I saw somebody. He's behind that tree, over there."

A rolling wave caught the prow of the boat, and began bringing it around.

Miriam's voice was sharp. "Will you for God's sake tend to what you're doing? Row, damn it."

"I tell you, I saw a man—"

"Don't be stupid."

I began to row, looking over at the royal palm.

There were only dark shadows now, stretching this side of the spotlights that played against the bulking front of the house, among the trees. I could see the bole of the palm quite plainly. There was no sign of anyone. Along the beach it was dark, but you could see the whiter sand. The fronds of the palms shivered against the paler sky, like black paper cut-outs.

Miriam's voice held a note of apology. "Besides, even if it was somebody, it wouldn't mean anything, don't you see? Us being in a boat."

"But who could it be?"

"I don't know, for Christ's sake."

I rowed very hard now, and we drew rapidly away from the shadowy line of the beach. We were already over deep water. You could feel the depthless surge. I didn't like it. I had never liked being in a small boat on deep water; it generated a curiously lost feeling along the backs of my legs and neck, and I imagined evil things. Drowning was such a drag. Something like when standing atop a tall building, looking down, or a high bridge, only the sensation was gloomier.

She said, "I'm going to start the motor."

I shipped the oars, watching her. In three seconds, the motor was roaring, and we cut out into the darkness.

"We should have lights," I told her.

"You're insane."

I stared down at the bulky tarpaulin.

She called, "I've got an anchor and some rope. We'll fix him that way."

I looked up at the sky and saw a jet, slanting off toward New Orleans. I wished to hell I were on it. I knew I should have brought a bottle of brandy along; I badly needed a drink. The anxiety was worse than ever now. My imagination tightened on the moment, as if my head were in a vise.

Ever since coming to the Kindott house, anxiety had grown. Nothing really helped.

Miriam switched off the motor. "We're out far enough." The boat ceased coursing into the blackness, and began to bob and roll. The water was not calm; small white caps burst nearby.

"Help me fix him with the anchor." she said.

She knelt beside the tarpaulin, holding a length of rope, which she began tying near the head of the bundle. I half lowered myself from the seat, and held my hands out. She stared at me, her face very white in the pale light. She was knotting the rope.

"You're no damned help at all," she said. "All right. It's fixed. Let's get it over with,"

I went about it automatically, in a kind of trance, not even believing at that moment what was happening. We lifted the anchor—a cement-filled bucket—and balanced it on the side, then hoisted the bundled tarpaulin up. The boat tipped precariously, and I saw us both, in my mind's eye, floundering in deep water, the boat drifting away. I was a lousy swimmer.

"Push, for God's sake—will you!"

We pushed and rolled the bulky tarpaulin. The anchor fell over the side, then the rolled bundle, splashing heavily. I gripped the gunwhale, and distinctly saw the anchor rope Miriam had tied slide off the head of the wrapped tarp. The entire package gave a lazy, twisting lurch. The flap of tarp came away from the head, and Sesto Vecchi stood up in the Gulf of Mexico, his face dripping, pale, hair drenched. Then the whole thing swung away, and slopped into a trough.

"The anchor came off," I told her.

"Jesus Christ." She tried to reach the floating package, but it swung bobbing away, and nosed down into the black water.

A streak of lightning sliced jaggedly across the sky, followed by racketing thunder. At that instant, the moon went behind heavy clouds. A storm was brewing. I realized the waves had grown; they splashed inside.

I grabbed the oars and fought to turn the boat.

"Where's the body? Which direction?" I Jabbed at the water.

"I've lost it. I can't see it."

"You've got to see it."

She shouted it. "Well, I can't see it!"

I sat there holding the oars, staring at her in the dimness.

She said, "If you'd helped, it wouldn't've happened. You just watched."

I said nothing.

"Oh, the hell with it," she said. "It's gone. I saw it sink. The fish will get it, you know that."

"Sure they will."

"What do you mean, 'sure?'"

"I mean we've got to find it if we stay out here all night."

She spat something and returned to the stern, began working with the motor. It came alive with a stuttering burst of sound. She cruised in circles, the boat pitching violently in rising waves. There was no sign of the body. She shouted something I didn't catch.

Then I heard her again. "We're going in!"

I knew it was too rough out here to continue searching.

What we had done became a realization, and I grew numb inside. I hadn't killed him. I kept repeating that in my mind, but it didn't help. He had been of the soil—now of the sea... gone.

Miriam had murdered Sesto Vecchi and I had helped dispose of the body. Up until the moment the wrapped body had struck the water, I'd been in a kind of dream. It changed now. I was as guilty as she. The entire world had altered, become something strange in a single moment. Conning somebody was one thing, taking their money. It was a skill, and sometimes you could actually feel proud, in certain ways, of how you handled the situation. But this...

This was murder, for hell's sake.

I was sick.

She cut the motor. We were already near the beach, the lights around the house glaring brightly.

"Row," she said. "Hurry up, it's going to rain."

Waves slammed the sides of the boat as I took up the oars again, began rowing toward the channel.

I looked over my shoulder, checked the bole of the royal palm where I'd noticed the black figure before, and I saw him again.

I said nothing. I kept heading for the channel. Soon we were there, the water calmer. I quickly took the boat close to the channel wall, dropped the oars, and leaped on top of the wall.

"What're you doing, now!"

"Saw him again," I said, and ran off down the lawn toward the royal palm. The wind was up, the moon shone again. I knew it would not rain. I had no idea what I would do if there was somebody waiting. I ran hard across the small clearing of lawn, past a spotlight, and straight to the place. Nobody was there.

The winds were dying off the Gulf, bringing a tang of saltiness. I looked up the beach, but saw nothing.

Whoever it was, he had a real knack for disappearing.

A long broken frond dangled down the side of the tree, lazily scraping the trunk, moved by wind.

I was breathing with my mouth open, rapidly, and my heart was quick. It was almost too damned quiet out here. I looked up at the house, hulked against the sky. Silent, it was, over-secure. I felt a sense of loneliness, of late night, and began walking back toward the channel wall. I came between two rustling cedars. The boat was gone.

Across the back lawn, I saw her tying the boat by a pier, her white shirt flitting in the shadows.

When I reached the pier, she was just coming out of the small boathouse, where she had obviously taken the outboard motor.

"There was nobody there."

"Goddamn It, Tolbert. You've got to cut this out. There was no one to begin with." I could see those huge eyes, staring at me, blinking slowly. "Now, we've done it. There's nothing to worry about now."

I chewed the inside of my cheek.

"You're so damned scared, you see things," she said.

"It was somebody by that palm tree."

She gave a short laugh. "Oh, boy."

I thought, Could it have been Brundell?

She said, "You stew about everything, don't you?"

I kept my voice steady. "There is another thing, Miriam. You told me you hired an investigator. If—"

"I said I'll take care of that," she broke in. "There won't be a single hitch." Her tone rose. She seemed to catch herself, and smiled, and stepped up to me. She gripped the sides of my arms, and wormed her hips against me, looking up at me. "Want a little? Huh?"

I did not move.

She said, "Doing that, out there—in the Gulf. It made me kind of itchy."

"Not now, Miriam." I thrust her away, and turned toward the house, began walking.

She stood back there. I could hear her chuckle.

She was something people tell you about. I came across the stepping stones, between the glass walls, and reached the door, opened it carefully.

Nobody was in the hall. I closed the door and made for the stairs. Moments later I stood in my room, feeling a sense of relief. I sat on the bed, and picked up the brandy bottle, took a long swig, shuddered. I did not want to think about Miriam. Now, if I could just sleep.

I stripped and showered and crawled naked between the crisp sheets. The room light was still on. I got up, turned it off, came back to the bed. I was trying to block off my mind, shut out everything that had happened, refuse to admit it, even. But each time I closed my eyes, visualization became bright, clear; the face of Sesto Vecchi, dripping and awash under the open flap of the tarpaulin as he stood erect in the water, and then slid foaming away.

Oh God... I thought that, and tried to think hard about something else.

The first thing that came to mind was Ann Elliot. She had been there all along, probing.

If I'd been at all sure of myself, I would have admitted there was something going between us, something unsaid, but felt.

Only I could not be sure of myself any more. Not since being in this damned house.

Poor O'Shaugnessy, I mused.

I tried slow rhythmic breathing. Sometimes it helped. You had to keep it up steadily, and force everything else from your mind. It took effort, but often in a little while there would be peace. I remembered Pop Carmoody saying, "If you can't get to sleep, wiggle your toes. It makes you breathe deeper. Just keep on wiggling your toes, and you'll drift off."

I wiggled my toes and breathed steadily.

This went on for some time, and I must have actually been conscious that someone was in my room for long moments, but I kept refusing the possibility, continuing to breathe carefully, with my eyes shut. Normally, I envisioned my little submarine, and got aboard, and plowed deep into the sea, but this did not seem to work now.

Then I couldn't stand it, and opened my eyes, turning on my arm.

She was hunched over the bed, looking at me, wearing something white and filmy. Moonlight lancing in the window, bathed her with pale silver.

She touched my arm. "Oh, God," she said. "I can't help it, Joseph Lancaster." She swallowed, sat on the bed, and thrust against me with her hip. Her mouth was dark and sober.

At first I couldn't be sure who it was. I lay there, rigid and confused.

Then I recognized her, and Ann Elliot was all over me, her lips against mine, her quick hands fumbling beneath the covers, running across my bare skin.

...TEN

I tried to say something, She leaned back and put her hand over my mouth. "Don't speak," she said softly, quickly. "Let me speak first." She whispered breathlessly, "You must have felt it, too. Didn't you?" I nodded against her hand, and she took the warm palm away. She was smoothing my belly with her other hand. "Are you much surprised? I couldn't help myself. I've been lying in there—I'm a woman, Joseph. There's something about you that just..."

She sprawled on me, kissing me with open lips, her silky tongue probing, breasts thrusting against my chest. I was conscious of that expensive perfume again.

She gave a gasp, twisted free, tore off the filmy white lace, and flopped on me absolutely nude.

"Don't make me wait—please!"

I did not make her wait. I held her close, and her thighs moved apart, and the moment began to swell. She was urgency itself, terribly excited. She trembled all over, and I began to tremble myself, and halfway through the business I was conscious of the fact that I really enjoyed her. We didn't linger. It became something imperative, filled with nighttime, and need. We were both gasping hoarsely. We crested in a violent battle that left us both wrecked in the ditch, covered with perspiration, breathing long and deep, clinging to each other as if we might fly suddenly apart forever. Her skin was smooth and marvelous. She was marvelous.

"Good God," she said. She leaned her head up, and in the moonlight I glimpsed the tip of her tongue.

She buried her face against my neck.

"I love your tongue," I said.

She became hot, pressed against me, a flush.

"You're blushing."

"I can't help it—my tongue, I mean. I've been to doctors. Nothing can be done. I can't control it."

"I love it."

"I saw you watching it. I was embarrassed."

"I couldn't help watching."

"You absolutely stared."

"It's sexy as hell."

"It's a curse."

I squeezed her and at the same instant heard a step in the hall. Miriam called softly from beyond the door. "Joseph?"

Ann gave a tiny shriek.

"In the bathroom—quick." I whispered.

"Joseph?" Miriam said softly. The door began to open in the moonlight. Ann was off the bed, and into the bathroom. I grabbed the white lace thing and hurled it after her, and leaped to the door. Then I realized Miriam might say something wrong, and Ann would hear. Amen...

Miriam stood there staring at me. There was a dim light in the hall, She wore shorty pajamas of pale blue, and she was frowning. She walked past me into the bedroom and stood there. Moonlight made her paler than ever. She stood like that for a long moment, watching me,

"Let's go downstairs and get a sandwich," I said.

"I don't want a sandwich." She hesitated, still frowning, and said, "I just wondered if you were all right."

"Perfect. Everything's perfect." I glanced toward the bathroom. Miriam could blow the whole thing, right now. For an instant I realized how I was thinking again. I was still going along with this thing.

It was then I knew I was standing there, naked.

Miriam came toward me where I was in the doorway. I moved aside and she stepped into the hall. Inside, I was shaking and my stomach was beginning to burn.

I stepped into the hall beside her, and took her hand, squeezed it. She looked at me steadily, straight in the eyes, and said, "I'm going to bed."

"Yes. Fine." It sounded like hell, but I could think of nothing else to say.

"See you in the morning, Joseph," she said coolly, and went on along the hall.

I came back into the bedroom and leaned against the door. Miriam had acted a touch strange. "She's gone," I whispered.

Ann came out of the bathroom. She was still nude, carrying the wadded white lace.

"My God," she said.

"You can repeat that over and over."

She said, "You didn't have anything on—you were naked."

"I stood behind the door. She couldn't see anything."

I waited.

She was silent for a moment. Then she said, "I behaved like a pig."

"You're an angel."

"You suppose she suspected anything?"

"No. Of course not."

"I'll go now," she said. She slipped quickly into the filmy white lace, moved over to me. Her lips touched my chin. I pressed her hand. She turned and was gone.

I closed the door, went to the bed, and slumped down. I was breathing high in my chest. It had been too damned close, both ways. When I thought of the things Miriam might have said, the bridge of my nose ached.

Ann Elliot was a surprising package.

It had been a very strange night. I lay there, trying to think, but it was all mixed up with Miriam and the body of Sesto Vecchi out there in the Gulf, and Ann Elliot's sudden revelations. It worried me plenty that Ann thought more of me than I was worth. She knew nothing about me. She thought I was Joseph Lancaster. She was dynamite, with a short fuse, and I saw myself being blown to bits. She was quite serious, and obviously had a case of the hots that wouldn't quit. Thinking about that, I changed position in bed. She was lovely and tender and sweet and her body was tender and lovely, and when I thought about her, my mind slid into high gear... racing with the wind. I had to admit there had been inclinations on my part, intimations of currents between us. But now...

I knew I had to get some sleep.

I checked my watch. It was 5:20. Soon a bright new day would begin, and I would be in the middle of it, like a fly pinned to a sheet of paper.

I got up and took two seconals to calm me, and lay down again. Then I tried closing my mind to everything, even Ann. I tried not to think of this house, Miriam, Sergeant Brundell, Grandma Kindott—Sesto Vecchi, the bloody monkey. It wouldn't work. There was too much happening. The entire caboodle pecked at my aberrant skull with trying persistence. I lay first on one side, then the other. I tried face down, but came close to smothering in the pillow. On my back, thoughts in technicolor streamed across the tight screen of my forehead, and my eyelids fluttered. I checked my pulse. It was in the nineties. I needed a Tum. I took a Tum. I lay there, loaded with grief, and the next thing I knew, Miriam was poking my arm.

"What?" I said thickly.

"It's eight o'clock, darling. I do hope you had a good night's sleep. Did you?"

I let that pass, and just mumbled.

She said briskly, "Your breakfast is ready. Get up—and make it snappy. We're running in to Tampa."

I blinked grittily. She was bright and crisp in hot pink, a minimal dress, with white lace stockings, a tiny white jerkin, flaming beads that swung to her belly. The pale hair was lustrous, and the eyes were clear and large. She rubbed her chin with a slim forefinger.

She said, "Are you all right, Joseph?"

"Certainly, What's this about Tampa?"

"Howard Fisk. He's the investigator I told you about. We're going to see him."

I thought about that for a second, and came up with nothing but faint panic, "Miriam—I think—"

She broke in smoothly. "I don't give a damn what you think, Joseph. It's what I think, this time. I know what I'm doing, and we're going to see him. I won't take any chances, and this is the absolute only way."

I could see she was a trifle worked up. She imagined I would balk.

"Up, up," she said. "Jinny's bringing your breakfast. She'll be here any minute, so get going."

"But what will we tell him?"

"Please leave that to me. I've got it all worked out. You're Joseph Lancaster, that's all. When we hit him with that, he won't have a leg to stand on."

I swung my feet to the floor, grabbed shorts, and slid them on. She frowned at me. She checked the leather-banded watch on her right wrist. "You're going to take a shower, now—hurry it up, huh? I want to get going."

"All right."

I got up and went into the bathroom, and smashed against the doorjamb. My head gave a lurch and everything started spinning. A step in the opposite direction, and I had the brandy bottle. I bee-lined for the sink, rinsed my mouth, then tossed down a wild slug of brandy. It didn't want to stick. My eyes watered, and my neck ached at the back. My heart pounded, and I waited for the drink to bounce. It did not bounce. I took another, letting it trickle down. I could feel it working.

I took a shower, toweled off, and came back into the bedroom with the bottle, trying to keep my mind closed. A breakfast tray, with covered dishes, was on the bed. There was coffee. I managed some of that, black, steaming. I knew I had to get some food in my stomach. I stared at an egg, juggled it carefully on a fork, and swallowed it entire. A Frenchman had once told me that if one is badly hungover, eat bread—lots of bread. There was only toast. I ate two slices, and managed another egg. I felt like a Thanksgiving turkey.

I shaved and dressed, my hands shaking faintly, and was just knotting a red- and yellow-striped tie, when Miriam again entered the room. She was frowning.

"Grandma asked about you. I told her I was going to show you around a little, the beaches, so on. She'll see you later."

"Fine."

"Ready?"

"My jacket—I—Miriam, are you sure...?"

"Just hurry up."

I slipped on a seersucker jacket, black and white stripes, went to the closet and picked up a fresh jug of Martell's. "Okay."

We came downstairs without speaking. There was a morning aura about the house. I looked for Ann, remembering pleasurably, but saw nothing of her.

"I forgot my Tums."

"What?"

"Be right with you." I hurried back upstairs, took two rolls of Tums from the carton on the bureau, and went on down again. She waited halfway along the hall.

Ann Elliot came out of the dining room doorway, and stood there looking at me. She was blushing.

"Hi," I said. "We've got to run."

She just looked, but said nothing.

Miriam insisted I drive the Chevelle. The trip to Tampa was fast, across the Courtney Campbell Causeway, and Miriam did not want to answer my questions. It was a brittle, glaring morning, though most of my mornings were like that. Birds stood out like paintings in black ink against the lemony sky. The bay was calm, with boats here and there. People were swimming from the causeway, lunching this early in sun-burny gaggles around picnic tables.

"All right," I said, "I'll just leave it to you, child. But you might've warned me last night that we were coming to see the guy."

She looked straight ahead, "Turn here."

I made the turn. "The place is on James Street."

She said, "It's the Wilkerson Agency. Kind of a big deal, y'know—posh."

"Heard of them. They're nation-wide."

"I figured I should choose the best. Another right, and we'll be there. Just halfway down the block."

We came into James Street, and I saw the sand-colored building, the austere sign. The place was richly landscaped, with expensive tropical trees and shrubs abounding. I drove into a pink gravel parking area, stopped the car. Miriam immediately climbed out, and motioned to me. I got out, came around, looked at her. "You're all business this morning."

"I'm scared to death, for your information. But it's got to be done. All you have to do is be Joseph Lancaster, see? I'll do the rest. I think the guy's a touch soft on me." She gave a tiny smile, and dug me in the ribs with her elbow. "My God, I'll be glad when this is over with."

We approached the door.

Wilkerson. Personal Investigations.

The name was in small gold letters. The building was large, and I knew they would employ a minimum of one hundred investigators. We went inside, through a small foyer, and into a large, heavily furnished reception room. Two very striking girls sat behind desks, looking faintly strained.

Three women sat together on a couch, and two middle-aged men blinked over magazines.

"I'll check with the receptionist," Miriam said.

She started toward the first desk. A door at the other side of the room lettered *Managerial Suite* opened, and a heavy set man with thin streaks of black hair across a pinkish skull, carrying a sheaf of papers, stepped out. The door closed. He saw Miriam, lifted his eyebrows, cleared his throat, and said, "Miss Kindott?"

Miriam paused, then said "Oh?" Then she smiled and said, "Mr. Fisk. Actually, I came to see you."

"Well, well," he said, stepping up to her.

Miriam's smile was gone. Her eyes looked hard.

"Something the matter?" Fisk asked.

"Yes." Miriam was brusque now. "You know that investigation you carried out for me?"

"Yes. Surely."

"Well—" She turned and motioned to me. I came up to her. "If you recall," she said to Fisk, "I wanted you to check on my cousin, Joseph Lancaster, in England, I paid a lot of money, if you remember?"

She was socking it to him, and everybody was listening. One of the receptionists had her mouth open.

"I recall, yes," Fisk said.

"And you discovered Joseph Lancaster had died?"

"Of course. Yes."

"Well, meet my cousin, Joseph Lancaster."

I nodded, took his hand. It was like shaking a dead fish. He stared at me. His mouth opened and closed. Suddenly he turned and glanced quickly at the office door behind him. Then he sort of gathered us together in his arms, hustling us toward the front entrance. "If you'll just come along. Look, there's a pub across the street. We could have a quick one. Okay?"

"All right." Miriam was slightly reluctant.

I was happy about his suggestion.

We plowed through the door and crossed the parking lot.

"So, this is Joseph Lancaster?" He gave a short laugh. He moved with a steady, lunging pace, still carrying the sheaf of papers. He kept running one hand across his thin-haired skull. His mouth was rather tight and small, a straight line, and his color was none too good.

We crossed the street, and he ushered us through the door of the James Street Bar & Grille. It looked cozy enough, and cool. The lighting was dim. One of these very plush joints, where the clientele can remain hidden. We silently moved past the bar, and entered a booth with soggy leather seats, and high leather backs. The table was a mirror.

"Wait," Fisk said.

The barman came along, and I ordered a double brandy. Miriam chose beer. Fisk settled for a shot of gin. We waited, watching each other, until the drinks came. Then Fisk tossed off the gin, and forced a grin.

"What kind of a place do you run, anyway?" Miriam wanted to know.

"I work there," Fisk said. He was downhearted, and he knew what was coming. He fiddled with the papers on the table in front of him. He sighed and tried to look at Miriam. We were on opposite sides of the table, Miriam beside me. I felt a touch sorry for Howard Fisk.

"Well, we drove over, just to let you know," Miriam said, "And, of course, to collect the money I paid you. I do not throw money away."

"But I don't see how I could've..."

"Obviously, you traced the wrong Joseph Lancaster."

He turned to me. "You lived in England?"

"Yes. London, actually."

She hadn't prompted, she had left it all up to me.

"I don't see how I could've..."

"You said that," Miriam put in. "This is my cousin, and I don't think you did a very good job. Perhaps I should report you, I don't know."

"Wish you wouldn't," Fisk said soothingly. "That's why I brought you over here, rather than my office. My secretary would be sure to hear, and she's a damned informer. Look, now. I'll see that you have your money, but let me handle it." He paused, took a long rattly breath, ran his pudgy palm across the thin hair again. "Mind if I have another drink?"

"No."

He ordered his drink. It came and he drank it.

"The truth is," he said, " things haven't been going too well for me. I can explain this situation to my boss, all right. And he'll refund your money. But if you go to him, I'll probably lose my job. See?"

"I understand," Miriam said coolly. "I just want to be certain of that money. And I should say you'd better make sure about things in the future."

He sighed again. He smiled bravely at me, and slowly moved his head from side to side. "I even saw your—*the,* I mean—the gravestone. A small one, but there it was."

"Sorry about that," I said.

Suddenly he was quite serious. He spoke to Miriam. "Will you forgive me? Mistakes do happen, you know?"

She gave him a gentle smile. "I do know. And I forgive you. We forgive you."

It relieved him immensely. He knew now that she wasn't going to wreck his life. Watching him, I saw that he had a tic in his right eye. The eyes were freckled blue, slightly bloodshot and watery, and his right eye kept snagging itself at the corner, jumping faintly, I supposed it was much worse when he was in a tight spot.

He looked at me now, satisfied that he was not going to be turned over to his superiors. "I just can't understand how I came to make such a mistake," he said. I knew he was trying to save face. He had regained some nerve, and he wanted a better edge. "I was quite thorough. Everything pointed to that gravestone in Hedgeton—everything." Abruptly, he gave a looselipped laugh. "You'll have to excuse me. I didn't mean to be morbid."

"How do I get my money back?" Miriam said.

He turned to her, hunched his shoulders. I could see now that he was covered with a layer of plump hide. His hands were heavy, soft. The plumpness thrust at his clothes, like cloth stretched over a balloon. He was not protuberant in any special area; it was a general condition. "An itemized accounting will be forwarded to you, along with our check," he told Miriam. "I hope this doesn't discourage you from using our services in the future."

"I certainly hope I don't have to." Miriam gently pushed against my arm with her elbow. "Since there's nothing further to discuss, we'll be running along."

I slid out of the booth, and stood up. Miriam rose beside me. She smiled at Fink. "Good-bye, then."

He half stood, propped plumply between the seat and the table, eye twitching, He smoothed the dank strands of hair, nodding.

We left. I glanced back, He was flagging the barman for another shot of gin, probably congratulating himself on a thin thing.

It was not until we were on the causeway, headed toward the Clearwater thruway, that the anxiety hit me. It was a sudden, debilitating strike, and my heart began pounding. Since last night, even before we went out in the boat with the wrapped body, I had not been myself. I realized this now. I had escaped to a strange plain of matter-of-fact acceptance. Now it was rather like being gassed.

"Hold the wheel," I said to Miriam, and reached back into the rear seat for the bottle of brandy. She drove as I opened it, and swilled as much as I could, fast. The sense of panic was like a feather around my heart, a fluttering shard of bird's wing, and there was a new tightness in my head, at the temples. I wanted -to crack my cervical vertebrae. My head was a-swarm with un-nice possibilities. I tried to force them away. I took another swallow of brandy, put the bottle away, and gripped the wheel.

"Your hands are trembling," she said. "What *is* the matter?"

"Nothing."

"Perhaps we should stop by some bushes." She gave a little giggle. "I still have that itch, y'know?"

"Not now, Miriam."

"All right," she said. I sensed a change in her tone. She cleared her throat, and looked out her window, and said, "When I came to your room last night..." She waited.

"Yes. What about it?"

"Wad she there?"

"Who—who there ?"

"You *know* who, Tolbert. Damn you. I could smell it. She's the only one wears that perfume. It was like what I imagine some whorehouses are like. Now, I can't see any reason for her to be there. But I wouldn't put it past your to take advantage of her."

"Who the hell are you talking about?"

"Ann Elliot."

I laughed. "Miriam. You're a case."

"Don t fool with me."

"She wasn't there. You saw me. I was naked."

"All the more reason."

"She wasn't there, I tell you."

"And *I* tell *you*. I smelled her perfume. It's damned expensive and I don't know how she affords it—but I smelled it. I've got- a nose like a hound-dog."

"Maybe she was there when we were out in the—boat."

Miriam did not speak. I decided not to pursue the matter, and neither of us said anything for a time. Ann Elliot had made a dent in me, I knew that. When I thought of her, it was with a curious softness, remembering. And at the same time, I knew I had no right to think like that. Nothing could come of our moment last night.

Miriam and I didn't say anything until we drove along the gravel into the parking area behind: the Kindott home. I was trying to deal with the most trying surges of anxiety- I'd ever experienced, and she, probably was attempting to reconcile herself to the possibility that I had told the truth about Ann.

In the parking area, I stopped the Chevelle fast.

A green-and-white police cruiser, with a crimson dome light, stood conspicuous and glitteringly polished in the middle of the drive.

"Well," Miriam said. "Visitors."

I coughed and felt like throwing up.

•••ELEVEN

"There's a Sergeant Brundell here," Jinny Kirkus informed us as we entered. She had apparently been hovering near the door. "He's very anxious that you both should be here. Mrs. Kindott is with him."

"Where are they?" Miriam asked coldly.

Jinny Kirkus's eyes snapped subtly. "I'll take you," she said.

We came along the hall. I realized we were headed for the same room where we had talked with Brundell before. I stepped over to the mahogany chest on the right of the hall, picked up my pipe. My fingers twitched. There was a fat unsmoked heel, and I was happy about this because my tobacco was upstairs.

Brundell, I thought...

We entered the room, Miriam was there a moment before me. Jinny Kirkus backed away, poking at her red hair, and vanished down the hall.

Miriam said, "Well, Sergeant. You've come again?"

Grandma Kindott had been crouched in a straight chair beside the sofa in front of the fieldstone fireplace. She leaped up with a gasp, fluttering her hands, wearing a startling canary yellow dress of some shiny material, the sharp blade of her nose slicing the air. The dress sagged over those brittle bones, and the pink cloud of fantastically teased hair was even more enormous today. Those jet eyes behind the tortoise-shell glasses were a touch wild.

"Oh Miriam—my dear. Joseph, darling—where have you been? Sergeant Brundell is here, and he insisted we wait for you. It's been—"

"We were taking a ride, Grandma," Miriam said.

Martin Brundell stood up from the exact center of the tan sofa, where he had sat the other time. He held a small brown paper bag. Maybe he carried his lunch with him, I wondered. He nodded. The square framed glasses glinted from sunlight shafting through a window, and I couldn't see his eyes. The lenses were opaque blanks. He looked like a Martian. He wore a fawn-colored jacket, with over-broad lapels, dark slacks, a pink shirt, a maroon tie, the knot so large it was all you saw at first. As usual, he had just stepped out of a haberdashery; so neat it was almost painful.

He smiled, then looked a bit grim. "Hello, there."

I grunted, and stood quietly waiting.

He scratched his chin. His straw-colored hair, gently waved, was immaculate. I could see him mornings, working with the hair spray.

"Would you please sit down?" he asked.

Miriam and I went to the same chairs we'd been seated in yesterday.

"This is simply awful," Grandma Kindott said. "It's horrible. Just horrible." She was shaking her head, the eyes darting about the room.

"You'd better sit again, too, please, Mrs. Kindott," the sergeant said.

When we were all seated, he sat. It was like a board meeting.

"Oh, Joseph," Grandma Kindott said.

I smiled at her, feeling sick inside.

"I'm afraid I have rather overwhelming news," Brundell said in his soft, fleshless voice. There was absolutely no timbre. It was like white wisps of milkweed astir on a gentle balm.

"Oh, my," Grandma Kindott said, "There's a—"

"Please," Brundell put in lightly. "If you'll allow me?"

"Oh, yes—I'm sorry—of course, you..."

He gripped the small paper bag with both hands and held it against his tight knees. He looked directly at me and said, "Sesto Vecchi has turned up, I'm afraid."

"Well, you've found him," I said. "Good." I looked at Miriam whose face was like stone, and said, "You see? I told you he'd ooze out of the woodwork."

"I'm afraid there was no woodwork, as you put it," Brundell said.

I had taken a breath, and it stuck agonizingly in my chest. I could not release it. I sat there, struggling, and finally it came out with a rush. I covered it by sticking the pipe between my teeth. I probed for a match.

Miriam said, "Just what exactly do you mean?"

I found the matches. A small box. I dropped the box. It bounced twice. I leaned down and retrieved it.

"Sesto Vecchi is dead," Brundell said.

"It's horrible—simply ghastly," Grandma Kindott said hoarsely. "Maria is in a pitiful state. Terrible."

"Please," Brundell said.

"Oh, yes—I'm so sorry—continue, Sergeant."

Brundell glanced at Miriam, then at me again. "Vecchi was murdered, then dropped in the Gulf. The body washed ashore on a sand bar three hours ago, at John's Pass. Middle-aged couple eating breakfast at the Windjammer Restaurant, out on the terrace overlooking the pass, spotted it. They saw what looked like a coconut bobbing in the water—but it was a head instead." He shrugged, very solemn now. "That's neither here nor there, of course. But I thought you'd be interested."

"Shocking," I said. I shook my head. I struck the match and held it to the bowl of my pipe. I was over-aware of my hands. I had been in many rugged spots, but this was the worst. I searched with a kind of diabolical extremism for some nook of calm within, to cling to. There was none. I was a great wrack of panic. "Have you any leads?"

"No. Not as yet."

"How did he die?" I put this in just to be saying something, confident of a modicum of composure.

"Shot three times with a .32," Brundell said, "We're pretty sure it was an automatic..." He went on talking about firing pins and ejectors, while I nuzzled the icy rush of new fear. They had been lies. I turned lazily toward Miriam. She was shaking her head, one hand against the side of her face, the big eyes sad. She was an actress; an actress and a monster and a liar.

"*...and hit him with the flat-iron. On the head.*"

I struck another match, re-attempting to light the pipe. I drew great clouds of smoke into my lungs as surreptitiously as possible.

"Poor Sesto," Grandma Kindott said.

"Three times," Brundell said, "In the abdomen, in the stomach—and in the heart."

"Had he been dead long?" I asked, amazed at the smooth, coordinated sound of my, voice.

"Yes. Obviously several days. But he hadn't been in the water long, that's what's surprising.

Of course, we'll know more after the autopsy. They're on that right now. Time Is always of the essence."

"I can imagine," I said.

I realized I was sending thick clouds of blue-white smoke into the room. I rested the pipe on my knee. Sweat trickled down my sides, from the armpits. I wondered if my eyes were glazed.

Then I thought how usually cops did not reveal so much about murder victims. Why was he telling us all this? His way, I assured myself. It's how he is, O'Shaugnessy.

"Now," Brundell said. He cleared his throat lightly, and it had the same sound as the tone of his voice. "Isn't there a Miss Elliot who lives here, too?"

"Yes," Grandma Kindott said. "She's my companion. She also acts as my secretary. But why should you wish to see her?"

"Please," The sergeant said. "Try to stay calm."

Grandma Kindott had sounded distraught, as well she might. Brundell gave his tiny laugh, spitting a beebee out on to the floor. "But I'd like to have Miss Elliot here, if it's convenient."

Miriam rose quickly. "I'll get her." She left the room and we sat there looking at each other. My pipe was out now, and I had no tobacco. Brundell wore a fixed smile on his lips, and he glanced at this watch twice, an enormous skin-divers chronometer with a thick black strap.

"Ah," Brundell said, as Miriam and Ann Elliot appeared.

Miriam came back to the same chair she'd had before, and Ann, avoiding my eyes carefully, nodding to Brundell, went over behind Grandma Kindott, and stood with her hands on the back of the straight chair.

I suddenly blurted, "Have you any notion—?"

"None at all," Brundell cut in. "But we'll get there eventually." He glanced at me with his eyebrows slightly lifted, the glasses glinting, mouth sober. He turned his head. "You may be wondering why I came here so precipitously. It's because you all are a starting point, as it were. You see? Any one of you may have something to offer, without really knowing it." He looked at Ann. "That's the reason I prefer having you here, Miss Elliot."

"Oh, I understand," she said. "I'll try to do whatever I can."

"It's obviously a planned murder," Brundell went on in his smooth, textureless voice. "But the motive eludes me." He faintly shook his head. "There seems no reason. From what we can determine, Sesto Vecchi was well liked by everybody. Now, as we talk, here, please try to think, too. If there's the faintest thing troubling you about this, please mention it. He spent moat of his time here, and—well—"

He ceased talking, began banging the small paper bag against his knee. Then he stood up abruptly. "I have something here," he said even more softly than usual.

I watched him. He carefully opened the paper bag, reached in and brought out a pair of crimson nylon panties, trimmed with white lace.

"I wonder," he said, "Do these belong to anyone in this room?"

He held the panties up with one hand. Then he dropped the paper bag, and gripped the flimsy nylon with both hands. He looked straight at Miriam, and I thought his face had become a touch pale, I was certain mine had.

Ann was watching me, now.

"Why," Grandma Kindott said. "Why, my soul, they're panties, aren't they?"

"Yes. Red panties."

The letters *M.K.* were embroidered hugely on the panties, in black.

"Why," Grandma Kindott Said, "I do believe—"

"They're mine," Miriam said. "Certainly they're mine." She gave a little gasp. "Where did you find them?" She rose from her chair.

"I just wanted substantiation," Brundell said. "I was sure they were yours." He stood there holding the panties up, watching Miriam. He was an actor, and he would milk every scene. But exactly what went on inside that neat head would never be revealed until he was ready.

I felt as if a vise were slowly pressing against my chest, squeezing tighter every second. Right then, I couldn't have moved if I'd had to. I was rigid in the chair, searching frantically for some mental calibration so I could adjust to the situation.

"Where did you get them?" Miriam asked again.

"Sesto Vecchi was wearing them when he died," Brundell said. "They were on the body." He jiggled them slightly. "Still damp, as a matter-of-fact."

Everybody was quite silent.

"Tell me," Brundell said. "How could Sesto Vecchi have gotten them?"

I managed to turn my head and look at Miriam. She was back in her chair, with one hand over her mouth, eyes wide. She, too, was an actress.

"Miriam," Grandma Kindott said with a frown in her voice. "Did you ever give Sesto your panties?"

"Oh, Grandma!"

"Let's put it this way," Brundell said. "Did you miss these panties?"

"No. Not exactly."

Brundell's glasses glinted.

"But—I've been missing lots of panties," Miriam said.

"Didn't this fact trouble you?"

"Well, yes."

"Why didn't you say something, do something?"

"Really," Miriam said, "I hadn't had a chance, Sergeant. It's only quite recent. Within the past few days. I thought perhaps they had been misplaced."

"How many pair were you missing?"

"I don't know exactly. Several pair."

"You have many pair?"

"Yes. A drawer full, actually."

"I see."

A heavy silence came down over the room, and it seemed as if I sat in the exact center of this mute contamination. Nobody had to tell me anything about Martin Brundell. He was a careful son-of-a-bitch, a piece of thinking machinery. The way he used those glinting glasses was enough to scare anyone into confessing mayhem. He knew very well the light caught on the lenses, and he utilized this, tipping his head slightly, glancing from one to another. I had never seen a more sober face. It was absolutely expressionless. He probably practiced before a mirror.

When I looked at Ann, there was a faint yearning inside me. I wanted to speak to her, to hold her in my arms—perhaps just to touch her hand. She was watching me, gently. She looked so good, it sort of caught in my throat as I remembered what had happened during the night. I could faintly detect the odor of her perfume, too, and that did not help. The heavy dark blue eyes watched me with a strange kind of patience.

"There's something missing," Brundell said. He quickly lifted one hand. "Oh, yes—there are many points missing. But I mean, there's something missing here." He spat another beebee, and smoothed his hair without touching it with his palm. A gesture, nothing more. "You see, somebody here must have noticed something about Sesto Vecchi. It just doesn't stand to reason he went about stealing panties, without giving himself away, somehow. You must remember, he was wearing them."

"Have—have you questioned his wife?" I asked.

"Only briefly. She's in the hospital. She took it all very hard, and—well, it's rather delicate, you see?"

"Was he homosexual?"

"Indications are that he was not."

"What indications?"

"I'd rather not go into that at the moment."

"Just trying to come up with something." I felt suddenly expansive, and loose generally. I knew it was a false moment of elation, induced by absolute fear, but I pressed helplessly on, completely unable to stop. "It occurred to me that if he was homosexual, one of his boy friends might've done him in. It happens, Sergeant—you certainly know that. Shouldn't you begin with the element of —"

"You mean jealousy—over the panties?"

"Over the connotation. Something like that, anyway. In fact, that's a point, right there. If Sesto had a lover, and the lover discovered he was wearing Miriam's panties, perhaps the lover thought something might've been going on between Sesto and Miriam." I paused. I was desperate. I had seen a tiny peek into a way to throw suspicion off this house. "I think..."

"Please," Miriam broke in with tight exasperation. "Stop it, will you? Nothing *was* going on. This is all pure conjecture, and I don't like it. I don't like any part of it. Isn't it bad enough, what he's done, stealing my—"

"Sesto Vecchi is dead," Brundell said. "He was murdered. I realize it's not nice, but we must discuss these things. You'll just have to get a brace on yourself, Miss Kindott."

"I—I forgot," Miriam said.

"If many pairs of panties are missing," Brundell said, "then we must find them. Sesto probably took them, secreted them somewhere. This is normally the case. They steal them, and in a secret place they wear them, and, well—we're all adults," he said, hesitating. Then he said, "Actually, they usually masturbate. You see? Perfectly harmless, unless there's some other hidden attribute that's—"

"Oh!" Grandma Kindott exclaimed. "This is too horrible. I cannot imagine any such thing of our Sesto. He was the kindest, gentlest young man you ever met."

"The fact remains that he stole your granddaughter's panties, from a drawer—and he wore them."

Grandma Kindott made throat noises.

I said, "Have you searched his home?"

Brundell did not answer. He changed the subject, back to what we had discussed previously. "Did Sesto Vecchi ever approach you, Miss Kindott? Sexually, that is?"

I broke in, "Actually, if he went around wearing women's panties, he wasn't likely to approach a woman, was he? I mean, isn't that a type of exhibitionism, too, sort of?"

"In a way. But that doesn't preclude his being sexually attracted to some woman," Brundell said. "I've made rather a study of this." He turned to Miriam again. "How about that, Miss Kindott. Did Sesto ever show any signs—you know what I mean."

"No. I had no idea." She was almost nastily abrupt.

He stared at her. "Nothing at all?"

"No." She spoke flatly.

He glanced over at Ann Elliot. "How about you, Miss Elliot? Any overtures that you recall?"

Ann slowly moved her head from side to side. "No, I'm afraid I can't help you. I really didn't have much to do with Sesto."

Brundell heaved a sigh.

He looked at me. "You arrived here yesterday, you said?"

"Yes."

"Then you really wouldn't have known Sesto at all."

"No."

Brundell sighed again, but he kept looking at me, the glasses glinting, the mouth sober, the face still rather pale.

"Did you, in fact, ever see Sesto Vecchi dead or alive?"

The "No, of course not," came out like syrup. I rattled my pipe against my teeth, watching Brundell. I knew I looked completely composed, but inside was a tentacled spider of apprehension that snarled in my chest. I hoped my eyes wouldn't give me away. I tried to think of everything I could other than what we had been talking about. Pop Carmoody had taught me that. "Sometimes they can read your eyes," he'd said. "You've got to watch out. The more ignorant they are, the less you should take chances. Some of 'em are like animals. They sense things, and they go by their feelings. So watch out—every minute."

The way Brundell was looking at me only increased the fright. He had nothing to go on, no reason to suspect me—but I knew I was guilty. Facing him was tricky.

"You've met Sesto's mother?"

"Yes."

"Another thing," he said abruptly, glancing at Miriam, then at Grandma

Kindott. "There were knotted loops of twine on the body. It seems plausible Sesto was wrapped in something,"

"No chance finding what it was," I said, feeling a sudden touch of bravado.

"You can't say that." Brundell's voice was gentle. "We're dragging the area around John's Pass, anyway. You never can tell." He gave that sigh again. "If we only had the gun. Well, that's too much to ask for—and a motive, of course. It could be anything, you know? What with this panty business." He leaned down, picked up the brown paper bag, stuffed the panties inside, and gave me a small caustic smile. "That'll be all for now."

I rose too quickly, fumbled with my pipe.

"Never mind," Brundell said, flapping one hand. "I can find my own way out. By the by, I'll probably want to talk with you all again. Things come up, and you people saw him the most. Sesto, that is."

He said, "all," but he was looking directly at me.

He turned and left the room.

Everyone watched him go. My only thought was how I wanted to get at Miriam. That, and what had been happening.

She realized this. I could tell by the way she avoided my eyes, twisting her chin away, half smiling at Ann and Grandma Kindott.

I stepped over to Miriam.

"I'd like to talk with you, cuz, if you have a minute? In my room?"

She said nothing, but it was strong in her eyes. I broke into a sweat, everything was wrong,

Grandma Kindott came out of her chair, swooping yellowly toward me, brittle hands out. "Joseph, Joseph. We've had so little time together—"

"I know, Grandma," I managed, swallowing. "We'll remedy that, too."

She started to say something else, but I turned fast and walked as nonchalantly as I could from the room. In the hall, I rushed for the stairs, ran up to my bedroom, then into the bathroom.

I made for the toilet and was immediately, wretchedly, sick.

...TWELVE

I had just finished brushing my teeth when Miriam appeared in the bathroom doorway. I stared at her reflection in the medicine cabinet mirror, and rinsed my mouth. I was drenched with sweat, and quite pale, shaken. I felt no better, either.

She said, "I know you want to see me. I won't avoid you. You have every right..."

"Don't pull that little girlie stuff, baby."

"I'm not pulling anything, You've got to believe me." She was faintly contrite, trying to brave it out.

I turned to her.

She must have seen something in my face, because she whirled and moved quickly into the bedroom. I followed her, wanting to throttle that lovely white throat. Instead, I went to the bedroom door, glanced out into the hall. Nobody was there. I closed the door, took a turn over by the front window, wondering whether I should hit her or what, and stopped, staring out and down at the lawn.

It was that investigator, from the Wilkerson Agency, Howard Fisk. He stood by some bushes, looking at the house.

The way I felt, I hardly knew what to do.

"He's out there," I said, and went to the door.

Moments later I was hurrying down the stairs, carrying a whirlpool inside me. I didn't know what I was going to say to Fisk, and it was all mixed up with how I felt about Miriam. I heard her call to me, from back there on the stairs as I came along the hall.

I opened the front door, and stepped outside.

He saw me. He turned and immediately started walking off toward the beach, the sun gleaming on his thin-haired skull. He wore a light gray suit and his plumpness punched at the cloth.

"Hey, there," I called.

He stopped and turned slowly, staring at me. As I came up to him, I saw that his mouth was as tight as ever, eyes still bloodshot, and the tic was going it strong.

"I'm sorry," he said. "I really didn't want to disturb you."

Miriam came up beside me, "What is it, Mr. Fisk?"

He was looking at me, and so much had happened that the look scared me, even knowing his position. Why was he here? Did he suspect something?

He said, "I came with your money, Miss Kindott. I was—just looking around the lovely grounds."

It was lame as hell. He'd been snooping. Inside, I was beginning to come apart.

"You could've mailed it," Miriam said.

"I know, I know—but I wanted to deliver it, personally. My boss—well, never mind." All this time, he was running through his pockets, and then he came up with a crumpled, yellow piece of paper from his trousers—a check. He handed it to Miriam, watching me.

She opened it and looked at it. I took a quick shot at it and saw it was a check for $2,500, made out to Miriam by Harold Wilkerson. The name Wilkerson Investigations was in red across the top of the check. She folded it, and said, "Thanks."

I was scared to the toes, because of the damned way he kept watching me, and that eye of his jumping around.

"I'll have an itemized accounting," Fisk said. "The fact is, I have the account, but I blundered—I left it on my desk."

"That won't be necessary," Miriam said coldly.

He was still staring at me. It was is if I were a magnet. Then he began popping his pudgy palms together in front of his waist, and trying to smile.

"Hope I didn't inconvenience you," he said. "I mean, not mailing—"

"Good-bye," Miriam said.

He nodded, and looked a touch glum. It made me feel no better at all. He wasn't satisfied, and I knew it.

He hunched his shoulders, and popped his palms again.

"Well, I'll just—run along, then."

"Yes," Miriam said. "You do that."

He gave me one more look, then turned and shuffled off around the house. He walked far out by the cedars, along the channel.

I turned to Miriam. "My room," I said. "Now."

I headed for the door. She said something, and I knew she was hurrying after me, but I did not wait for her. I went to my room, and she came in. She no longer had the yellow check.

She went over and faced the bed. I was burning up with all that had happened before, and now this Fisk character again. I closed the door, and came across to where she stood with her back to me. I took her shoulder, whipped her around, lifted my hand to slap her face.

"You do and you'll be sorry!"

I held it, staring at her.

"Now *he's* snooping around," I said. "Isn't it bad enough?"

"I can't help what he does."

"What about down there with Brundell? You lied to me."

Her voice was pitched low, but there was plenty strain in the throat. "I had to tell you that—what I did. I don't know why. I mean, I thought I shouldn't tell you I—I shot Sesto—it would look bad to you. I don't know *what* I thought." Her chin bunched and her eyes filled with tears.

"Cry, you crazy bitch. You start that and I'll fan that smart ass of yours."

"Don't you dare talk to me like that."

"I'll do more than talk."

"You have no right."

"Haven't I? Oh wow. You give me a glob of crap about a flat-iron, and I find you shot him three times with your trusty automatic. And they've got the body. The fish didn't get it. See? And they're searching for the tarp."

"They'll never find it. Besides—"

"Besides what?"

"You were sick, weren't you? They're spots on your shirt."

I tore my tie off, then stripped off jacket, shirt, and hurled them across the room into the corner. I found a blue pullover, slipped that on, glanced past Miriam and saw Long John Silver's eyes on the poster. He glared at me fiendishly. He seemed to be laughing.

"You bitch," I said.

"Don't call me that. I've a right. I'm a person, too. I have as much right as you."

"To what?"

"To anything, damn you."

"Miriam. Can't you see? Brundell's thinking things already. I can tell. The way he looked at me was enough to blow the top off my skull."

"It's nothing. Nothing at all. He doesn't think anything. It's your fool imagination."

"We've got to get rid of that gun."

She gave an exasperated sigh. "We don't have to get rid of the gun. It's your stupid guilt complex. I knew something was the matter with you when I first met you. The same night. The way you act. But I couldn't figure what it was, till I got that information about what you are. You're all loaded with guilt, because of the things you've done. Conning little old ladies, stuff like that. Jesus." She put both hands against her cheeks, then lowered them to her hips and stared at me boldly. "You are a mess, Tolbert. Some Con Man! Where's your head, stupid? Get a grip on yourself."

My stomach was burning now. I took Tums from my pocket, and chewed three. My heart was beating like a West Indies bongo. Brundell—and now that Howard Fisk.

"You keep on like you are," she said, "somebody will suspect something's wrong. Jesus."

I went over and slumped on the bed. I took up the bottle of Martell's and had a long swallow. It finished the Indian. There was one more in the closet, and another mostly full in the Chevelle. I got up and went into the closet, grabbed the other bottle, opened it, and drank. It burned its way down and squatted like a fiery fist. I lowered myself to the bed again.

"That's right," she said. "Guzzle yourself senseless."

"Shut up, will you?"

"I won't shut up," She came over to me, standing close to my knees. "And you'd damned well better begin thinking about what you're really here for."

I sat there, holding the bottle, staring at nothing.

There wasn't a thought in my head. Just her voice, that was all.

"Did you hear me?"

"How did you happen to shoot Vecchi?"

She gave another of those sighs. She was as bad as Brundell, in her way. "It's just like I told you," she said. "Only I went after him with the gun. I *knew* I had to do something."

"You don't have to impress me."

"He went into the cellar, and I followed him, and I caught up with him. He said how he was going to tell everything unless I did things for him, and what difference would that make? I ask you. He'd still know. So I shot him. That's all."

I watched her.

She said, "Now, what I said." She had lowered her voice and it was almost a whisper. "We've got to do this thing, you hear? And the whole idea is to do it now, fast. Before you've been here long."

"We can't do it with Sesto dead, with the body..."

"We can!" She grabbed the bottle out of my hands, and took it across the room, set it on the bureau. "We can do it. That's the angle, don't you see? If she dies right away, there'll be no suspicion. Not on you, and certainly not on me."

I heard myself groan.

"I figured how I want it done, too," she said.

"Great."

"Don't be sarcastic. I want her smothered. It'll look better. She could smother all by herself, and that's how I want it."

She moved slowly up to me again.

"It's a million and a quarter, honey. Face it, even you can stand that, can't you?"

"You make it sound easy."

"It is easy. Listen to me, Joseph—you have absolutely no other choice. None."

"Miriam, you're all mucked up."

"Are you stalling?"

I said, "I don't like anything about it. I don't like this Howard Fisk character. What if he gets to thinking about things? What if he reads something in the paper? I mean, it'll be in the papers. Admit it."

"So what?"

"So he can lift the dust. Don't you see?"

"No. I do not see. Fisk is finished with us now. He won't want anything more to do with us. He feels he's lucky getting away with what he did. Suppose I had gone to his boss. He'd have lost his job. That's what he was afraid of. We worry him. It's that way, not how you're imagining."

"Okay," I said. I felt tired, but at the same time there was a knot in my solar-plexus. I did not like Fisk. "But what about Brundell?"

"Our Sergeant Brundell is concerned with Sesto's murder. There will be absolutely no relation between Sesto and Grandma. Don't you see?"

"No. I do not see."

Her voice rose. "It's why I want her smothered, dope! It's got to look natural. That's what I wanted from the start. We can say she was distraught, worried about Sesto's murder. She drank too much. See?" She leaned down, grimacing at me. "It's simple. There'll be no reason to connect the two deaths. None at all."

"You beat everything."

She was loud now. "And you're a fool—an idiot. I swear, I've never met anybody like you." She took a quick, deep breath. "That's why we've got to get with it—immediately. It'll seem still more natural if it just happens any time now."

I stood up, grasped her arms, and said harshly, "Miriam, baby, I'll take care of everything in my own good time. I'm telling you, I'll take care of it."

Busy hearing my own words, and what they meant, I didn't hear the door open. But I did hear the clearing of a throat. It was Grandma Kindott, She stood hovering in the hall, one stick-like hand on the doorknob, looking at us, frowning beneath the pink fog of hair.

"Grandma," I said brightly. "Miriam and I were just talking about your birthday I said I wanted to take you on a trip." It kept coming out, like a kind of deodorant spray. "She said you seldom leave the house, and I was trying to convince her that I could convince you. Wouldn't that be a great idea?" I gave a short laugh. I had no idea when her birthday was. If it had been mentioned among the items in the folder on Joseph Lancaster, I had forgotten it. There was only this beseeching desperation to talk, to keep on talking, to cover up. "We could go out west. Wouldn't that be wonderful? That's what I was telling Miriam. Maybe Denver." Denver would be the last flaming place we ever went, but it was the first thing on my tongue. "Have you ever been to Denver? I haven't, of course. But I always wanted to go there—"

"Joseph," Grandma said. "Could I see you, please?"

"Sure, sure." I patted Miriam's arm affectionately. "We'll discuss it later," I said to her.

Miriam's eyes were like burned holes. Slowly she turned and gazed at Grandma Kindott.

Grandma did not smile. She was quite sober, the dark shining eyes blinking behind the tortoise shell glasses. Her lips were set, and she looked pale.

"Now, Joseph," she said. "Please? Now?"

I moved past Miriam into the hall and took Grandma Kindott's hand. I squeezed the dry palm. "Sure."

We started along the landing, and around to her room. I held the door and she entered. I stepped inside behind her, and closed the door.

The damned monkey, Gargantua, was over on the studio couch, sitting with his hands folded on his lap. He was rolling those lips sickeningly. He wore red- and white-striped diapers. He blinked savage eyes at me, and emitted a horrible, rending shriek, without moving a muscle. The eyes rolled in his head. All I could think was Fisk—Sergeant Brundell.

I looked at Grandma and she gave me a tentative smile with that crimson mouth. The broad lips curled high at the corners. Her ring-bedecked fingers twined about each other as she tilted the crazy-looking head.

"Sit down, Joseph."

She lowered herself on to a chair near the secretary desk, like a folding ruler, and pointed at the chair I'd sat in when we'd drunk the sherry wine.

"I'm terribly sorry about yesterday afternoon," she said primly, fluttering her hands. "You must think I'm horrible, acting like that. It shan't happen again, I assure you. Lands!"

"It's nothing, Grandma. Could happen to anyone." Why hadn't Fisk come to the door? He was snooping—that's why. Could he suspect I wasn't Lancaster?

Grandma leaned forward in her chair, and became very serious. The grooves at the edges of her lips deepened. There was a grotesque clown-like quality about that face, that head. It was somehow intense in expression, even in repose. Just now she revealed determination. "Desmond is concerned," she said quietly.

"I don't believe I understand."

She glanced quickly toward Gargantua, then back at me. I looked at the monkey. He had not moved from his position on the studio couch. He blinked solemnly at me, and made gurgling noises. She said, "Desmond thinks something bad is going on in this house."

I couldn't help tensing. I had just begun to relax, but now that changed. "Surely—" I began.

She lifted her hand. "Don't try to tell me I don't know what I'm talking about. He's disturbed, and he's let me know about it. It has to do with you, Joseph—and that's what bothers me."

The dry little laugh that had surprised me before, burst past my lips again, unbidden, deriving from nervousness. Not for an instant did I believe Desmond lurked somewhere beneath Gargantua's furry hide. His soul, either...

"Was he specific?"

"Not very," she said. "As I told you, communication is extremely difficult." She made another prim face, and sat back in the chair, "But he lets me know. And he is disturbed—about you. I can't imagine what it's all about."

"It's nothing, believe me."

"You're taking it entirely too lightly, Joseph." Her voice was edged with crispness, now. "I know what you think. You believe Gargantua is really just an animal, a monkey. I've tried to explain that this isn't true. Desmond is there, and he's watching out for my welfare. He's made it plain enough. Even under the circumstances."

I gave that little dry laugh again, at the same time trying to contain it, without success.

"You can laugh," Grandma said. "But it's not funny, Joseph."

"I really wasn't laughing."

"Well, it sounded like it."

"Grandma. What could Desmond mean?"

She tightened her lips, "What were you and Miriam discussing when I came to your door?"

"Just what I told you," I lied quickly. "About your birthday. I thought it a fine idea—"

She broke in sharply. "Joseph—?"

"Yes, Grandma?"

"You lie no better now than you used to, as a child. Surely Miriam told you my birthday is in May. This is September. That's eight months, Joseph. And, anyway, you were arguing. I heard you quite distinctly."

Old Pop Carmoody had said, "Always stick to your first word, even if it's the worst imaginable lie—never retract, Tolbert. When you give the lie to your first words, then everything after becomes a lie in the mark's eye. This is basic."

I said, "It's true. We were arguing. But it was about your birthday, Grandma. Please believe it, will you? I want to do something for you. I have a little money, and I'd like to spend it that way. Miriam told me about your birthday being in May, certainly—but that doesn't prevent us going on a trip, does it?"

She watched me steadily. Her eyes blinked. She apparently was satisfied. She sighed, and said, "I never leave the house, Joseph. Miriam was right in telling you that. I couldn't possibly go on a trip. It's thoughtful of you, but quite out of the question."

"Why don't you leave the house?"

"I go to town sometimes with Ann. That's all."

"But why shouldn't you leave the house?"

"Desmond is very implicit. He doesn't want me to."

"Has he told you that?"

"Yes. He's made it quite clear."

"Does he give a reason?" I heard myself saying these things, and marveled.

"Something might happen," she said, She sighed again. Everybody was sighing today. Brundell, Miriam, and now Grandma. She went on, "Desmond never gives alarm without good reason."

"Alarm?"

"Yes."

"But, Grandma!"

"And now, this Sesto Vecchi business," she said. "It's terrible to consider. Imagine, the poor fellow was murdered—shot three times. And those panties of Miriam's. And dropped in the Gulf. It's awful, degrading, and I don't like to think about it. There's something back of it all, Joseph, you can be sure. Frankly, I'm frightened. But I don't know what to do."

"Why should you be frightened?"

She hesitated, then said. "Desmond believes my life is in danger, Joseph." She hesitated again. "Joseph, darling—you've got to help me."

...THIRTEEN

I stood in the hall outside Grandma Kindott's door. I had excused myself as quickly as possible, explaining that we would talk later. As a reason for leaving, I told her I hadn't eaten, and felt faint.

That was not the reason. If I didn't talk with somebody half sane right away, I was afraid I'd be as crazy as the rest of them. Miriam, bent on murder. Brundell. Howard Fisk. And worst of all, Grandma Kindott, suspicious, and frightened for her life.

I wanted desperately to know more about what the damned monkey had somehow imparted to her, but I could not remain another second in that chair. Facing her was bad enough. But how I felt made it much worse. I was sick.

Walking swiftly, I came around the landing to my room, closed the door, and took three Tums. Then I slouched on the bed and eyed the bottle. My stomach was empty. I did need food, that had not been a lie.

I thought of Desmond... Grandpa Kindott.

Should I go to Miriam about this?

I felt half stunned. I had not been paying much attention to my physical condition, and the least relapse in concern always brought on illness. The tension in this house, the remote silences, that bloody Gargantua, everything that was happening—none of it helped; all of it was pressure of a type I could not bear.

Something inside we cried out for surcease—surcease, nepenthé. I would never find it, never. I knew that.

And, sitting here, I came face to face with myself as a con man, and knew something clearly, something I had avoided like plague. I was a failure in every damned way possible. For years I had kidded myself along, living in an aura of imagined happenings, stories told to myself, while dimly aware it was all a prodigious lie.

Now it was here, the culmination.

Had Grandma Kindott been trying, in her own way, to tell me she knew what was going on? Did she, in fact, actually know?

Could her husband, Desmond Kindott, really be somehow awfully inside that frightening beast?

It was hideous to brood about.

I felt utterly abandoned. This was not unusual, but normally I could tease myself along, feed myself a line of opiate-like thinking that kept the monsters from coming too close. There was none of that now. Somebody was chipping away at me.

It was self pity. I could detest myself because of that, but it did no good either. I had always sneered at self pity, and look at me now. Yes. I had always sneered at the very thing that was the machinery of my being.

"My life is in danger, Joseph." she had said.

When she said that I had nearly leaped from the chair, screaming. My moments of calm were jam-packed beneath a lava crust of precious hope that had cracks pasted over with Scotch Tape. Every now and again that tape loosened and the momentary calms burst up, geyser-like, spurting into the once sunny air, changing, becoming blood and horror.

I wanted a drink, but avoided it.

I had to talk with somebody. I wanted it to be Ann.

In the hall, I realized I did not know where her room was, and she might not be there anyway. I didn't want to meet up with Miriam.

It was imperative; I must see Ann.

She would be something to cling to, someone who would help assuage the wound.

I made for the stairs, and started down. I heard, faintly, from Grandma Kindott's room along the landing, the screech of Gargantua. I kept going, and came into the downstairs hall.

Jinny Kirkus was just entering the dining room.

"Jinny?"

She turned, hesitant. Her red hair was brushed to a sheen. Her blue-gray uniform crisp and fresh.

"Could you tell me where I might find Miss Elliot?"

"Oh? She's in the writing room, doing up some letters."

"Where's that?"

"You go through the room where you were with that policeman, and down a hall, and it's your first right. She's in there."

"Thank you, Jinny."

"By the way, I made you two sandwiches. Maria isn't here, of course."

"Thank you, again." I felt as thought I could use a sandwich. "Where are they?"

"On the table, in here."

We stepped into the dining room. She handed me a plate covered with a white napkin.

"I'll just take it with me," I said.

"There's some iced tea."

I smiled and nodded and went out into the hall, carrying the plate of sandwiches.

Walking through the room with the fieldstone fireplace, I discovered the hall, and then turned into a bright white room, with high bright windows, sparsely furnished with elegant Chippendale. A period desk stood near one of the windows, polished to a high gloss, topped with a slim vase holding a single yellow rose.

Ann Elliot sat at the desk, writing.

I paused in the doorway. She hadn't heard me. I stood there with the sandwiches, and watched her.

She was a picture of another day. From a dream, I thought. The sunlight glinted atop her dark head, altering the jet tones to burnished copper and gold. She had her head propped in her left hand, the fingers along her forehead. She wore white. It suited the occasion perfectly. There was a slimly delicate silver chain about her narrow, neat waist. Her ankles were curled together, slanting out to the right of the chair.

I came softly across the room until I was within two paces of her. "Ann," I whispered.

She looked up quickly, with a faint blush touching her cheeks. She saw me. "Hi." The pink tongue tipped between her lips.

I knew then that this was my woman. I must have her for all time. It was an extreme moment, a second's interim of flat-out knowledge. I wanted her so fathomlessly, so desperately at that instant, it was all I could do to prevent myself leaping upon her and committing rape.

The sandwiches tilted and one nearly slid from the plate. I rescued it.

"Ann, you're beautiful."

"Thank you, kind sir."

I stepped still closer, and hunkered down on one knee. "Did it mean anything to you, last night? Did it mean something other than just—I've got to know. What are you feeling right now?"

"In order, Yes, it did mean something. I tried to tell you that at the time. And at the moment, you excite me."

"Christ," I said, almost gritting my teeth.

"What have you there?" she asked.

"Sandwiches. Jinny made them."

"Why don't you eat, then?"

"All right."

Still hunkered. I flapped off the napkin, and took up a sandwich, had a bite. It tasted like turkey.

"There's some wine, over there," she said.

"Yes. Wine. By all means."

I rose and the blood surged to my head.

I saw twin bottles, resting on a silver tray atop a small, delicate-looking mahogany sideboard. At that same instant, I remembered what Grandma Kindott had said, and I recalled clearly why I was here. It was like a knife. For a moment I had been free, standing in a life of sunlight and content.

I went to the sideboard. It was port wine, both bottles. I did not care. There were small, stemmed glasses. I filled one, then the other, set the sandwiches down, and carried both glasses across the room, chewing.

"Here," I said, handing her a glass. "To us."

We drank. I drank, that is—she took a normal sip, and set the glass on the desk.

"Are you all right, Joseph?"

"Yes."

I was far from all right. I was sick.

I said, "Did you know about Desmond Kindott?"

She frowned, laid down the black pen she'd been holding in her left hand. I glanced at the letter she'd been writing. It was a check.

"Paying some bills," she told me. "What d'you mean about Desmond?"

"He's back. Did you know?"

"You mean — Gargantua? Yes. I know."

"How bad is it?"

"You mean—?"

"I mean, is she really batty?"

Ann gave a little giggle. "You have every right to think that, I suppose." Her face sobered. "No. She's perfectly sane—in every way except one, that is. And that's not really crazy. She's studied a lot; reincarnation, transmigration of souls, and she's convinced her husband's come back in the form of the monkey. I know it sounds screwy. But you should've known Mr. Kindott. He was a student of the occult, especially ESP—all sorts of supernatural stuff. Spent all his time at it."

"I see." I was watching her, not hearing everything she said.

"You should see his library. She spends a good deal of her time there."

"Library?"

"It's only across the hall." She stood up and walked swiftly past me to the room entrance. "Come along," she said.

I followed her, carrying my near empty wine glass, retrieving the turkey sandwiches. She opened a door on the opposite side of the hall, and stepped through. I entered the room. Ann was just switching on a light. There were no windows in this room.

The walls were covered from the floor to ceiling with books. Five rows of stacks, with ladders for each aisle, lined the right side of the room, and they were deep. There was another broad fireplace, of red brick this time, a wide, flat, leather-topped desk that looked dusty, with a telephone on the far edge, a high-backed chair, and two glass-covered cases of mounted butterflies, vari-hued, delicately beautiful.

"Lepidopterist, too?"

"Yes. The old man. He ran around in shorts with a net. Joseph?"

"Huh?"

The room seemed secluded from, the rest of the house, more silent, almost secret.

"Last night," she said. "I don't want you to think..."

"Please don't say it, Ann. It's trite. Anyway, you don't really mean it."

"No, I guess not."

"You just felt you had to say it, didn't you?"

"Yes, But, really." She suddenly stepped up to me. "*Will* you put down those damned things!"

I laid the plate on the desk, set the wine glass beside it, and took her in my arms. Her mouth touched mine, and I tasted her tongue. The same pink tongue that so delightfully appeared between her lips when she spoke. And in the middle of the kiss, with her urgent hips pressing against me, feeling the thrust of her breasts on my chest, I knew it could never be.

Miriam would see to that...

It was always Miriam.

Kissing her, I thought that. It was as if everything flew apart inside me. There hadn't been a time in my life when anything turned out right. And this was once when I wanted things perfect. I knew I'd never met anyone like Ann.

She slipped her hands up between us, to my shoulders, and tilted her head back, regarding me with those deep blue eyes.

"Something the matter?" she whispered.

"No, My God, no."

"Something is the matter, I can tell."

"Ann. I feel stupid, saying this. Honest. It's just not like me. When you get to know me better, you'll realize I'm speaking the truth."

"What is it?" She was half smiling.

"Ann—I think I love you."

She gave a little laugh, and put her arms around my neck, squeezing.

"I think I knew how I felt when I saw you at the door, and you couldn't believe I was Joseph Lancaster, home at last."

Then, abruptly, it was my turn to pull her close, look over her head and make faces at myself in the fluorescent shadows. Because I wasn't Joseph Lancaster. I would never be Joseph Lancaster. There was murder on my mind—it was the real thing, and there was Miriam.

And there was also a million and a quarter dollars. Waiting to be picked up. Which, then, did I really want?

I had no choice, I knew.

The phone on the desk rang. Ann pushed against me. "I'd better answer it, I always do. If it's for someone else, I'll call them." She moved to the desk, picked up the receiver.

"Hello?... Yes, Ann Elliot... Why, yes—he's right here. You want to speak to him?... Just a second." She looked at me. "It's for you, Joseph —a surprise." She handed me the phone.

I took it grimly, wondering, and said "Yes?"

"Joey. You old son-of-a-bitch, you old bastard!"

It was a man's voice, hoarsely raucous. "Joey Lancaster. Guess who! You'll never guess. C'mon, guess who! Christ, you old fart, how the hell are you?"

My heart slammed in my chest. "Who is this?"

"Ah, you'll never guess. It's Winky Waters. There, what you think of that?..." Right then, I heard a click, and knew somebody had lifted a receiver someplace else in the house. I actually heard someone else breathe, a short gasp. They were listening. They did not hang up, and he went on talking, "Christ—you said it. Been a long time, hey? But, say, don't call me Winky now, Joey. Just Bill will do." He laughed, loudly. "How the hell are you, anyways?"

"Fine, Bill—just great. How's it with you?"

"Listen, baby, when I heard you were back. Say, remember the tree house? Boy, what a thing that was. Hey, when your grandmother phoned my mother and she told the wife, I just couldn't believe it. We were little hellers, huh? Listen, Joey—am I right, calling you Joey?"

"Well, Joe is better."

I was conscious of a tightening in my head. My temples began to ache.

"Well, ol' buddy, this is something—really something," he went on. "They don't make kids like we were any more. I think..."

"Bill? Where are you?"

"Across the bay. But, listen, we've got to get together. Right away, old times, y'know? I can think of a thousand things I want to talk over with you. Ah, them memories. Hey, what you doing tonight? We'll go out an' paint the town, ol' buddy. I can't wait—how about..."

"Look, Bill. I'll have to let you know. I'm kind of tied up right now."

"Oh." He was silent for a second. Then he came on strong again. "Well, how's for making it soon, huh? You can't get off this hook, you old bastard. I'll come over there and..."

"Bill? I'm sorry, but something's come up. I've got to go. I'll call you again. Okay?"

"Well, now. That's a—well, okay, then." He was a touch disgruntled. I did not share his wild enthusiasm.

"I'll call you, Bill. Good-bye."

I waited and he hung up, and then I waited some more. There was a gentle rattly click as someone else hung up another phone. I hung up and looked at Ann through a reddish haze. Bill Waters, an old chum from childhood days. He would want to share memories. And he was a nut, to boot. I felt groggy. He was the type who would get angry if you didn't remember what he wanted you to remember. Then he would become suspicious. And then he would call the sheriff. Great.

"Bill Waters," I said. "He and I played together when we were kids."

"Mrs. Kindott's mentioned him."

I studied her face, trying to come back.

"What are you thinking about?" Her voice was soft

"This house, I guess."

"Strange place, huh?"

"Yeah." Strange wasn't the word. The phone call played hell with me now. I imagined all sorts of things. Bill Waters frightened me, along with everything else.

"Joseph? I've already told Grandma Kindott about how I feel. I mean, about you. We're very close, she and I. We share everything—I mean, our thoughts, like that. She's a great old girl, really. And I had to tell her."

"I see."

"Do you care?"

"Christ, no."

"She's worried about something, though. And she hasn't told me what it is. It's not like her. It's happened since you came."

I said nothing. I slipped my hands around her waist, and our hips pressed together. She was faintly frowning, and I felt like committing suicide. "Has she mentioned anything to you—I mean, about anything?" she asked.

"About. us?"

"No. Not that. Has she mentioned anything troubling her? She dotes on you, Joseph, But—there's something. I don't know..."

"What d'you mean?"

"Well, she keeps asking me about you. We went over some old snapshots early this morning. Pictures of you."

She went on talking, but I wasn't hearing what she said. The sickness was strong inside me, now. Knowing this girl was mine for the asking, and knowing I could not have her. It was too damned much.

Just the same, there was *now* to consider.

I drew her to me, and stopped her talking with a kiss, and Miriam said, "Well, I hadn't really expected this so soon. Or did I?"

We came apart like coiled springs. Miriam stood just inside the door, one hand on the knob, her face pale even for her, mouth drawn.

I was sure, then, that she had been the one who was listening on the phone.

...FOURTEEN

"We didn't mean—" Ann said, startled, obviously not knowing what to say.

"Never mind," I said. "Hello, Miriam. Did you want something?"

"Yes." Her gaze was stiff. "I have to see you. It's about Grandma. Could you come immediately?"

She turned and left the room, slamming the door.

"What could that mean?" Ann asked.

"Nothing, I'm sure."

"What right does she have, behaving like that?"

Her tone had bite. She had spirit. I said, "I suppose it's merely Miriam. You know her better than I. Does she always act like this?"

"She's never had occasion," Ann said. "How well do you know her, Joseph?"

"The hell with her." I took Ann in my arms, and kissed her again. But it was no good. It was an embrace that was an effort, perhaps on both our parts. As for me, I wanted to discourage suspicion. The cold con, coming to the fore. What the devil was I? Could I be a monster, too?

"I'd better see what she wants," I said.

"Yes. Run along."

"Are you all right?"

"Certainly." She smiled. "It's all right, really."

I squeezed her hand.

She said, "I probably won't see you till evening. Loretta and I are going into town."

That brought me down a bit more. I wanted to be with Ann. And why would Grandma and she go to town today?

I could not ask. I winked at her, tasting the ultimate in frustration, turned and left the room. In the hall, I ran a hand harshly through my hair, and made for the front of the house. My statistics all added up to one thing: a bottle of brandy, and to the very devil with Miriam Kindott... at least for the nonce.

I ran up the stairs, came around the landing, and entered my room. Miriam was staring at the John Silver poster. She did not look at me. I said nothing.

I went over by the bed, sat down, picked up the bottle of brandy, opened it.

She kept on staring at Long John.

"All right," I said. "Say it."

"Say what? That you're a tool, a stupid ass? You know that." Her voice was cool, matter-of-fact. "I've told you often enough, and I presume that you've lived long enough with yourself to realize it's absolutely true."

I took a quick swallow of the brandy. It was mellow. I wished I had eaten more than I had. I felt like getting stoned.

"What time is it?" I asked her.

"Look at your stupid watch."

It was one-thirty. The day was progressing. What else would it bring?

"Miriam, for hell's sake, stop standing there as if you were my wife, caught me in bed with the upstairs maid."

She said, "And now we've got that Bill Waters character to worry about. But I'll take care of him if he shows his face around here."

"Then it was you listening in on the phone call."

She did not answer. I took another swallow of the brandy. "You pass Waters off lightly enough. It's my neck, you know."

She looked at me, drew a deep breath and shook her head.

I said, "What happened to your parents, Miriam?"

"They drowned, right out there in the Gulf. My mother was drunk and she swam too far out. My father went after her. Neither of them came back.. He was Harvey Kindott. He would've approved of what we're doing. He kept trying to spend Grandma's money. But he never made it. I was five years old."

"You've lived with Grandma all this time?"

"Yes. And it was years ago I knew I would do something."

"Didn't she give you any money?"

Miriam made a nasty face. "Doled it out in measured stipends. So much for a trip to Switzerland. So much allowance, for school. Just exactly so much. Damn her."

"You don't look as though you went without."

"No, I never went without. But it was always just exactly the right amount. Everybody knew. It got so I couldn't face anybody."

"You never met Joseph-Lancaster, then?"

"No. But I heard enough about him. And how Grandma mourned her own children. She said they were cursed. That's why she lavished so much attention on Joseph. But never on me. Sometimes she would just sit and stare at me, sort of nodding to herself. As if she had plans. Well, I've got the plans."

"Too bad about you."

She drew another long breath, turned and left the room. I heard her going along the hall. She was a bitter little piece.

I sat there. There was no banishing of discontent, but it seemed a moment's respite while I stood at the boiling center of my personal hells.

Poor Miriam. And real tough, about her childhood, not having enough money; just exactly the right amount. I remembered my last foster home, before I ran away for good. It had been in a little northern California town, and the bastard used to beat me up, a real monster. So then one time I turned on him and broke his jaw. I was fifteen and big for my age, and given to mean thoughts. I left him lying in the back yard, groaning and cursing, and I took off and never went back. That was one of the beginnings. I was always beginning again, always trying to improve myself. There were correspondence schools, and petty thefts, a few nights in jail—and then I met Pop Carmoody. He saved my life.

Sure, I had big ideas. But he told me I would never amount to anything. And then came all those intervening years, always managing to live it up, somehow, so I could forget myself. And now look.

For once my stomach was behaving, and there was no pain. I took my pulse. It had slowed down, but there was an erratic tumble after so many beats.

I was caught in the bull's-eye, and there was no way out. If I ran, Grandma would hire them and they would find me and my whole miserable life would explode in a grisly wash-out. There was nothing to do now, but—go along, and hope.

I remembered Ann with a kind of warm sick feeling. I didn't want to think of her, either.

I heard Miriam coming back along the hall. It was getting so I could tell the sound of her footsteps. She entered the room quickly, bright-eyed. "Grandma and Ann have gone into town, I sent Jinny on an errand. There's something we've got to do—because tonight's the night. I've made up my mind. Tonight is when we take care of Grandma."

A creepy feeling came over me, looking at her. You really would not suspect, just seeing her. She looked lovely, if rather pale, wearing tight, flared jeans now, and a loose, maroon sweatery thing that clung to her hips. You had to know her before the loveliness, the almost childlike appeal, changed to ugliness; before you could see the evil in those huge brown eyes.

She said, "There's something we've got to do first."

I didn't say anything.

"We're going to catch Gargantua. He might scream and play havoc with anybody who tried anything with Grandma. We can't chance it, with him around. Then you're going to take him out in the country someplace, and dump him."

"You're mad," I said. The whole thing seemed like a kind of play, with us the principal actors.

"I told you what we're going to do," she said, her voice rising, "Now, c'mon, get with it. I'll help. He'll come to me. I'll even go along with you. Don't you see? Grandma will mourn him, and you can get her drinking that damned sherry wine. We'll tell her Gargantua ran out the door when it was open—that we chased him, but he disappeared. We'll be all broken up." Miriam paused, and looked sly. "She'll have fits. You'd better believe it."

"She'll call out the police, I said.

"So long as they're not after you, darling," she said quietly.

I got the implication. I stood up.

"Now, come on," she said. "Jesus, the way you slop it up."

"Beautiful."

"What d you mean by that?"

"Nothing." I set the bottle down.

She went out into the hall and I followed her. I thought of what she had said about tonight being the night. She really meant it. She gave me a stiff look. I grinned at her.

"You'd better be all right tonight," she said. "I want this done right. Understand?"

"Why don't you do it yourself?"

"Because you're a man, that's why. If she fights, you can handle her. Anyway, you've got to do your part. I thought it up."

"And you took care of Sesto, huh?"

"Listen," she said. "Right now we'd better get something straight. You agreed to this. And you're living here, posing as her grandson. I'm getting just a little irked at you, if you want the truth. If you keep your stupid head, it'll all work out. We've got to be together for a while, at least. And there's a million and a quarter tied up in this deal. So quit acting like an old woman."

Marvelous," I said.

Her face flushed some then, but she was holding it down. She swallowed, and there was something nasty in those eyes, but she only said, "Come on, now," and we started for the stairs.

I tried to let the feelings I had about Miriam wash out the fear. It didn't work. I knew she was crazy. She had to be. But there was nothing I could do. I had to think of my own skin.

We came down the stairs into the hall. "Now, where the hell is he?" she said softly.

"In his cage?"

"He might be. Only not locked up."

We started along the hall toward the cage room.

I said, "Will he ride in a car?"

"How the hell should I know? He's never been in a car."

"Enchanting."

The jungle scene in the cage room was apparently kept blindingly lighted day and night. The rank odor was powerful.

"There he is," Miriam said.

Gargantua was perched on a steel bar at the entrance gate to the cage. He spotted us immediately, and began chattering. He wore the red- and white-striped diapers, and for an instant he just poised there, watching, making staccato, strident noises.

"Here, Gargantua," Miriam said, moving slowly toward him. "Tolbert, you go around to the right, and come along the front of the cage."

She was nearly up to him. He looked down at her from the gate, which was head-high, and blinked, rolling his eyes. "Grandpa," I whispered. I kept telling myself I was going along with this to save myself, but it didn't do much good.

Miriam reached for him. "Here, boy."

Gargantua emitted a shriek that sounded as though he had been stabbed. He sprang off the bar at the gate, sailed over Miriam's head, and landed rattling in among the fronds of an artificial palm tree. He was still higher now. He bounced up and down on the springy, wire-enforced fronds, clinging to dark green leaves, and began grunting. He looked at me and blinked those animalistic eyes that at the same time held a human quality, and then he leaped directly at my head. His mouth was open, baring yellowed tusks, arms and legs spread-eagled as he tumbled through the air. He struck on my head and shoulders, gave a guttural "Eyolp!" and jumped to the floor, dodging away.

"Grab him!"

I'd hardly been able to move.

The monkey stood erect on the floor some six feet from me, staring at me. Miriam stepped carefully toward him.

"Here, Gargantua."

He paid her no heed. Abruptly, he ran at me with diabolical speed, tore at my thigh with a clutched fist, and ran over behind one of the metal containers that held the plants and trees.

It was a wild scene—the matted artificial grass, bright green in the brilliant light, the awesome smell of the place, the monkey's shrill screams.

"We've got to get him," Miriam said. Her voice was strained.

He turned, blinking at her. She had one hand out. He gave a running bound, jumped to her right shoulder. She tried to hold him. He chattered violently, leaped to the floor and ran from the room. We both headed for the doorway. He was in the hall, watching us, blinking, his mouth sagging open, arms loosely dangling at his sides. His back was hunched, and he looked at us sideways, like Quasimodo.

"Circle him," she said.

"Sure, sure."

"Don't be funny."

She ran at the monkey, hands reaching out.

He seemed to laugh. The lips spread broadly, revealing those teeth, and he screamed, "Eyolp! Eyolp!"

Whirling, he leaped across the hall toward the door, where an umbrella stand stood against the wall, holding what looked like canes, and rolled umbrellas. He sprang on top of the stand, savagely jerked an umbrella out, and hurled it at us like a spear. Immediately, he grabbed for the canes and the other umbrellas, brandishing them in both fists, then flinging them at us.

Miriam cursed him brightly, trying to protect her face. Canes bounced against the wall, rattled on the floor. An umbrella struck my legs.

"I thought you said he'd come to you," I said.

"Shut up and catch him. He can't hurt you."

The brandy I'd drunk did not help matters. It was all beginning to get slightly comical. Then I remembered again why we were doing this, and a raw depression abruptly settled into me.

Gargantua hurled himself off the umbrella stand, ran fast, ape-like, hunched over with arms dangling, along the hall and turned into the short areaway that led to the dining room. We went after him.

The monkey stood on the dining room table, waiting.

"Get around to the side," Miriam said.

He blinked, breathing rapidly. Then he flew straight at the chandelier. He made violent grabs at the crystal. As he grabbed, the tear-drops of glass came away and tinkled smashing on the table. He had the fixture itself by his hand-like feet, and he clung swinging. The fur stood out thickly around his head, and he began screaming at us in earnest, then.

Miriam started climbing onto the table. He swung by one foot, hanging to the fixture, and swiped at her with vicious strikes of one arm. She dodged, and he dropped straight on to her head. She made a crazy attempt to grab him, but he leaped off, still screaming, and ran past me like wind, out into the hall again.

We both went after him.

"You bastard!" Miriam yelled, "Come here, damn you!"

The monkey went on screaming, running.

"We've got to catch him."

We both ran along the hall, and it was then I saw the front door stood open, and there was somebody by the entrance.

Miriam stopped dead. The monkey turned the other way, ran frantically past us, and vanished into the cage room.

It was Sergeant Brundell.

"The door," he said. "I was going to knock, but it opened all by itself. Is something the matter?"

Miriam, breathing heavily, stared at him.

I sagged against the wall.

...FIFTEEN

The monkey vanished, and Sergeant Brundell stood there staring at us.

I gasped for breath, looked over at Miriam. Guilt had touched her face in an expression that could easily be read. Then she smiled. Her breasts were rising and falling rapidly.

"I'm sorry," she said quickly, "Gargantua was acting up. We were trying to get him back into his cage. Sometimes it's a real chore."

Brundell just nodded. His face was quite sober.

He said, "It must be a problem."

"You've no idea," Miriam said, still breathing sharply, but trying to hold it down. She brushed pale hair from the side of her face, and smiled again.

Brundell stood there for a long moment. He was completely practiced. His mouth was a straight line. He still wore the fawn jacket with the too-broad lapels, the maroon tie, and his hair was as flawlessly neat as ever. The square-framed glasses glinted, even here in the hall. Maybe he had special lenses made, so he could intimidate people.

Gargantua chattered steadily from the cage room, the grating sounds faintly muted here in the hall.

"Well," Miriam said, "what brings you, Sergeant?"

Brundell cleared his throat and gave a little twit of a laugh, spitting the usual beebee on the floor. "Something I have to check with you about."

"Oh?"

"Yes."

I was breathing a bit better now, but I felt no easing off of pressure. Brundell was getting to be a habit. I did not like it at all.

"That is quite an animal," Brundell said.

"Yes." Miriam kept on smiling.

"Not many people keep monkeys."

"No. That's true."

"I have something to show you," he said. "Could you step out to the car a minute!"

I didn't like the way he said it. He was watching me again, now.

"Sure," I said. "Anything to help."

"Well—" He did not finish the thought.

We followed him outside, and down into the parking area, where a shining green-and-white cruiser sat. Brundell motioned to us, and we walked to the rear of the car. He gave a little jerk of his head, and opened the trunk, lifted the lid into place so it remained open.

The tarp lay there in the trunk, partially folded, giving off a fishy smell. My heart began to hammer.

"We discovered this just outside John's Pass," Brundell said. "Pure luck, I'm sure. We're fairly certain Sesto Vecchi's body was wrapped in it. There is some evidence. Of course, it has to go to the lab. But I wanted to check with you people first."

"Why us?" I said deliberately. "What is it, a tarpaulin?"

"Yes. As to the 'why?'" He reached in and folded back the length of tarp, and I saw Miriam's lips twitch. Written in large white letters was the name *"Desmond Kindott."* An address, this address, was beneath the name. It was all done with a heavy brush in white paint.

"Curious, isn't it?" Brundell asked. He was staring at the tarp. "Pure luck," he said.

"By gosh," Miriam said. *"I* remember that tarp. It was in the basement, I'm certain. Sure. I remember it."

She was cool and smooth.

"Oh," Brundell said. "You do remember it?"

"Sure." I haven't seen it in some time. And that's my grandfather's name. He was always writing his name on his possessions. But, my goodness, he's been dead ten years. That must be ancient."

"Well, it's pretty old." Brundell reached in and refolded the tarp, covering the name. He lowered the trunk lid and snapped the catch. "Could we go inside? There are a few things—"

"Sure."

We came back into the house.

Miriam closed the door, and Brundell said, "I'd appreciate it if you'd show me right where you last saw the tarpaulin. Could you do that, d'you suppose?"

"Sure."

I tried not to look at Miriam, but it was like a magnet. When I did glance at her, she was keeping her eyes carefully away from me.

"Down here," she told Brundell, motioning toward the basement door. We reached the door as she opened it and flicked on the light. Silently, we descended.

I could not take my eyes off Brundell's hair. I thought of what was inside that skull. I wondered if he had any real suspicions. My stomach began burning.

"Ah," he said. "A wine cellar. Don't see those often these days."

Miriam smiled again. She was overdoing it. "It depends on the company you keep," she said.

"I suppose you're right."

Miriam's voice was bemused. "I think it was someplace down here. It's been so long—years, really. But nothing's been touched here since Grand-pa died. Not really, that is. I haven't been down here in at least three years, myself."

Brundell nodded.

We turned to the right, away from the section where the body of Sesto Vecchi had lain. Miriam switched on another light, and we entered what looked like an old fashioned laundry room. Ancient zinc tubs lined the wall, and rotting rubber hoses lay on the floor. There was a metal drain, the floor sloping toward that.

"Yes," she said suddenly. "This is it. It was right over here."

She pointed to some broad shelving.

Brundell said, "Ah."

Miriam said, "It was folded, right there, under those shelves. I remember it, because I was looking for a can of blue paint one day, and I stepped on the tarpaulin so I could reach higher."

Brundell leaned down, looking. I glanced at Miriam. She avoided my eyes. The sergeant straightened, and said, "It's a puzzle." He slowly shook his head. "Let's go back upstairs."

We returned to the downstairs hall and went into the room with the fieldstone fireplace. Brundell was thinking hard behind those glasses. "You've noticed no door latches forced, anything like that?"

"No," Miriam told him.

"Seen anyone hanging around, outside? Someone who shouldn't be there, I mean?"

Miriam said, "No," again, and smiled.

He was staring at me. I knew it would be good to say something, and hoped it would sound all right. "Have you spoken with Sesto's mother?"

He nodded, but did not speak.

The doorbell began bonging, and at the same time somebody pounded hard on the door. I heard a muted man's voice calling, "Joey! Joey!" The pounding continued, loudly.

Miriam gave me a quick look, and said, "Excuse me." She hurried from the room. There was only one person whom I knew used the name "Joey."

It had to be Winky Waters.

I stood there looking at Brundell, feeling like a zombie. If Waters got in here, anything might happen. I had the feeling that the slightest suspicion, and Brundell would mount his horse.

He said, "Interruptions."

I gave him my bright new little laugh. "It's nothing, I'm sure."

"This whole thing puzzles me," Brundell said. "So far as we can discover, Sesto Vecchi had no enemies." He shrugged. "Of course, he *did* have one. But we can't turn anything up."

I could hear Miriam's voice, and the loud, demanding tones of Winky Waters. He sounded much too loud for the circumstances.

Brundell cleared his throat. "How well d'you know Miss Kindott?"

"You mean, Miriam?"

"Yes."

I let that little laugh loose again. It must have sounded as nervous as it felt. My heart was trying to rise into my threat, "As well as cousins ever know each other, I guess."

"Then you've lived here before?"

"No. Not exactly. Not for some years, that is."

"Then how could you know her?"

"Well, we're rather close." I had gotten myself into a corner. "It's by mail, actually. We write back and forth a lot."

"I see." He did not see. And he was letting me know it just by the way he looked. His face was sober, and he was chewing his lower lip.

The hall had gone silent. Miriam suddenly appeared in the doorway. "Well," she said. "A drunken acquaintance. Sometimes they can be trying."

Brundell looked first at Miriam, then at me again. "Where is Mrs. Kindott?"

"Today was her day to visit her doctor," Miriam said. "She's in town."

"And Miss Elliot?"

"They went together. They always do."

"I see. Then you two are all alone with the monkey, eh?"

Miriam coughed slightly, "Yes. That's right."

He said to me, "Have you a cold?"

"No."

"I wondered. Your eyes are rather red." He paused then, and glanced toward the door. He was not certain what he wanted to do. He sighed. "I'd better get over to the lab. Will you please explain to Mrs. Kindott about the tarpaulin? And tell her to contact me at the police building if she can recall giving it away, anything like that."

"We'll do that," Miriam said.

He scratched his chin. He did not want to leave. There was something he wanted to say, but then I knew he would not say it. He turned abruptly, and left the room.

Miriam moved quickly after him. I listened to their footsteps in the hall, a mutter of "Good-byes," and the door closed. I did not move. I heard her running back through the hall. She came into the room.

"That damned Waters," she said. "He was lushed up."

"Will he come back?"

"It don't think so. I told him you weren't here. If he'd known you were, he'd have insisted on staying. He's a clown."

"Aren't we all."

"We've got to catch Gargantua."

"Miriam. You're out of your mind."

She stepped up to me. Her voice was low, "Now, get this, O'Shaugnessy. I'll say it once more, and that's the end. Tonight is the night." Her pale face with those big brown eyes was turned up to me, and she was very much in earnest. "It's the perfect time. Please consider. If we do it properly, there won't be an iota of suspicion. None at all. And it's all the better doing it now."

"Why?"

"Because everything else is happening. There's Sesto, see? And you've just come to the house, after being away so long. You'll be clear, just because of that fact alone. That is, if they ever suspected she didn't die of natural causes. But don't you see, with everything happening at once, it'll look right."

"Your reasoning is superb, Miriam."

"Don't be sarcastic. All you have to do is smother an old, helpless woman."

I said nothing.

"Come on," she said, "We've got to get that monkey out of the house somehow."

I heard the door open, and voices out there in the hall. It was Grandma and Ann Elliot. The door closed.

"Oh, Jesus," Miriam said. "Well," she said, "we'll just go ahead, anyway. I'll keep Gargantua out of the way."

"What If Waters comes back?"

"I'll take care of him, too. Leave it to me. You just get prepared. Wait till It gets dark, and she's sleepy—in her room. Then we—"

Ann appeared in the doorway. "We're back."

Grandma was by her side. "Where's Jinny?" she asked. I thought for a moment she was avoiding looking at me, but then she did look at me. She smiled, and said it again, "Miriam. Where Is Jinny?"

Ann had vanished.

Miriam said, "Jinny was ill, so I sent her home."

Grandma gave a sigh. She was wearing a broad-brimmed floppy white linen hat. She took it off, and poked at the enormous pink fog of hair. "Then you or Ann will have to prepare something to eat."

"I'll take care of it," Miriam said.

She was taking care of everything. I felt ill. Too much was happening all at once. Already, I sensed a chill on this house. Again, it was like a play. Once more that objectivity came to me, and I stood off, watching. That old woman was supposed to die tonight. Miriam was watching her, smiling.

Abruptly, Grandma turned and vanished in the hall, her footsteps dying away.

Miriam turned to me, whispering fast, "I'll fix some sandwiches. We'll have beer. Beer will disguise the taste of the sleeping pills."

"Sleeping pills," I said. I heard my voice saying that, and it was like a remote echo from somewhere else in the room.

"Yes. To give to Ann It'll work. She's got to be out of the way, don't you see?"

"Of course. Naturally.

She was exasperated, but she tried not to let me see it. She was excited, too, her eyes shining with it. "I've given her a pill before when she couldn't sleep. Just one knocks her loopy. I'll give her four."

"That'll do it."

"You bore me to death,"she said. "Just remember what you have to do— and remember what can happen if you don't. Remember who you really are. All right?"

"Okay." I heard myself say that, too.

"It'll be dark in another hour—"

I could not stand it any more. I brushed past her, and walked steadily out into the hall, heading for the stairs. The house was silent again. There wasn't even a sound from Gargantua, wherever he was. It was a death house, I knew. It was cold, and I tried to tell myself this was just because of the air-conditioning, but it did not work. The cold was something you could see as well as feel. There was a gray quality to the light, now. And I tried to tell myself this was because the sun was going down, perfectly natural, but that did not work, either.

It was a house of death...

The old woman was probably up there in her room, waiting for her light lunch that her granddaughter was going to prepare. She had no notion this was her last night of life.

She would be snuffed out.

The thought was a violent contamination.

Then I got a grip on myself, and started up the stairs to my room. Once there, I partially closed the door, went over to the bed, and sat down.

I stared at the brandy bottle on the floor.

The whole enormity washed over me, then, and I thought for a moment I would actually weep. I could not control it. Tears sprang to my eyes and my nose filled up. I went to the bureau, found a Kleenex, and blew my nose. I took another Kleenex, came back to the bed, and slumped down again.

This was *his* room, his electric train, his toys, his posters and colorful books. And he lay in his grave in England, and Grandma Kindott waited in her room. And O'Shaugnessy sat here, waiting, too. And O'Shaugnessy was sober. And I kept knowing what I had to do. If I did not do it, I was finished.

It was a vicious tangle and I nearly wept again. I blew my nose and sat there holding the wadded Kleenex. Even this was a form of self pity. Somewhere the gods were laughing.

I was staring at the brandy bottle again. I rose, stepped into the bathroom, and dropped the Kleenex into the toilet. I flushed the toilet. Then I returned to the bedroom, picked up the brandy bottle, and took that into the bathroom.

I poured the liquor down the sink. It gurgled beautifully. As it vanished in the drain, I knew I would never take a drink again. I did all this in a kind of dream, knowing full well what I was doing, approving it, tasting only faint bitterness.

The strange thing was, I felt an almost immediate relief when the last splurt of brandy trickled away. It left a slight amber stain on the white porcelain of the sink.

In the bedroom, I dropped the bottle into a brightly colored waste basket. Then I returned to the bathroom, rinsed away the last lingering amber traces in the sink. An odor was all that remained.

"Joseph?"

It was Ann. I came slowly into the bedroom, and she stood at the doorway, leaning against the jamb.

She smiled, holding a sandwich, half eaten, in one hand, a tall glass of beer, mostly finished, in the other.

"Miriam fixed a lunch. Pot luck, huh? You'd better go down and eat."

"I'm not hungry."

I stared at the glass of beer, knowing it was loaded with sleeping pills. She finished it with a swallow. I wanted desperately to say something, but remained silent.

She frowned. "Are you all right?"

I nodded, watching her. She was lovely, still wearing the white dress with the silver chain at the waist. The deep blue eyes regarded me calmly. And I could never have her. No matter what I did, I could never have her.

"What are you thinking?" she asked.

"How good you look."

"You, too."

I thought how those sleeping pills would be working, now. I had a crazy urge to just tell her. But I couldn't do it. I was still considering myself, trying to save myself. And all the time I knew there was no way.

"Joseph?"

"Yes?"

She moved closer to me. "I don't want you to think wrong, now. But, if you like, maybe I can come to your room again tonight. We could at least talk. We don't get much time to talk."

It was difficult keeping a hold on myself. "Yes," I said. "That would be great."

"Just to talk, though," She paused, then said, "I think we should discuss what we're going to do."

I was slightly abstracted. "Do?"

"About us. I mean—Joseph?"

"Yes?"

"I think I feel the same as you."

I touched her arm.

She said, "I'll come, that is, if I don't fall asleep. I suddenly feel sort of all gone." She turned back toward the hall, "See you, then." She went away.

I stood by the door and watched where she went. It was a room across the landing, toward the rear of the house.

It was right then that I knew we were not going to kill Grandma Kind-cott.

...SIXTEEN

Three quarters of an hour passed, while I walked up and down the bedroom. It was dark outside now. The notion that we would not do anything to Grandma was an exciting one, and at the same time evil to consider, because it would mean the end of me. I knew that.

But my mind was a blank, for the most part. I was here in this house, posing as Joseph Lancaster, and if I went away, they would find me. I would be held for complicity, if nothing else.

Christ, I thought, I had been in prison. I knew what it was like and I did not want that again.

But just the same, there was this excitement. I felt a sense of freedom, even if it was nebulous.

What should I do?

I moved to the front window, and stood there looking out at the night. The spotlights were on, trained against the house, glaring.

Then I saw it again, out by the royal palms—a dark figure moving. As I watched, the figure seemed to hesitate, as if watching the house.

I did not wait. I ran from the room, down the hall, and down the stairs. Something was going on, and I had to know what it was.

I remembered the man I'd seen swimming in the Gulf with Miriam. Abercrombie, she'd said his name was. Maybe he came up this way, hoping to get a look at her. He might have a thing for her.

It was a lousy explanation, but it was the only one I had.

In the lower hall, I hurried to the front door, and opened it. I ran then, closing the door as silently as I could, down the lane toward the royal palms. The lights glared in my face, and I could see nothing.

It was absolutely still, with only the lazy sounds of the surf on the white beach.

I paused. The bole of one of the palm trees had moved, and I knew there was a man standing behind it.

I ran at the palm.

The man stepped out with his hands in his pockets, as if looking around, and smiled at me in the light.

It was Howard Fisk, that damned investigator from the Wilkerson Agency. Just the sight of him, knowing who it was, did bad things to my solar plexus.

"Hi, there." he said. "Just having a walk on the beach, looking around—beautiful at night."

It couldn't have been more lame.

I came up to him, and I didn't know what to say. He suspected something, and the only slight relief I had was the knowledge that Grandma Kindott was not going to die. Little help that was. He was after me, and if he caught on, then I was dead.

Hell. I was dead, anyway.

"You want something?" I asked.

"So, you saw me out here, eh?"

"Yes. We're wary of prowlers."

We stood there staring at each other, and his right eye began jumping with the tic. He wasn't smiling, either. He was trying to, but it didn't come off—it just made him look grim.

"Walking on the beach," I said.

"Yes. I love it out here. Can't get enough of it."

"Seems a long way from Tampa."

"All how you look at a thing, I guess," he said, shuffling his feet around in the grass. He glanced up at the house, then at me again. And then he started popping his palms together, as before. "Haven't been here long, have you, Mr. Lancaster?"

"No."

"Ah."

He hunched his shoulders, and I was again aware of the tightness of his clothes, the layers of plumpness beneath. Then he began to look harried.

"Well," he said. "I'm probably holding you up." He paused, then said, "Oh, yeah. Meant to say, and almost forgot again. I don't know what the devil's the matter with my head. I have that accounting list with me." He grinned now, that tight mouth. "You could give it to Miss Kindott. I know she doesn't care much, but I still think things should be done right."

"By all means."

He hauled some folded yellow onion-skin papers from his breast pocket, and held them out. They were clipped with a brass fastener. I took them and stood there, with my stomach on fire.

"Well," he said. "I'll just move along, then."

I didn't say a word.

He said, "She sure is a looker, isn't she?"

I still said nothing. I couldn't. My throat was blocked and my mouth was dry, like brown leaves.

He hunched his shoulders again, eyeing me. "Well, Mr. Lancaster, I'll bid you adieu."

"Nice of you," I said, my throat cracking.

He flapped one hand, turned and began trudging down toward the beach. I watched him until he was out of sight. Old Pop Carmoody had said it: *"It'll come, and you'll dog it to the ground."*

I felt as if somebody'd shot me in the tail with rook salt; as startled, as muzzy, as helpless... and as hopeless.

He was onto me some way. He was onto me, and there was Sergeant Brundell, too. My head was beginning to throb.

I turned and started back toward the house.

Miriam stood in the doorway, the light from the hall against her back, the spotlights shining on her pale face. She looked like a waif in those flared jeans, the loose maroon sweater.

"What's the matter?" she asked.

"I saw him out there. He was out there. Fisk, that damned Fisk."

"There you go again. So what?"

"He was snooping. He thinks something's wrong, I know he does. He's onto something about me."

"What've you got there?"

"The account list—he gave it to me. That was his excuse. Said he was looking at the grounds, he liked it at night—liked to walk on the beach."

"So?" She took the papers.

"How can you just stand there like that?"

"Get inside, will you?"

I entered the hall. She closed the door and leaned against it. "Never mind about Fisk. He's stupid. He's not 'onto' anything. Now. Relax."

"Oh, sure."

"Ann's asleep."

I took a long slow breath. Nothing was settled in my mind. She hadn't helped a bit.

She was very pale. Her lips stood out like a wound in that strangely childlike face, the eyes large and haunted.

"Joseph?" It was Grandma Kindott, calling from the stairs. "Joseph, are you there?"

"Yes, Grandma."

"I'd like to see you a moment, if you will?"

"All right."

Miriam gripped my arm. "Now," she whispered, "We'll do it right now—"

I took her by the shoulders and stared into her eyes.

"Not 'we' Miriam. *Me*. Get it. straight. I've made up my mind, and *I'm* going to do it—alone. You'll leave everything to me."

"But—!"

"I mean it, Miriam. It's all up to me, now. I don't want anyone else around. I'll do it, and that's the way it is—dig it."

She stared at me. "Well, if you think—anyway, I never thought you were that heavy. All right, then. You do it. But do it right now."

I just gave her a look, then released her, and walked toward the stairs. My head was in a vise. My stomach burned and I automatically took out the Tums. Then I threw them to the floor, and kept moving for the stairs.

Fisk. That damned Fisk. And Sergeant Brundell with his panties and his tarpaulin.

I went on up the stairs. There was no sign of Grandma.

Miriam had not calmed me. She'd made me a little crazy, that's all. Crazier than I was already.

I came around the landing and rapped on the door.

"Come In, Joseph—come right in."

I stepped slowly inside and closed the door. The room was humid, stifling.

All I could think was what I had told Miriam, and I wondered what I was going to do about that.

Grandma Kindott sat stiffly in the chair by the secretary, with a glass of wine at her elbow. She looked up at me and fluttered her right hand.

"I need your help," she said, "Something's wrong with the air-conditioning. It must be the duct. No cold air is coming into this room. I'm positively suffocating."

I was already beginning to sweat. I had on the blue knit pullover, which was quite warm itself.

"Sure," I said. "Where's the duct?"

"Up there." She pointed toward the far corner of the wall, against the ceiling. Just then, from the other room, adjoining this sitting room, I heard "Eyolp," and Gargantua bounded in with us. He stared at me. He still wore the red- and white-striped diapers. He began banging his chest. Like Tarzan, chattering and grunting.

The hall door opened, and Miriam looked in.

"What is it?" Grandma asked.

She was checking on me.

"I've fixed something real good for Gargantua. I'll take him downstairs."

"You know very well he won't go with you," Grandma said. "He doesn't like you, Miriam. You tease him."

"He'll come along if you tell him to."

Miriam glanced at me, then back to Grandma.

"All right," Grandma said. "Desmond—go with Miriam. Go, now."

Miriam had her hand over her mouth. The monkey gave me another long blinking look, and moved slowly to the door.

"Go," Grandma said, "Miriam's fixed you some dinner. Run along, now."

Miriam held the door open. The monkey moved slowly into the hall. Just before she closed the door, he turned and looked at me again, pulling his lips back from those yellowed teeth. Miriam looked too.

The latch clicked.

Grandma said, "For goodness' sake, take off your shirt. It's much too hot in here. Get comfortable."

"That's all right," I said.

The air-conditioner duct was near the ceiling, up over the studio couch. I looked at Grandma. She was sipping her sherry, watching me. I took off my shoes, stood on the couch, and inspected the duct, It was tightly closed. I tried to open it, but the flanges were jammed.

"I'll need something to pry with. A screwdriver. It got closed somehow."

"I don't see how that could've happened. I have a screwdriver, right here." She opened the desk drawer and came up with one.

I jumped off the couch, took the tool, and looked at her pink-haired head, thinking what I should do.

"Please," she said. "Will you take off that shirt? You make me sweat, just looking at you."

"All right." I stripped off the pullover, and moved toward the couch, I dropped the sweater on the couch and climbed up again.

"That's much better, isn't it?" she asked.

"Yes." I pried at the flanges. They were jammed badly. I finally got the end of the screwdriver under the bottom flange, and worked it loose. It gave a snap. I opened the duct, and cool air began washing into the room.

"There," I said. "It's fixed."

I jumped down off the couch, went over and handed her the screwdriver, and she said, "You're not Joseph Lancaster, are you. You're not my grandson at all. Who are you?"

I said, "What?"

She put the screwdriver in the drawer, and closed the drawer, and looked up at me with those wise, dark eyes, behind the tortoise shell glasses.

"You're not Joseph." She didn't seem frightened. She just sat there, now, with her hands folded in her lap, watching me.

"What is it?" I asked. "A birthmark?" Because I knew then that she had wanted me to take off my sweater for some very good reason. And I knew what that reason had to be.

"No." she said. "It's a scar—on the right shoulder. You don't have that scar, and Joseph would surely have it. It was over an inch long, and very deep. He fell from a trapeze he'd rigged in a tree in the back yard, and landed on a milk bottle. It bled horribly, and he had to have stitches. It was quite red, and the doctor said he would always have it. Joseph was proud of that scar."

I went slowly over to the couch and picked up the blue pullover and slipped it on. I put on my shoes. Then I came back to where she sat. I stood there looking down at her. I looked at the weird mass of pink hair, and the sharp blade of the nose, the gaunt face, the tortoise shell glasses. Everything had suddenly and completely gone to hell now. There was nothing I could do and I knew it.

"What are you doing in my house?" she said.

I could not speak. It was that bad.

"Who are you?" she asked again. "Why are you here?"

And then I was talking fast. I told her everything, and finally about how I had known all along at the back of my mind that I could never go through with it. "I'm Tolbert O'Shaugnessy," I said. "Tolbert O'Shaugnessy, not Joseph Lancaster. Do you understand now?"

"What will I do?" she asked. "I've got to do something."

I stared down at her. "Grandma," I said. "Will you just play along? I'm going for the police."

She continued to stare at me that way.

Then she said, "But, Joseph—I mean—Tolbert, I don't know what to do. Don't you understand? What should I do? I'm all mixed up."

"Just play along," I said. "I'll be back as soon as I can." I touched her shoulder. "I really don't want anything to happen to you, Grandma."

She just sat there, blinking slowly behind those glasses, staring at me with an expression I could not read.

...SEVENTEEN

I came along the landing, until I reached Ann's room. Opening the door, I looked inside. The pink bedlight was lit, glowing down on her face. She lay there, her head propped on a pink pillow, the hair fanning out around her face, framing it. She was sound asleep. I went in and stood by the bed, looking down at her. I could hear myself breathe, long and deep. I touched her hand. She did not move.

Turning, I left the room, walked along the landing to the stairs, and started down.

Miriam was at the foot of the stairs, looking up at me. It was written in those enormous eyes, the big question, the eagerness, the impatience. Those eyes seemed to glow. She had one hand on the banister, and the knuckles were dead white,

I paused at the second from last step.

"Did you—?" she asked.

"Yes." I said, hearing myself speak again with that strange remote inflection, "Yes."

Miriam started to say something, but I broke in sharply. "I'm leaving now, understand, Miriam, I don't want anything. I'm just going away, and that's an end to it."

She stared at me. "But—Tolbert. Wait."

I gave her a shove and started for the door. She grabbed me, hanging on. I tried to pry her loose, worried now, but she clung like a leech, shouting, "Hurry up, honey! Get out here."

I heard the basement door slam, and looked along the hall. A man strode rapidly toward us. It was the investigator from the Wilkerson agency, Howard Fisk. I tore loose from Miriam, and turned again for the door.

"Hold it, right there!" Fisk snapped.

He gripped a gun solidly in his right hand. It was pointed straight at me. I decided I'd better do as he said.

It was a blue steel .45 automatic, from the looks. I knew what one of those could do to you. Fisk's face was rigid.

"Try something," he said, breathing rawly through his nose. "Try it, and you're dead, right here." He meant that, too.

Miriam was pale. "He said he was leaving," she told Fisk. "Christ, he was actually running out. I had to hold him."

"Did he do it?"

"Yes. But I'm going upstairs. It won't take a minute. I've got to see."

"Hurry up, then."

She turned and raced up the stairs, and my stomach was a knot. Fisk and I eyed each other, and he held the gun steady. There was what might have been a smile on his lips.

Then Miriam was running down the stairs.

"He did it, all right," she said. "Grandma's lying there with a pillow over her face. I took it off. He really did it!" There was excitement in her tone.

I sent up a little prayer, thinking about Grandma Kindott. Somehow, I had to reach the police.

Fisk spoke. "We're losing time," he said, "Let's go."

I watched him. There was none of that worry and fear that he had shown when we last met. He was entirely in charge. But the right eye was twitching, so I knew the strain told. The eyes were quite bloodshot, as if he badly needed sleep. He wore a thin white turtleneck, a lightweight pale gray suit. The gun was absolutely steady.

How did Fisk figure in this?

"All right," he said. "Out the door, O'Shaugnessy "

I looked at Miriam.

"Move it," Fisk said, his voice nasty.

Right then Gargantua gave a shriek from down the hall and came leaping furrily toward us.

"The monkey," Fisk said. "Shall I shoot him?"

"Are you crazy?" Miriam was sharp. "How would that look?"

"Then get going."

I knew now who'd been lurking around outside the house, and why he'd acted so fishy. Miriam and he were in it together.

Miriam opened the door. The monkey ran toward Fisk, and the man lashed out with his arm. Gargantua dodged, and stood with his arms hanging, watching with bright, mean-looking eyes.

We came out on to the porch, and Miriam closed the door.

"Let's hurry, she said, "We can't take any chances."

"What car?"

"The Mercedes."

"Where we going?" I asked. I was sick inside and really scared now. Nobody answered me.

We came to the garage. The night was soft with the smell of jasmine, and the moon bathed everything in pale silver. Miriam vanished into the darkness of the yawning garage and a door opened and slammed. A car's lights glared. She backed the gleaming gun-metal Mercedes out into the parking area, and Fisk dug at my back with the gun.

"Just don't even consider trying anything." He spoke softly now. "Get in." He held the door open and I slid in beside Miriam. Fisk climbed in beside me, slamming the door.

Miriam drove fast, hunched at the wheel. She said, "We've done it."

"It's not over with yet," Fisk said.

"But the worst part is over."

We came along Gulf Boulevard, and I could feel the layered fat of Howard Fisk, pressed against me.

"Take it easy," he said, "All we need is a cop stopping us for speeding."

Miriam slowed the car. We drove for a time, and nobody spoke. We came into Indian Rocks and I thought, it can't be. But it was, just the same. Miriam turned the Mercedes in at my place, narrowly missing a yellow open convertible parked across the street.

Fisk was out quickly. "Come on," he said.

Miriam and I got out. Fisk gestured toward the house with the gun.

Lights gleamed through the Monk's cloth draperies at the north window. I knew now they had been using my place for themselves.

Miriam went inside and held the door, watching me.

Fisk pushed behind me. She closed the door and leaned against it. He motioned with the gun, meaning I should step toward the center of the room. I just stood there, waiting. I was conscious of the place, remembering its secureness. It had been kind of a sanctuary. That was all gone now.

"Tell him," Miriam said.

"Look," I said. "You and Fisk have something beautiful going for you, obviously. But you can't get away with it."

Miriam gave a little laugh. She gestured toward Fisk. "O'Shaugnessy, you're an idiot. Meet Joseph Lancaster—the real Joseph!"

I looked at Howard Fisk, understanding now. There stood Loretta Kindott's grandson.

I had sensed it even before she spoke. But just the same, it was weird.

...EIGHTEEN

I stood there, realizing my position, and inside a kind of wildness was beginning to take over.

"Don't you think it's neat?" Miriam asked.

My voice was hollow. "Sure. It's neat."

"And now we have to kill you," Fisk-Lancaster said. "And, believe me, it's been a long, weakening haul, getting this far."

The gun in his hand was steady. He was taking no chances. There was a certain smugness about his expression now.

I said, "Miriam, you went up and checked on Grandma. But you made a mistake. You see, child, she isn't dead. Now bite on that and see where it gets you."

All the time I spoke, I was watching for an opening—any opening.

Miriam started to say something, but Lancaster turned and flung a harsh, "Shut up. He switched to me. "Say that again."

"It's simple," I told him. "Grandma spotted I wasn't Joseph, because I didn't have a scar on my right shoulder. So, hell, I told her the whole thing."

Miriam said, "Joe—Joe—"

It was all clear enough to me now, and I knew I had to get away.

Lancaster rubbed his hand across his face, staring at me. The gun drooped a little. He said through his hand, muffled, "He's probably telling a lie, but we've got to believe him."

"What'll we do?" Miriam wanted to know. Her voice was a touch strident. "It's all your damned fault, Joe— you wouldn't kill Grandma—"

"I told you I'd never kill an old woman, like that. I depended on you, and now look. You botched it. It's not my fault, Miriam—it's yours."

She gnawed her lower lip. "Will you take care of him? Will you kill him?"

"We've got to—and you'll go back there and do it right to Grandma. It's the only way out."

"Jesus," she said. "To think. You didn't have the guts. Look what's happened."

I said, "I told Grandma I'd call the police. Hell, she's probably done something by now."

I didn't believe she had, but that's the way I played it.

Lancaster glanced at Miriam. "You get over to the house and fix her, right now. I'll take care of O'Shaugnessy." He took the hand away from his face and his lips curled.

"Well," Miriam said. "Do it, then, damn you! I don't trust you. Not after how you acted with her. Shoot him—or do I have to…"

She lunged and reached for the gun in Lancaster's hand. The man turned to glance at her. I moved. There might not be another chance. I dove straight at that gun with both hands out, and nailed it. There was a mingling of hands; Miriam's, Lancaster's, and my own.

I wrenched at the gun. It fired. The explosion was deafening. Miriam fell back, her throat pumping crimson. She'd been struck with the slug. She tried to speak, but sprawled against the wall, bleeding, and slid down to the floor.

I still had hold of the gun, and Lancaster's hand. He was staring at Miriam. I tore at the gun.

"You bastard," he said. His face was red with strain and shock and fear.

I kneed him in the groin. At that moment, the gun came free in my hand. Without thinking, I hurled it across the room into the kitchenette. It clattered among some pans out there, and at the same time he rushed me. He had the hitting power of a maniac.

I dropped low, caught him around the knees, and lifted. He came up and fell sharply backward with a smash. He was dazed. I whirled, seeing Miriam crawling along the floor toward him, trailing blood, and I rushed through the partially open door.

I didn't know where to go. I headed for the Mercedes, flung the door open, and saw immediately that the keys weren't there. Miriam had taken them. I could not wait, but headed back along the side of the house, toward a field, and a wooded snarl of mangroves beyond that bordered the bay. I didn't know what I was going. All I knew was that I had to get away. And as I hit the field, heading for the mangroves in the moonlight, I heard him call back there, and the gun fired. The slug went wild. He had gone and picked up the gun from the kitchenette, and he was after me.

He had to kill me, now. His life depended on that. He would be as deadly as they come.

I paused and glanced back. I saw him, a black shadow, running toward me across the field.

"O'Shaugnessy!" he called. "O'Shaugnessy, I'll get you!"

I turned and ran for the mangroves. I knew Miriam was back there at my place bleeding. And I knew that would be O'Shaugnessy's troubles, too. Not Lancaster's. He wasn't connected with me, so far as anyone knew.

I reached the mangroves, and broke through the heavy tangled barrier of limbs and leaves and gnarled stems. He wasn't far back there. I could hear the pound of his feet, and just as I shoved among the twisted trees, he fired the gun again. The slug snickered through the branches, cutting sharply, but far to the right.

What was I going to do? It would be a stalking game, and Lancaster was as desperate as any man could get; he knew he had to kill me, or he was finished. I wondered if he was thinking of somehow getting back to rid himself of Grandma. He would have the nerve now. He'd been chicken, or human, maybe—but now he was a cock, and if I didn't get away, I was dead.

I didn't want to be dead. Too much had happened. Anything but dead, dead was the ultimate, and I did not want that.

"O'Shaugnessy—you'll never make it."

He was among the mangroves now, too. We both crashed and thrust toward the bayside.

Then I was breaking through the last spreading and snarled mangroves, and I came upon the beach. Fiddler crabs scurried around my feet, and the fish odor was strong. Moonlight revealed the water, some lights over to the right, and the dark shapes of keys not too far out on the gleaming bay.

I turned to the right and ran hard along the soggy, mud-splattery beach, leaping twists of driftwood, and kicking an occasional beer can.

The hell of it was, I had no idea where I was going. He could keep chasing me, and he had that gun. Sooner or later, he would get me. I knew everything that went on in his mind, and it was all evil.

I thought how I'd told Grandma not to worry, to lie on the studio couch with a pillow over her face and play dead. I'd said I would get to the police and she'd trusted me.

I looked back. The shadow of Lancaster was running swiftly after me through the muck.

There was a million and a quarter, and a dead man, Sesto Vecchi, tied up in this, and if I talked, it would be Lancaster's neck—and Miriam's, too—if she lived.

It had been beautiful, what they'd done.

I kept running, and there was a stitch in my lift side now. It hurt bad. I was breathing in sharp gusts, and for some reason, then, I thought of Ann Elliot. God, how I'd wanted that woman. I'd wanted her for mine—to be my own. My throat was thick with it, and what had very nearly happened. They had meant to kill me, then tell how I'd instigated the whole thing. Miriam would talk plenty. She knew my background, knew I'd been in prison. That cell out in Colorado seemed very peaceful, right now.

I kept running, not looking back, just hoping for something, and not knowing what it could be.

If he got me now, no matter how it seemed, it .would still send him riding high.

He fired at me again from back there, and the slug sent up wads of mud and water near my left foot.

That was much too close.

I kept running, dodging in close to the mangrove branches now.

"O'Shaugnessy!" His call echoed over the water, in the moonlit night.

It would be simple enough for them to explain why Lancaster hadn't shown himself to Grandma Kindott, since he was in the area. All he would say was that he'd been playing detective with Miriam's help, trying to keep Grandma safe, and get something on me, so I could be held by the police. It was very neat. They would verify everything.

And Ann—Ann would think what they wanted her to think. It was a lousy feeling.

Then I saw it up ahead, a small marina, dimly lighted, with docks and boats and a couple of sheds. It would be some sort of private marina, for use of the people who lived nearby.

The mangroves ended, and there were lawns, now, stretching back up toward large homes, walls and gates.

I made for those boat docks, the saffron-hooded area of the marina.

I glanced back at Lancaster. I was farther ahead of him than I'd figured, and I increased my running, even though the stitch in my side was paining like hell. I knew that because of that I couldn't run much longer. I was gasping and staggering.

He had to kill me. That was all I could think now. He had to kill me, because otherwise it was all over for him.

It was all over for me, too. But I didn't care about that. I just didn't want to die out here, like this.

I was thankful for the night, what little help it was.

I searched frantically for a boat, as I ran, and spotted an outboard not far along one of the cement docks. I ran along the dock of the tiny marina, and unfastened the boat, and was in it, starting the motor, just as I saw Lancaster make the turn onto the dock.

The motor caught, and I swung the boat slowly out away from the dock. At the same time, I watched Lancaster. He stood still for a moment, then ran again, and I cursed to myself because he was heading toward a larger Chris-Craft that was moored nearby. And as I held the throttle wide open, pushing the smaller boat out into the dark waters of the bay, I saw him pull away from the dock in the Chris-Craft, with a swirl of water and a smoking roar.

I knew I was sunk. I could not outrun him, and I didn't see how I could outmaneuver him, either.

I headed directly for the nearest black, wooded key. Already, the Chris-Craft was gaining on me, and I knew he had that gun ready, too.

All I wanted to do was reach the police.

Taking the boats would cause a stir back at the marina, but what good would that do?

I couldn't go on to the small island. He would only be after me, stalking me, again. I came around it, to the right, close in by the shore, under swirling branches. I was in darkness, out of the moonlight, and there was the chance I might lose Lancaster that way.

But as I came around the island to the bayshore side again, I saw the Chris-Craft nosing toward me.

I cut straight in to the left, above the marina, and as close to the bayshore as I could get. It was then that I saw what looked like black stalks sticking up out of the water. Then I realized they were immense pilings, dozens of them, with the remnants of a huge pier that had once thrust out into the bay, but was now nothing but a wreck.

I was among the barnacled pilings, the gleaming shadows, before I could do anything. I swerved in and out, barely avoiding striking the huge leaning posts. I looked back.

The Chris-Craft was coming straight behind me.

I burst out into clear water again, and cut further in toward the shore. Lancaster had a spotlight on now, and he was headed for the pilings, with the Chris-Craft obviously wide open.

He didn't make it. The explosion rocked the night, and flames spat into the darkness. He had struck a piling. Pieces of the Chris-Craft arced up and settled down and struck the water. I didn't like to consider what had happened to Lancaster.

I turned the outboard and went back there.

Floating, burning chunks of the boat were floating about the smashed hull, but I spotted no sign of Joseph Lancaster.

I got out of there, heading north up the bayside, in close to the beach, hugging the shadows. When I figured I was about opposite my place, I beached the outboard, and jumped ashore. I shoved on through the mangroves, trying not to think about anything.

I finally reached the field, and dog-trotted across that to the house. There was nobody around. The Mercedes still glinted in the drive, and the front door of the house was open, revealing a path of yellow light. I stepped inside.

Miriam lay dead, stretched on the floor with one hand out like a claw, her eyes wide, her mouth gaping. There was a lot of blood.

And it was now I knew something. I wasn't going to the police. All I could think about was Ann Elliot, and Grandma Kindott, and all that I'd done.

The keys to the Mercedes gleamed on the floor near the doorway. I took them, went to the car, and drove back toward Belleair.

As I drove beneath gesticulate shadows from palms and oaks, I thought about Lancaster and how he had posed as Howard Fisk. The meeting at the office with Miriam and myself had been simple enough to rig. He hadn't been working for the Wilkerson Agency, he had just been there, waiting. He didn't take us to his office, because he had no office. That was why we'd gone to the bar across the street.

But he'd worried about Miriam and me. And that was why he had come to the house, lurking around the grounds. He had known I would be worried, too, but that had not fretted him. And with me dead, ending it all, it would have been very neat for them. Grandma dead. Me dead, caught posing as Joseph Lancaster. Caught by the real Joseph, who had become suspicious from what Miriam had written him.

It had been sweet, all the way.

And I was numb with all of it. I was finished, too. I knew that now. Grandma Kindott knew who I was.

...NINETEEN

I turned the Mercedes in at the Kindott residence entrance, and crunched along the gravel drive. Then I saw that everything was lit up brightly, all the spotlights surrounding the house, along with another light on a police car. The red flasher was winding prettily.

I parked the Mercedes, got out.

Then I saw Grandma, over by the potted roses, holding Gargantua's paw. The monkey was picking at his leg, and eating what he found.

Ann Elliot stood beside the police car, talking with the driver, a uniformed cop.

I came steadily on, sick inside, knowing it was all over for me.

"Joseph!" Grandma called.

I heard her say that, but I couldn't believe what I'd heard.

"Joseph," she said again. "Where have you been?"

Ann Elliot turned and looked at me in a dazed fashion.

Sergeant Martin Brundell walked toward me. There was a jaunty swing to his shoulders, and his glasses glinted in the bright light. He had not changed.

"Hello, Mr. Lancaster," he said.

"Hello, Sergeant."

"I just came out to check on things," he told me. "What with the way everything's been going. Mrs. Kindott was worried. She said you went away without saying anything."

I looked across at Grandma Kindott, and she nodded and smiled at me. I was stunned and disbelieving. The monkey continued picking at his leg.

A wild thing came into me, and I heard myself speak, marveling.

"Just took a little ride in the Mercedes. It's something, driving a car like that. Sorry I worried you, Grandma."

Brundell's face was sober. "Anyhow, Miriam—Miss Kindott, that is— she's gone, too. It seems that Mrs. Kindott suspects she's in some kind of trouble. And I've had a funny feeling about her. Searched her room and came up with a gun. It's the same calibre that killed Sesto Vecchi. I think something was going on there. Of course, ballistics will have to check."

"Of course, "I heard myself say.

"Well," he said. "You'll want to be alone with your grandmother, now. If Miss Kindott is implicated in Vecchi's death, would it surprise you, Mr. Lancaster?"

"I wouldn't like to say."

"Joseph?" Grandma said. "You don't have to shield Miriam. You know the kind of person she is."

I said nothing.

Brundell nodded, and walked over to the police cruiser, and opened the door. Ann Elliot stopped away, then came toward me. Brundell got into the car, and they drove off, slowly, gravel splattering in the drive.

Ann held her hand out and I took it. She smiled at me. O'Shaugnessy was dead and gone, or at least in a semi sort of fashion.

"Dear Joseph." Grandma said.

I looked at her. I was still dazed, and didn't know what to do about what was going on inside me.

I said to Ann, "I see you're awake. I looked in on you."

"I just don't know what happened, "Ann said. "Grandma slapped my face to bring me to. It was as if—but that's impossible. Then she threw water on me. I'm still damp."

"It becomes you. Must've been that beer."

She still wore the white dress with the silver chain, and her thick dark hair went with the night. Those eyes regarded me heavily, and the pink tongue tipped her lips.

We walked over by Grandma Kindott. The old lady was smiling at me still. The pink hair was a foggy mass around her sharp face.

"Joseph, dear," Grandma said. "We'd better go inside now, so you can calm down—"

"Calm down?"

She matched me. "I mean, after your drive, and all. And I'll bet you're hungry. Am I right?"

I just nodded, and Ann tugged at my hand. We walked toward the house.

Ann leaned close and whispered, "You're not really Joseph, at all—are you?"

"No."

"Will you explain it to me later?"

"Yes."

The way she looked at me was filled with promise. By the glass walls, I turned and looked back at Grandma.

Loretta Kindott was watching me, pulling at Gargantua's paw. He was leaning far down, scrawling something with a bent finger. I stretched to see what it was.

There were three letters, quite large and erratic, but still plain, written in the pale sand.

"D. E. S.—"

Then Grandma yanked him along toward the house, saying softly, "Come Desmond—come, now!"

I turned to Ann and we walked between the glass walls, heading for the door.

Well, I thought. O'Shaugnessy, everybody's got a bit of the con in him.

Ann pressed my hand and we went inside.

THE END

Dig That Crazy Corpse

BY BAILEY MORGAN (GIL BREWER)

I hadn't decided to hire the blonde yet, but when the phone rang she looked at me and I nodded. She got the receiver off the cradle and began to think we were in business.

"Clint Carlisle, Investigations," she sing-songed into the mouthpiece. I made it a point to tell her this was not a travel agency or the office of a lingerie manufacturer. It had sounded like that.

"Digging," she gasped. "Did you say digging, madam? I'll have to check with Mr. Carlisle. One moment please." She clapped her graceful fingers over the phone and rendered me a desperate look. "Do you dig, Mr. Carlisle?"

"I've been known to do a little of everything," I informed her. The way business was going, I'd have dug a tunnel partner to the Brooklyn Battery job, if there was money in it. I smiled, "Find out what they want dug."

"Madam? What... uh, do you want dug?... Yes. Yes, I heard you." My dizzy new blonde seemed suddenly alarmed. She scowled at me and shook her pretty head negatively when I arched my eyebrows. "No," she said into the phone. "Definitely not. Mr. Carlisle does not do that kind of digging." She hung up.

I gasped. I clawed my way to the telephone and bounced it off the cradle, dropping the receiver with a loud clatter on the desk. "Hello!" I shouted into it. "Hello!" I listened to the dial tone.

"She hung up," my dizzy blonde said.

I replaced the phone carefully. "Miss Spears," I said. "That *is* your name, isn't it?"

"Yes, Mr., Carlisle. That is my name."

"We don't hang up on potential clients. Ever. We listen to them patiently, and then we let me speak."

My dizzy blonde appeared crestfallen, dropping her rouged lips at the corners. "The woman must have been a practical joker, Mr. Carlisle. You are an investigator, I was lead to believe by the sign on your door. An insurance investigator."

"Wrong. I am a *private* investigator. A detective."

Her blue eyes got wide. "No."

I shrugged. I'm tall enough for the stereotype, I guess, but not wide enough, not deep-voiced enough, not scarred, lecherous, snarling, sadistic or brutal enough. I wear shell-rimmed glasses, because I'm near-sighted. I wear tweed suits because I like tweed. I favor a pipe and don't hand smoldering cigarettes from my mouth because the smoke makes my eyes water.

"But you don't look... "

"It's an asset." I assured my dizzy blonde. "A definite asset. Hey, the phone! No, don't answer it."

She didn't. I did. "Carlisle Investigations. Carlisle speaking."

The voice purred pleasantly. Female, I catalogued. Young. "I hope you will reconsider, Mr. Carlisle."

"Reconsider what?"

"I neglected to tell the girl there's a five hundred dollar retainer in it for you. And five thousand, if we're successful."

"Yes," I responded mechanically, my brain swimming in an orgy of riches. "I have reconsidered."

"That's splendid, Mr. Carlisle. Shall I bring the retainer to your office, or mail it?"

"Better bring it, so we can discuss this further."

"Splendid. This afternoon? Ten o'clock."

"Splendid." I thought so too. I hung up. "By the way, Miss Spears," I said. "Just what does the lady want dug?"

"A dead man," my dizzy blonde told me, removing a buff colored buff from her handbag and buffing her fingernails.

The clock on my desk pointed ominously to 1400 hours, then drifted beyond it. No purring-voiced client. No retainer. No, nothing. I retrieved a Coke from the refrigerator cubicle under the water cooler and chug-a-lugged it. Miss Spears click-clacked busily on my beat-up Remington at the smaller-desk in my one-room office, typing the report on my last case, which I'd concluded two weeks ago. The report had been delayed because my client's husband had died suddenly and violently, with three inches of steel parting his breast bone. I felt unhappy about it, although not unduly. I felt guilty not at all, for I'd been paid as an eye and not a bodyguard.

At two-twenty-five a shadow bobbed into view on the other side of the frosted glass pane on the door. The shadow formed an obscuring background for *snoitagitsevnI* which, anyone with or without a Phi Bet Key can tell you, is Investigation seen from the wrong side. I began to feel I was on the wrong side of something, definitely on the wrong side, when the door opened and the shadow became a man. A big man in gray sharkskin and a too-small fedora perched above and between his ears like a thimble. The ears were something to see, large and thoroughly mashed and flushed an angry red color, so thoroughly captivating that you hardly saw the pinhole eyes and the rest of him.

"Clint Carlisle?" he said, rushing across the small office like a twister.

"Why, yes. I... ."

He had a ramrod attached to his shoulder, a rock-hard basketball at the end of it. He brought it up about a foot and stiffened it and I started to hear it go splat! against something. A basket, two points. The thing it went splat! against was my face. And by then I realized it wasn't a basketball after all, but his fist. It hardly mattered.

I admired the patterns on the linoleum floor without my glasses and made a feeble try at a pushup. As a gymnast I was a washout. I collapsed in perfect time to my dizzy blonde's scream.

He didn't kick me while I lay there attempting to get the little sand grains in my ears in order so I could stand up. He waited til I crouched on all fours, then kicked me. I went down again and my groan coaxed a whimper from the dizzy blonde.

I drooled bloody spittle on the linoleum and wondered if all my molars were in order. I had in mind to compose myself and come up swinging when the roaring in my ear differentiated itself into syllables, words, and short declarative sentences.

"You're looking at a gun," he said. "Stand up. Don't get wise."

I was. I did. I didn't. I glared at him hopelessly and wished a trapdoor would open in the floor and swallow him, although his angry pink ears would have stuck in anything smaller than a bomb bay. He said, "About that phone call."

I grunted, removing a handkerchief slowly from my back pocket, making damned sure he knew it was only a handkerchief, then blotting the blood off my lips with it.

"About that retainer."

I was still grunting.

"No, Carlisle. You don't want it." He had an impossibly mild voice for all the trimmings that went with it, but there it was.

"I don't know a thing about it," I said. "The lady indicated merely that she'd be here this afternoon to discuss —"

"Yeah. But she won't be. Don't get in touch with her. Don't do nothing. Forget it."

"I can't contact her. I don't even know her name."

My dizzy blonde, who looked somewhat sickish, was about to say something, but I glowered at her and saw her simmer down to silence.

"Huh?" the man mumbled, turning his .45 up slowly and staring at the muzzle as if he expected something to pop out of it. I hoped a reflex would make his trigger finger jump. It would be messy, but gratifying. "You mean you don't..." He scratched at the furrows on his overslung forehead with the front sight of his automatic. "You mean I got tough for nothing?" You mean... "

Clearly, he was perplexed. Like a boy who was told he couldn't touch another bite of candy because it would kill him. He lost the gun in the immensity of space under his sharkskin jacket between left armpit and wrist. He stuck out a hand he could have wrapped around the business end of a Louisville Slugger and said, "Shake."

It meant he was sorry, and who am I to hold a grudge? I shook hands with him, then turned southpaw long enough to cross my left fist from way out yonder to his jaw. His flinty little eyes followed the arc. He must have seen it coming, but he didn't duck. Neither did he wince. Up to the elbow my arm felt suddenly and completely numb. He let go of my other hand, which I drove against his paunch. I numbed that one too.

He smiled and said, "I had that coming. Pretty good, too. Hey, you're OK, Carlisle." He dropped a white business card into one of my numb hands, pumped the other one vigorously and added, "Look me up some time, guy."

He winked at my dizzy blonde, closed the door behind him. His shadow retreated behind the frosted glass pane.

I read his card. GIZMO TUCKER — Private Detective.

Well, he looked the part.

The phone shrilled. My hands had begun to tingle but had not yet achieved the functional stage where I could actually employ them to lift the receiver and place it against my ear. Miss Spears obliged with the time-tested preamble, then screeched. "He certainly does *not* want to talk to *you!*"

"Miss Spears," I said.

"Oh. Well, here." She threw the receiver at me and I managed to wrap my chin around it and start talking.

"Carlisle speaking," I said.

There was a background of music, far away and scratchy over the phone. The scratchiness got punctuated every two or three seconds by strident blasts from a horn. Trumpet, I figured. It made my ear curl. "Cat, I'm pleased I got through to you. Cat, listen. Don't you dig that rumble about none of this here body-snatching. Give it a wide pasture to graze. Cat, I mean wide. Start yakking if I'm sending solid."

"Uh, yes," I managed.

"The doll nixed me since I sang about body-snatching, but I anticipated you'd want to tumble. We've got a stake-out on this, cat. It's a kind of jive you don't dig, don't dig at all. Don't even try, cat. Vamoose from that there rumble, let me advise you."

"I'm advised."

"Five Gs will produce a solid funeral you you. Solid. But who worries about funerals when they're gone? I mean gone, cat. Not like a mainliner, but departed. You tumble?"

"I certainly do."

"It's our combo, cat. Don't you forget it." There was one last wailing note from the trumpet, then a click.

"Miss Spears," I said, somewhat dazed. "Gizmo Tucker and that there cat agree with you about this rumble."

"Mr. Carlisle?" she said doubtfully.

"Never mind. Point is, I don't. I like that woman's angle better. Five thousand dollars worth. If everyone's so interested in stopping me from helping her maybe the five thousand is for real. Too bad I don't even know the lady's name."

"She told me" said my dizzy blonde.

"She told you what?"

"Her name, Mr. Carlisle. You won't like this. I know you won't."

"How do you know?" I glared at her.

"Because I read that other detective's card. The woman who called was Mrs. Gizmo Tucker."

I found the Gizmo Tuckers listed in the Manhattan phone directory, stashed up in a fashionable upper East side apartment. Apparently Gizmo, big ears or no, did much better at this investigations business than I did. I hoped Gizmo and his unusual sensory organs would be off on a case somewhere, for I'd decided to pay a call on Mrs. Tucker.

When I parked, mine was the only pre-war car on the street. Hell, it looked like practically the only pre-1934 car on the street and the only heap smaller than a Roadmaster, unless you considered the rakish little MGs and other foreign sports jobs. I found the Tucker's apartment number and took the elevator up without telegraphing my intentions on the downstairs buzzer. The lack of a doorman surprised me.

I squeezed my Windsor knot outside the apartment door and dug my heels into the plush hall carpeting. There was a murmur of sound from inside, then silence as a pressed the buzzer. I tried again. Someone was on the other side of the door, all right, but apparently he, she, it, or they, wished I'd go away. Instead, I got ornery and tried the door. The damned thing wasn't locked.

First I saw the woman. She lacked Gizmo's ears, but I assumed she was his wife. She held a revolver in her hand, without pointing it at anyone or anything in particular. It had already done its pointing.

Another woman lay on the floor where she had fallen with awkward finality, her skirts up a good foot over her dimpled knees. I started wondering which dame was Mrs. Gizmo Tucker. The one on the floor, from the size and location of the ugly holes in her dress, was dead.

"I know what you're thinking," the standing woman said. "I know this looks bad."

I suddenly knew which one was Mrs. Tucker, for I recognized the woman on the floor. Two weeks before, she had been my client. For a modest sum, but I'd have taken half of it. Her husband had died under peculiar circumstances while I was in the process of trying to find out if he had a love nest or something. By peculiar circumstances, I mean he was murdered. I couldn't help thinking it ran in the family.

"It was self defense," Mrs. Tucker bleated. Her face was run-of-the-mill, but her body would make even an octogenarian think lecherous thoughts. Deciding I didn't want to get side tracked, I fought down an impulse to catalogue its sundry points of interest.

For the first time, Mrs. Tucker realized she still held the murder weapon. She got that repeat-performance look in her yes and said, "What are you doing here?"

"You called me, Mrs. Tucker. I am Clint Carlisle, though why you thought it necessary to hire a private detective when your husband makes like a good one, I don't know. Unless you're suing for non-support"

"That's just it. Gizmo is trying to stop me. You're job is to stop him from stopping me."

I gestured at what was on the floor. "Doesn't this alter things?"

Mrs. Tucker squared her slim, feminine shoulder. "Must it?"

"It must," I said sadly.

"Sit down, Carlisle," Mrs. Tucker waved her free hand toward a chair. I sat. "I have the five hundred dollar retainer right here. It's all I can afford right now, but if we're successful tonight there's five thousand more for you."

I shook my head. "Sorry. You can bet I was sorry."

"Well" said Mrs. Tucker, stepping toward me, lifting the big revolver and bringing it down, barrel-first, across my forehead. I began wishing for faster reflexes. I remember groping for my glasses as they fell off, then racing them toward the floor. Isaac Newton proved his point. Glasses and I hit the floor in a dead heat, then I blacked out impolitely on Mrs. Tucker's final words, "You don't look much like a private detective."

There was a ringing in my ears almost like a telephone when I regained consciousness. I found my glasses, put them on, sat up and realized it *was* the telephone., The dead woman on the floor reminded me to pick the receiver up with my handkerchief.

"Hello?"

"Did you say murder?"

"I didn't say anything."

"A wise guy, huh? This is Sergeant Maguire of police headquarters. A lady called up and said there was a killing at that address. Some kind of gag, huh? She sounded like she was joking, so I figured I'd better call back before I sent a squad car and got homicide all in a stew."

"You're very considerate, Maguire," I said.

"Yeah, but as for you two wise eggs, I've a good mind to —"

"Wait a minute. You're very considerate, but there's one thing you don't understand."

"Tell me."

"There has been a murder here. The corpse will appreciate a thorough investigation. Next time you get a call, Maguire, do your duty."

"Huh? Who's this? What's your name?"

"Hurry over, Sergeant," I said, and hung up. I got out of there in a hurry, drove my heap over to Central Park, purchased a bag of peanuts, found a bench, sat down and commenced feeding the pigeons."

I was also thinking.

Magda Flint — the dead Licorice Flint's wife and my former client — had visited Mrs. Gizmo Tucker at her apartment, after Mrs. Tucker had called me, after Gizmo had tried to scare me off his wife's offer, after some denizen of a be-bop booby-hatch had done likewise via the telephone. He fit into the puzzle as well as any of the others, for Licorice Flint had been a band leader, so named because he played the clarinet or licorice stick. Magda thought Licorice was two-timing her and hired me to find out. Licorice had been murdered. I had waited the customary time in such unhappy circumstances, then had my new dizzy blonde prepare the report. Now that Magda was dead, the blonde could do her practice typing on something else.

I had to assume Mrs. Magda Flint and Mrs. Gizmo Tucker had been embroiled in an altercation. One of them had come to the debate heeled with a revolver. Mrs. Tucker had used it. Then, I deduced brilliantly, perhaps Mrs. Tucker was the co-respondent I hadn't been able to find. Perhaps Magda had found herself and got killed for her trouble. That clearly made Gizmo Tucker not only the wearer of big ears but the wearer of big horns, right in the middle of his forehead. So Gizmo was plenty mad.

But Mrs. Tucker, bless her little murderous heart, had offered me five thousand dollars for a job tonight. The job seemed to deal with a corpse, or so my dizzy blonde and the be-bopper had indicated, the one indignantly, the other in warning. Aside from an anonymous collection at the morgue, the only other corpse I knew about was Licorice Flint himself, dead and buried these two weeks.

I left the remainder of my peanuts for the happily cooing pigeons and steered my heap downtown. I found a telephone booth in a stationary store and called a friend of mine who worked at one of the big morning dailies.

Phil," I said. "This is Clint. You should have some copy on a band leader, a Licorice Flint. Died about two weeks ago.... Yes, that's our baby. I want to find out where he was buried .. Uh-huh, I'll hold on." It didn't take long, and I repeated Phil's words. "Heavenly Hills Cemetery, right across the Suffolk County line. Uh-huh. Thanks."

I was going to heaven. I was going to the heavenly hills tonight, because that was when Mrs. Gizmo Tucker had indicated the digging would occur. But first I had to see my dizzy blonde.

"MR. CARLISLE! You look terrible."

"Thank you," I said. "That's no way to ask for a raise. Anyway, you just got here."

"No. It's your head."

Maybe that's why all the other pigeon fanciers in the park had been looking at me queerly. I went into the john out in the hall around the corner from the bank of elevators. I scowled at myself in the mirror and washed the blood off my forehead. When I returned to my one-room office Miss Spears smiled and said I looked much better now.

"Listen," I told her. "I have some extracurricular activity for you."

"I have to stay late on my first day of work?"

I shuddered when I thought that maybe there was a secretarial union or something. "Not unless you don't have a telephone at home or can't find a pay phone in your neighborhood. I just want you to make a call for me at nine o'clock."

"Oh. Certainly, Mr. Carlisle."

"Thank you very much. You are to call Police Precinct 14 and ask for Sergeant Maguire. If he's gone home to his wife and kids, ask for Homicide. Or ask for anyone. Tell them it's about the murder this afternoon on East 93rd Street. Tell them they better come running out to the Heavenly Hills Cemetery, in Suffolk County, or inform the Suffolk police or the State Police or somebody. You got it?"

"I'll write it all down. Did you say murder?"

I nodded and watched her face turn green-tinted white. The way she seemed determined to stick this job out, she must have enjoyed suffering. "And one other thing. Wait till exactly nine before you make the call, because I may decide to call you and tell you to forget about the whole thing. Better give me a number where I can reach you."

She did. She was writing furiously. She scribbled herself enough notes to tell my story five times over. She was still writing when I left to get something to eat. I wore the long afternoon out with a double-feature movie, three or four gin and tonics, a shave and shower and a long nap in my apartment. At seven I took the Queensboro Bridge over to Queens, filled my tank with gas and drove along Queens Boulevard with a forest of apartment houses on either side and the sun setting behind my back. I began to think it might be a good idea to turn around and go home, making an early night of it or perhaps calling my dizzy blonde and getting to know her socially. I'd done the job for Magda Flint, it naturally terminated with the death of her husband, whom I was shadowing. But Magda had found what I couldn't find, and Magda was dead. It made me mad. I felt guilty somehow. A conscience and a private detective don't jibe, I thought, still arguing with myself.

I swung left on Grand Central Parkway, right on Cross Island, then around a big cloverleaf to Southern State. The hell with it, I thought. I'd used up enough gas already. I might as well go through with it.

People talk of California as the place of fancy cemeteries. Could be, but for its size Long Island has California beat, at least in the sheer number of its happy hunting grounds. Take the Southern State Parkway out far enough: the cemeteries will crowd around you like motels on the New York to Florida highways. It was still light enough to see them when I got out there, but darkness had asserted its nightly prerogative by the time I took the cutoff to Heavenly Hills.

I parked near a pair of massive fieldstone columns supporting a metal arch over a dirt driveway in the moonlight. It was a clear night and a firefly night. All around me it looked like hundreds of people were busy lighting cigarettes. The place smelled pretty, but the tombstones were disturbing oblong shadows.

I felt like a ghoul.

The watchman's shack looked like a mausoleum. Maybe it was. Maybe someone had built the thing and then changed his mind and went on living. I checked the .38 in my shoulder holster, hoping I wouldn't have to flash it to impress the watchman, then pushed the door in and followed it. A small lamp shed half-hearted illumination. I saw a desk, a large filing cabinet, a big wooden chair, a collection of picks and shovels in one corner, and a body on the floor.

It was the watchman. I kneeled and felt him. He wasn't cold, but he was on his way. I must have resembled my dizzy blonde when I'd mentioned the word murder. Someone had used the edge of a pick on the watchman's head, crushing it to pulp.

I took a deep breath and crossed over his body, taking the shortest course to the filing cabinet. The first drawer contained "A" through "G" but it was locked. I debated searching the dead man for his keys, decided against it and smashed the lock with one of the picks. In its proper alphabetical place was a card on Desmond Flint. No wonder he had called himself Licorice. At the bottom of the card there was a notation to the effect that Mr. Flint resided permanently in plot B-11.

I consulted a map on the wall and found B-11, off in a corner of the cemetery, bordering on the highway. Licorice didn't want to be surrounded, but my fellow ghouls had to come past the watchman because a ten-foot wire fence had been erected to discourage trespassers. Whoever dreamed up the sturdy fence had signed the watchman's death warrant.

Easing the .38 from its holster, I hefted one of the pickaxes experimentally in my left hand, decided I was all for it and started wending my way between the tombstones. I expected to find Mrs. Gizmo Tucker, but while she seemed the type who could perhaps shoot and kill Magda Flint in an argument, she didn't seem the type who could bash in the watchman's head with a pick. I expected company, possibly lots more company.

Moonlight failed to dispel the cemetery's gloom. I waited for a hand to tap my shoulder from behind with every step I took. I anticipated barging in on a convention of ghosts or something and proving how little we humans really know. When I got close to B-11 I heard noises.

Scraping sounds. Shoveling. And hard breathing. Suddenly the scraping stopped, getting replaced by squeaky hammering. Someone was forcing a lid. Nice.

I couldn't see much in the moonlight. At the head of Licorice Flint's grave stood a small wooden plaque which seemed lost among the crowds of larger tombstones and which one day would be replaced by a stone itself.

Whoever was doing the digging was downstairs with Flint in his single room accommodations. I got goose pimples just thinking about it, then became so interested in what I saw that I stopped thinking.

A shadowy figure stood over the open grave, near the large pile of dirt. The figure's hand pointed down into the hole. There was a loud roar and a flash of fire. Someone yelped, then cursed. I decided it was time I announced my presence, so I aimed my .38 in the general direction of the grave and fired. The slug whanged off a tombstone. There was more yelling and cursing.

"All right!" I cried. "This is the police! Hold it!"

Nobody held anything. Apparently they didn't think much of police, but I began to wish I *were* police, a whole riot squad of them. Something flashed and roared again as I dropped behind a stone and got peppered with splinters. I fired a second shot, but it was like shooting up into the sky and hoping to hit a star — any star. I began crawling forward, dragging the pick-axe with me.

After locomoting six or seven feet like a baby, I collided with something too soft for rock and too hard for foliage. It whimpered and attacked me and by the clothing and perfume I knew it was a woman. I thought it was Mrs. Gizmo Tucker. With all these people, we were having ourselves a regular ball out here.

I subdued Mrs. Tucker and didn't feel much like a hero for doing it. I dropped the pick long enough to clip her on the jaw and hoped it would keep her out, but available, til I settled affairs up ahead.

They must have heard us scuffling, for I squinted ahead and saw no one. I figured one of them was in the grave, possibly wounded. It was a good bet the other one crouched behind the pile of earth.

I slithered forward and climbed up on my haunches this side of the dirt mound. If I was wrong I'd feel like a damned fool, but I gathered my muscles and my courage and sprang up and over, getting a faceful of dirt because I misjudged the height. A startled oath greeted me. My pick-axe sailed over the man's shoulder and my fist, gun and all, crammed the startled oath back down his throat. Even without the gun it should have been enough to knock him out. When he only grunted and wrapped his arms around me I knew — with despair — I had found Gizmo Tucker.

We fought there. Gizmo did the fighting. I held on and tried to bring my .38 around where I could empty its clip in his mouth. The muzzle kept pointing off in the wrong direction, though, and Gizmo kept squeezing my ribs and I thought, so long Clint Carlisle. My right hand was between us with the gun, and although I started seeing exploding red dots on a yellow background, I still could smack his chin with the butt of the gun. I did it until my arm got stiff and my chest ached and I forgot what it was like to breathe.

It actually began to wear Gizmo down. He no longer embraced me with such finality. His arms grew slack. I'll concede this much: he never fainted. All those blows probably would have broken a bull elephant's jawbone, but Gizmo just got dazed. Good and dazed. So thoroughly dazed I was able to lead him off docilely by the hand while I sucked in all the air in the cemetery.

I peered down into the grave and saw a man down there with a tiny hand flashlight, the kind with a peephole of light.

"Are you hurt?" I said.

He was busy counting money. I could just see it. Even if they were small bills it was more money than a man has a right to take into his final bed with him, more money even than any one man has a right to keep in the bank.

"Cat, I am bleeding badly," he said. "That square separated my shoulder. I will never beat my drums groovy again. Go away."

"Come up here," I said.

"I can't."

"I'll reach down and you reach up. We'll pull you up and we'll get you to a doctor and you'll be as groovy as can be in no time at all."

"You think so, cat?"

"I certainly do." I shoved the dazed Gizmo away from me and watched with relish as he sprawled on the ground. I leaned over the grave as far as I could without falling and reached down. A hand caught mine. We played seesaw for a while and I thought I'd join him down there. I finally got him up, though.

"Cat," he said, "never dig a money rumble. Money is the seed of the root of all evil."

I pushed him ahead of me and prodded Gizmo to his feet. I marched both of them back to where I'd left Mrs. Tucker, then heard her voice. "Stop moving," she said. "Freeze there. I've got a gun."

I didn't know whether to believe her or not. She convinced me by blasting at the moon and then recocking the hammer audibly.

"Gizmo, you louse," she said. "You had to spoil everything. Sure, I was playing around with Flint. What do you care? You're not lily-white. He was all set to leave me a fortune — only he was worried his wife would contest it. He was a sick man, see?"

"He knew he would die soon. He'd thought he'd leave the money where no one would think to look for it, unless he was told. In his grave..... But you had to get nasty and jealous and bump him off right before he was ready to go, anyway. You big dope, you ruined everything."

"How should I know?" Gizmo gasped.

"Our cat here," Mrs. Tucker went right on, "was Flint's go-between. He carried the plan out for a while, then I guess he lost sight of his loyalty to a dead man with all that money lying around and rotting, so he decided to get it himself."

"I regret to say you latched the rumble thoroughly," the Cat admitted.

"One of you killed the watchman," I chimed in. "Probably Gizmo."

"Yeah," Gizmo said, in his ridiculously gentle voice. "He thought I was looking for trouble."

"I ought to kill you, Gizmo," said Mrs. Tucker. "You ruined everything. I... think... I... will."

"No you won't baby." Gizmo plodded forward toward her. Gizmo was mistaken.

The gun barked, flaming and bucking four times. Gizmo almost reached his wife and fell on his face. The gun clicked on an empty chamber. The gun hit me in the chest as I moved forward. I subdued Mrs. Tucker again, not feeling particularly happy about anything. I hadn't made a plugged nickel but at least the mess was straightened out and I had a clean conscience. It would never get me rich, but I could live with myself.

"Don't lose the money," I told the cat.

"It's stashed," he told me.

I sat down and waited for the cops to come. I hoped my dizzy blonde remembered to call them. I had a hunch she would. I began to think about telling her to rip up the report tomorrow and at least I got a kick out of that.

THE END

Love... And Luck

By Gil Brewer

Cora Fleming slowed the white Saab, and waved to the obviously striking woman beside the mountain highway.

"Who's she?" Rush asked.

"Catherine Parrish. A friend of ours."

"Stop the car, baby. I like meeting your friends. Never can know enough about little Cora. Right?"

Cora stopped the car. Rush, blond and over-handsome, grinned at her, revealing teeth like even white carved chips of soap. She felt furious, helpless, inside, but what good did it do? Rush Taylor had her right where he wanted, and it was strictly evil. He'd stepped out of her busy past, come to Albuquerque, located her in the Sandia Mountains, and he was the same as ever, sadistic and insatiable. That she was married to Ernie did not stop him. Rush posed as her cousin. Cora tried not to reveal anything of what she felt as Catherine Parrish stepped over to the car.

"Wow," Rush said softly.

The other woman, quite obviously, as was her way, chose the passenger side, and moving gracefully in skin-tight black denims, a skimpy white sweater, those full red lips half parted expectantly, winked at Rush. Thick auburn hair framed a flawless, oval face set with slanted, Oriental-like, green-blue eyes.

"And who, may I ask, is this specimen?" Catherine said, tipping her head at Rush. "My, my, honey-bear—you keeping everything to yourself?"

"No, of course not," Cora said, feeling uncomfortable. She introduced them. "Rush is my cousin, stopping over for a little while."

"Now, baby," Rush said. "You know I'll be here more than a little while." He turned to Catherine. "Nice meeting you, Miss Parrish. And what do you do, way out here in the wilderness?"

"I carve stone," Catherine Parrish said. "How hard are you, Mr. Taylor?"

They laughed together. And their gazes held.

Cora watched them look at each other, and she could almost feel the electricity. Catherine tossed her hair back, and laid one hand on Rush's arm. She glanced at Cora.

"You and Ernie must bring Mr. Taylor over to my place some time. Okay?"

Cora nodded. "Sure, Cathy."

"How is Ernie?"

"He's fine."

"Still writing up a storm?"

"He's on a new book. It's going well."

Catherine smiled, squeezed Rush's arm. "You make them bring you around, Mr. Taylor."

"Rush."

She gave him a down-under look, squeezed his arm again, then stepped away from the car. "It sure is lonesome out here." She sighed.

"So long, Cathy," Cora said.

They all waved, and Cora moved the Saab off.

"She just lives over the hill, eh?" Rush said.

"Yes." She paused, chewing her lip. "Rush? What do I have to do to make you leave?"

"You can't make me."

"I could tell Ernie—"

"Tell him what, baby? What could you tell him? You want to break his heart?"

"No."

"Come away with me, then."

"Don't talk rot. I love Ernie."

"Oh, rats. Cora, baby. Those are words. Anyway, you can't tell him anything. And I'm not leaving. I like it with you. You know that. We have a thing few people have."

"My body's all marked up."

"So what?"

"Ernie's already asked where I got some of those bruises."

"What did you tell him?"

"I said I fell."

Rush chuckled softly. "Ah, me. You know you like it. Anyway, you tell him anything at all, baby, and I'll spill like a bucket with a hole in it. Your past, remember? I do. Cora Cult, exotic strip queen."

"He wouldn't mind." She knew Ernie would mind.

"Hell, you know that's not the nub, baby, I'd tell him what you really worked at. Big-time call girl. All the houses you been in, later on. And then, all that time with the syndicate. I think he'd curdle, knowing Ernie. It's too much."

"I've changed," she said tightly. "I'm different now, Rush. I'm happy. I've finally found it. I'm married. I love Ernie. You've got to understand that. I don't want you around!" She gripped the wheel tightly, turned in the drive beside the large, rambling, rustic, lodge-type mountain home.

"I'm staying, Cora. I like that red hair of yours. I like that piquant little face, that body, everything. I go for you, I always did. You never listen to me." He leaned her way, grinning. "I love you, Cora, baby. That's what you don't understand. So I don't mind sharing. I'm not like other guys. You know that. Just so I can be with you then."

She squeezed her eyes shut, turned off the ignition. Maybe he would go away if she just kept her eyes shut. She opened them. He was watching her.

What could she do? Ernie would find out sooner or later, and everything would go bust. She knew it.

Abruptly she opened the car door, got out, and ran for the side door of the house. She wanted to get as far away from Rush Taylor as she could. But she couldn't get away.

She burst into the house, closed the door, and stood there listening in the hallway.

The resounding clatter of a typewriter reached her through the near wall. It was like popcorn popping. Sometimes he used the tape recorder, but usually the machine. It was a good sound. It had always made her happy, because Ernie was doing what he wanted, and he was a good writer.

Someday a lot of people would know that. Maybe this was the book that would do it. Ernie was very excited about it.

Then she remembered Rush again.

His sexual demands were horrifying. He was brutal. He actually beat her, and she knew he was twisted, and Ernie would begin to question those bruises. She couldn't get by forever.

What could she do?

If Ernie ever learned about her past, that would be the end. She knew this. His character was such that he could never forgive her, even if it had happened before they knew each other. And Rush would tell Ernie. He'd take a sadistic delight in the telling, Cora knew.

Rush came in the door behind her.

She hurried off down the hall, took the front stairs up to her bedroom. She spent a lot of time in her bedroom these days, reading, reading, trying to think a way out.

The nights were lonely, too. Ernie worked half the day, and nearly all night long now. He wanted to complete the book. He apologized for leaving her alone, but he told her they would make up for it.

She stood there beside her bed.

But Ernie was getting a little frustrated about Rush, too. Several times he'd questioned her about Rush leaving.

"He has nowhere to go."

"He's a man, Cora. He drinks too much. He's lazy. I just don't like him."

"I'm sure he'll leave one of these days soon."

"Well, he's your cousin, and all that, I know. But there's something about him. I just can't quite put my finger on it."

And she would rub his curly black hair, and nuzzle his throat, and try to make him forget. She seemed to succeed.

The bedroom door opened. She whirled, expecting Rush. He sneaked around the house, came upon her unexpectedly. It was Ernie.

"Hi, love."

"Hi."

"Where you been?"

"Rush and I took a drive up to Golden. He wanted to see the old mines again. He's like a kid."

How would that go over? Ernie stood there, watching her. He wore blue denims, a baggy black sweater. His curly hair was matted, and he needed a shave.

He said, "Oh."

"What d'you mean, 'Oh'?"

"Nothing."

"Honey, I know you wish he weren't here. But I can't just tell him to leave."

"Yes, you can."

"You want me to tell him to leave?"

"Yes."

"All right." She turned away. "I will, then."

"Thanks."

She turned back to him. They looked at each other. Finally Ernie grinned, and stepped up to her. He took her in his arms. "We haven't had much time together lately," he said. "Another month, and things'll be different. Back the way they were. Okay?"

She smiled up at him, happy in his arms. "Yes."

"You'll tell him, then?"

"Yes."

"Well—" Ernie sighed. "Back to the salt mines. It's going good just now." He turned and left the room.

She went over and sat on the bed and held her head in her hands.

They had money. Ernie's father had left him plenty. Only he wanted to make it with the writing. They had their love. Ernie trusted her. He thought she was some sort of angel, she knew. He'd told her. He put her on a high pedestal, too high. God, when she thought of the things she had been and done. He must never know. He would leave her in a wink.

She *had* changed. She was no longer the same woman.

But what good did it do now?

Well, she would have peace for a few hours, anyway. Rush remained in his room nights. He knew it was taking too much of a chance, their being together during the evening hours. Even with Ernie in his study, he might come out at any time.

Cora would stay in her bedroom, reading, waiting for Ernie. Sometimes he never came; working all night long. Then he would sleep during the day.

And Rush would corner her. She admitted there was something magnetic about Rush. Too much of him might turn a girl's head. Once she'd been deeply in love with him, even with the things he did. Or so she thought.

Two days went by. Ernie asked her on the second day, "You speak to him yet?"

"No. I haven't the nerve."

"Want me to?"

"Oh, no!" She tried to hold his gaze. He turned away. "It's just that—" she said, "that I should do it. I will speak to him, Ernie. I will."

"He's *your* cousin. Not mine."

"He's so alone."

"Yeah." Ernie left the room, and soon she heard the typewriter hammering away again.

That night, after a light siege with Rush during the afternoon, she was preparing for bed, trying to convince herself she had an interesting book to read. She was by the window, brushing her thick red hair, when she happened to glance down into the driveway.

She saw a man hurrying along from the house. Glancing toward the road, she saw a car, recognized it immediately as Catherine Parrish's yellow convertible. It was Rush down there. He was meeting her.

She had to make sure about them.

She threw down the brush, left the room at a run, came downstairs, went through the side door. She heard Ernie's typewriter going strong, so he wouldn't notice if she went out. The convertible was just drawing away from the front of the house. She ran to the Saab, started it, and followed the other car. She was excited. Rush was having some fun with Catherine.

She followed them down the road, expecting they would go to Catherine's home. Then she knew they wouldn't. Catherine's mother lived with her, and she was a strict old woman, straitlaced, suspicious.

The convertible turned off the road not far from Cora's home, drove through a sparse woods, and Cora knew where they were headed.

Lovers' Leap. It was a high cliffside, not far in the woods, surrounded by huge boulders. An Indian maiden and her lover were supposed to have dived to their deaths off that cliff, because the brave's father, a chief, wouldn't condone the marriage. Something to do with the maiden's infidelity.

Cora parked the Saab in the woods, moved quickly toward the cliffside. She saw the convertible. She could hear them murmuring in the back seat, see their heads. The top was down.

She knew what she had to do. She would never be free of Rush Taylor, except one way. She gave no thought to Catherine Parrish. Catherine didn't matter. Maybe it was a sharp inclination out of Cora's past. She hadn't used to care about anything. She felt that way now.

Excitement streamed through her. It was perfect. She knew the terrain ahead of her in the pale darkness, the slant of the clifftop where the car was parked. All she needed was nerve. All the nerve in the world.

But she was desperate. She did not want to lose Ernie. He was already plenty suspicious. Today he had looked at her curiously during lunch, stared at her, actually.

She was breathing rapidly as she walked softly up to the back of the convertible. She could hear them whispering, hear the movements of their bodies, the rustle of cloth. They wouldn't notice her. They were very much wrapped up in themselves.

How long had it been going on?

Naturally, Rush wouldn't tell her.

She slipped up alongside of the convertible, bent low, and reached the door. She lifted her head carefully. They were really at it in the back seat, their breathing furious. She heard Catherine moan.

She stood, leaned sharply, reached in and released the emergency brake. She went with the car as it began to roll, pushing it with all her might, crying inside.

"Hey," Catherine Parrish said. "The car's moving."

She saw the black figure of Rush struggle to a half-sitting position. She was already behind the car as it gained momentum.

Catherine Parrish stood up then, in the back seat, half-naked, and screamed.

It was already too late.

The yellow convertible leaped out over the smooth rock on the edge of the cliff.

Cora saw Catherine waving her arms as the car somersaulted and vanished into darkness. A long, rending scream echoed in the night. This was followed by a distant shuddering crash, the rasp of crushed steel. The car struck several more times before it hit bottom.

Cora ran to the cliff edge, looked down.

She was just in time to see the car burst into flame, explode. Black smoke poured up into the night, brightened by fierce fire that lit the tops of pine trees far below.

She walked back to the Saab, got in, started the engine, and drove home.

She parked the car. Her hands trembled slightly, but she kept sighing, thinking how it was all right now.

She came in at the side door, started down the hall. The sound of the typewriter was reassuring through the wall.

"Hi, baby."

Rush was just coming out of the kitchen. He held a thick sandwich in one hand, a glass of milk in the other. "You been out?"

She stared at him. Something frittered away inside her, like a ripping and tearing of silk.

"Baby," Rush said. "What's the matter?"

She turned abruptly, and walked quickly past the entrance to the side hall, and opened the door to Ernie's study.

"Ernie! "

But Ernie wasn't there. The chair by the desk was empty. The typewriter clattered merrily away.

Then she saw what it was. The sound came from the tape recorder, the spools slowly revolving. The recorder was on Ernie's desk.

She knew.

Rush came into the room.

"Honey?" he said.

And she knew she would have to tell him. She knew what he would say. And there was plenty of money, too, because Ernie had certainly left it all to her.

She stared at Rush, and suddenly wept with fierce and desperate frustration.

Rush, frowning, took a big bite from the sandwich and said thickly. "Wonder where Ernie is, love?"

THE END

Indiscretion

BY GIL BREWER

She woke into a pink morning, the first in many a moon. It was pink, the way it used to be when she'd first met her husband. This morning promised to be pink all day long, and she found herself at the breakfast table with her two children and her lawyer husband with the roses on the table and the late summer through the French windows of the dining room, and everything was as pink as could be. The breathlessness that had been with her since stopping at the valley gas station a month before was as tingling as ever.

His name would be Jeff. She couldn't get over that.

His name would be Jeff, like that of her love so long ago when all the days were always pink and ravenous.

So long ago? So few years seemed so much sometimes.

She hadn't heard her husband speak.

"As I said, you look dizzy with delight this morning."

"I didn't sleep too well," she said with care.

"I really meant it," he said. He was finished with breakfast and he came around the table, tall and easy, first ruffling the young junior's hair, and gave her a kiss on the forehead. And she thought of the valley gas station. "Won't be home for dinner, either," he said. "I have to run over to Riverton. A client's in trouble."

"Doesn't he own a car?"

"It involves something of the sort. License revocation, so forth. Dirty business. I don't like it. But we do have to live, don't we?"

"You make it sound as if we're starving, Daddy." This from the young miss. Blonde curls and all, and properly used to wealth. She had probably picked up the sensitivity at school. "I'll need help tonight, too," she said, looking at him. "We're having a composition contest, it's on next summer's vacation. I want you with some big words. If you've learned any new ones."

"A deal. See you early, though," and he was gone. Then moments later through the fine pink wonder, they were all gone to their daily business, and there was only the too thorough maid's unwelcome deliberateness to endure as she avoided helping with the breakfast dishes, avoided the maid's tireless presumptive glance. But she wasn't reading anything into that, was she?

And there had only been the one slight jar, the dizzy delight he'd seen in her.

His name would be Jeff.

She went to her room, giving the blue point Siamese a light jostle on the way and remembering the cat show on the hill that afternoon, and how she wouldn't be there. She would have to think up something.

Everything was proper.

Even the improper way his yellow hair curled over his collar, somehow, and there was never any grime beneath his nails, either. Her heart rocked slightly and she decided against trying to read, or anything. Because in a short while he would be off work and she would be with him. Then just to get ready, was all.

It was the first time for anything of this sort, and she felt carried away with it. There was no wrong in it, save the intellectual wrong and that lay buried beneath a veritable storm of pink, so what could she do? She knew she should be experiencing some sort of guilt, and she actually tried to bring the thinking part of it within the realm of her emotions, the way that psychiatrist had explained two years ago. But it wouldn't work. The pentness of the emotion was too strong one way to bend another at will.

It was just all Jeff and the valley and soon and pink.

And the husband part was the second layer, undealt with, and to remain so. Beyond that she did not avoid; but she could not fathom.

Once, at the dressing table, intent on the pink mirror, she parted her perfect red lips and said half aloud, "Sordid." It almost made her laugh, but strangely the laugh degenerated into a smile. A beautiful smile, too.

She remembered the luncheon engagement with Elizabeth, knew suddenly that she could not endure it, started toward the jeweled phone, then came up with the jeweled argument that she would go to the luncheon, because she had to, because that's how it was still done.

Even if his name was Jeff.

There were the long hours of the day. Now there was Jeff. She heard the maid downstairs. She thought of the word *dishabille* and remembered a French novel, and then it was that his name was Jeff again.

Lunch was classic in its proper simplicity at the club and Elizabeth was on the horse show, and with talk about a new family building near their home, and somehow everything went all right, even if Jeff did work at a gas station. In fact she rather enjoyed having that knowledge and knowing all the time what Elizabeth could do with such a thing.

Oh, yes, of course, even if they—any one of them—ever drove into the valley, or happened upon her out there. Well, there wasn't any need for excuse. Cars did need gas, didn't they?

And the luncheon went pinkly on and came to a pink close and she drove toward the valley with a feeling of ice cream melting in her throat.

Would he notice how carefully she had dressed? Did the rather severe suit look well? Did it fit as perfectly over the hips as she presumed? Had the mirror ever lied? No, the mirror had never lied. Would it ever?

You're indiscreet, she told herself. As indiscreet as you can be.

Jeff had this friend and the friend had been drinking rather too much, so we would take him home first, you see?

So Jeff drove with her between, cramped a little, her left hand playing with the curl of yellow hair over the collar and the friend breathing heavily on her right, noticeable even in the open convertible, his harsh breathing somehow hurting the newness of the car.

The way led through the canyon, and up beyond the woods.

"It's not too far, honey," Jeff told her quietly. And then, the other said, "Right here'll be perfect, you damned fool!"

And the car was stopped under a tree just in the woods without a house, not anything in sight, and they were pressed close to her, and the one on the right was pulling at her skirt, and Jeff held her left arm, and with his left hand unbuttoned the flimsy jacket of her suit and began on her blouse.

And his name would be Jeff was what she thought, just once.

"My God, she's great," the one on the right said. "She's the best looking dame we've had for a while."

"You're a hot one, honey," Jeff said, bending her back and kissing her and she tried to bite his lip, and the other was forcing her legs, and had her skirt up to her waist. She wanted to scream. She couldn't. There was argument short, terse, as to who would be first. She was a commodity. Not even that. Not for sale, and without her realizing how it happened, she was in the back seat with Jeff, nearly all undressed, and nothing she could do about it, but kicking all the same. And the other hanging over the side of the car with his breathing mouth by her eyes as she saw too the curl of the yellow hair over his collar and thought did his fingernails have grime under them today, and she screamed.

"Shut up!"

"Let her yell."

"It don't matter, does it?"

"Hell, look at those legs. Jesus! Hurry up."

"Shut up."

"Hurry up. I can't wait. Jesus."

And she wanted to scream and the pink was red now. And the car rocked and even not screaming, she was screaming thinking of home, and the pink mirror and then insanely of the French novel and of how she'd forgotten to tell anyone she couldn't make it for the cat show, and without her realizing it, they had changed and it was the drunken one on her now, rougher than Jeff, drooling some, his eyes glazed like an animal holding himself up so he could see her, telling her, "I've got to look at you, too, oh you pretty, pretty honey, you, oh, you pretty, pretty honey."

Torn, she watched as the drunken one went off toward home through the woods, and she drove Jeff nearly to the highway before choking with it, she made him get out of the car and she drove off toward home.

She drove like a demon. I won't cry about it, she thought. My face will be red. Did he scratch me badly? Can I cover it up?

Angered and sick to the point of absolute craziness, she drove, thinking the police, call them, yes, swallowing. Oh, God, his name would be Jeff. Like that. Walked right into it.

At first she couldn't say the word, driving the new convertible, soiled somehow now, into the garage. Then, yes, raped. Raped.

The maid. The maid. The cat was at the side door as she slipped through, holding the shred of jacket and blouse and the torn skirt, with her insides feeling like shredded cabbage, cold in her abdomen. Her room. The door locked. She wanted to fling herself on the bed, like in the movies, and bawl it out with someone coming to her.

Doctors. The police.

The shower. She showered carefully.

She went over every inch of her body thinking all the countless things. She showered oh, so carefully, then dressed lightly in a white dress and sat before the pink mirror remembering the pink. Would it ever be again? Would she ever forget the gas station in the valley?

After dinner he came home and she sat there on the couch in the living room with the French novel on her lap and the word in her mouth.

"Hi, there. I didn't eat."

"You'll find something. I fixed it special. The maid's gone."

"All right."

He would be back. She heard the young miss prompting him. "You didn't forget about the composition, did you?"

And it would all have to wait until later. And what was it she would do about later? And it was now the first bright tear came. She couldn't help it, sitting there on the couch, thinking the word of it out there in the woods. What the word was and should she tell him, and how would she tell him.

He returned into the living room. The tear was gone now. She laid the book aside, and she knew it would have to wait until later, but she knew what she had to do.

Because it had to be right.

There had to be some of the pink again.

THE END

The Three-Way Split

by Gil Brewer

One

Have you ever watched them get drunk? *They* call it deep-sea fishing. They talk it up plenty back home in Ohio or Pennsylvania, about the big ones, the sunburns, the way the rods bend double.

That's how it was today.

We'd been out since nine-thirty. It was three now, the Gulf smooth, with no sign of weather. I let her drift. I figured no use wasting gas, even if they wanted to pay for it.

There were these two from Dayton, Morris and Brandon, with two good-lookers who were friends' wives.

"Bring us some more ice, Skipper!" Brandon called.

I was on the bench behind the wheel, thinking how one mess leads to another. If I didn't connect with some loot soon, I'd better high-tail.

Then there was the telegram from my old man this morning. Just in time to start the day off right.

I looked aft through the screen door of the deck cabin.

"Skipper?" Morris said. "Bring that other bottle of gin, too. This here one's a dead Injun."

They all laughed. They were great ones for telling me to bring them things.

"Carl," the plump blonde said. "You're a dog!"

"Watch out for my bite."

You could see trouble coming with both of them sniffing after the blonde. The other woman with the dark hair lounged on the bait wells. She stared at me. She wore red shorts, a blue handkerchief, and a heavy diamond choker, like a bull-dog collar.

I folded the telegram I'd read ten times and jammed it under the throttle on the wheel housing. He'd said he was coming down for a rest in Florida, a rest on my boat. It made me kind of sick. He'd never brought me anything but trouble. He had some good points, maybe, but they sure were dim.

"Hey, Skipper," Brandon called. "The ice?"

They were both big men, soft, like cotton batting. Big bumbling twins. Brandon wore glasses.

"Boy," the blonde said. "Am I tight!"

I went aft. "You want something?"

"We want a drink," Morris said. He wore coral-colored shorts. All of them wore shorts. "I told you to bring me some ice, Cap."

Now it was "Cap."

"Hurry it up," Morris said.

Brandon laid one hand on the blonde's plump thigh and looked up at me. They were all seated in deck chairs, except the dark-haired one. She was still on the bait wells holding an empty glass, that diamond choker knocking your eye out when it caught the sun.

"And don't forget the gin," Brandon said.

They had another good laugh over that. The sun was pelting them good, but they didn't seem to know it.

I went back through the cabin, down into the galley. I opened the icebox and whacked some ice off the cake into a wooden bucket. I'd arranged for the ice before daylight, thinking how it would be nice for them to have a long cool one in the afternoon, after a hard day's fishing. They'd put out one line for about half an hour.

Since then it had been drink and work on the blonde till she was dizzy. Pretty damned quick I'd have to take them home.

I took the bottle of gin out of the sink and jammed it into my hip pocket.

They started arguing back there. I looked, and this Brandon was on the blonde's lap, using both hands. Morris stood behind them, plucking at Brandon's shirt. He said if Brandon didn't stop mauling his woman, he'd crack down. The dark-haired one watched coolly.

I just stood there.

All I had was this boat.

She was mine so long as I kept up the payments on the loan. I was behind there, too. Twenty of the forty-five I'd get from them today would go on the loan. Twenty more for slip rent. That left me five dollars to buy gas and oil and food. And Sally would come down to the boat. We would sit across from each other on the bunks, and stare. Silent.

She insisted we get married. I wanted to wait.

Because, *We can't marry without money, Sally. It's no good that way. You lose something. You never get it back.*

All right, she had her job at the map office. I couldn't get a job; not one that would do any good. She and her sister lived in that big old house their mother had left them. Her sister Vivian was off the rail, bad. A mess.

And now, the old man. The Holland tornado. I'd lay the twenty-five, and the boat, too, he'd show driving a Cadillac.

My old man, sweetheart. Meet my old man.

Morris and Brandon started arguing in earnest. One of them threw a punch. I heard the "Whoof!" They were fighting in the stern. The blonde began yelling.

I put the bottle of gin back in the sink, and went aft again.

They looked like a couple of kids, sunburned and sweating. Brandon's white net shirt was torn down the back. They faced each other, fists up. It was comical.

"Come on," I said. "Cut it out."

The blonde and the dark-haired one stood by the bait wells, watching. The dark-haired one was still cool.

"Go away," Morris said. "I'll settle this."

Brandon muttered something and swung. He was still wearing the glasses. Morris leaned backward, making wild passes with his fists. His finger caught Brandon's glasses and they flipped over his head and dangled from one ear.

I stepped between them.

"You'll hurt somebody, you don't watch out."

"Get away!" Morris said.

I gave him a shove. He windmilled across the deck, bounced against the cabin, and sat down hard.

Brandon fumbled around, trying to put on his glasses. He muttered to himself, his shirt hanging.

"Why'd you stop 'em!" the blonde said. She stepped in close to me, her face beaded with sweat, nasty-eyed, her hair in damp ringlets. "Who you think you are?"

Morris crawled up and dove at Brandon.

"Treat a woman that way!" he said.

"God damn," I said.

I grabbed Brandon's arm, flung him out of the way.

Morris charged like a bulldozer. The dark-haired girl said something and jumped right into Morris' path.

"Look out," I said.

Morris smashed into her. Off balance, they fell back against the stem.

"Another man's wife," Morris said.

He whirled, pushed the dark-haired one out of his way. He pushed hard, all hands.

I stepped in again, grabbed him by both shoulders, and yanked.

The dark-haired one yelped. Her hands flashed to her throat.

"My choker!"

I'd seen it. As nice as you please. That diamond choker snapped under the pressure of Morris' hand when I yanked him; it sparkled twice, brightly, spiraled over the side, and plopped into the water.

The Gulf was clear as glass. It was like dropping something into the bathtub.

We all hung over the side. Looking.

"Your fault," Morris said. "You shouldn't've done that. My God."

"My choker," the woman said. "My diamonds!" She gripped my arm with fingers like ice-tongs. Her eyes were wild. "Do something. Get it back. You go in there and get that back!"

I stared at her, then looked over the side again.

You could still see it flash and twinkle up through the sunlit water.

Two

"Don't get plugged," I said.

She turned and smashed her glass against the side of the cabin.

"Get that necklace back."

She didn't have to tell me again. She would go to the Law, and it would be my fault. Who was I against a handful of diamonds?

I stripped off my shirt, kicked off my sneakers, and went over the side wearing only khaki trousers.

I dove straight down. The water was cool and it was good to be away from them. It was quiet and clear. I swam for the bottom, trying to figure current for drag, watching for the diamonds.

For a full week, during the first part of the month, this section of the coast had been ripped wide open by storms. A hurricane had started it, circling inland from the Gulf of Mexico. Only the winds and seas hadn't let up. But things had had a week to settle and the water was clear as gin. I'd be able to see the diamonds if I came near them. I'd done a lot of skin-diving because I liked the feel of it down there, the things I saw. I'd picked up some tricks from the natives when I was in the Pacific during the war. You can go a lot deeper than people think with a lung full of air and a head full of nerve.

But swimming down, I figured, no, it would be too deep along here—and right then I saw bottom. About five fathoms. I swam toward a smooth sand dome, like an immense circus tent-top. I let out some air, and kept going.

Smack on top, where the tent flag would be, was that diamond choker. There was no seaweed.

I swam over toward it, conscious of the way the far side of the dome slanted down sharply into darkening depths. If the diamonds had missed and gone over there, it would have been goodbye.

A three-foot shovel-nosed shark was inspecting the choker. It was the only fish in sight. I knew I couldn't make it, this time. I went back up, hurrying, swimming for the surface.

They yelled as I came into the sun-slant. The boat was about twenty feet off.

"You get it?" Morris said.

"You damned well better get it," the dark-haired girl called. "You be damned sure."

I rested with my back to them. I hadn't done any of this for a long time.

It made me dizzy and tired. Finally, I sucked air, thinking, *Those bastards*—and went down again.

This time I took it easy, making each stroke count. Wouldn't it be fine if that shark swallowed the diamonds? The water was like pale green glass, crystal pure, touched with silver.

I was glad for the slight weight of my trousers, but wished I had some lead. Then I spotted the choker. The shark was still there. I popped my ears and kept going. I came in close. The shark looked at me and nosed the choker. Then he vanished like a shot, his belly a white blur.

I swam across the dome. I got the choker, braced my feet, turned... then I stopped dead.

It was like a stab, seeing what I saw. My head buzzed and ached around the temples. I swam quickly toward the edge of the sand bank.

It was mystery, promise. I held myself down, said crazy things inside my head.

The storms had done it.

There she lay. A ship. A hulk, with her masts stumped off, lying right in against the side of this tremendous dome. It was like a black ebony plaque carved in the side of the sand. Not a modern ship. An old one, maybe a couple of centuries. Pictures thronged my mind. I remembered all the stories old Mike Wales had told me.

The first thing you think of is treasure.

It hits you right between the eyes. It's no joke. There are men who make a business of it, only sometimes a guy runs smack into one. Like now. It kills you.

She lay down there in about twelve fathoms. Maybe more, because the water was very clear and therefore deceptive.

The currents from the storm had done it. Sand had shifted, exposing the ship. It had been buried for God only knew how long.

I had to surface. I stuffed the choker into my pocket and started up. I'd stayed down much too long.

They yelled again. I lay there on my back, exhausted. I floated, resting, with my heart trip-hammering, and my head ready to tear loose. I turned and looked at them.

"I saw it," I said. "I'll get it this time."

They yelled a lot of things. The dark-haired one made more threats. I knew I shouldn't try going down again. I was all out of shape. But I had to. I took some air and dove hard.

It was no dream.

But there were lots of hulks around, weren't there? Especially on the Florida coasts. Then why hadn't this one been reported long ago? Why didn't I know about it? I'd spent a lot of time with Mike Wales and he'd never mentioned a sunken ship out here. Mike had dived in these waters plenty. He'd gone after treasure ships all over the world. He knew the score. If anybody knew of this one, he would. Even if there was nothing aboard her, he would have mentioned her.

But she hadn't been seen. That was why Mike didn't know her. The currents had gouged the sand dome, opened it up. The hulk was in the middle of the gouge. It was as if somebody had scooped a huge long hole in the sand. The ship was only about a quarter buried.

Like a picture on a wall.

The hulk was just stuck there, over nothing. If she ever let go, that was the end....

I was bursting. My ears screamed and cracked. My head ached.

When you haven't got anything, you jump at what looks good. Nothing ever looked so good to me as this. There had to be something in her. There had to be.

A school of fish came along. They swam tight, shooting crimsons, oranges, purples through the silver-shot green above the blackening depths. They nosed toward the hulk and hung there amidships like a swarm of humming birds.

It was some picture.

I went back up. I kept telling myself, *She's just an old empty wreck, that's all. They probably scuttled her.* Only it didn't do any good, telling myself those things.

"You're pretty good, aren't you?" the dark-haired one said. Her eyes had that weird light, like a kind of scheming, in them.

"You've got your diamonds," I said.

They were quiet. I dripped on the deck, thinking about what was down there and what it might mean to me. The blonde, Brandon, and Morris sat in deck chairs, watching me. The dark-haired one looked me over, like she wanted to buy. She had that damned look in her eyes.

"You're really good," she said.

"Glad you feel that way."

"Sarcastic, too."

"Anything you like."

"You know what *I* like. Don't you, sailor?"

I shrugged.

"Strong and silent. Big and bold. A lion."

"Oh, drop it," Morris said. "Drop the whole thing."

"Write it into a book," I told her. "You're good."

All I could think was that I had to mark this place, somehow. They hadn't seen a thing. You couldn't, from where we were. You could just make out the top of the sand dome, but not well because of the slant of the afternoon sun. But you couldn't see the hulk. The pitch of the bottom was in the way. A good thing. It would have started something, all right.

"Don't you want a reward?" the dark-haired woman said, her breasts thrust out. She moved her hips and smiled brightly.

I frowned. "Forget it."

"Look at him scowl," she said. "Isn't it wonderful?"

"You got your necklace," I said.

She looked at it in her hand.

"True," she said. "You did bring it back, like a good little dog. But the clip's broken."

I watched her.

"It's just no good any more."

She gave a flick with her wrist. The diamonds winked as the choker went over the side. *Plop.* Into the water. I didn't look. Nobody moved.

"Well," I said. "You can do what you like."

Now it was her turn to frown. Then her voice went nasty. "I bought it yesterday afternoon," she said. "At Woolworth's." She waited. I didn't say anything. Something else came into her voice. "Aren't you mad?"

I grinned. "We're going in," I said. "No, I'm not mad. I think somebody should clue in your husband, though." I looked her over good: the breasts, the belly, the hips and thighs.

She slapped me twice. Hard. Across the face.

"We're not going in, either," she said. "You hear that, sailor?"

I shrugged and went into the cabin.

I spotted where I was as best I could. From points ashore. Egmont Light was to the southeast, and the shoreline was a dark green snake. I had to mark the wreck some way. I went belowdecks, up past the bunks, and got some line and a three-foot piece of two-by-four. I climbed up through the open forward hatch and out on the deck, and cut the anchor off the rope. I looked aft where they were; they couldn't see me up here. I tied the line to the anchor, computing distance by eye, and tied the two-by-four to the other end of the anchor line. I hoped I had it right; I wanted the wood to float just below the surface.

They were talking back there.

I let the anchor go. It splashed and went on down. All the line had to do was break when it whipped at the two-by-four— It didn't. It went down, the wood floating about two feet under water, very plain to see.

It would have to do. I figured I could find the spot.

A breeze was making from the port quarter. The Gulf was beginning to hump.

Down through the hatch. I got a towel and rubbed myself down, think-ing about the dark-haired one and how crazy she was with it. I put on clean khakis, a T-shirt and went out there with them. I put on my sneak-ers.

"All right," I said. "We're going in. You've had a fine day, haven't you?"

I went in to the wheel, started the engine. She turned over *bang,* and caught. A not-so-young 120 Gray Marine, but I had it running sweet. I ruf-fled it a little, blasting it above their talk, then came about and headed for Egmont Light.

Just think what's down there, I thought. Morris came forward for the gin.

I left the wheel, got the bottle out of the sink, returned to the wheel, and opened the bottle, while Morris watched. I dropped the cap on the deck, and knocked down about a third of the bottle. It was Gordon's. It was just what I needed.

For Sally, I thought.

Then I remembered my old man, and the gin was sour.

Morris took the bottle, and went aft.

At the slip, I told them what the bill was.

"Thirty-five dollars is too much," Morris said. "How do you figure?"

"You're getting off light," I said. "You didn't do any fishing, so the equip-ment wasn't used. But there's gas—and my time. Hell, it's the price."

"You didn't burn much gas. We just sat out there." They hadn't looked like deadbeats. But that's the way it goes. I hate it this way. It always embarrasses me.

"Look at that," Morris said. He pointed to a big sign advertising rides on Higgenbotham's *Island Belle.*

"Three dollars," he said. "That boat's three times as big as yours."

"It's an excursion boat."

"This is just a rowboat, compared," he said.

The others were on the pier. The blonde looked down at me and winked over his shoulder. I could see she was a good scout. She'd just got drunk, that's all.

"We're going out to the car," Brandon said from the pier. "You take care of it, Leonard."

They walked off. The dark-haired one's shoulders were stiff.

"I'll give you ten dollars," Morris said. "It's plenty for what you did. We didn't catch a thing. Not even a bite."

"Strike," I said tiredly.

"Here."

He held out a ten dollar bill.

"I told you forty-five when we left this morning," I said. "We agreed on that."

"I didn't hear you." His eyes got fishy. He reached out and jammed the bill into the pocket of my T-shirt. Then he turned and started up the ladder. Halfway up, he paused. "There's half a fifth of gin left. You can have that, too," he said. "Damned if I ever charter a boat again. It's a racket. Somebody ought to do something about you men."

I took a long stride, grabbed the back of his belt, and gave a yank. He came off the ladder, hit the deck, and went down. He got to his feet, lumbering, his lower lip stuck out. Obviously, there was a nasty cut in his pride.

I took hold of the front of his shirt and twisted it up, stretching it good. His eyes were like mirrors.

"Let go," he said.

"No. I've taken all I can stand from you people. It's a damned wonder I didn't leave you out there and let you swim in. You'd make nice plump fish bait. Now, you still owe me twenty-five dollars."

"I'll get the cops."

"Go ahead. They'll laugh you out of town. Now, you want to go over the side?" I dragged him to the rail and bent him over so he could stare at the waters of the basin. "That what you want?"

He spoke with a weak whine. "All right."

"Get it up, then."

I let go of him. He took out the money and handed it to me. I jammed it into my pocket. I still wanted to pitch him over the side.

He turned and stumbled for the ladder. He took two steps, and banged his knee a nasty crack. Limping, he made the pier, and then half-ran, half-walked toward the gate.

The hell, I thought.

I went into the cabin and sat on the bench by the table. There was nothing you could do about them. It takes all kinds, like the man said. And to begin with, it was off-season. I could make out during the season, but right now things were rough. I knew I should have made him come up with the forty-five.

I put an ashtray on the money so it wouldn't blow away, and started looking for the bottle of gin.

Three

The gin bottle was empty. It had tipped over and the gin had drained between the deck planks into the bilge. You could smell it fine. I threw the bottle out into the basin. It splashed, began to gobble water, and sank.

I took the money and started out for where Hillman, the dock master, parked his car. I needed every cent of the money. It was all I had.

"Can you let it ride a few more days?"

He was ready to go home. He was behind the wheel, sober, with his cigar, his white yachting cap, his air of contentment. He was a good enough egg, with a rotten job. He lived for fishing, and had to sit there all day, watching the water, taking in slip rents. This must have chewed the hell out of him.

"Hell, Jack. You're way behind. There's a guy been asking for your slip, you know that."

I watched him rub the ash off his cigar with his thumb. "Thought you had a charter."

"I did."

"Well, you owe me sixty bucks. It's got to be paid."

"Here's thirty."

"Thirty's not sixty."

I didn't say anything. He rubbed the end of his cigar down on the top of the car door. *Well,* I thought, *it's his job.*

"I'll tell this guy you're keeping the slip." He blew smoke at the steering wheel. "But he knows your electricity's been turned off. And they pulled your phone."

"What the hell?"

Hillman shrugged.

I thanked him and started down the sidewalk, along the municipal pier, where the slips were. I had to get something to eat. I didn't feel like cooking anything aboard the boat. I knew I was postponing seeing Mike Wales. That was the big thing.

Maybe I was scared to tell him what I'd seen out there. Mike would know the truth damned quick, and I was afraid to hope. Excitement was inside me like a caged bird.

I came along the sidewalk by the benches under the palms. A car honked in the street.

It was Sally. Her sister, Vivian, was driving the old Buick convertible. Sally waved, got out, and slammed the door. Viv drove off, roaring in a U-turn on the pier across from the tennis courts.

I watched Sally come toward me. She was a picture, a slim, dark-blonde girl, with a way of looking at you that made you seem important. She wore a white linen skirt that snugged against her round hips, a white, very thin cardigan buttoned to the throat, and white loafers. There was vitality in the way she moved.

"Hi, Jack."

She stood there with that little smile, her eyes soft in the early twilight. Her firm, full breasts thrust against the fine fabric of the sweater, heaving a little as she breathed, and the nipples showed. She had a shy way about her, making everything still stronger. Her full red lips were hesitant. The look of her ate into me.

"I was just coming down to the boat," she said.

"Good to see you."

"I can't stay long. Viv's coming back for me in a few minutes. I've got to work tonight. We're getting out some blueprints for a new housing project."

It stirred inside me. We stood there.

"We could walk up to the boat," she said.

She came close, took my arm, and we walked along the sidewalk. Three young girls in tight shorts passed us, eating hotdogs. The streetlights came on, glowing faintly in the twilight, like a string of pale diamonds. I didn't want to tell her about what I'd found; not till I was sure. But I had to tell her about the old man coming down here.

"Everything all right, Jack?"

"Sure."

"Any luck today?"

"Took some tourists out."

"Oh, I'm glad. You get the phone connected?"

"I will."

"Then I could call you. I miss that."

I pulled her close, feeling the easy warmth of her thigh, as we turned in toward the slip gate. We stood on the grass by the sea wall, looking down at the bow of my boat. You could faintly smell the gin.

"What's the matter, Jack?"

"Nothing."

She moved close against me, and I held her. I kissed her. She began to tremble, and so did I. She breathed heavily, her body so vibrant and urgent it nearly drove me nuts. I knew what she was thinking about. So was I. It was bad. Her breasts mashed against my chest, and her legs pressed against mine. I wanted her worse than ever.

She drew away.

"What are we going to do, Jack?"

I shook my head.

Water lapped at the boat, slapping in the growing shadows. The bow would rise just a little, and you could smell the gin.

"Could you sell the boat for anything?"

"No."

"I'd sell the house. Only Vivian won't go for that. When mother died she told me never to sell the house, but we're just managing with the old place."

Light from the streetlights shone in her hair, and her lips looked black.

"You think I want to go on working in that damned map office?" she said. "When every minute I can't get you out of my head?"

"I know."

"And Vivian's awful. The things she does. She had another wild party last night. She's drinking too much. I can't say anything to her." She paused. "Jack—how long can we go on like this?"

I told her about the telegram from my father. "He's coming down here. Wants a vacation on my boat."

"You've never mentioned him."

"Good reason. He's never brought me anything but trouble. He's all right, but he can't help getting himself all fouled up. I don't like the idea of his coming down here, but there's nothing I can do about it." I hesitated. "You won't understand, till you see him. It's been this way ever since I can remember. It means he's broke again. Either that or in some kind of jam. He never grew up, my old man. He's always in trouble of some kind."

"You're probably exaggerating."

I didn't say anything.

"Is that what's bothering you?"

"Maybe."

The Buick came down the street, slid into the curb. The top was down, and Vivian waved from behind the wheel.

"Sally. I've got something. I mean—I can't tell you, not now."

"What d'you mean?"

"Something big, maybe."

"Why can't you tell me?"

"Just keep your fingers crossed."

I held her arms and she pressed tight up against me, hard, with her ripe body. She looked straight at me. It was wild and dizzy.

"Sally," Vivian called. "Hurry it up, huh?"

"She wants the car," Sally said. We walked over to the car. "Phone me," she said.

I squeezed her arm and opened the car door.

"Hi, Jack."

Vivian was high. She was a damned attractive girl, with sharp features and bright wild eyes, yellow hair down over her shoulders, and a straight slash of red mouth. There was a hardness about her, though. She wore a tight, dark dress. The skirt was up over her knees.

"You look sad, sailor," she said. "What's up?"

"G'bye, Jack," Sally said.

Vivian gave a little snort and started the engine. They whipped away. Sally looked back at me. Her face was white and serious over the top of the door.

Vivian had had part of the money from the estate when their mother died. She went through it, fast. She borrowed from Sally, and that went, too. There was plenty wrong with Vivian.

I went down the pier to the hotdog stand and ordered three hots and a cup of coffee. I ate, wolfing it down. Then I cut across toward the slip where old Mike Wales had his yacht.

It was a big boat. Mike had memories of long years in sailing ships; had taken some of the big ones around the Horn in the last days of the big square-riggers, the five-masted giants. Out of that, he'd gone into his hobby, diving, and had done some famous salvage work. He'd managed to drag up quite a bit of treasure, here and there. Mike was wily. There was no telling exactly what he had stored away.

I thought, *If there is anything in that hulk, you got any idea what it costs for salvage?*

I came through the slip gate. Mike was sitting in his rocking chair up on the bow, smoking his pipe. He waved as I came alongside.

Four

"Did she have a poop?" Mike said.

"Yeah. A big poop."

"Hot damn," Mike said. He sucked on his pipe, then spat over the bow into the water.

Mike was about seventy-two, maybe more. He would let his beard grow gray and scraggled for a couple months, then shave. He looked like hell most of the time. He was still a big man, but he would lose it all one of these days. His eyes were clear. He lived for his ship, his pipe and tobacco, his endless supply of black Martinique rum, and an eight-by-twelve photograph of his wife. She'd been dead only three years.

"What'd she look like?" he said.

"Like I said, I couldn't tell much."

"How far down did you go?"

"Maybe five fathoms." I explained bow there was this dome of sand, and how you could look over the edge and see the wreck down there, a long way down. "The water was clear as hell. No fog at all. But even going down thirty feet gave me a head."

"It would kill me, Jack. Like that!" He snapped his fingers, holding the pipe in the same hand. He sat there in the old Boston rocker on top of the forward hatch cover, spitting over the side. He never missed. Someday he would miss, and then he'd never sit up there again.

"I seen you over to that hotdog stand," he said.

I was plenty nervous. He was trying to avoid talk about the hulk. *We'll have to do it his way,* I thought.

"That's a rotten thing," he said.

"What is?"

"Man eating hotdogs. How's for an omelet?"

"All right."

"I can still spit," Mike said. "So long as a man can spit..."

He climbed out of the rocker, about six-two of him, and looked at me, gnawing his pipe. He wore white ducks, a white shirt, and white tennis shoes. His hair and beard were iron gray. His eyebrows were black, and his eyes as black as hell. He had shoulders and chest like an ox.

"All wound up, aren't you?" he said.

"Yeah."

He turned and started down the deck. I followed him. You could see the channel lights out beyond the basin, and the breakwater. Mullet jumped in the basin. The cars went up along the pier, around the drive, and back again. Cars were parked fender to fender up by the hall. Streetlights played across the palms, silvering them in the dark.

The excitement was strong.

"Treasure's what you're thinking," Mike said.

"I never said the word."

"Afraid of it?"

"I don't dare think it."

"Six eggs all right?"

I sat down at the table in the galley, smelling rum and coffee and fried meat. He broke a dozen eggs into a cast-iron frying pan and walloped them around with a fork. The coffee boiled. He turned it off and broke an egg in there, too, shell and all. He slammed a loaf of bread on the table, got another frying pan, and filled it with bacon. He banged two pint mugs on the table, poured in steaming coffee until they were two-thirds full. Then be brought down one of those bottles of rum, black as tar, popped the cork, and filled the mugs to the brim.

He filled the plates and we ate. The rum was like a hot rasp running across the tongue.

We sat there with the coffee and rum, belching at each other. There was just enough swell so you could feel her roll.

Mike dunked hunks of bread in the rummed-up coffee. The smell would gas you. His face was like a slab of red beef that had been scarred with a sharp knife.

"Can't let it rest, can you?" he said.

I couldn't tell him what it meant; how it ate at me till I was nearly sick with it

"You want me to cheer you up, right?"

"I've got to know."

"How in hell do I know?"

I sat there. He didn't want it. He wasn't interested.

"Look," I said. "She's an old one, that's for sure. You've done salvage work. You've used diving equipment. You've been through all this, Mike. Do you know anything about her?"

He shook his head.

"What about all those stories you told me?" I said. "Like taking candy from a baby. Remember? Treasure ships. You told me there's plenty lying on the bottom, waiting to be picked up."

"You've got the bug."

"Could it be?"

"It's off the usual run, Jack." He waited a long time, packing and lighting his pipe. He took a swallow of coffee and rum. "But they're down there. They're in these waters. But I never knew of any hulk out there. I've been all over these waters. It's practically in a ship lane, isn't it?"

"Not quite."

"Does she sit solid?"

"Like I said. No more."

"The storms cleaned it out." He frowned, stared at his pipe. "I was through all that." He spoke with faint resignation. "It's too dangerous. I gave all that up long ago. That stuff is for a young man."

"I'm twenty-seven."

"I know it, damn it!"

I watched him. *Come on, Mike,* I thought. *Come on.*

"I was on a job, right along there," be said. "We raised a freighter. Brought her up. She was for Port Tampa. Load of machinery. Popped her rivets and swamped. There was nothing out there."

"There is now."

He got up and poured more rum, beetling his brows. The story was getting to him.

"Is there a chance there's something in her?" I said.

He looked at me. "There's always a chance."

"How do you find out?"

"Knew you'd get to that."

He was driving me nuts. "Look," I said. "I don't know a damned thing about it. I've never been in a diving suit. It's the first sunken ship I've ever seen. I can't pass it up."

"That's the hell of it, Jack."

"God damn, Mike. Don't hang me up like this."

"Have some more rum." " He filled my cup with straight rum this time. "In wildness is the preservation of the world," he said. "I got enough stores aboard so we could swim in it, we want to. You want to?"

"Not right now."

He sighed. "All right. I'll find out for you."

"How?"

He waggled his eyebrows, peering into the mug of rum. He said, "How you know I won't tell somebody about this?"

"I know."

"All right. You go on along, then," he said. "It's befitting that an old man should have his rest."

"I'll bet."

"I've got the location, near as I can tell. There's nothing else we can do tonight. Things I can do, but nothing you can do. So take your bloody excitement someplace else. I don't want to catch it worse than I got already."

I grinned, standing up.

"You'll see what you can do?"

"If anything can be done," be said.

I left him sitting there, staring into his mug of rum.

I used Mike's phone and called Sally. Mike knew something. He would have been emphatic if there was no chance. I wanted to tell Sally.

"I'll be down when I'm through work," she said. "It won't be too long. Tell me what it is, will you?"

"No. When you get down. I'll see you at the boat."

Heading back for the boat, it all went out of me like mush out of a paper bag. I didn't know a damned thing. I'd seen a sunken ship and I was nuts because of it. A rotten business.

I came along the pier, and remembered I had no lights. The hell with them. I closed the slip gate, went over to the pole, and broke the seal on the box. I flipped the handle and plugged the extension cord in. Now I'd have lights. Let them scream.

I came aboard, smelling the gin.

In the cabin, I closed and locked the screen door, reached over and lit the wall lamp. It flooded the cabin with orange light. Real homey.

"Turn the light out," a man said.

I stared at him. He stood down there in the galley, looking up at me. Light fell across his face. I had never seen him before.

"Second thought," he said. "Leave it on. Come on down here."

"Who the hell are you?"

"Never mind. You're Jack Holland, that's all that counts."

"Get the hell off my boat!"

He shook his head and grinned. He wore a light blue tropical suit that looked brand new, a white shirt, a rose-colored tie with a very neat knot. The grin went away. He stood there watching me, and blinked twice. The blinking was the only expression on his healthily tanned face. He flicked his jacket open, hitched at his trousers. I saw the gun hanging there, snug against his left armpit. Then he buttoned the jacket. He did it with one hand, his left.

"Suppose I get a cop?" I said.

We watched each other.

"You can keep right on standing there," he said. "Only you'll get tired, eventually. To say nothing of how I'll feel. So why not come down here, and flop on your bunk."

"What do you want?"

He shrugged. "I'm waiting for somebody."

"Who?"

"Sam Holland," he said. "You may as well know."

So my old man had finally gone and done it. This bird wasn't the law, either. This one meant business. There are two kinds. The ones who are big winds, and the others. This one was one of the others.

So it had started already.

"He isn't here," I said.

"You coming down here?"

I went belowdecks. He flicked on one of the little lights I had rigged over each bunk.

"Sit down, Jack."

I sat on my bunk and he got on the other, leaning back with his feet up. You could tell by the pillow that he'd been sitting that way before I came aboard.

"Nice quiet place you got here," he said. "Anybody on the boat next to you? The *Jezebel?*"

"She's for sale. Nobody aboard."

He relaxed a bit. His voice was soft and smooth, only it was as if he held it that way. Everything about him was leashed down.

"You get up," he said. "Go unlock the screen door. You locked it when you came in."

I did as he asked, and came back again.

"When you figure he'll pull in?" he said.

"What's it all about?"

"Tomorrow? Next day?"

"Why not tell me?"

"It's a little thing, got to be taken care of."

Trouble. Every damned time. Trouble.

"Make yourself comfortable," he said. "Forget I'm here. Just don't leave the boat, understand?"

"What'd he do?" I said.

"You know your old man? It's something he *didn't* do. It's a little bit of business."

He was like a whip, lying on a shelf.

"How'd you know he was coming here?"

He shrugged. "Telegraph office in Jacksonville. They keep a copy."

"He'll say one thing and do another."

"Could be."

It wouldn't be good if Sally came along now. I kept trying to figure what to do. I wondered if I could jump him. When I looked at him, he just sat there, watching me.

"Take it easy," he said. "Everything'll come out in the wash."

"That gun supposed to scare me?"

"It better."

I stretched out on the bunk and stared at the open port by my head. You could smell the water. You could see the moon coming up, round and fat and yellow, out there over the bay. A bird flew black and lazy across the moon. It was real quiet, with the water lapping.... I pictured the hulk, laid in tight against the sand, with the old sea chest down in her. And when I cracked the top with a bar, gold coins would glitter and roll out around my feet....

Sam Holland. All my life it had been this way. From one place to another, never knowing when my old man would show and foul things up. Nothing small about it, either. Always in a big way, with lots of bluster, and that gold tooth of his flashing like yellow neon.

"Well, Jack, kid! Howsa boy!"

Christ. He browbeat and smashed my mother into her grave and left my stepmother in a sanitarium where she thought the head nurse was a madam from St. Louis. The rest of the patients were "the girls." If she saw a man, it was too bad, and even her doctor had a time convincing her he hadn't come with five bucks for a quick trick.

He hounded me like a rat, sometimes. He'd wrecked jobs I'd had as a kid by getting drunk and pulling some cockeyed stunt.

Only sometimes, I remembered, he'd roll in with wads of money bulging out of every pocket. And always a new Cadillac. We'd have a ball, then. Yeah. With his damned gold tooth and his shoulders swaggering.

Later on, he'd have bad times. He'd take my money, my shirts, my food. Rob me clean and vanish.

Always talking about the big piles of dough he'd made and dropped someplace.

I got married after Korea. June wasn't too much, somehow, but I figured we'd get along after a while, especially with the kid coming. We both tried hard, but with the money the way it was and me lamed up with an arm full of shrapnel.... As usual, I couldn't seem to connect. Then one day my old man blew in from Texas. He'd lost a pile wildcatting around the oil fields. I saw right off he liked June's smile.

A few days and things began to hum. One afternoon, June went downtown. I put it to him, about June, and told him to get out. He laughed. I would have jumped him then, even though he was my father, but I had this arm full of shrapnel. So I got the rifle and held it on him.

"...and don't come around again," I said. *"I'll put one right in there, above your belt."*

He knew I meant it. He got out of the house fast, with me standing over him with the rifle. Somewhere, he picked up June; undoubtedly a planned meeting. They went down the street in the Cadillac. We were living in

Alexandria, Louisiana, then. He sailed through town and turned left for the bridge over the Red River. He never quite made the bridge. Christ only knew what they were doing. The left front wheel caught the abutment that used to be there, and the Cad took the bank head on. Right smack down into the water.

My old man climbed back up and started looking for a drink. They fished June out, dead, six hours later. I went a little crazy when that happened, but there wasn't a damn thing I could do. By the time the news reached me, it had all been settled in the eyes of the Law. *Accidental death.* And to make it that much more convincing and sentimental, Sam Holland came up with the bright yarn that he had arranged a meeting with June downtown so they could shop together for birthday presents for me. They had planned a surprise party. He was all broken up over the "accident." He had a "deep sorrow" over his son's loss. June had been a "truly remarkable" girl and a "marvelous" wife.

He was very convincing.

The bad thing was, the next day *had* been my birthday. There was absolutely nothing I could do. It really had been an accident. There was nothing for a lawyer to go on. There were no witnesses. Nobody had ever seen them together.

Besides, he was my father.

Two weeks later, he left town in a new car.

"Jack, look at it this way. Accidents happen. The good Lord adds it up, that's all. Look, I'll send you some cabbage. Send you a real wad. I got a big deal on in Chi."

No matter what, he always brought trouble.

So I wandered a lot, after that. Then finally ended up here in Florida, and managed to get this boat. There'd been no word from him for months. Only now....

I looked out the porthole again. The moon was coming up fast.

I sensed something, felt it....

Somebody was boarding the boat. Just a touch, nothing more. Attuned to the rise and fall. A feeling. I glanced over at the guy on the bunk and he had his eyes half closed. He hadn't felt a thing.

Somebody had boarded the boat.

Then I heard it good. By the forward hatch behind our heads. I'd left it wide open. The guy on the bunk came to his feet, reached for his gun. He was too late.

My old man came down through the hatch. He took one big bounce and stood there looking mean, with that gold tooth flashing, and a belly gun in his fist.

The other guy froze.

"Hi-ya, Jack," my old man said. "What's the word?"

Five

The boat rocked.

"You go for that gun," my old man said to this guy, "you'll make trouble for everybody. Not to say what a mess you'll be in yourself."

The guy didn't say a word. He didn't move, but his fingers were just under the lapel of his blue jacket.

"I don't know who you are," my old man said, "but I know where you're from. Didn't he tell you Sam Holland wouldn't stand for this truck?"

The guy stood there.

"Jack," my old man said. "I'm sorry all to hell about this. Couldn't be helped. Lucky I figured on it. You poor slugnutty," he said to the guy. "I saw you. You let yourself get spotted. Saw you board the boat. I parked my car out there. I was standing right across the street. Hell, man, I snuck over on that boat next door. I could see Jack through the porthole."

I noticed then that his big feet were bare. He wore size fourteen shoes. His shoes and socks were jammed into the side pockets of the jacket of the cream-colored, lightweight suit he wore.

"Stretch your arms out," my old man said to the guy. "Or you want me to stretch you out some other way?"

"It'll never work," the guy said.

"Sure, it'll work."

They watched each other for a minute. Then the guy stretched his arms out, one over each bunk.

"Okay. Lay down on your face, between the bunks. Keep your arms out. Kneel and lay down on your face."

The guy gave my old man a hell of a look. Then he knelt down. If he kept his arms out like that, he wouldn't be able to get down without falling.

"Go ahead," my old man said. "Fall forward on your face, slugnutty."

The guy looked at my old man, with his arms spread. His right hand almost touched me. His fingernails were neatly manicured, and he wore a little gold ring on his pinky.

My old man stayed back between the cupboards, just this way of the open hatch. He was sweating. His face was huge, with the eyes shining, and that neat pencil-line mustache above his thin lips. His hair was combed neat and gleaming, with lots of oil. Once, I remember, he ran out of hair oil, so he used salad oil. It kept running down his neck. But he was hell with the women, just the same.

"Move!" my old man said.

The guy fell face down on the deck. His arms jammed up on the bunks. You could tell it hurt him.

"Jack, you get his gun. But be careful."

So far there hadn't been any shooting. I didn't want any. My old man stuck the barrel of the belly gun against the guy's head.

I reached under the guy and got the gun. When I touched it, it popped right out into my hand; a spring holster. I sat back on the bunk.

"Give it here," my old man said.

I handed him the gun.

"Now, get up," my old man said to the guy.

He got up. You could tell his arms hurt plenty. They had twisted in their sockets. The aisle between the bunks was narrow.

The guy stood there nursing his arms, and he cursed Sam Holland up and down and sideways. My old man just laughed, with a gun in each fist, and his big bare feet sticking out, the toenails cut square like shingles. And those shoes sticking out of the pockets of his jacket. It was a picture.

"Well, Jack," he said, "we got him now."

I didn't say anything.

"When you take their guns away, they're done. Ain't that so, slugnutty?"

"It'll never work, Holland."

"Sure, it will. Well, Jack, it's good to see you. See you got my wire, eh?" He flipped his jacket back and jammed one gun into his belt. "You got a nice boat, here. Real nice."

"What's he want of you?" I said.

"You mean this guy? He wants some money." He looked at the guy. "No, it ain't exactly that. Not any more. Is it, slugnutty? You came to get me, did-n't you?" He looked at me. "He was hired for the job, Jack. Now, listen. Let's get out of here. Start up this tub, and take it out in the bay."

"The hell."

"That's right."

"It won't work, Holland," the guy said.

"It will too work," my old man said. "You take it out, now, like I said, Jack."

"I'm not taking this boat anyplace," I said.

"Take it out. Don't fool with me." He paused, then forced a grin. "It's sure good to lay eyes on you, Jack. You look good. You look fine. We'll have a real blast together, Jack. We sure will. Now, start the engine and let's go. Head her right out into the bay."

I thought about Sally.

"What you want to take the boat out for?" I said.

"I just want to, that's all. We'll have us a little ride in the moonlight." He kept looking at the guy. "How's your guts?" he asked him. "Your guts hold-ing out?"

The old man was like a dynamo, a big nervous machine, sweating and laughing and looking and swaggering his shoulders around. His eyes were like black chips of glass, small and beady and close together. Like an animal's. As if never under control. Only you knew better. He was scheming and planning every minute. He wore a handpainted tie with a palm tree on it. He reached up then, hooked a finger in his collar, and popped the button. Ripped his collar open. He was the same, all right, with that big gold ruby ring on his right hand.

"You," he said to the guy. "Back up the stairs into the cabin." He gave the guy a shove. They went up into the deck cabin. He gave him another shove onto the bench by the table, and the guy sat there. "Turn her over, Jack," he said. "Twist her tail."

He was all wound up. I didn't want any part of it. I didn't know what he was planning, but it smelled, any way you looked at it.

"Jack!" he turned on me with a sudden viciousness, and showed me the gun in his hand. "You heard me. Get this tub moving."

The other guy looked at me. "You better do it," he said. I looked at the gun, and said, "Jesus," and looked at my old man, and he hadn't changed.

I went out and took in the bow lines. Then the two stern lines. I looked up and there was Sally, coming along the sea wall, up the street a way. It got me in the stomach. I didn't want her to have any part of this. I pushed away from the pier a little.

Sally was coming along fast. The streetlights shone on her hair. She walked along the sea wall with her hands jammed into the pockets of her white cardigan.

She saw me and waved.

I knew I had to get the boat out before she reached it. No telling what might happen if she came aboard. I ducked into the cabin and went over to the wheel. She started with a roar. The damned battery always seemed to be up these days. I kept looking through the windshield. Sally was moving toward the slip gate. I pushed the windshield open, reached out and caught the electric light cord, yanked it off the pole. It sparkled blue-white up there on the box. I hauled it in quick, turned the switch for the generator, and the lights came on again.

I shoved her into reverse, and yanked the throttle. She backed out of there, churning. I turned on the port and starboard running lights. I was soaked with sweat.

"That's the way," my old man said. "Keep it moving, Jack."

Six

Sally stood up there on the pier. She looked at me and waved her arm.
Then she quit and just stood there. I felt like hell, but I had to do it. I kept
on backing her out into the basin. Sally stood there, watching.

"Somebody on the pier?" my old man said.

I didn't say anything.

"Your girl?"

I still said nothing.

"Sorry to spoil it. She looks good from here. Why didn't you tell me she
was coming down?"

I turned the boat and headed out for the bay. We came down the channel between the cement sea walls. Over to the right by a clump of palms,
I saw a guy and a girl eating sandwiches. By moonlight.

It was a clear night. The bay glistened with the moon, but there were
some clouds to the east. I kept her out opposite the municipal pier.

"Take it out to those lights," my old man said. He meant the channel
lights. "Head for the Gulf."

"You don't know what you're getting into," the guy said. He sounded
plenty serious.

I looked back to where old Mike Wales had his yacht. You could see the
lights from the galley, through the ports. What the hell was I going to do
now? I felt black with it.

"Jack," the guy said, "I thought you were smart."

"Not so smart yourself," my old man said. "You mucked up, didn't you?
What will they say in Miami?"

"Listen," I said. "What did you want to come out here for?"

"Just keep headed the way you're going," my old man said. "How you
been making it, Jack? Doing any good? You got *some* tub here. How long
you had it?"

"Quite a while."

"In the chips, hey?"

The sweat started on my palms.

"You ain't married yet, are you, Jack?"

"No."

"What's your racket?"

The hell with him.

We came along by the first marker. The bay was big and black out there,
even with the moon. You could look back and see the lights of the munic-

ipal pier. You could hear the PA system—music fading in and out, roofing the night.

"Head for the Gulf, Jack."

I didn't say anything. But one thing was for damned sure: we weren't going out into the Gulf.

"He welched," the guy said. "He welched so big there can't anything be done now. No matter what he does, there can't anything be done. It's too late."

"That's what you think," my old man said.

"You'll see," the guy said.

"How's your guts?"

"My guts are fine. Just perfect. Remember that, too. He welched and he lied, your old man did. He's no good. There's nothing he can do about it now. If it isn't me, it'll be somebody else."

"Shut up, slugnutty."

"Nuts to you, fatso. You know what I say is true."

I looked around at the guy. He sat there with his hands folded on the table, watching my old man. He still looked as neat as a pin, only he didn't have the gun now. The things he'd said sounded plenty bad.

"You're some talker," my old man said.

"Jack," the guy said. "If I was you, I'd jump overboard."

"You better turn it off," my old man said.

"Don't like to hear the truth, do you?"

My old man didn't say anything. We were headed toward the Gulf. You could look back off the port side and see Tampa all red in the sky.

"I'm heading back," I said.

"Just keep going."

"I'm heading back."

"Just don't try it."

I looked at the gun in his hand. It was a mean looking gun, and he acted wild. You could see it in his eyes, and in the line of his mouth.

We went on for a while like that, heading toward the Gulf. Why don't you turn her, I asked myself. What's the matter with you? Go ahead and take her back in. You scared or something?

Now I could see the keys in there, lying in a solid black line. If we headed into them, they'd break up as we came closer. I could see the Gulf out there, too. It was calm tonight. Calm and weather-black. Every now and then a car's headlights over at Pass-a-Grille shone through the trees.

I had her at about fifteen knots, cruising. She was running great, but it didn't make me feel good. I wondered why I'd brought the old man out like he'd asked. All the time I knew it was that damned gun. He would have put the gun on me, and I knew it. The more I thought about it, the madder I got. The hell with that gun. And right then I knew I wasn't going to take him out into the Gulf.

"I'm not taking you out into the Gulf."

He stared at me, blinking slowly.

"You do like I said, Jack." He spoke softly.

"I mean it. Get it through your head. We're not going out there."

He raised his voice, the gun steady. "You listen. We're going out, just like I said!"

I got hot. I reached over and cut the throttle with a slam of my fist. The boat slowed and began to rock and wash around. I was plenty churned up inside.

"All right," I said. "You want to go out there so damned bad, you swim out. Get it?"

He stood there watching me, blinking. He raised his left hand and rubbed it around on his mouth and chin, staring at me.

We stood like that for a few seconds, watching each other. Finally he turned his head away.

"Okay, that's the way you want it," he said. "Head for one of those islands, in there. Take it right up on the beach. Is that so goddamned much to ask?"

If I put it on the beach, we might never get off. I told him so.

"Okay. Just get as close as you can to one of them islands.

I turned away, shoved the throttle up, came about and headed for Shell Key.

"You stand up," he told the guy. "On your feet."

The guy was pale, and his eyes were like glass.

We came along by the island, and I kept trying not to think. I wanted to close my mind to everything, but it wouldn't work.

I knew there was a small jetty somewhere on the bay side. It was old, and never used, and going to pieces. But maybe it was still there. I didn't know what my old man planned doing, but this was better than going out into the Gulf.

I found the jetty, and brought the boat in.

My old man didn't say anything. I went out on the forward deck and tied the boat to a rotten piling. My old man herded the guy up along the deck, with the gun.

"Get off on that pier," he told the guy.

"What you going to do?" I said.

"Nothing. It's all right."

The guy's face was a white mask and he was fighting inside. I didn't like it. I didn't know what the hell to do. They climbed off onto the pier.

"It's all right, Jack. Be right back. You wait here for me." I saw him wink at me.

They walked off the pier and down onto the sand. I watched them vanish into the tangle of mangroves and cabbage palms, moving toward the gulf side of Shell Key.

It was quiet. Just the sound of the water. You could hear the waves striking the island from the other side, coming in from the Gulf. I was nervous as hell. I thought of taking the boat away and leaving them there.

I waited. It kept eating at me.

Finally I couldn't stand it.

I stepped off onto the pier and started toward the shore, moving as fast as I could. I was breathing heavily, and my heart rocked in my chest. Then I saw my old man, a big shadow. He stepped across the sand, walking heavily, and up onto the rotten boards of the old pier, and nearly fell through. I kept hearing my own breathing. He came along and we stood there on the pier.

All I could think was how that guy had acted, and what he'd said about Sam Holland welching, and how they would send somebody else. It had sounded bad. "What'd you do!" I said.

"Look, Jack. Try to understand. I didn't do anything, really. Just trying to put a scare into him, teach him a lesson. I tied him to a tree, over the other side of the island. That's all." He gave a short snort of laughter. "You should've seen his face. He'll be all right. I had to do something. It's good for him. He'll work himself loose. He can swim back."

He turned away, walked to the bow, stepped aboard, and moved down into the stern. I went after him. I noticed he only had one gun now.

"What'd you do with his gun?"

"Left it there for him."

"How come he didn't yell?"

"What would he yell for? Who'd hear him? No sense to that. He knew I'd do something—probably thought I'd beat him up. But what use?" He sat down and started pulling on his socks and shoes. "Serves him right."

"Suppose he can't swim?"

"Tough. We're leaving him there." He paused, and looked at me. "Listen, Jack—he talked big, but that's all there was to it. Talk. Just talk."

I thought about everything the guy had said. "Yeah?"

"Yeah. Now, look. There's no damned sense stewing about it. You don't know the whole story. It's a smalltime outfit, and anyway, they can't get blood out of a rock. See? I threw a scare into him, and that'll be all there is to it. I scared him off. They were just trying to bulldoze me, sending him up here. I don't blame 'em. I'd have done the same. He was bluffing. He had a good act."

"He said they'd send somebody else."

"Bull. Don't you see? They try to scare you, but they don't really do anything. Not the bunch he's with." He shook his head, and laughed again. "He was sure mad when I tied him to that tree. Cussed me to beat hell. But he knows it's all over. He's mad because he'll probably get wet, and maybe mosquito-bitten."

I was still skeptical. I didn't like it, but there wasn't a hell of a lot I could do. I had to admit it sounded halfway reasonable, anyway.

He slapped harshly at his neck. "Let's get the hell away from here. Mosquitoes beginning to find the boat."

I didn't say anything.

He looked at me. "Okay?"

I went up, took in the line, got the engine going, and headed back across the bay. He paced up and down the cabin. He was heavier than be used to be.

"Where'll you head for, now?" I said.

"Me?" He laughed real loud. "Noplace, Jack. I'm staying with you for a while. Going to take a rest, here in Florida. The land of sunshine."

I looked at him.

"We'll have a ball," he said.

We came into the slip. My old man hooked the stern line off the piling and tied her. I backed and cut the engine. My head ached. I went out and plugged the light cord into the box, came back aboard.

He was down there, stretched out on my bunk, with his feet on the pillow.

"Air makes you sleepy," he said.

I went aft and coiled the lines, then up onto the bow. I closed down the hatch cover, and stopped it with a piece of wood so it lay part open for ventilation. Then I checked the lines so she wouldn't rub against the pier or the piling and returned to the cabin.

Somebody stepped on the pier. My old man sat up like a shot, all ears.

"What's that?"

"Jack?" It was Sally. "Jack, are you down there?"

My old man winked at me, hitching up the side of his mouth, and sprawled back. I went on outside, and up onto the pier. She was waiting there. I never saw anybody look so lonely. Wind blew down across the pier. She stood there, watching me.

"Jack," she said. "Where were you?"

She had been waiting all this time.

Seven

We walked out through the gate.

"You saw me when you pulled out, Jack."

"I know."

She closed the gate and slipped the hook into place, and looked up at me. I turned the floodlight off up over the gate. It was dark and cool.

"What you been doing?" I said.

"Sitting on the bench, out there."

"Sally—"

"You could have waited."

"I couldn't."

For the first time I felt a sense of real fear. I couldn't exactly pin it down, but it had to do with my old man and the guy he left out on Shell Key. It was a blackness inside me. I looked out across the street, and something by the other curb took my eye. My jaws went tight. Parked against the curb, under the streetlight, was a Cadillac. The left front fender had a bad wrinkle. The car was covered with mud and dust; the top was down and the white sidewalls were smeared and streaked. I knew it was his car.

"Jack, what's wrong?"

"Nothing."

"You said over the phone you had something to tell me. "

"Yeah. I've got something to tell you. But first, hear this." I went into it about my old man; I told her about him, about the trouble he'd always brought me. Then I told her about tonight, out there in the bay. "It's got me worried," I said. "Plenty worried. He's mixed up in something bad. I don't want to be in it with him."

"Jack. Honestly! I think you're just building things up. You've painted him awfully black. There must be some good in him."

"Sure," I said. "I suppose you're right. You might say he's big-hearted. He's done a lot of things for me, maybe. But he's like a kid. He's always in some sort of jam, and this one looks really bad." I paused. "Sally, that guy was here to kill him. "

"You're imagining things. It can't be that bad."

I wasn't going to convince her of anything. She'd pulled the shade, like women can. When they do that, there's nothing you can do.

"If you're so worried, why not go to the police?"

Just her saying that gave me a hell of a jolt.

"I couldn't do that."

"Of course not. Not to your own father. So, then, it's not so bad, really. See?"

I didn't say anything. She couldn't understand. I had a feeling. And it was bad.

"Hey," my old man said. "You haven't introduced me."

He had his head and shoulders up out of the hatch. He flipped the hatch cover all the way back. I wondered if he'd been listening to everything I'd said. Probably, knowing him. I felt the sweat pop out on me, because right then I'd been going to tell her about the hulk. I didn't want him to get wind of that. He'd never quit.

He climbed up through the hatch. He was outlined against the paler sky as he stepped to the bow and looked down at us.

When I introduced them, Sally seemed to brighten. The old story. Father appears in the picture, and the picture is all sunshine. She'd forgotten everything I'd told her. Either that or she didn't believe it.

He gave a jump off the bow and landed heavily on the pier. He swaggered through the gate, slammed it shut, and grabbed her hand, grinning down at her.

"I'm sure glad to meet you, Sally. Jack here's told me a lot about you. I been looking forward to it."

Boy, he was sure something.

"You sure can pick 'em," he said.

I had my teeth together so hard they began to ache.

"We'll see you," I said. "Come on, Sally."

"Why not come aboard, and talk," he said.

"It's late."

I pulled her away, by the arm. She balked a little. I pulled her some more, feeling her irritation.

"Well, so long, kids!" my old man called.

"Jack," Sally said. "That's no way to treat your own father."

We went on up along the sidewalk.

"You want to hear what I was going to tell you?"

"Well, all right. But I still don't think it's right."

So I told her about being out in the boat that afternoon, and about the diamond choker, and how I'd gone after it. Then I told her about what was down there. The excitement was in my voice. I tried to take her right down there with words, and let her see that old hulk, laid in against the sand bank. "Then I talked with Mike Wales. He's seeing what he can find out, right now."

"Jack."

That's all she said. Just the one word. It sounded like a stone dropped in the middle of an empty street. It was as if she'd suddenly discovered I'd lost my mind.

"Don't you understand what it might mean?" I said.

She sighed and bit her lip.

"You think I made it up?" I said.

"No."

"Doesn't it get you?"

The only thing she saw was old newsprint telling how sunken treasure had been found someplace by somebody she didn't know. Hearsay. She'd heard Mike talk, I knew now. She had listened to his stories, thinking, *The poor old man, let him have his dreams.*

"Never mind," I said.

"You've got to listen," she said. Her fingers gripped my arm. "You're desperate, that's all. Don't you see?"

"Oh."

"It's childish, Jack. Those things just don't happen. You've got to..."

"Let it lay," I said. "Come on. I'll take you home."

Night winds swept the length of the municipal pier, rattling palm fronds. All along the basin, boats bobbed and rolled, hundreds of masts jerking and slanting against the night sky, like the frantic legs of an insect caught on its back.

We cut down the street toward the Cadillac convertible.

"You'll go home in style, anyway," I said.

"Please, Jack." There was confusion in her tone, but there was a bite to it, too. "I wish to God you'd forget all this nonsense! Can't you see? You're grabbing at straws." She came close to me. Her sweater was undone at the throat, halfway down. I could see the lush, round curve of her breasts. "I want you, Jack. I want to get married. I don't give a damn about money, don't you understand that?"

"We can't work it that way."

"Then why in hell don't you get a job? If it bothers you so much?"

Her voice carried in the night.

"You say your father's like a child," she said. "Well, I think you're acting like a child. Damn it, Jack, I'm burning up. Sometimes I lie in bed at night—I think I'll go crazy, thinking about you."

"How do you think I feel?"

I drew her close and she shuddered in my arms. I slid my hands up under the sweater, along her back, on her bare skin. She thrust against me. Desire pounded through me. I slipped my hands around front, inside her sweater, cupping her breasts. She writhed against me, and opened her thighs slightly, her body abruptly rhythmic, pulsing. She pushed her body against me, and her breasts were urgent, the nipples hard against my palms.

"Oh, Jack," she gasped.

We kissed and I felt the slash of her tongue. We clutched at each other, crazy with it.

She breathed. "My God, Jack—I can't stand it!"

"We'll take the car—"

She thrust herself away. "No, damn it. No!"

She stood there, breathing heavily, staring at me. "Not like that," she said. "Not again, and again. I want it right."

"Sally."

I reached for her.

"Take me home."

"Sally, damn it. You've got to understand. We've been through this before."

"Well, I'm sick of it."

"Sally."

"I want to go home."

"All right." The old man always left the keys in the car.

I opened the door and she got in. I went around and got under the wheel. She sat staring at the, dashboard. I reached for her again, but she drew away.

"It'll only make it worse," she said. "Once isn't enough, twice isn't enough. I want it for always, Jack." She paused. "I'm sorry. I'm all wrought up, I guess."

I didn't say anything. All I could think was, *There has to be something in that hulk, and I have to get it.* Then I thought of my old man, in the boat. And the guy out on that island. How long would he be there?

"Sally. For God's sake, try to understand. We've got to have some money."

"Get it, then."

I drove her home. Vivian had some kind of shindig going on in the house. I hated to leave her there. We kissed goodnight, but she had drawn into herself.

"Think about what I said, Jack. It's getting worse every day. Don't you see?"

There was nothing to say.

"We can't go on this way," she said.

I started to say something, but she got out and went up toward the house. Impulse brought me halfway across the seat, with my hand on the door. But she was already on the porch. A moment later she vanished inside.

Driving back toward the slip, I wanted to smash the car into a building. It was that bad. I parked at the curb in front of the slip, got out, and went aboard.

You could hear him snoring clear out at the gate. The snores lifted into the night like a new kind of bird.

He was sprawled out on his back on my bunk, with his mouth open, choking and gurgling.

"That you, Jack?"

He'd come awake.

"That's a hot little piece you got there. You can see it in her eyes. I can always tell. She's got that thing."

"Shut it off."

"She got a sister?"

I went back up to the deck cabin and sat at the table, thinking. Everything was in a tangle. There was the hulk, out there, and Sally and my old man. And there was the guy on that island.

Maybe he'd come to kill my old man, maybe he hadn't. Either way, it wasn't right to leave him out there. Anything could happen.

It ate at me.

I got up and went out on to the pier. I stood there for a time in the night, then found myself walking fast, out through the gate and down along the sidewalk. The next thing I knew, I was at the phone booth down at the end of the municipal pier.

I dialed Police Headquarters....

"... yes," I said. "That's right. Shell Key. There's a man out there. He's stranded and he's alone."

"Who is this speaking?"

I hung up fast.

Eight

I woke up sweating.

Sunlight streamed through the porthole on the starboard side, slanted directly into my face. I felt like I'd been on a long drunk.

I slung my feet to the deck and sat there on the edge of the bunk. My old man was gone. There was a suitcase on the other bunk, flung open, with a pile of dirty clothes strewn over the bunk and spilling onto the deck.

This wasn't my boat any more. That's how I felt.

I slipped on trousers, socks, and sneakers, and started for the head. I saw him. He was standing at the screen door, looking aft into the brilliant white sunlight that was like an open furnace at the edge of the basin. The boat rolled and his shadow changed, flung backward, slanting back across the cabin. He wore a clean pair of my khaki pants and a clean T-shirt that probably was mine.

I glanced back at the cupboards. Sure enough, he'd been there. Drawers hung open, two clean T-shirts were lying on the deck, and he'd discarded three pairs of socks before he'd settled on the ones he liked.

I went into the head. There were soap splotches on the mirror. My razor was in the sink, lying uncleaned amid the drainage of whiskers and dirty water. I felt my toothbrush. It was dry. A goddamn wonder.

I went out again. He turned and looked at me.

"Morning, Jack. What's the word?"

"The word is keep your hands off my clothes."

He frowned, with his mouth still open on a grin, the gold tooth gleaming dully. His hair was slicked down and he looked clean and fresh and hungry. The bastard. I wanted to tell him to get off the boat.

The grin finally went away. He sighed. He patted his belly. He hitched at my trousers. They were new khakis I'd bought at the Army surplus store only a few days ago; I hadn't even worn them myself yet; the store creases were still in them. It's the little things that get you.

"What in hell you talking about?" he said.

"You know what I'm talking about. You've got a car out there. Why don't you get in it and drive away?"

He raised his eyebrows and grinned. Like a banished king. "Saw my car, eh?" He stood there with that damned grin. "Now, Jack," he said.

I turned and went back into the head. I cleaned the wash basin, cleaned my razor, and shaved. I kept cutting myself.

Then I remembered the phone call I'd made to the police.

In the galley, I put on the coffee pot. I got the stove going and leaned against the sink, looking over at the bunks. Sweat ran down my chest, gathered around my belt. There was a small swell this morning. The deck lifted and fell.

He began to hum, up there. Humming happily to himself. I heard him clump back through the deck cabin. He stood in the companionway, looking down at me. He drywashed his hands and made faces.

"I smell coffee," he said.

The water hadn't even begun to boil yet.

"You're damned good," I said.

"I'm hungry as a whore at dawn," he said.

I turned and clanked the coffee pot on the stove.

"Christ, Jack," he said.

I looked through the murky port over the stove. With a dish towel, I reached up and wiped some of the dust and grease off the port. A pair of white ducks flashed by outside the port. It was Mike Wales.

I dropped the towel in the sink, went up the steps into the cabin, pushing past my old man.

"Ho, Jack?"

I went on out the screen door into the sunlight beyond the awning. Mike stood up on the pier. He grinned. His hair blew in the morning breeze. He was smoking his pipe, and his eyes were a little wild. He looked as though he'd slept in his clothes. The wind turned and you could smell the rum. It didn't show on him, though.

"By God, Jack," he said. He gave a jump to the side, then down into the stern. The boat heaved.

My old man came through the cabin and stood in the screen door. Mike looked at him and chewed his pipe stem.

If he opened up about anything now, it would be bad. But if I told him to shut up, or go away, my old man would wise up there was something in the wind.

You could really smell that rum now.

I was nervous as hell, wondering if Mike had found anything.

I introduced them.

"Well, well," Mike said.

"Glad to meetcha," my old man said. He stepped outside and grabbed Mike's hand. "How's for some breakfast?"

"I do smell coffee," Mike said. "I got a hankering for some java."

"Mike," I said, "I'll see you later." I tried to let him know something was up. "I've got to get a move on."

"That's no hospitality," my old man said.

Mike looked off the stern into the basin. Some gulls flew by, screaming.

The coffee was boiling over. I went back and shut the stove off. The coffee was frothing over onto the stove. I grabbed the pot and flung it into the sink. Scalding coffee splashed all over the place. I left it that way and went back out there.

"Figured I might as well have a rest," my old man was saying. "Nothing better than a rest in the sea air. Jack's been after me to stay on his boat for some time. We don't see much of each other."

"Oh?" Mike said.

"Yes sir," my old man said.

I could see that Mike understood. He glanced at me, knocked his pipe out over the side. He snapped his fingers.

"Come to think of it," he said. "I just remembered something." He nodded at my old man. "Won't be able to stay for that coffee, after all. Jack, why don't you drop by the ship, later?"

"All right."

"Oh?" my old man said. "You live down here too, eh?" It was all pretty damned obvious. Sam Holland was on the scent.

Mike climbed up on the side. He looked down, hanging onto the awning rail, then stepped over onto the pier. He told my old man he was glad to meet him. "See you, Jack." He walked away fast.

I stared at the sunglare on the basin. A schooner was tacking in through the channel, and they were furling. You could hear the engine begin to tick over.

"Nice old gink," my old man said. "What's his racket?"

"He's retired."

"Let's have some breakfast."

"You want breakfast, go buy it."

"What did the old gink want?" His eyes were suspicious.

He said, "You an' him got something cooking?"

I didn't say anything.

"Where does Sally live?" he said. "She could show me the town—you feel so grouchy this morning."

I went up onto the pier. He stood there, watching me. Then he shrugged and went back into the cabin. I walked along the pier and through the gate, heading down toward Mike's boat.

A lousy state of affairs.

It was like walking in a fog.

Mike Wales was standing against the gate to his ship. I turned and glanced back. My old man was up on the bow of my boat, watching me.

Aboard Mike's boat, I wanted to get right to the word about the hulk. But Mike wasn't having any of that. He kept asking about Sam Holland.

"You shied off him, plenty," Mike said. "And I heard you heave the coffee pot. Why?"

We were down in the galley. Mike started the stove and began making coffee.

I didn't want to tell him, but it was best he knew what my old man was like. So I gave it to him; the whole business. All except the part about leaving the guy out on Shell Key. At least Mike would know the score about Sam Holland. And knowing Mike knew helped lighten the load on my back. Not much, but a little.

Except for that guy out on Shell Key. That kept eating at me, and I wondered what the police had done about it. Had they found him out there? Had he talked?

"I think I can see how you feel," Mike said.

"Yeah." Excitement crowded my voice. "Now, what did you find out? Did you check on that hulk?"

Mike sat down across the table and folded his gnarled hands. The suspense was bad, but there was no way to hurry him.

"I knew when you told me yesterday," he said. "Only I had to see about something."

I waited.

"It's likely there's something there, Jack."

I came off the bench so fast it crashed to the deck. He'd spoken so casually.

"Calm down," he said. "I've joked a lot. Diving and all that goes with it—it's no easy job."

I watched him.

"Pick up the bench and sit down, will you?"

I did that. He got coffee and poured two mugs.

"You mean it's a treasure ship?" I said.

He drank some coffee. "Damn it," he said. "Treasure ship! Will you stop it?"

"Listen, Mike. A lot depends on this."

"That's the part I don't like. On top of about ten other small matters."

"You going to keep it to yourself?"

Mike made a face. "There were three of them, according to what records I could find."

"Three!"

"Yes, three. Supposedly, anyway, damn it. Now, calm down. Spanish galleons. They were lost in a hurricane somewhere outside the mouth of the bay, in the Gulf, off Long Key. What in hell they were doing 'way up here beats me. Near's I can make out, it was around seventeen thirty-eight."

"Over two centuries."

He nodded. "You said she was hanging together?"

"What I could see."

"They were buried, that's what."

"Three of them!" I said. It made me wild inside.

"Don't forget," he said. "You saw one. Or you think you did. We get a storm, that one will probably go."

I could hardly trust my voice. "Mike. Was there anything in them?"

He cleared his throat, watching me.

"Listed as approximately seven hundred thousand dollars in gold and silver. That's the three of them." He paused, still watching me. "Might not be anything in the one you seen."

"How'd you find out?"

Mike waggled his eyebrows. He said, "Jack, they've looked for those ships. It was given up as a false report years and years back."

"Where do we start?"

"I knew it would be like this," he said. "I wish I'd told you there was nothing out there."

"You've got diving equipment, haven't you? You told me you have."

"They were unidentified," he said. "Those old three deckers." His eyes were dreamy.

It gets you. We sat there looking at each other, but seeing nothing, thinking about those ships.

"Still hanging together," he said. "Lord, how they did build them."

I came to the surface again.

"The bottom shifted and uncovered her, all right," he said. "But if it's shifting out there, it can shift back. Remember that. The other two are probably still buried."

"You didn't answer my question," I said.

"About equipment? Jack, where we going to get a diver? I can't dive any more. And you never done any diving, did you?"

"Only skin diving. About forty feet, with weights and a mask. That's the deepest. I never worked with an aqua-lung."

"We're not using any aqua-lungs. Not for this kind of work. No skin diving. You said the wreck was maybe twelve fathoms, or more, from where you saw it at thirty feet. That water's so clear sometimes it's deceptive as hell. Could be a hundred feet, or more, down to that hulk. It acts like a magnifying glass. And neither one of us is Mike Nelson."

"I know. It could be a lot deeper than I thought."

"Well, that lets aqua-lungs out, anyway. You go below sixty, sixty-five feet with a lung, and try to work any length of time—it's dangerous, damned dangerous. Besides, I don't know enough about it. Equipment is expensive, and you have to train to use it. It'd cost plenty to hire a diver. Not only that, if this got out—and it would, if you hired somebody—it'd be goodbye. Too near everything. Every rowboat on the coast would be out there. They'd have sightseeing tours." He shook his head.

"You told me you had equipment."

"It's old," he said. "But I took pretty good care of it. Hell, though," he said, "it's old. No telling. The suit, that is. I already checked the line. I got about a hundred and sixty-odd feet of good hose. That's old, too. But I checked every inch of it. Only the suit. Christ!"

I waited. There was a strong urgency inside me.

"I had an old Fairbanks-Morse air pump. Double-action. But it needs overhauling. Hell, it needs to be new. I got a hand pump mounted on deck. I've always kept it there, and it's all right. Checked all of that."

"Great."

"I suppose I could patch the damned suit."

"I'll do the diving," I said.

"It's a crock," he said. "A crock of very sweet honey. It's no good at all, Jack."

I waited some more.

"You can't go down. I wouldn't let you. Not with that equipment. You never had any training. And if we hire a diver, it's going to get out. But we can't pay for a diver, anyway."

"You just don't want to go out there, right?"

"Sure, I do! But, damn it, I can't dive any more."

"We could go up to Tarpon Springs and borrow anything we need. The sponge fishermen use suits all the time in their work."

"They can talk, too," Mike said. "They'd ask you what you wanted the stuff for."

"We could tell them anything."

He got up and left the galley. I followed him out on deck. I was sweating and so pent up I could hardly contain myself. And he kept backing away from it.

"Mike, I've got to get some money. This sounds like a good chance."

He burst out laughing. Then he filled his pipe, and lit up. "So," he said. "You're going after treasure to get some money. This is the best yet."

"You've done it."

His face sobered. "I know."

We stood there.

"I got a Jacob's ladder, too," Mike said, smoking and looking out at the palm trees. "Let's say a hundred and twenty feet down to the hulk, at the outside. That's a hell of a ways down, Jack."

"Maybe it's not that far."

"Don't matter. Fifteen feet can be far, if something happens. You ever hear of the bends?"

"Sure."

"Listen, you get bubbles in your blood. Maybe one settles in your knee and stays there the rest of your life. If you're lucky, you begin to itch like hell and it pops through your skin, see? Or maybe you go into convulsions and die."

I didn't say anything.

"You got about nine hundred pounds pressing on you, every foot you go down. Figure it up. It's like a building squatting on you."

"Let's look at that suit you got," I said.

Mike made an obscene remark, and turned away. "I wish you'd forget the whole thing."

Somebody called my name. It was Sally, coming through the slip gate.

"Jack? Come here a minute."

"Go on," Mike said. "I think I'll get drunk."

"Jack?" Sally called again, her tone impatient.

I went onto the pier. Sally had gone back through the gate. She waited on the sidewalk. She wore a thin soft yellow dress that showed off her shape. She looked terrific. Only then I saw the way she looked at me, and it was bad. She carried a small white-net purse. She kept wadding it in her hands. As I came through the gate, she moved over by one of the benches under the palms and stood there.

It was noon already, and hot. Across the street they headed toward the spa in their skimpy bathing suits, wagging their behinds, carrying caps, with their blonde heads flashing in the sunlight.

"I took a bus down," Sally said. "I haven't had lunch yet. I've got to get back to the office, right away."

She didn't smile.

She said, "I've got to know if you're still going through with that fool notion. What you said last night."

"The sunken ship?"

"Yes."

"Listen," I said. "It's true. There is one out there. I'm not lying. Mike checked, and there's gold aboard."

"I thought you had some sense, Jack!"

"You don't understand."

"I understand, all right. You're like a little boy, digging in a vacant lot. Captain Kidd. Don't you know any better? If there'd been anything out there, they'd have gotten it long ago." She paused. Her voice caught. "What's the matter with you, Jack?"

"How'd you know where to find me?"

"Your father. He said you went down this way with an old man who smoked a pipe. Mike, he said."

"You think I'm crazy."

"You know it."

"Mike has the records, I tell you. Here I am with a break, and look how you act."

She looked at me steadily. "I came down to tell you, there's a job open at the office. It pays forty a week." She let it lie there.

"The map office?" I said. "Where you work?"

She nodded. "With your forty, and my fifty-five, it's ninety-five a week. It's enough, Jack. One of the men left, so I spoke to the boss about you. It's just taking orders at the desk. You could work up, learn map-making, and photography."

"Why didn't you get it for Vivian?"

"They want a man."

I didn't speak.

"We could get married, Jack. It's enough money."

"I can't do it. I've got to take this chance. I'm going down into that hulk, Sally. If I get anything, we'll have it made. There won't be any worries, and you won't be working, either. See?"

Her voice was bitter. "You can't get it out of your damned head, can you!"

"I can't take that job."

"Okay."

"Look, come and talk with Mike."

"I don't want to talk with Mike." She hesitated, looked off down the street. "Besides, here's your father."

My old man came swaggering down the street. He had on my gray gabardines and a white sport shirt, with a blue straw cap cocked down over one eye. I knew he'd got a bottle someplace.

Nine

"Well," my old man said. "Well, well, well!"

"Hi, Mr. Holland," Sally said. She straightened up, and smiled at him. She breathed deeply and her breasts thrust out.

He eyed them. "Call me Sam," he said, grinning at her. "Jack," he said. "She's a beautiful creature. She belongs on the cover of *Life* magazine."

"Yeah."

Sally looked at me, then at him again. She was letting me have it with both barrels. The only trouble was, she didn't know my old man. With anyone else you could do something, say something. But when it's your father, it's still your father. There isn't much you can do, except maybe humor him.

"Sure a peach of a day," he said.

"Isn't it grand?" Sally said.

"What you two doing?"

"Oh, I'm not doing anything," she said.

He looked at me and winked. That damned blue straw cap. I remembered how in Alexandria he'd borrowed somebody's Irish setter. He used to ride around town with that dog beside him in the convertible, with the top down. He'd wear a blue straw cap and smoke Egyptian cigarettes in a long black holder, and just cruise around town with that damned dog sitting up there. All day long, up and down streets, driving real slow and making eyes at the girls.

He hated dogs, though. That was the comical part. And they sensed it. Sometimes he had a bad time. The Irish setter finally bit him in the shoulder.

"Had your lunch?" he said.

"No," Sally said.

"Well, now," my old man said. "Jack, here, went off without no breakfast too. I bet you're hungry," he said, looking down at her, rocking on his heels. He smoothed his shirt sleeve, flashed that ruby at her, and held his lips so the gold tooth gleamed.

"I'm starved," Sally said.

She was really rubbing it in, and it hurt.

"Well, now. How's about having lunch with me? Then maybe you could show me some of the town. What you say?" He paused, then said, "You too, Jack."

It was stupid, but I got sore. Let her find out for herself, I thought. "I'm busy," I said.

"Anyway," he said, leaning toward Sally, so it would look good, "we don't want an old sourpuss along, do we? And, you and me, we ought to have a talk about our boy Jack, eh?"

"I'd like it very much," Sally said.

"Car's right up the street," he said. He started to glance at his wrist watch, but caught himself just in time. You could see the pale band of skin where the watch used to be. "Well, Jack, we'll see you later."

Together they would figure out what was right for Jack.

Then it hit me, what she might tell him. If she ever mentioned anything to him about that hulk— But they'd already started walking away. They cut into noon traffic on the pier. I started after them, then stopped. What could I say, in front of him? The way she was, she wouldn't listen, anyway. I hoped she had sense enough not to tell him.

It worried me, plenty.

I watched them get into his car and drive off. She was really giving me the business.

Standing there, I looked down the street and saw a long white car stop at the curb in front of my slip. A man got out and stood there on the grass, looking at my boat. I'd never seen him before. Somebody else was at the wheel of the car. The guy walked over and stood on the sea wall, looking down at my boat. He lit a cigarette, turned, and went back to the car. I was jumpy. But he got back in the car; they made a U-turn and drove off. Probably a tourist.

The hell with it. I was getting spooky.

"Mike," I said, "let's see the diving equipment."

He was in his rocking chair, on the forward hatch. I wanted to get out there to that ship before somebody else found it. That could happen, too.

"It's not that easy," Mike said.

"Make it as hard as you like, you won't discourage me. You know damned well you want to get out there yourself, Mike. You couldn't live with yourself if you didn't do it."

A big Chris-Craft roared around in the basin, sliced close to the yacht, then slammed out through the channel, leaving a beautiful wake, the foam flashing in the sunlight. Gulls barked and screamed. Way out on the bay, a freighter crept along the horizon, trailing a black finger of smoke.

The main pier was crawling with people. If any of them knew what was on our minds, they'd get out there to the hulk and wouldn't leave a stick in her. They'd clean her. The newspapers would go crazy.

I thought of Sally and the old man. Then forced them out of my mind.

Mike got up, walked back down the port side of the deck. "Here's the pump," he said. He loosened ties on a big tarp, threw it to one side, lifted a large wooden crate that was standing upside down, and there was the pump.

"Sure you really want to go through with this thing, Jack?"

"I've got to."

"You tell Sally?"

"Yeah. She thinks I'm nuts."

"She won't say anything to your father, will she?"

"No. Of course not."

I wished I could believe that.

Mike shrugged. "We can't just go out there and try for it, Jack. We got to see if you can dive. Guess it's all right, you risking your neck. You're not working for anybody."

"What do you mean, 'if I can dive'?"

"Some can't take it. We'll have to test the suit, everything. No telling how that suit'll stand up in deep water. And suppose I get a heart attack, or something. Then what?"

"Forget it. Let's look at the suit."

It was like an obsession. Banking life on the chance I'd get something out of that wreck. It frightened me a little, now. But I couldn't avoid it.

The other route was worse, though. Take the job Sally mentioned. Learn how to make maps and draw a pay envelope every week. Live like the next guy. Get married and have kids. Tell Sally she can stop worrying. Take her out of that house, away from her crazy sister. Sure. Then, later on, you can go out to the wreck week-ends, and make a try for it.

Well, I couldn't play the game like that.

And what about that cool bastard I had for a father?

Mike broke into my thoughts. "What the hell's got you nailed down, Jack? You're in a fog."

"Just knowing what might be out there, that's all."

He looked at me closely. "All right," he said, turning away. "We'll take the suit and go out in the bay. I'll let you try it. How'd you feel when you dove down there, by the wreck?"

"I got a rotten headache out of it. Like to cracked my lid."

"Had anything to drink this morning?"

"No."

"Nothing to drink, nothing to eat, till we get back. Hope to hell it works." He walked down the deck. I followed him. "I wish you'd forget whatever's bothering you, Jack. If it was just going down for that hulk, it'd be all right. But I know it's something more than that. It don't take half an eye to see it."

Ten

Mike had a winch operated by a small gasoline engine. It was set up right next to the hand pump. He told me he never liked anything but a hand pump. With a fuel operated compressor, what happened if a spark-plug fouled up? Anything could go wrong. He said that with the hand pump it was different.

I didn't like that idea, myself. But I said nothing, for the time being.

"We should have one more man with us," he said. "But you wouldn't stand for that."

"We don't want that."

We came along past the channel, running toward the Gulf, and it was a good day for it. There was just a small breeze, the water riffling only on the surface. The water was very clear.

"All we got to do is have somebody start snooping," Mike said. He had the wheel lashed and was oiling the engine on the winch. "They get wind somebody's diving out here, they'll have ideas. We'll cut in by the keys. I know a spot where you can go down about sixty feet. If you spot another wreck, by Christ, I'll leave you there."

He started the engine. She caught the first time. He levered the belt and the winch turned. He already had the lines on the drum. He shut the engine off, straightened up, and looked at me hard.

We came past the Navy Base, leaving a nice wake, heading straight for the Gulf. I looked off toward town. Sally was in there someplace among those buildings and trees, with my old man.

"I learned to dive in the Navy," Mike said. "There were six men to take care of things. Now there's only one, and he's an old wreck. It's a good thing I'm crazy."

"If it wasn't for you I couldn't do it at all."

"Lucky me," Mike said.

He went on checking the pump and the engine that operated the winch. He was like a bug crawling over every part, an oil can in one hand and a rag in the other, wiping, oiling, turning, pulling, twisting. Suddenly, he threw the oil can to the deck and looked at me.

"Damn it, I don't like working without a tender. How in hell can I do all these things?"

"We can't work it any other way."

"A diver should have a man tending the lines. Today maybe we can get by. But we get out there in the Gulf, you got to have a tender."

There was more to this than I'd imagined.

"Let's forget it for now. Nobody's around to foul things up. Maybe it'll be better this way."

We couldn't have anybody else in on it. I knew that.

"Something else. We're going to use that old gasoline compressor. I went over it last night, and it runs. It's the only way. I don't trust myself with the hand pump." I was glad he'd said that.

"If anything goes wrong," he said, "I can always switch over to the hand pump."

So we got the other pump and bolted it to the deck beside the hand pump. It ran fine. He connected the hose.

"Feel better," he said. "Let's hope it doesn't quit. This is the damnedest diving work I've ever done. Let's hope we don't have to use the winch."

He went into the cabin again. When he came out, he carried a basket with him. There were weights in the basket, and a pair of diver's shoes.

He dropped the basket. "Put the shoes on. You can go down in the clothes you got on, only take off your belt."

I looked at him hard and saw he was drunk as hell. He'd been going in and out of the cabin a lot. I knew he had that rum in there. His eyes were getting more bloodshot all the time. He walked all right and he talked all right, but he was stoned.

"Tape and chewing gum," he said. "Fix anything. How's your spit—sticky?"

I took the diving shoes out of the basket.

"Come on," he said. "We'll get the suit. There's some things you got to know about the helmet."

We got the suit out of the cabin, carried it out to the deck, and laid it down. It was heavy. Then we got the helmet. That was damned heavy, and I began to see what Mike was getting drunk about. But everything looked in perfect order. I'd half expected the suit to be like an old inner tube, all cracked. It wasn't. The heavy strong rubber was shielded with a kind of mesh of tough-fibered cloth, and I could tell Mike had taken good care of everything. Even the glass on the helmet was clean and clear.

He vanished into the cabin again, and came back with a breastplate and another wicker basket full of what looked like junk. A couple wrenches, bolts, screws, odds and ends.

"The shoulder pad's beat up. Hope you don't mind."

I looked at him.

"All we got to do is attach the ladder. Going to help me with that, or shall I do it myself?"

"I could help better if you gave me some of that stuff you've been sampling."

"Never mind about that."

He went back to the wheel, brought her around, and headed in for the keys. I thought how I'd been out here last night. I wondered about the guy on Shell Key. It gave me a bad feeling inside.

We came across some shallows, and you could see the bottom real clear. I spotted a big redfish lying in there, waiting, with his mouth open. Then Mike cut the engine and we started drifting. We were still in the shallows when he went up on the bow and heaved the anchor.

I wondered, *What the hell?* Because there was only about six feet of water. I started to say something, and right then the bottom went away. Pretty soon we dragged on the anchor, drifted around into the breeze, and sat there.

He knew these waters well.

"All hands," he called. "The ladder."

We finally got the ladder rigged on the side, and somehow Mike got me into that suit. I felt trapped and dead, especially with him breathing powerful gusts of that rum at me. I began to sweat. Mike looked wild as hell, with his eyes all bloodshot and his hair blowing around.

He had me seated on an upturned box. I felt like I'd never move again.

"Now, there's some things you got to know."

"Glad you're telling me before we start."

He picked up the helmet, nearly dropped it, and set it by my feet. Then he carefully explained about everything, showing me the helmet. "We don't have no phone, though," he said. "But they're a bother, anyway."

"Sure."

He told me about the different pulls on the life-line and the air hose; the signals so we'd know what the other guy was doing.

He dropped a weighted line over the side, for me to follow when I went down. He held up the rope. "This is the bitter end, Jack." He fastened it to the rail.

The bitter end. Great to contemplate.

He got the pump going, finished helping me dress.

He motioned me over to the ladder. "I'll put the front plate on your helmet. just take it easy."

It was like trying to walk while carrying a bank vault. I finally made it to the ladder. Mike screwed on the face plate, then rapped on the helmet with his knuckles and pointed down. I said something out loud and it almost blew my ears off. His mouth was open, laughing at me.

I went on down the ladder into the water, then down to the last step, and hung there. I reached for the guide rope.

It's like no feeling you've ever had. You're all nailed and bolted up, and you know it. You're trapped. If the slightest thing goes wrong, anything can happen. I tried to look up at Mike, and almost fell over backward.

Then I left the ladder, holding to the guide line, and dropped.

Elevators couldn't touch it. My eardrums ached. I popped them and kept on going down.

My feet struck solid. I half let go the guide rope, and my feet went out from under me. I grabbed for the line again and went down some more. I'd landed on the edge of a shelf. It seemed as if I couldn't see anything. Panic hit me like a light, quick fist in the face.

The water was clear-pale green and silvery. I landed on level bottom. I heard the pump going. Air hissed through the helmet, and there was a rushing sound as it burst from the exhaust valve. I kept swallowing, and wondered how far down I was. Probably sixty feet, just as Mike had said. I felt cumbersome and useless. Then I began to relax.

I clawed around and got the life-line, and just then it jerked sharply in my hand. It scared me until I realized it was only Mike, saying, "How you doing?" I yanked once, like he'd told me. Then it was peaceful again.

A school of sheepsheads riffled by, glimmering in the sunlight. It was a new world, down here in the green water. Dry and strange, behind the glass in the helmet. I took a step and rocked, and took another, then tried one backward. I liked it fine. A snook breezed by, hesitated, had a look, then scooted off.

I wandered around. I knew I could do it all right. Getting into the hulk should be a cinch. I felt like going out there right now, but I knew Mike wouldn't hear of it.

Then I thought of Sally again. It was different, thinking at the bottom of the sea. I suddenly felt a deep sense of helplessness.

Mike gave three yanks on the life-line. I knew it meant for me to come up. I was glad to.

He unscrewed the front plate on my helmet, while I stood on the ladder, still half in the water.

"Well?" he said. I got a whiff of that rum.

"We got it made," I said.

I wanted to get back to my boat, and fast. We'd been out longer than I thought, and it would take a long time to clean up the gear and get back to the pier. I couldn't put it out of my mind how Sally had gone off with my old man. What worried me was the chance of her telling him anything about the wreck. I hadn't warned her not to tell him. It had been a big slip on my part. All I could do was bank on the chance that she hadn't told him.

Then I remembered that guy out on Shell Key again.

Eleven

I heard my old man laugh on the boat, as I came through the slip gate. Then a woman laughed.

I came aboard fast.

"Jack!" my old man said. He stood in the screen door, pretty well crocked, watching me.

"Out of the way." I shoved past.

It was Vivian. She was down there, lying on one of the bunks. The suitcase was still on the other bunk, with dirty shirts trailing out. Lying across the shirts was Vivian's dress.

She lay there, spread out, watching me.

She wore nylons rolled high on her thighs, a pair of tight black scanties, and nothing else. She held her hands cupped over her melon-like breasts, leered drunkenly at me, and winked. She had her knees bent up, and she let her legs lie open, watching me from between them. Bright red lipstick was smeared on her mouth.

"Hello, honey," Vivian said. Her tongue was thick. Her eyes gleamed fuzzily, but she didn't move.

I turned to my old man. "Where's Sally?"

'Working," he said. "You know that. We had lunch, then she went back to work. We happened to run into Viv, that's all." He was owl-eyed, but holding it pretty well.

"Get her the hell off the boat," I said.

He took hold of my arm, motioned me over by the door, and said in a stage whisper, "She's a little drunky. You know how it is."

"Get her off. Why'd you bring her aboard?"

"You know how it is, Jack."

"Baby," Vivian called. "Come to mama. Mama wants to do bad things."

"You heard me," I said.

"Don't be so damned intolerant, Jack," he said. "She's not hurting nothing."

"Get her off," I said. "Quick."

"Sally and I had a long talk about you," he said.

"Damn you!" Vivian said. She lurched up the steps in the companionway and stood there. She flipped the yellow hair out of her face. She looked horny as hell, and plenty mean. "Broke up the party," she said. "Damn you!"

"Get dressed, sweetheart," my old man said.

"Nuts to you, Sam."

"That any way to talk?"

"You let me down."

"Not for long—not for long."

She gave him a big leering smile. Her black scanties were skin tight. They were some kind of net.

She said, "We going someplace?"

"That's right."

"Swell," she said. She looked at me, stuck out her tongue, turned and waggled her plump behind, and went down by the bunks again. She almost fell on her face. "Sammy," she called. "Come an' help mama get dressed."

"I see you've found a home," I said to him.

"She's all right. She's a good kid. Just a little pie-eyed is all." He winked. "She's a boiler-house, though."

"You go with her," I said.

"I'll take her home. Then I'll be back. Something I want to talk over with you." His eyes were round and unblinking.

I walked back by the companionway and looked down at Vivian. She was skinning the tight white dress over her hips, watching me, shaking the hair out of her face. She got the dress on, grabbed her purse, took out a mirror, and cursed her smeared lips. She vanished into the head. When she came out, her mouth was neatly scarlet again. She ran a comb through her snarled hair, and right away looked good.

"How I look?" she said. She came up the steps and bumped me with her hip. "Okay?"

"Great."

"You always want to get rid of me," she said. "Someday you'll want me to stick around. You know what?"

"I couldn't guess."

"I would stick around."

"Come on," my old man said to her. He steered her through the cabin door. "Go up on the pier. Be right with you."

A moment later her heels clipped along the pier.

"Well, Jack," he said, "Viv told me what you got."

My heart hammered. "What?"

"That sunken wreck, out there. Viv told me."

"Vivian?"

"Yeah, Jack."

I turned and walked down the steps, went over to my bunk, stretched out, and closed my eyes.

"We'll talk about it when I get back. Okay?"

I didn't answer him. I kept my eyes shut, staring at the reddish blackness behind the lids.

I heard him clump aft and up the ladder. I listened to him walk down the pier. He was humming to himself. Then I heard Vivian call to him. He laughed and closed the gate. Then she laughed. The sound of their voices died away. The slam of his car door added the final exclamation point.

I lay there for a long time without thinking. My mind was a blank. I smelled Vivian on the bunk; it was very hot and the pillow was damp from her head. I began to sweat. Water leaked out of me. I was like a sponge being wrung out.

Sally must have told Vivian. But why? How come?

What did it matter. Vivian had told him.

Goddamnit, I thought. Goddamnit!

What could you expect? I thought. *You didn't ask Sally not to say anything.*

I lay there. I began to worry, plenty.

It was as if I'd known all along that he would find out, somehow.

I lay there till it was drawing on toward dusk, smoking cigarettes, listening to the rocking thump of my heart.

I sat up, flung my feet to the deck, and stared at my old man's suitcase on the opposite bunk. He should have been back by now. I went into the head and splashed water on my face. The water was warm, smelling of the tanks, metallic and stale. I went out, put on a clean T-shirt, then went up by the wheel and stared at the crack in the windshield.

The sun was an orange ball of fire. The first of a cool breeze came through the screen door, gasped, and passed out on the hot deck.

I went out onto the pier, and out toward the gate. It was cooler out there. The sun was gone now. Just as I reached the gate, the Buick slid into the curb.

Sally was at the wheel.

"I've got something to tell you," she said. "Get in."

I slid onto the seat and slammed the door. She drove away from the curb. She kept looking straight ahead. We came around the park, and headed north past the Vinoy yacht basin and around on the road to the bayside.

I didn't know what to say to her. All I kept thinking was, *He knows about the sunken ship, and there'll be hell to pay, now.* I couldn't get it out of my head. I was sore at her for telling Vivian, but I didn't want to say anything. Certainly she hadn't done it purposely. At least, I hoped not.

"What's up?" I said.

"I had to see you."

"I wanted to see you, too."

She drove along, and parked the car by the sea wall. It was growing darker now. There were no streetlights on this section of the street. It was more or less a parking place for lovers. The cars would start lining up later in the evening. You could look out across the bay, and it was very still. I wasn't still inside, though. The bay was smoky with early evening. Tampa was a red tent in the sky.

"Something's been bothering me," she said.

I waited.

"I was so damned mad at you."

"Yes?"

"I told Vivian about that sunken wreck, Jack. I never should have done it. It just came out, and I've been worrying about it ever since. I told her everything you told me. I don't know why I did it. I was mad at you, I guess. That prompted it." She hesitated. "What bothers me is, she might tell somebody else."

"She did."

"What?"

"She told my father."

She just sat there. Then she said, "Well, that's not too bad, then. Maybe we can find her and see that she doesn't tell anybody else."

"If I know my old man, he's already put the clam on her. He wouldn't want her to tell anyone else, either."

"I don't get you."

"Never mind."

"I will too mind. What do you mean?"

I looked at her. "He's the one person I didn't want to know," I said. "You can't get that through your head. But it's not your fault."

I patted her thigh and stared at the bay. She was wearing a printed skirt, wildly flowered, and a white blouse with a rolled collar. She hung onto the steering wheel.

"It's hard to explain," I said.

She turned toward me, hitching her skirt up over her knees. Her eyes were deeply troubled. A hell of a lot of good that did now. There just wasn't anything I could do about it.

"I told Vivian I thought you were crazy."

"Fine."

"Do you honestly think there's something out there?"

"I've been trying to tell you that."

"I couldn't believe it. I still can't."

I didn't say anything.

"Then Vivian was with your father?"

"Yeah."

"We bumped into her. I introduced them. They seemed to hit it off, right away."

"They hit it off."

We were looking at each other. I reached for her, and suddenly I wanted to forget about everything. She came over against me, and we kissed, and it began to get hot, like always.

Her lips were close to my ear. She whispered it. "I didn't wear anything but a blouse and skirt. Maybe this is why I really wanted to see you. It's driving me crazy."

"I know what you mean."

"There's no place to go."

"What's wrong with right here?"

She reached up and, with a single gesture, unfastened the front of her blouse, baring her breasts. I started kissing her again, her warm, wet, part-ed lips, then her neck, and her breasts. She began to moan faintly.

"Jack!"

She came on fire. There was a wildness in her. I moved my hand under her skirt, and the flesh of her thigh was warm against my palm. She rolled over against me with abandon, her body pulsing.

"Please, Jack—yes...."

We were both breathing hard, now. It was harsh and brutal. I didn't give a damn if cars came by, or anything, right then. Neither did she.

We clung to each other like two maniacs, and the world was a wild wel-ter. Her fingers gouged into my shoulders, and she bit my neck. It was sav-age and crazy.

"What are we going to do, Jack?"

"I don't know."

"Are you still going after that sunken ship?"

"I've got to, Sally."

She nuzzled me, and we sat there, looking out across the bay, numb with satiation.

"Suppose somebody'd come along, right then?"

"What would you have done?"

"Nothing. I couldn't have done anything," she said.

"That's what I mean."

"It would have been some show."

I didn't say anything. I held her, and sat there. She kept running her hand up and down my chest, inside my shirt. Neither of us spoke for a time, and I began to think about that ship out there. I knew we had to get to her as soon as possible. I had no idea what my old man was planning, but I knew it would be no damned good, whatever it was.

"Jack?"

"Yeah?"

"Please. Can't you forget about it?"

"About what?"

"About that treasure? You know there's no treasure. Please, forget about it. It's silly, Jack."

I didn't say anything. It was as if something had come between us again. I kept thinking about my old man, knowing what he knew. And Sally. She'd been trying to soften me up. That was all I could think.

"I'm going to try for it," I said.

She drew away. "All right. I've got to get going."

"Don't say anything to Vivian. I mean about how she shouldn't have told my father. It's better that way."

"All right."

I told her to drive on home from where we were, that I would walk. "It'll do me good."

"Jack. Please, be careful."

That was the last thing she said. Then she pulled away from the curb, and left me standing there. I watched her drive off.

I walked along the sea wall, all the way back to the municipal pier, half sick with everything that was inside me and unable to control any of it.

Coming along the sidewalk toward my slip, I paused under a streetlight, where there was a newspaper rack. I never bought the evening paper, but often stopped to glance at the headlines. But this time, something else leaped out at me in bold black type from the right-hand corner of the front page. I dropped money in the box, and grabbed the top copy.

It was like being hit in the stomach.

MYSTERIOUS KILLING
ON SHELL KEY

An anonymous phone call last evening led police of this city to a gruesome discovery; the dead body of an unidentified man, his skull smashed in, obviously murdered, lying amid the wastes of white sand and tangled mangroves on Shell Key.

Police were summoned to action by a male caller, who gave only brief details and hung up. They took a launch to the remote island in Tampa Bay and soon found the body. There were no papers of identification on the body, and the labels of his clothes were missing. A .38 caliber revolver was found nearby, obviously the murder weapon, as its butt was clotted with dried blood and hair. The victim's skull was smashed in from several powerful blows that ranged across the back of the head.

The victim was about 30 years of age, neatly and expensively dressed, and had been wearing a hat. He had worn a holster for the gun found beside the body.

There are no leads to the killing, but authorities assume...

Twelve

I quit reading.

I started walking fast up toward my slip, then stopped, and stood there with the newspaper crumpled in my hand. My old man had killed that guy. And I'd been with him. He'd lied to me about leaving him tied up on the island.

At first it was like something you couldn't believe.

Then you did believe it, and it was bad.

He had left the boat with that guy, walked onto the island, and, when the guy wasn't looking, smashed his skull in with the butt of his own gun.

It was a hell of a picture.

And I had been the anonymous caller.

All sorts of things thronged my mind; none of them were any good. It was hard to believe at first. A rotten thing to try to believe. But I knew it was true.

What the hell would I do?

The Cadillac was parked out by the curb. My old man was over talking with a guy named Russell, who owned a sloop down the pier a way. Russell waved, and I waved. My old man broke loose and came over across the grass, grinning.

"Get on the boat," I said. "I want to see you."

"Okay, Jack. What's up?"

We came down into the stern. I handed him the paper, smoothing it out, and pointed to the write-up.

"That," I said.

He looked at it, then at me, then read it through. Then he looked at me again.

"You killed that guy," I said. "Christ!"

"Now, Jack."

"You killed him. You son of a bitch."

He squinted at me. "And you phoned in about it, didn't you? What the hell's the matter with you, doing a thing like that?"

"You said you tied him up, out there."

"Tied him up?" He looked as if he wanted to spit. "Are you crazy?" he said. "That guy was here to kill me. I got to him first. I was lucky. He was a punk, Jack—he deserved to die."

I stood there looking at him.

He crumpled the newspaper up and hurled it over the side into the basin.

"They'll get you for this," I said.

"They'll never get me. There's nothing to tie me in with it."

"Except me."

He looked hard at me for a moment, then let go with a laugh. "You," he said. "You forgetting you took me out there? We went out there in your boat, Jack. You forgetting that? You're as much to blame as I am." He hesitated. "Don't be a fool," he said. "That guy was ready to die. He was probably even prepared for it."

"I can turn you in," I said.

"Sure. Sure you can."

We watched each other like that.

He said, "You can turn in your own father, can't you?"

"You bastard," I said. "You don't even realize what you've done. It's a joke to you."

"It's no joke."

"They'll send somebody else for you."

"Maybe."

"What then?"

"There's other things on my mind. I'm not worried. Why should you be worried? That was a fine thing, reporting it to the police like that. What'd you think it'd get you, some kind of medal?"

I didn't know what to do. I turned and went inside the cabin and flicked on the lights. Then I went on down through the companionway and stretched out on my bunk.

It didn't mean a thing to him. He had other things on his mind. It didn't register with him. For him, it had been like knocking off a fly.

The crazy thing was, I *had* taken him out there. In the eyes of the law, I was as guilty as he was. But he had done it; he had killed that man.

I knew I should notify the police; but I knew I couldn't do it. Right then, I began to fight it out with myself.

I heard him come through the cabin and stand at the head of the steps. "Jack?"

I didn't say anything.

"What about that ship out there? Are you sure there's gold aboard?"

He'd forgotten all about the other. And his mentioning the wreck got it all tangled up in my mind too. "Why didn't you tell your old man?" he said. "Were you going to tell me? You might at least have told me."

I still said nothing.

"Well," he said. "We can hope there's gold aboard, can't we?" He waited a minute, then said, "How much you figure? How much you think is there?"

I lay there.

"Goddamnit, Jack. I'm talking to you. We'll be rich," he said. "We'll stink with it."

"You stink right now."

"By God," he said. He said it like he was talking in a dream and hadn't even heard me. "I knew you'd come up with something, some day. One of us. By God. We'll take off," he said. "Hit the big places. All the dames we want, Jack. The real classy ones. You touch 'em, they're like velvet, Jack—they're all yours. Money does that. That dough. You got to pay for 'em, to get the real thing. I know where to find 'em, Jack."

I turned my head and looked at him. His face was all loose, glazed with a kind of remembrance of lust. You could read it. My old man. It didn't concern him a bit, killing that guy. He'd forgotten all about it.

"Sally's a great little kid," he said. He cocked his head and grinned. "She thinks I'm quite a guy, too. Took to me right off, like that." He clapped his hands. "I knew she was troubled about something. I told her just to cry on my shoulder. She wants you to be something, Jack. Say, funny she never mentioned that sunken ship." He paused, shoved his hands in his pockets and rocked on his heels. "But when Viv told me—say, man, I knew this was it. This is what we been waiting for."

It kept coming up inside me, like a black whirling ball.

"I'll take care of Sally," he said. "Don't you worry. I'll see she comes around for you."

"You go near her again and I'll kill you," I said. The words came out and I heard them. He looked at me, his eyes widening slightly.

"That's right," I said. "You stay away from her."

"She'll be fine," he said. "It's just she don't understand things. Women are like that." He belched and scratched his head. "Hell," he said, "where we're going when you get that dough, you won't even remember her. I know a redhead in Jax, she could make you forget so quick you wouldn't even remember this morning. She'll make your nose run, by God."

He sounded crazy. "What you figure on doing?"

"We'll get it and blow this town."

"Oh."

"What you got with this here Mike? Vivian said he was a salvage diver. How you think we should work it? Listen, Jack. Is this a sure thing? Remember, we got to find out how to fence it, though."

"What?"

"The government will step in. Hell, yes."

In his mind, he had that money already, and was spending it.

I hit the deck, walked up past him, and outside. I went out along the pier, thinking about him, and I knew he was right square off his rocker. He didn't react right. It was as if he were deaf. He lived in a shell he'd copped somewhere, like a hermit crab, and nobody could get at him.

You could hear him humming on the boat. He had it made, all right.

I walked along the sidewalk, down to where Mike's yacht was, with all of this bubbling and seething inside me. I saw Mike sitting up there in his rocking chair. I started for his boat, then paused. He didn't see me.

He was sitting there, drinking rum, staring out across the basin, with that black pipe hanging out of his mouth.

I turned away and cut diagonally across the street, toward the sandwich bar.

I chewed on a hamburger, and drank black coffee. It didn't clear up inside me. It just got worse, all the time. I thought how Mike had taken me out there today, shown me the equipment and how to use it. I remembered the feeling of being underwater. I knew how easy it would be to get to that wreck and see if there was anything inside her.

But if my old man got to Mike with his windy ways, Mike would throw the whole thing into the trash can. He would forget it. Like that. Because Mike Wales was square, and this was ticklish enough as it was.

I quit eating. I couldn't eat.

It was like being in a room with no windows or doors. You kept running against the walls, slamming into them. You knew there was no way out. But back in your mind, something told you there had to be a way out. So you rammed, and rammed, smashing against those walls. You'd reel around and try again. Something had to give—either one of the walls, or you.

Human nature being what it is, you kept trying.

Or you quit.

I was mad as hell. The sensation of being trapped worked up through me. I left the sandwich bar and started up the street toward my slip.

He was on his bunk, sitting there with his shoes off, inspecting his toes. He looked up, grinned, and scratched his ankle. Three moths fluttered and banged around one of the lights.

"Jack," he said, "I been thinking. You didn't tell anybody else about that ship, did you?"

I brushed past him, headed for the cupboards in the bow.

"We want to keep it as quiet as possible," he said. "We'll want to get out there, right away. If this Mike won't do it, then I'll hire a diver. I can get somebody who won't talk. Just a question of money, that's all. How much money you got on hand now, Jack?"

I opened the first drawer under the cupboards and lifted out the flannel-wrapped shotgun. I felt kind of crazy inside, and my hands trembled. I unwrapped it, standing there, and I could hear him breathing. Then he began to hum again.

"This Mike won't say anything, will he?"

I didn't answer. He hummed some more. I got the gun all unwrapped and looked it over. No rust. I wiped the oil off and pawed around in the drawer till I found the glass mason jar full of shells. I kept them in the glass because of dampness. I unscrewed the top of the jar, feeling excitement, and took out two shells. I broke the double-barreled gun, dropped the shells in, and clicked it shut. Then I put the top back on the jar and stuck it in the drawer again.

"What you doing?" he said.

I stood there with the gun in my hands, and looked at him. I shoved the drawer closed with my hip, and stared at him.

"All right," I said. I pointed the gun straight at his gut. I was so tight inside, I could hardly breathe. "You get off this boat now. Go out and get in your damned car and take off. You come back, and I'll kill you. So help me."

"Jack. Now, for Christ's sake!"

"Maybe I'll kill you anyway."

He stared at me.

"Get up," I said. "And get out."

He stood up and slapped his thigh a whack, and started laughing. After he got his breath, he looked at me, swaggering a little, and said, "Jack. I honest to Christ thought you meant it for a minute, there. I did, by God." He laughed again, banging his leg with one hand. "By God!"

He kind of lost his balance. I saw it coming, but too late.

His hand snagged out, flashed, and caught the barrel right at the muzzle. He was brave as hell, you had to hand that to him. He whipped it right across his front, where it could have blasted out his guts. His face was all snarled up, now. The gun left my hands.

He leaped back with the gun and he wasn't laughing. His face was evil. I didn't move.

He broke the gun and banged the shells out on the deck and stomped them with his bare heel. They squashed. Buckshot ran out on the deck.

"For hell's sake, Jack!" He flung the gun behind him. It flew back through the companionway and crashed up into the deck cabin.

It had been a beautiful gun. An old Ithaca, with silver inlay. I'd had it for years.

"You're a great one," he said.

There was a big purple Y right in the middle of his forehead. It pulsed.

I took two quick steps and dove at him. I was as mad as I'd ever been. I was glad he'd smashed the gun. I wanted to use my bare hands.

For a minute, we stood there like a couple of crabs, clawing at each other. Then I went in and let him have my right fist with everything behind it, straight in the gut.

He grunted and looked at me with amazement.

Then he came at me. He had the weight, too. And he was fast and clever, and dirty. He was light on his feet.

I remembered he was my father. It only made me that much madder. I stepped in close.

He brought his fist up. It caught me in the throat. The cabin broke into pieces like a smashed jig-saw puzzle. I sprawled flat up between the cupboards.

"You asked for this," he said. "By God, you're going to get it."

Thirteen

If I didn't get up, he would stomp me.

He came down the length of the cabin, swinging his arms. His face was bursting with blood and sweat. The Y in his forehead throbbed darkly. He drew his right foot up.

I came up, rolled forward, and grabbed for his leg as he kicked. We both missed. I rolled over beside the bunks. He whirled and stomped. He cursed and grunted savagely.

I clawed up onto the bunk and rolled back against the side just as he dove. I got my feet under me and leaped straight over him. He grabbed out, caught me, and twisted.

He began to pound my side with his fist. Pain wrenched up through me. I pulled with everything I had, and yanked clear. He was on one bunk, me on the other.

We both came at each other. We met in the alley between the bunks. I let him have a wild one to the side of his head, then again. Fast.

All the time, he grunted and cursed. Maybe it gave him strength, assurance. Just like an animal. He rammed his hands up into my throat, and I backed away. I ran up the steps in the companionway, turned and dove at him head first. I was wild inside. He met me head on with his fist, straight in the face. He missed my nose, but all his weight was behind that blow. I plowed into the deck, seeing black.

He began stomping and cursing. I came out of it, grabbed for his foot, rolled. Spots blinked in front of my eyes. I wrenched at the foot, twisted with a lunge, and he kept cursing.

He got off balance and sprawled back on the bunk. I got on top of him, looked down into his ugly face, and let him have it, thinking about the dead guy on Shell Key, the wreck and Sally, all of them mixed up in my head. I got in three good ones to his jaw, but he was strong.

Somehow he wriggled free and stood up, gasping, spitting sweat off his lips. He kept looking around, his eyes batting, searching for something to hit me with.

We both stood between the bunks, the backs of our legs against them. He looked like a mad pig. We slugged it out, there, throwing wild ones anyplace we saw an opening. His fists hurt plenty. That ruby ring of his kept cracking and scraping every place it struck. He saw it. You could see the light in his eyes. He switched to raking with it. He balled his fist and raked it through the air. I caught the first one. He feinted with his other arm, and this time he made it. It sliced clean along my cheek, scratched and clattered across my teeth. It felt like he'd laid my face open right into the mouth.

"Wise!" he said. "Wise, aren't you! Wise guy!"

I broke clear. He got my arm and twisted with all his weight. I yanked free, got to the steps, and crawled up on my hands and knees. I was in the deck cabin. I turned for him. He lunged and grabbed my foot, and wrenched at that. My knee twisted. The pain was bright. It reamed me like a white-hot rod.

I sprawled out, got on my back, lifted my left foot and let him have it square in the face. He lost his grip. I got up again, looking for that gun now. I'd use it as a club on the son of a bitch—club him senseless.

The gun was under the table. It gleamed in the shadows. I made for it, with my head under the table. He came down on the table just as my fingers touched the gun.

The table cracked away from the wall and slammed me across the back, with his weight on top. The pain was terrific, right across the kidneys.

You could hear the table wood rip. He tried to rip it loose, so he could beat me with it. He tore off one of the hinged legs, and I came out from under there, hurting bad, but with the gun in my hands.

We both struck at the same time. I swung up and he swung down. We blocked each other's blows. The shock smacked my elbow and wrist. I got the shotgun by the barrels and chopped at him with the stock. His arm dropped and I beat him brutally across the shoulders.

I felt wild with sudden elation, and heard myself cursing now. Nothing could stop me. It was like being some sort of machine. It seemed we'd been fighting forever. I chopped with that shotgun, slamming it against his head and shoulders.

The table leg dropped from his hand, and he kind of washed out on his knees. It was pretty dark in there, and I couldn't see his face well. Only his big bulk going down. I kept hitting him, breathing in sharp shallow gasps, the air hot in my throat.

He got something from someplace, and just stood up, with me slamming him. He reached out and grabbed the shotgun stock, his eyes absolutely crazy. We whipped it back and forth. I felt his strength. It slipped out of my sweating hands; the barrel was like grease.

He yanked so hard, it flew out of his hands too, smashing against the bulkhead. He turned and headed for the companionway, tripped on the first step, and plunged down, crashing between the bunks. He got up and looked at me, reeling, with his hair flopping in his face, sweat streaming off him. His eyes looked red.

I took a step for the companionway, and fell to my knees. I crawled to the steps, and got down one. Then we looked at each other.

Neither of us could speak; we were both gasping. We looked and gagged for breath. I saw my left shoulder and shirt and chest, blood-soaked. Blood was spattered on the steps in front of my eyes. It ran down my arm, trickling off my fingers, dripping onto the steps.

He had really sliced my face. It felt like the flap of an envelope.

"Damn you," my old man gasped.

He spat off some sweat and blood and smeared his hands across his face. He teetered back and forth, watching me, nearly out on his feet. The left side of his face started to swell; you could see it blowing up.

"I won't give it up," he said, still breathing in gusts. "Something I won't do, you hear! You hitch onto something like this, you don't give up, see?" He began to snort through his nose.

I didn't speak.

"I don't give a damn what you do," he said. "I'm staying here, goddamn it. I'm going out there, and you're going too. We're going to get whatever's on that ship. Just—don't forget it."

He nearly caved in then.

I told him where he could go. My throat hurt bad when I spoke, and the blood still dripped from my face. I felt dizzy, and knew we were both knocked out.

"Just—just want you to know that," he gasped. "If there's money to be had, by God, I'm in on it." He shouted now. "Much mine as yours. You hear! Nothing you or anybody else can do will stop me."

I stood up. My head seemed to crack open.

"Now," he said, still fighting for breath. "Now, I'm going out and get a drink. Jesus, I need one—I really need one—after that. Then I'm coming back. You want to keep on fighting, it's jake with me. So it don't—it don't matter."

He lurched heavily up the steps, staggered by me and on out the screen door. I watched him climb onto the pier. He was really shot. There wasn't anything left but words, and not a hell of a lot of them.

It was no better with me. Fighting him had done nothing. I wished I'd broken his head with that shotgun stock. Abruptly, I turned and ran out of the cabin, leaped onto the pier, and headed toward the gate.

He was already driving off toward town.

I just stood there for a long while, trying to think.

Fourteen

In the head, I looked in the mirror.

He had laid the side of my face open from the hairline by my left ear all the way to the comer of my mouth. It was deep. It resembled lightly cut rare steak. I washed it and watched it bleed. The blood was almost black, with crimson highlights. It was like black fever blood. I knew it should be sewed up. If it wasn't sewed up properly, there would be a memorable scar.

It wasn't going to get sewed.

I swabbed it with iodine, and beat the side of the sink with my fist till the pain subsided, then swabbed it again. There was a flap of skin that was beautiful.

I took down the adhesive tape and cut strips with a razor blade. Then I snagged the flap of skin down tight with the tape. It had ceased bleeding now. I wiped it clean with rubbing alcohol. That burned, too.

Back beside the bunks, I took my old man's suitcase and his shirts and the rest of his truck and bundled it in my arms. I went to the stern and heaved the whole mess overboard into the basin. It floated around out there. Some of the stuff sank. You could hear the mullet jumping in the slow darkness and there was no wind at all now. There was no moon tonight. From a boat in the distant dark came the sound of a radio.

For a time, I stood in the stern, listening to the big nothing of the night, and some of the sweat dried on me. There was nothing I could do right now. Mike wouldn't be worth a damn until tomorrow morning, and maybe not then if he was hitting that rum too hard.

I was thinking all around the murder.

I went back and flopped on the bunk. One of the moths that had been flitting around the light was dead on the bed beside me. He had knocked himself out trying to find a new world of light. Everybody tries to find a new world of light. There were a lot of bugs around the light now. I left the light on. The bugs would stay around the light and wouldn't be down on my face.

I kept thinking about the murder. That guy, lying out on the island. I wondered if the crabs had got to him. Probably, though it hadn't mentioned that in the paper.

My old man had killed him.

I should call the police. I knew that, but I couldn't bring myself to do it. He was right. He was my father. How could you turn in your own father? Then, I thought, *Come off that. It's stupid. Some old man he turned out to be!*

So I put it off. I ached all over, and I was tired. I knew I was falling asleep. It was a nice, thick, sick, motionless feeling.

But I dreamed of blood.

Waking in the hot, sweating sunlight of morning, I was hungry. Then I remembered everything, with a black rush. I rolled over, and looked at him on the other bunk. His big yap was wide open, snoring like an over-heated radiator. Sweat bubbled and seethed on his face, gleaming on his neck. He was still dressed, half on and half off the bunk. I could see he had tied one on last night after leaving the boat.

It must be he had some money. *Hell, no,* I thought. *He either got it on the cuff or robbed somebody.*

Every time he snored, his upper lip jiggled, lifting off that gold tooth. *Now's your chance,* I thought. *Get the pliers and snag that tooth. It's the one good thing about him; solid gold.*

When I sat up, my T-shirt buckled like cardboard. The blood had dried. I was a mess. I got up and peeled off the shirt, took off my trousers, socks and sneakers, and went outside and dove off the stern into the basin.

The water was cool and good. There wasn't much garbage floating around. All I spotted was one hunk of orange peel and a beer can floating with some seaweed. I swam out toward the center of the basin. I was stiff and sore all over, but the water felt good. It must have been nine-thirty, ten o'clock.

I swam around, then back to the boat, grabbed the stern and humped over. I stood there in my shorts and let the wind and sun dry me some. Then I went in and dressed.

He kept right on snoring, with that gold fang gleaming.

The boat was a mess. There was dried blood everywhere, in splotches, in fine flower—like designs, and in bigger puddles where I had paused for a moment. The table was torn loose and smashed. The shotgun stock was cracked and splintered. It had been a fine curly-maple stock. I used to sit by the hour, rubbing that stock by hand with hot linseed oil. It goes to show you, I thought.

I went out by the gate. The Cadillac was parked with one front wheel up on the curb, the driver's door hanging open. There was a whisky bottle tipped over on the seat. I took a look. It was uncapped and it had sloshed out onto the seat and the side of the car. There was some left—about two fingers. I drank it; it was hot from the sun.

I went on down to the sandwich bar and had some bacon and eggs and coffee. The short-order cook was all full of talk about the man who'd been found on Shell Key with his head smashed in.

I felt my hands begin to sweat. I wiped them on my trousers, but it didn't help. I left the place. It was riding me bad, but I didn't know what to do, and couldn't come to any decision. I didn't want to turn him in, but it was the right thing to do. It had me crazy, thinking about it. There was no way for action.

I went back to the boat. He was sitting on the edge of the bunk.

"Get away and don't bother me," he said.

His face was swollen into bumps on the left side, and you could tell it hurt him to talk.

He said, "I know what you're thinking. You can't get off it, can you? Well, just remember—you were there, the same as me."

I didn't say anything.

"You think I wanted to do what I did?" he said.

"You did, though."

He stared at the deck. He was silent.

I went out and sat in one of the folding canvas deck chairs in the stern. I heard him bumping around back there. Finally, he came out, with lots of morning polish, wearing some more of my clean clothes. Except for his face, he looked all right. His hair was slicked down, and he was full of bounce. I knew that bounce. It was a great job of acting, but it was bounce, nevertheless.

"Well, I'll see you," he said. "Going to put on the feedbag." He slapped his belly. "Care to join me?"

"Not now."

"I'll be back," he said. He looked at the sky. "Good day for going out there in the Gulf, eh?" He laughed, slapped me across the shoulder, then grunted up over the side onto the pier. "See you," he said.

They made them all kinds.

I went to the head, and shaved one side of my face. My mouth was pulled up at one corner from the slice on my face. It looked as if I were grinning.

So this was it. We had to go out there and it had to be right away. They would trace that dead guy back to this boat. They always did.

I decided to give Mike another hour. I sat there in the stern, and tried not to think. It kept getting hotter. The side of my head hurt bad. I ached all over. My joints pained every time I changed position, and the sweat began to start again. I sat there and smoked, and tried to keep my mind closed.

It wouldn't work.

I began to feel mad again. It was a good feeling. I don't like that dead feeling that can get inside you. That's the way you feel just before you start walking in front of trains.

I kept lighting cigarettes, one after the other. Finally, I couldn't stand it. I left the boat, went up the pier to the public phone booth, and called Sally at work.

"You all right?" I said.

"I was coming down."

"Wish you could."

"I was worried."

"Take it easy."

"I thought you'd come by later last night, for some reason. Your father came by pretty late. He and Vivian went out. He was pretty drunk, Jack."

"Yeah. I can imagine."

"He said something about having a fight with you." I could hear her breathing at the other end.

"We had a brawl," I said.

"Are you all right?"

"Sure. It didn't solve anything."

"But, Jack—that's awful."

"It's nothing. There's something I've got to tell you."

"I just want to know if you're all right, Jack."

"I'm fine."

I wanted to tell her about that guy out on the island. I had to talk to somebody about it. It was eating me up. The one thing that I should have done—called the police—I couldn't bring myself to do.

"Jack. You sound as if something terrible's the matter."

"Yeah."

The phone booth was hot and stuffy and my head ached the worst it ever had. I felt sick and couldn't get enough air.

"What did you fight about?" she said.

"We just fought."

"It had to be about something." She was irritated. "Can't you tell me?"

"Can't explain it. Listen, Mike and me—we're going out after that, like I said. Pray, or something, will you?"

She didn't say anything for a time. I changed the receiver from one hand to the other and knew I had to cut it off. I couldn't stand there. I'd do something crazy if I kept on standing there in the booth. I kept thinking about everything at once. Control was slipping away. It scared me. I had to do something. Just walk, I thought. Take a walk, that'll help.

"I'll get down as soon as I can," she said. "Can't you tell me over the phone?"

"No. Goodbye."

"Jack?"

"It's all right. I'll see you."

I got out of there fast. I walked down the sidewalk, trying to get hold of myself. I was soaking wet with sweat, and I felt dizzy and wild inside.

I came down by Mike's boat.

He hailed me from the bow. "We can't go out there today," he said.

"Why the hell not?"

"You need more practice under water."

I didn't know what to do. I figured we had no time for practice. We had to get out there and make a try for it. They would trace that body to the boat, and then it would be all over.

I began to realize for the first time what was really going on inside my head. I wanted to tell the police about that dead guy. I had to tell them. But the thing was, I wasn't going to do it until I'd got out there in the Gulf and found whether or not there was anything in that ship. It had to be that way.

Either that, or I was putting if off—maybe putting it off for good. I felt as if something was going to happen. Something bad. Like the calm before the storm. That's exactly how it felt. I didn't want to turn in my own father for murder. But what else could I do?

Maybe I would never turn him in.

One thing for sure—I had to get out there in the Gulf, and as quick as possible. And I didn't want the old man around.

"It's got to be that way," Mike said.

He prodded some rough cut into the old black pipe and lit up. The smoke hung in the air around his head. He peered at me through it. The rum he'd drunk last night didn't seem to have touched him, this morning.

"We haven't got time for practice," I said.

"There's always time for that."

"I'm fine. What's there to worry about?"

"It's going to be deep out there. You've got to learn how to work under-water. It's not the same as on land, Jack."

"Christ, Mike."

"It's no use arguing."

"But suppose a storm comes up. Suppose the bottom shifts. What then? We'll lose out, Mike."

"I can't do it any other way."

"Goddamnit!"

"I thought it over last night."

"I was by last night. Were you thinking then?"

"That's right. I was in a deep study."

We stood there.

He said, "You going to tell me what the hell happened to you? Or have I got to ask? You look like you mixed with a dragon."

"I got in a fight."

"I can see that much."

I told him about it. I didn't mention what I'd seen in the paper, the real reason for the fight. I wasn't sure how he'd react to that. He might say, "No dice," on the hulk. There was no telling.

He nodded.

"Sally phoned me this morning," he said.

"She did?"

"Yeah. She was worried. She said your father looked like the type who'll want to get in on this deal we're working on."

"She told you he knew?"

"That's right. That Vivian told him."

I didn't say anything.

"It's a rotten fix," Mike said.

"Nothing I can do about it."

"Tell him to go to hell."

"It wouldn't work. You don't know him."

"I can guess." He paused, then said, "Well, we going out?"

"All right."

He stood up, went over and knocked his pipe out against the rail. He blew through it and a gob of tar whistled across the sunlight. He turned and started down the deck. "You can cast off," he said. "Pull the lights and the phone. We'll head right out there now."

It rained on and off while we were out. Mike said he thought some bad weather was coming, but he didn't know exactly when.

"I can smell it," he said.

I went down in the suit, not far from the spot where we'd first anchored. He sent me down tools on a line, and I goofed around, seeing how it was manipulating things under water. At least I got an idea.

He brought me back to the surface in stages, so I'd know what that was like, too—the waiting. I didn't like it, but in deep water it would be necessary to avoid the bends.

"It's a waste of time," I finally told him. "We should be out there, working on that hulk."

"Wait'll you get out there. Then, you'll see. That ship's old, so old maybe when you touch it the whole thing will collapse. It may have been held together by sand for a hundred years. You know what happens to wood after all that time?"

"If it was going to break up, it would've happened."

"It's probably broken up plenty, right now. Divers get caught inside a wreck, sometimes. A line snags. Maybe a line breaks. Maybe the ship falls on you."

"Jesus."

"You get pinned down there. They try to do something, only there's nothing to do. They pull the lines, trying to free you. The line breaks. Not good to think about. But you may as well know it. If anything like that happens, it's all over."

I didn't say anything.

"You're going to take one more dive," he said. "At about a hundred feet. Tomorrow, we'll go to a hundred and fifty. Then, maybe we'll make a try for it."

"You mean we've got to come out again tomorrow?" I said. We'd been out nearly all afternoon, already.

"Take in the anchor," he said. "Not a hell of a lot of time left. I don't want to be working out here in the dark."

At a hundred feet, it was different. Things happened more slowly. You got to thinking about all that water over your head. It was a long way up, and it took a long time to get there, the way it had to be done. Mike was ticklish about the bends, and what water pressure could do to you, if you let it. We didn't have any pressure tank, either, in case of emergency.

As we came back into the slip, Mike said, "Tomorrow morning, early."

I went back to the boat.

I was nervous, and plenty worried about everything.

Fifteen

Sam Holland was nowhere around.

The boat was just as I'd left her earlier in the day. From what I could see, he hadn't been back at all. It wasn't like him.

I wondered if he was on another bat.

That wouldn't be like him, either. Not with what was going on. He would want to get a word in with Mike, too. Not that it would do any good. But he would try to pin Mike down. He would be surprised.

He still wasn't back when it got dark.

I kept wandering up on the pier. I wondered what had gotten into me. I didn't want to leave the slip.

Then I got to thinking. Maybe he was worried about the dead guy. Maybe he took off. But then I knew that wasn't so. He would never leave a chance at the big dough... no matter what.

I was down in the stern when Sally called to me. She was up on the pier. She had on a pair of tight, white shorts. They were damned short. And a thin white sweater. Her legs looked voluptuous as she walked toward the boat.

She wanted to know if I'd seen Vivian.

"No."

"She and your father went out early today. I saw them on the street when I was going to work."

Then she saw the bandages on my face. She came down into the boat with me, full of concern. I smelled that perfume she wore.

"It's from the fight," I said. "It was some fight."

"Are you all right?"

I pulled her onto my lap and kissed her. I smelled the clean smell of her hair and felt the softness of it against my cheek.

I knew I had to tell her.

Finally it all came out, about the dead guy, and how I knew my old man had killed him. She caught some of my own fear then.

"I read about it," she said. "I didn't dare think it was true. But I thought, maybe—"

"Well, it's true, all right."

"He did that."

"He did it, all right."

"Jack. You'll have to tell the police."

"Easy to say."

She went on for a time, about how I had to tell the police. I let her talk and get it out of her system. Finally, she quieted down. Then she began again, and we started to argue. It went on and on till I thought my head would crack. She wouldn't let up.

"I've got to go back to the office," she said. "I'm working late again, tonight. Overtime."

"Okay. I'll call you in the morning."

"Jack. You've got to do what I said."

She hadn't been gone more than ten minutes when the Cadillac pulled up out by the curb.

Vivian and my old man came through the slip gate. Then I saw two men coming along behind them. They came along the planks of the pier, their feet clumping. "Get the hell on the boat," one of the men said.

My old man turned around. He laughed and said something I didn't catch.

Vivian cringed against him. All four of them stood there.

"You're wasting time, Holland," the same man said.

"All right," my old man said. "You got it straight?"

"We'll see," the man said.

"Sure. All right, Viv, honey, jump aboard."

"Listen to him," the other man said. "Listen to the way he talks."

"That's Holland for you."

And then I saw the dull gleam of the gun in one man's hand. He kept the muzzle right flat on my old man.

Sixteen

Vivian saw me first.

I was in one of the deck chairs, under the awning, over by the screen door. When she came aboard, she saw me. She ran up close to me, breathing hard. She clung to me, and kept breathing like that, with her mouth closed. It was a curious sound. There was deep fright in it.

Then my old man came aboard. He saw me.

I stood up, with Vivian pressed against me, making a burring sound with her teeth, like she was cold or something. She crowded me. There was something animal in it, a strong animal fright.

"He's here," one of the men said.

I couldn't see them well, because the lighting was bad. They all came down into the stern. We stood there, with Vivian burring. She leaned against me, watching them. The sound came from her throat, too.

"Jack?" my old man said.

"Who the hell you bringing aboard?" I said. "Tell them to get off."

He looked around. I saw his face in a streak of light from the streetlights out on the pier. He wasn't smiling. He looked at them, then back at me, and he didn't say anything.

"What's going on?" I said. "Get off this boat."

One shrugged and looked at the other. The one who shrugged was not holding the gun. He poked my old man. I felt a tight coiling inside me, and I knew they weren't going to get off the boat.

"Tell him to turn on the light in the cabin," one of the men said.

"Turn on the light, Jack."

The way he said that, I knew damned well the chips were down. Vivian kept burring. She clung to me, and once I felt her shiver. She was scared.

So was I.

"Please, Jack," my old man said.

"This what they told you about Sam Holland, Clyde?" the one without the gun said.

"Not by a long shot," Clyde said. He had a nasty voice, making it as hard as he could. "They don't have to tell about this. Everybody knows about this."

"He leaks the yellow," the man said.

"Turn on the goddamned lights!" Clyde said.

My old man cleared his throat. "Jack? You better do like he says."

I broke away from Vivian. She gave a little whimper, reaching after me in the darkness. I went inside the deck cabin and turned on the light over the wheel housing.

My old man came into the cabin. Vivian squeezed close to his side. The one called Clyde came in behind them with the gun pushing against my old man's back. I stood over by the wheel and watched them. This was it. I knew this was it. You could damned near smell it.

Because when you saw them in that light, you knew who they were. They were the same breed as the dead guy. They might have been stamped out by the same machine, fed same food, and it was pretty certain they all bought their clothes in the same place.

Clyde wore a broad-brimmed Panama hat, the other guy a gray felt snap-brim. Clyde's hat was cocked to the left side of his head. Their suits were gray or blue in the light, and immaculate; their shirts and ties the same way. Looking at them, though, I had the feeling that they didn't have the intelligence of the dead guy. There had been something about him.

Clyde had bright, hard eyes.

"Holland," he said. "Get rid of that dame. Get her off you. She bothers me."

"Vivian," my old man said. "Why don't you run down there and sit on a bunk, like a good girl?"

Clyde watched me. He didn't stare, he just watched, taking note of every movement I made.

"Jack," my old man said. "Something's happened."

"I'll—I'll go sit on the bunk," Vivian said.

"Sure. You do that." My old man watched her leave and hurry down the companionway. Clyde turned to his friend, his head snapping on his shoulders, the hat slicing the shadows. And for the first time I recognized him as the man who had gotten out of the white car the other afternoon and looked at my boat from the sea wall. There was something about the way he moved.

"Go close the hatch," he said to his friend.

"What?" the other man said.

"Close the goddamned hatch. Up in the bow."

The other guy understood, and went for the screen door. He moved on around the side. I saw his legs at the windows, dark against the paler sky.

"Well," Clyde said. "So this is the boy, eh, Holland?"

"Jack," my old man said. "Something's come up."

"You think I'm blind?"

"Now, Jack."

"Listen," Clyde said. He looked at me with that sharp hat brim slanting across his face, cutting the light, leaving the upper part of his face in shadow. "Your old man's done you in."

"It's not that, Jack. Not as bad as he claims."

"Oh, Jesus," Vivian said from down there on the bunk. The hatch slammed up on the bow. I heard the guy stomp on it.

They had come for my old man again.

He certainly had changed. There was none of that cocksureness, like with the other guy. It was all gone. He looked tired. But he looked mean, behind the tiredness. I knew he would be scheming till they packed him away below ground. He still grinned and showed that gold tooth. I knew that it did plenty for his ego.

"We can't do anything tonight," Clyde said. "Might as well make ourselves comfortable."

My old man tried to look apologetically at me. It was a farce. You could see the greed lurking in his eyes. It seemed the more we stood here, the brighter that light in his eyes became. Somehow, he was trying hard to build on his guts.

That dead feeling inside me grew worse—the sensation of being trapped. There had never been anything like this. But there had always been the knowledge in my mind that someday everything would be brushed up to a peak, and then knocked off by somebody.

I heard my voice. It was strained and dry and the weariness in it scared me a little. Maybe sensing that sound in my voice helped me a little.

"If you're going to stay on the boat," I said, "I want to know what this is all about."

The one who had closed the hatch came around and in the screen door. He looked at Clyde, then went over and slumped on the bench and stared at the smashed table.

"Look," he said. "Blood." He pointed at a splotch on the deck. He had a fat, well-fed face, unlike Clyde's. The heat bothered him. He was about the same height as Clyde, but stockier.

Clyde was the boss, and you could tell he enjoyed the role. He wanted everybody to know it.

"Shall we tell him, Willy?" Clyde said.

Willy shrugged and grinned at my old man. He grinned with his lips only; his eyes never changed. It was getting a bit stiff, standing here like this.

"Your old man's let you down, Jack," Clyde said. "Nothing we can do about that, either. We got to do what we got to do."

Willy said, "We ought to see about the other guy."

Clyde lifted his upper lip and picked at a tooth with his index finger.

"We got some talking to do," he said.

It came over me what they really wanted.

"What you say, Holland?" Clyde said.

"I suggest we retire to the other boat," my old man said. He glanced at me, then quickly away. The side of his face had tiny scabs on it. The swellings were still there, where I'd hit him with the shotgun stock. I should have hit him a lot harder. "Mike's boat," my old man said. "The man called Mike."

Vivian suddenly ran up through the companionway. She crashed full into Clyde. She held his arm in a kind of frightened frenzy, her yellow hair swinging across her face, trying desperately to speak. Finally, she got it out. "Then—then I can leave, can't I?"

"Honey," Clyde said. "Nobody's going noplace."

"Anything—anything you want," Vivian said.

"Honey," Clyde said. He spoke softly. "You been telling me that all afternoon. I told you, I got a wife. Besides, you been wearing it out, traveling with the people you do. Like him." He gestured with the gun toward my old man. "Told you this afternoon. You're a nice-looking kid, but you're getting shot. You're messed up in something now, an' it's over your head. You should of thought about things like this happening when you started running around. Baby," he said, "you're already getting limber in the joints. You aren't flab yet, but you'll get plenty flab, you keep it up. Anybody can see, baby. You're losing it fast. You get limber in the joints, and then you start walking with your knees bent, honey. You should of thought to of kept those legs crossed a long time ago. They're nice legs. But you'll spread out, see?"

She wasn't getting it. "Anything," she said.

"Pretty soon it'll be so you only can make it in a house, honey. You want, I could get you a contact." He shoved his face close to hers and laughed hard at her, with his teeth together.

Abruptly, she slapped his face—a harsh slash.

He didn't budge. "Honey," he said, "you still got that old spring in your tail. But I can hear it squeak. Your leaf's getting rusty in the middle."

She slapped him again, savagely. He didn't move. Then she turned sharply and went back down and sat on one of the bunks. He didn't know one thing, though—he had given her back her nerve.

"Well?" my old man said. "What you say, men?"

"Wipe it off, Holland," Clyde said. "Where's this Mike at? We'll go there, now."

"That's the ticket," my old man said.

"Willy," Clyde said. "You keep an eye peeled on them. I don't want anything to happen. Not this time. This time might be the big time. So remember."

"I don't like it," Willy said. "We come up here to do a job. And now what? You got us all mixed up in some fool thing. The boss won't like it."

"I'm the boss, now," Clyde said. "Holland's got something."

"You know what the boss'll say," Willy said. "He said about Sam Holland. He didn't say about anything else."

Clyde ignored him and looked at me.

"You're quiet, Jack," he said. "You thinking? I like them when they're quiet. Suppose you lead the way. We want to get to this Mike Wales' boat. Don't make a mistake. Don't think I won't use this gun. All right, Jack?"

I turned to my old man. "What's the story?"

He gave a big sigh, stared at his feet, then swabbed his face with one hand. That ruby ring flashed in the light. You could see the sheen of sweat on his face.

"There was nothing else to do, Jack. I didn't have a chance. I told them about what we got out there. The sunken ship. They want to come in on it with me."

Clyde laughed. "Listen to how he talks. I can't get over it. He knows he's done, still he keeps yapping." Clyde looked at me. "Figure it out, Jack." He called to Vivian. "Let's go, honey."

"I don't like it," Willy said. "I don't like it at all, Clyde."

My old man looked at me and winked.

Seventeen

I laughed.

It was a kind of purge. Tears came to my eyes. I saw my old man swimming there in the light, with his face puffed up where I'd smacked him with the gun stock. My old man had slipped up. He'd made himself a bed with dirty sheets to lie down in.

"Shut it off," Clyde said.

My old man eyed me quietly. His face was sober. I could tell he suspected something.

It was so damned simple. They would have to take him away. I could see it in my mind, how they would take him out and drive off in the Cadillac. The Cadillac would never come back. You would read about it in the papers, how they found the big old beat-up, dust-covered convertible someplace, on a country road. There would be this big slob of a man in it, and he would be dead. He might not even have the gold tooth any more. It was almost certain the ruby ring would be gone.

"Stop it, will you!" my old man said.

"For you, anything."

"Spill it," Clyde said. "You got something bright and happy on your mind. What is it?"

"You're right," I said.

"I told you," Willy said. "This is no good."

"Talk," Clyde said.

"Because," I said, "I'm the only one knows where it is, see? Nobody's going out there. And, listen—it's there. Gold and silver. Maybe three ships, you hear? I saw one, and I marked it, too. But Mike Wales don't know where it is, and my old man don't know." The sweat streamed down. "I'm the only one who knows."

My old man swallowed and tilted his chin.

"Nobody's going out there," I said. "I'm not taking you out there, and nobody else *can.*"

It was quiet as hell. The only sound was my breathing.

A steady breeze came up suddenly. It blew steady and strong through the screen door of the cabin, coming in across the basin. You could smell the Gulf.

Clyde looked at my old man. His hat brim slanted yellowly in the light; his eyes shone in the shadow under the brim.

"Holland," he said. "You talked all day up there in the hotel room. Now I'm telling you. You got me to wait. Willy and I came to do a job, but you got me interested. You got me so I won't give up on a thing. But he seems to have a point, Holland." He paused, the gun hanging down along his thigh. "We're going out there some way, because that's how it is. So you'd better start thinking."

"Clyde," Willy said. "Let's forget it. It don't smell right. Let it lay."

"Not this time," Clyde said. "I know it's real, now."

He lifted the gun slightly. "Well, Holland? There's always a way out. I heard a lot about you. Show us some of what I heard."

My old man grinned and rocked on his heels, but he wouldn't look at me.

"I figured on something like this," he said. "You don't think..."

"Say it," Clyde said.

"Simple. He has a girl, men. The girl is Vivian's sister. I know where she lives. Jack wouldn't want anything to happen to her."

I came at him. It was pure impulse. I smashed at him, feeling the bone of my fist grit against his teeth. He sprawled back. Something smacked against my head and my knees gave a little. Then I got my feet under me. Clyde had smacked me with the gun.

"Get back there," Clyde said.

I went to the bench behind the wheel.

"All right, Holland. Where does she live?"

Willy was bothered. "Clyde, I tell you, this is getting heavy in the middle. It's no good."

My old man rubbed his mouth where I'd hit him. Then he told Clyde where Sally lived, and how to get there. "You can take my car."

"Willy. You heard the man. Get going, and hurry it up. Meet us at this Mike's boat." He turned to my old man. "She know where that is?"

He nodded.

"Snap it up," Clyde said to Willy.

Willy went over by the screen door. He looked at Clyde. "Someday, you'll admit I was right." Then he went away. He stumped off along the wooden planks of the pier. Then a car started and roared off into the night.

"Okay," Clyde said. "Holland, you get Vivian, and we'll move out."

My old man turned, and slapped my shoulder. "Take it easy, Jack. Live and let live."

We came along the grass by the sea wall. It was a beautiful night, with a clear sky, but there was quite a wind.

Maybe they're a lot of talk and won't do a thing, I thought. *Try them and see.* Then I thought, *Sure. Feel the back of your head. Does that feel like talk?*

Coming through the slip gate, I saw Mike up there on the hatch, sitting in the old Boston rocker, smoking.

"That him?" Clyde asked me.

"Mike," I called. "We're coming aboard."

We came aboard with Vivian whimpering, her legs flashing in the high heels, her face pale in the windy darkness. She would whimper and scamper, her heels clattering. I hadn't thought Vivian would be like this. When somebody's up against it, the holes show what's inside.

Yeah, I thought. *Take a look at yourself.*

I hated to think of the grief I was bringing old Mike Wales. He didn't deserve it. He'd been going through this against his will, from the beginning.

"Mike, you're not going to like what you'll hear." We stood there on the bow. Mike stood by his rocking chair and smoked and looked at us. It was a little too dark to see what his eyes were like, but he wasn't smiling.

"Getting pretty late, Jack," he said. "Remember what I said about an early start?"

"Break it to him," Clyde said. He held the gun so Mike could see it. But Mike had already seen it, because he didn't look toward it once. "Go ahead. Tell him."

My old man stepped up to Mike with his hand stuck out, palm down, the way he does, swaggering and grinning, and even in the half-dark that gold tooth gleamed. "Good to see you again, Mike."

Mike just didn't seem to see that hand. My old man stood there with it sticking out, like he was telling you how tall his hedge grew. Then he dropped it. He went and sat in Mike's rocker and stared out across the bow. I wondered if my old man could spit, right then.

"What's the story, Jack?" Mike said. He knocked his pipe out and held it in his hand, tapping the bowl.

I told him. I let it all come out: how my old man had killed that guy on Shell Key, and how we were now in the soup. These two men had come to collect a body, but had seen a good thing. "Only, we don't have to do it," I said. "Except, Sally..." I remembered.

I had forgotten about Sally.

"This is true?" Mike said.

"That's the way it is."

"Why didn't you tell me?"

"There's nothing we can do about it."

Mike looked at my old man in the rocker, then at the man called Clyde. "We're not taking this boat out there," he said.

Clyde didn't even bother looking toward him. He was watching the street, waiting for Willy to turn up with Sally.

Maybe she hadn't been home. It was the one thing I could hope for.

I whirled and made a jump for Clyde. I had one chance, anyway. I had to go between Mike and my old man in the rocker. Clyde turned and saw me coming.

My old man looked up, stuck his foot out. I tripped and sprawled across the deck.

Clyde's hard heels clipped across the deck toward me. I sat up. He leaned down and whipped the gun across my shoulders, hard, twice. He used the gun as he might have used his hand.

"Don't be a dope," he said.

My old man wasn't looking at me. I got up and went over there.

"You bastard," I said.

"Now, Jack."

"Here they come," Clyde said. "Now we got a full party."

Out there in the street, the Cadillac pulled to the curb. Sally was in the front seat, her face craned toward the boat. Then the door flapped open. Willy came around and they both moved fast toward the gate.

Coming aboard, Sally saw me, and rushed over. Mike was speaking to Clyde. I had never seen my old man so quiet. It was as though he was frozen in that chair. Sally kept asking me what it was all about and Vivian kept trying to tell her.

"Shut up," Clyde said. Then he shouted it, and they were quiet. Sally kept looking at me.

"Did he try to get funny?" I asked her.

She looked at Willy, who was standing in the shadows, and shook her head. "Oh, Jack," she said in a small voice. It was then I realized she was wearing only thin shorty pajamas. Tiny pants, and a hip-length blouse, of very thin material. Her lush thighs shone in the darkness.

Clyde started talking to Mike. He made it clear things would go as he said, and no other way.

"Old man," he said to Mike. "Don't try to give me any guff. I had a gran'-pap, like you."

Mike grinned, his teeth white in the darkness. He packed his pipe and lit up, clouds of smoke billowing.

"I've run into them like you before," Clyde said. "You don't fool me, not a damn bit. So, listen, don't think I'm dumb."

"You aren't old enough to be dumb," Mike said. "You're just naïve."

Jesus, I thought. *Don't be brave, Mike.*

Clyde said, "I know it might take a while, out there—if there is anything aboard that sunken ship. I know it's a chance. But I know this, too. It's a pretty good chance, because now I've met you, Mike—and I've met Jack. And Holland was bargaining for something that means a lot to him. I saw the compressor on the deck there. And the ladder." He pointed into the shadows by the rail, where Mike and I had shipped the ladder. "So, all right. I don't expect everything to happen in an hour. I know it'll take time. Diving's no cinch. I had a brother was a diver in the Navy. He did salvage work, Mike. He used to tell me stories. But we're going out there. And something bad's going to happen if you don't bring the stuff up. It has to be that way. We got a job to do, and Holland is the feature attraction." He laughed shortly. It was a little like the neigh of a horse.

"You've got a lot of talk," Mike said.

"Yeah. So, now, you cast this tub off and take it out and anchor it out there."

Sally's hands clenched tightly on my arm. She pressed against me, the soft roundness of her bare thigh and hip tight up against me. I reached down and gripped her waist, feeling the resilience of her flesh through the thin, soft pajamas.

"Get on with it, Mike," Clyde said. He turned to my old man. "Holland," he said. "You're going to have to help watch these people. You make a false move—it'll be all over. This is just a job to me, remember that."

"What if I won't do it?" Mike said.

Clyde shrugged. "You will."

"Clyde," Willy said. "Let's do it the easy way, and go home. There's too damned many."

"All the time yapping," Clyde said.

Willy obviously didn't like any of this. I got to wondering if maybe he wouldn't be an asset.

Mike still hadn't moved.

"Didn't you hear me?" Clyde said.

"Not clearly, little man."

Something happened to Clyde. He took a single, long step and smashed Mike's face with his gun. You could hear the crack against bone. Mike's pipe flew and bounced across the deck, scattering a blowing trail of red embers.

I broke free of Sally. "Mike—you all right?"

It had staggered him. He rubbed his jaw, dropped his hand, and looked at Clyde.

"Do as he says, Mike."

"All right."

He went over and picked up his pipe, knocked it out, repacked it, and lit up again. He kept watching Clyde.

"I got an enemy," Clyde said.

"Ready to cast off, Jack," Mike said. "They want to go out there, we'll take 'em."

We pulled out of the slip, finally.

I kept watching for some opening, a chance to catch Clyde unaware. There was no such chance. He was jumpy and watchful.

All of it was bad.

Eighteen

The hours before dawn were a torture.

Mike anchored the boat in a channel between two keys. There was plenty of water on both sides. We rode there on the night swell, with the stars clear overhead.

We stayed in the bow of the boat, on deck. Clyde took careful watch of Mike now; the gun never once left his hand. He sensed something in old Mike that had him on guard. He would move the gun from one hand to the other—an implement of emergency, a loving memento he refused to part with. You could tell he would be good with that gun.

In the slow grayness of a false dawn, I looked carefully at Clyde. His hat slanted above his face, and the eyes beneath were as hard and bright as ever.

"Can't you refuse to take them out there?" Sally said. We were sitting on the deck, by the ladder, with our backs to the rail. The boat rocked gently. Morning was fast approaching now, and there was a soft mist.

"No."

"Why not!"

I didn't say anything. I kept thinking about Mike and my old man. They did not speak to each other. My old man still clung to his swagger and his grin.

"You worried about what they might do?" she said.

"That's right."

"What if they find something out there? What will they do? You'll be the one who does the work. What if something happens?"

"I don't know."

"They want to kill your father."

"He did something to them. To somebody they knew. They came to do that. But he talked them out of it."

Clyde had been sitting in the rocking chair for some time. He had moved it down, so his back was against the cabin. He sat there and watched and listened, very alert. Willy kept moving around a lot. Vivian trailed after him, like a bitch hound. She had spotted her game. She knew Willy didn't want any part of this. She was trying to get him to do something about it. He spent his time in trying to escape her. Why Clyde let this go on, I couldn't figure.

Mike had rolled up in the tarp beside the air pump, and gone to sleep. He slept quietly, breathing evenly, with his pipe in his hand, his face straight up to the sky.

"Willy," Clyde said. "Take the girl and go to the galley. Fix some breakfast."

Willy turned to Vivian.

"Not that one," Clyde said—"the other." He gestured with the gun toward Sally. He grinned at her. The first true dawn began to spread across the sky.

"Let me," Vivian said.

Clyde shook his head. "I been watching you."

She stared at him.

"Get going," he said to Sally.

"I'd better," Sally said.

She rose and looked at Willy. Willy was very tired and anxious, his heavy face oily and stupid with early morning. You could see the wheels going around behind his eyes.

They went down the deck. Sally was still in her pajamas. Willy kept looking back over his shoulder towards his partner. Clyde got up and went over by Mike and kicked him in the side.

Mike opened his eyes. He looked at Clyde.

"Take her out, now," Clyde said. "Take her out to where we start."

"That's the ticket," my old man said.

He had been sitting on the deck against the starboard side. He stood up, gaped, and stretched. He leaned on the rail, stared down into the water, then off toward one of the keys. He turned and looked at me and grinned.

"Morning, Jack. Ain't it hell?"

"Mike," I said. "It's up to you."

Mike sat up and tossed off the tarp. He stood, looked at everybody with a quick glance, then frowned at Vivian.

"Don't do it," Vivian said. "Don't do it, old man."

It was becoming lighter now.

"Don't you do it," Vivian said. I noticed something in her voice, and watched her closely.

It happened so suddenly there was something more than mere horror in it. It was abrupt, clean.

Vivian said something about God, and you could see the way it was in her eyes—the despair. She rushed at Clyde.

She yelled at him.

You could tell the fear had worked in her all night long. She ran right into him. He tripped, fell backward, his face white. As he fell, the gun went off.

The sound of the shot passed across the water, rattling into distance.

I was on my feet, much too late.

"Damn it," Clyde said.

He shoved Vivian off him. She rolled over on her back on the deck. He stood and looked down at her.

"It was an accident," he said. "I never meant..."

She was dead. She bled for a short time from the hole in her throat, then the bleeding stopped, and she lay there staring with half-closed eyes into the morning. It had happened fast, and it was over with, like that. She'd made a crazy try for something, and missed.

Sally ran along the deck and knelt by her sister. She didn't touch Vivian. She just stared at her.

Willy came up beside me. He stood with his mouth open. Mike and my old man didn't speak. Mike was smoking his pipe. He walked over very slowly and reached down and put the palm of his hand on Sally's head.

"I never shot a dame," Clyde said. "She shouldn't have done that."

"What'd she do?" Willy said. You could see he didn't like the episode, but death itself did not touch him.

Nobody spoke. Sally looked up at me. She touched Mike's hand and stood up and came over by me and stood there. She looked over at the body.

Vivian lay very neatly on her back with her legs together, and her hands at her sides, with the palms up and curled a little. She had been wearing earrings. One gold earring had come loose and it lay beside her head on the deck.

She had done nothing, been a part of nothing. She had minded her own business. Then she was scooped up, carried away and killed.

"Willy," Clyde said. "Find something to weight her down. Put her over the side."

Sally gasped. "No."

Clyde said, "Instead of that, Willy, you take Mike, here. Mike, you get this tub underway. Now. Take it out there."

"Go ahead, Mike," I said.

Willy and Mike went away.

"Holland," Clyde said. "See that pipe over there?" He pointed to a six-foot length of lead pipe, lying close to the rail. "Tie her to that with rope, and get rid of her."

"Right," my old man said. He went to work.

"Listen," I said to Clyde. "Can't you—"

"Shut up!" Clyde said. "Accident, see? You think I'm going to let her lie there?" His eyes were bright; you could tell it bothered him. "What's done is done."

I took Sally's arm and turned her around. We went over to the opposite side and I kept her facing that way. But I could feel what she was going through.

Mike had already hauled in the anchor. Now I heard the engines turn over and catch, and the water ruffled out behind the stem. We moved. The engines thumped and ticked. Then, slowly, we came about in the channel, turning tightly. The sun was all the way up now, sitting on the rim of the world. The day was coming bright. I could feel the warmth of the sun. I didn't want to look back there on the deck.

But I did look. My old man played the game the way the cards fell. He was very much alone. He must have felt that. He was tying Vivian's body to the pipe with a length of rope. He had laid the pipe lengthwise along her front, so it mashed her face in some, and her breasts. He tied her hands and ankles to the pipe, working steadily. Finally he was done.

Sally kept her face turned away.

"There's nothing anyone can do," she said.

My old man inspected his workmanship.

We were coming into the bay now, headed toward the mouth of the bay where the Gulf shone a misty blue-white with the morning sun slanting long shafts across the far water.

"Jack," Clyde said. "Get over here and help your old man with this."

"Take it easy," I said.

I went over there. My old man and I hoisted the body up onto the side. For a moment we stood there, holding the ends of the pipe. Vivian's hair blew in the wind.

"Get with it," Clyde said.

My old man gave a wrench, and the splash threw water up on the deck. I turned and started back toward Sally. Something rolled hard beneath my right sneaker. I looked and it was that gold earring. I picked it up and took it over there and dropped it into the water.

Nineteen

I knew when we reached the spot.

I was at the wheel. I knew this was it, just like you know your own back yard, or your kitchen, after dark.

All I had to do was find the two-by-four marker buoy, and that wasn't necessary. I had thought of taking them out into the Gulf, telling them I was unable to locate the spot. But it wouldn't work. Not the way Clyde was now.

Vivian's death had done something to the man. He had changed into a tight, nervous person who marched about with the gun in his hand. His attitude was one of intense hatred. It showed in everything he did.

"Mike," I said. "Take the wheel. I'll go up on the bow. When I give the signal, cut her out. I'll heave the anchor."

Mike stepped to the wheel and I went out on the deck and started toward the bow. Willy was with Mike, holding a gun on him. Clyde stalked along behind me. Sally was up in the bow, motionless against the sky and sea. She had taken Vivian's death badly. Not with any demonstration, but hard inside, and you could see it in her eyes. My old man was with Clyde. They came along behind me.

Everybody was keyed up, waiting. My old man seemed to radiate a tense, wary energy.

"If this comes out right," Clyde said, "maybe we can work something out, Holland."

"You know damned well we will," my old man said. "I'm banking everything on this." He laughed loudly, and banged his hand on Clyde's back.

"Just don't get familiar," Clyde said. "I can leave you here. You know that, Holland."

"But you won't."

"Just don't bank on that."

I glanced at Sally. Then I began watching over the side. The water was clear; the sun hadn't blanked it out yet. The sun was very hot, though, and I didn't like the looks of the sky.

Maybe it was meant to be, because right then the bow of the boat sliced the water not ten feet from the flash of white two-by-four. It was the marker, as sweet as you please.

I waved at Mike, and the engines cut out. I grabbed the anchor, hauled it over, and let go. It whipped the hawser over the side, and I caught it as it slacked. We drifted, then stopped. We began to come about in what wind there was. The Gulf was calm now, but much too oily-looking for comfort. The water was tinged with that slate color. I took another look at the sky, and didn't like what I saw.

Over the side, you could see the big sand bank down there. We were anchored not ten feet from the spot where my boat had been the first day I'd located the sunken wreck.

I tried to sight the ship, but the sand bank hid the view, just like before. Then the sun began to brighten and it glazed the surface. You couldn't see anything. It was so hot, the sweat dripped off me down into the glasslike water.

"What makes you think I won't leave you here, Holland?" Clyde said to my old man.

I looked at Clyde. His shirt was still buttoned, with his tie tied, and the collar of the shirt had wilted from the heat. His hat slanted and gleamed in the sunlight, his eyes as mean as ever.

"I could take this tub clear to Texas," Clyde said. "You know that, don't you, Holland?"

My old man's gold tooth flashed. "There's too many."

Clyde said nothing. He hunched his shoulders, standing there with the gun in his hand.

"This the spot, Jack?"

I ignored him. I went over to Sally and took her in my arms.

"Just hang on."

I kissed her and held her as close as I could. She drew up against me. I wondered when I would get to hold her alone again.

"Jack," she said, with a fierceness that surprised me. "If we get away from this, we're going to get married. No more putting it off—for anything."

"Right."

"Break it up," Clyde said.

He stepped in close, grabbed my shoulder, and knocked me away. For a moment, we watched each other. I nearly went at him. But my old man stepped up and came between us.

"It won't do, Jack," he said.

"Stay away from me. I might blow the whole works."

Mike came along the deck just then, walking toward me with his pipe in his hand. He motioned to me. I pulled away from staring at Clyde and my old man.

"This it?" Mike said.

Clyde came over and stood there. He listened, watching, with his hat slanting in the sunlight.

"This is the spot," I said. "She's right down there."

"We might have to blast," Mike said. He acted as if nobody else was there. "You try to get inside her, she might crumble."

"I don't want to think about that."

"I'd planned to take it easy."

"If we blast, we might lose her. There's that shelf. God knows where it goes."

"I've got the dynamite," Mike said. "And the equipment. It's just a suggestion."

Willy came up, his face worried. He glanced at Clyde. "I wish to hell you'd quit this. For Christ's sake, we got what we came after." His voice was hoarse. "No good's going to come of this."

Clyde said nothing.

"Is it possible to get inside her?" I asked Mike.

"Sure, it's possible. But if there's sand packed inside her bad, we'll have to blast. A lot of the wood will probably be teak. It's good wood, and it lasts. Just use your head and don't take chances. Check under the poop. Maybe if there is anything, it might be in there, someplace. But don't take chances, no matter what."

"You take all the goddamned chances you want," Clyde said. "If we lose you, we still got your old man to send down." He laughed shortly. "Isn't that right, Holland?"

"Sure," my old man said. "That's right."

Willy's voice was tense. "I'm through," he said. "I'm quitting, Clyde. It's too big a thing. I won't monkey with it." He turned sharply and started down the deck toward the cabin.

"Get the hell back here."

Willy hesitated.

"You know what I'll do," Clyde said. "I won't pass this up. You think I'm crazy?"

"You're damned right," Willy said.

But he came back.

"All right," Mike said. "Then you've got maybe a hundred and sixty, seventy feet. That means if you stay down thirty minutes, it'll take almost an hour to get you back up here. We better keep it at that."

"Can I stay down longer?"

"Every minute counts," he said. "The longer you're down, the longer it is coming up. Remember that. Work fast, but not too fast. For God's sake, Jack, don't lose your head. Watch out for sharks. They're not apt to bother you, but they might. They're in these waters. Some hellish things hang out in old wrecks. They make it their home, no matter what anybody says. I know. If she's filled with sand, it's bad." He paused, then said, "It's bad any way you look at it, so be careful."

"All right."

"All those stories you've heard about an octopus hanging around some old wreck," Mike said. "They're probably true, Jack. Just remember."

"Get started," Clyde said. "I eat octopus."

"I'll send down a bar to work with," Mike said. "There's an ax, over there." He pointed to a large, double-bitted ax, secured to the side of the cabin. "But you won't want that. All I can say, is use your head. And watch your lines. If the air gives out, hang on. We'll switch to the hand pump."

"Anything else?"

"That's it. But be careful."

In the suit, I stood on the ladder and looked at them. Mike gave the helmet an eighth turn, and it locked. He hung over the side. His face was hell to see. The face plate was still open on the helmet. I glanced at Sally, then quit looking. I didn't like the way her eyes were. My old man stood there and kept waving his hand at me. It was as if he wished to hell I'd go and get it over with.

I wore a shark knife, and in the suit I felt that trapped feeling. Especially now, because if anything did happen up here, I was out of it.

So far as I judged, we were anchored just up the side of the sand bank. But we hung almost directly over the wreck now. Mike had passed the guide line down. The anchor line slanted into the top of the sand bank, and the flukes were holding perfect.

"Got the signals straight?"

"I think so."

I looked up on the deck. Willy paced back and forth. He had his hat off now. He was bald. The sweat stood out on his face in beads, and he kept tearing nervously at his collar. He would look at me, then at Clyde, and pace some more. Clyde just stood there, waiting. You could see the gamble in his eyes.

"All right, Mike."

Mike went away. I heard the pump start working. He came back, leaned down close to the face plate, and secured it. And he said, right next to my face, "Storm's coming up, Jack. Something will happen. So hang on!" He closed the plate. I felt the air rushing into my helmet, and the pump transmitted its energy along the hose. I backed my head against the escape valve, as Mike had shown me, because I thought there was too much air. Mike tapped on the helmet. I went down the ladder, took hold of the guide line-and dropped.

Abruptly, I was sick with wanting to be back aboard. My stomach turned over. I took it a lot faster than I should have and passed brightly colored fish that winged past like flashes of light. The colors of the water changed as if on a screen.

My feet struck the bottom.

And there she was.

She looked like an enormous black monster. I was right down under her side where I could see her black keel in the shadows, with her sides swelling out above me. I was at a little over a hundred feet.

There was a current right along there. It was like a millrace. It nearly took my feet out from under me.

For a long black moment panic took over.

Twenty

I was scared.

Another two yards in the wrong direction and I would have dropped right down through the middle of her. I was scared of everything. This, down here, and what was up there.

I no more dared look around behind me than I dared move at all, right then. It was the weirdest sight I'd ever experienced. Tall ferns waved around, and there were rocks and coral and fish of so many different hues you thought you'd gone mad.

The water rushed by where I stood. I felt the stark, cold thrust of it. It bucked against my legs, and against the heavily weighted diving shoes. Sand folded and looped around my shoes, whistled off into nowhere. The sea around me was illumined by crazy flickerings of light, and ghostly shadows turning back into one another and then looping and leaping as in an insane dream.

There were sudden fogs, then sharp, clear patches. And through it all, that immense old black hulk loomed like all disaster. With the timbers rotted and cracked out of her sides and her dirty black skeleton showing, with the green and silvery waters glowing, and furling, and glistening like flaming silk.

Fish shot by and braked and looked and shot away, streaming brilliant color through the heavy water. The water seemed like boiling glass.

I still couldn't move. I stood there with the vivid sound of the rushing air only helping the dream. I hadn't imagined anything like this.

She was covered with weeds, and encrustations of kinds I'd never want to examine. But she looked pretty solid, like a gigantic black rock, sitting there.

I knew she could fall apart like burnt paper.

She was cracked badly amidships, and kind of buckled, but not broken. Her timbers gaped and the big old poop glowered over it all.

The signal came along the line. I yanked back that I was all right, but to take in some line. I was leery of the current. I didn't know just how, or where, to start. Then I saw another line dangling and swinging over by the stern, with a bar hanging on it.

The bar banged and slammed against the side of the old ship.

The lines tautened just then, and my feet left the bottom. I whirled around and saw the blackness out there, and down below where I'd been standing. I knew if we ever blasted, she'd be gone for good. She was lying right in there against this huge sand and coral bank, just as I'd thought. Like a plaque, with only about five or ten yards of what you might call bottom beneath her.

I came around, swinging in a slow arc, taking the guide line weight with me. I swung in against the bank, even with the top of the poop. There was no current right there.

You could see the old mast stumped off. My heart rocked. There were broken balustrades all around the high, hand-carved poop. The ship looked as though she'd been through hell, all right. There was something ghostly about the old hulk, with its jagged-holed sides, and broken-fingered masts, and shadows.

I got the bar Mike had sent down and worked myself along the sand bank away from the guide line.

I could see then that I'd be able to go up and over on the sand, and come right down the drift of it onto the poop deck. But when I got there, it seemed as if she was hanging on nothing, floating in space. It was a weird feeling. You could see the water washing the sand away, eating at it, a little at a time. She was getting a thorough cleaning and burnishing before she toppled down there into the empty depths and vanished forever.

When this would happen, I didn't know. But I watched the sand wash away, and I knew that all through her it was the same. There wasn't much sand and coral holding her now. She was just glued there, waiting for doom.

I brought the guide line with me, now, and hung onto it as I lowered myself onto the deck. I took it mighty careful. I had figured right. The sands that spread about one-fifth of the way across the top went right down through her.

The deck was badly broken. I drew back the bar and jammed it into the wood with everything I had. It was still attached to the line. It left my hand and went through an old plank. It stopped, sticking up. I hauled it back and pried. Hunks of black wood tore away, and tumbled along amidships like graceful strips of cloth. I couldn't see a hell of a lot in there.

I knew I'd have to go inside. There was no other way.

"Are you all right?" came on the line.

I yanked back that I was, and to give me about four more feet of line.

There were a lot of things jammed into the wood, showing here and there through the sand, piled around the shattered decks. Two crusty looking cannon, gnarled iron-work, and nails, and broken cooking implements, and a great deal of iron chain.

I slipped through the hole in the poop, hanging to the guide line, watching every step. It was then that I began to get conscious of time.

If I had to cover the whole ship, searching for a chest, it would be impossible.

I went on down. Then I saw I could have made it easier for myself. I was in a large old cabin. But the side of the cabin, facing out, was torn away. I could have walked right in over there.

There was a great deal of ornate wood carving, and an accumulation of debris and smashed timber that warned me to tread easy. I checked my lines to see if they were free, then had a look around. The deck was spotty and ready to cave in. She seemed to shudder every time I moved. I thought of the empty blackness down below, and how the ship hung over it.

There was a drift of sand against the port side. I kept looking around.

A doorway led out into a companionway, and beside the door was a huge walled cupboard, or bookcase, with junk strewn on the rotting shelves. Rotten chunks of iron. Then I glanced down and along the base of the cupboards, and stopped breathing.

This was it.

I didn't have to go anyplace else on the ship. Mike had been right. There was a chest there. It was packed neatly in under the bottom shelf of the cupboards. It was banded, just like in the museums. Excitement took over. For a moment, I couldn't believe my eyes. But it was there, all right. As big as life.

I forgot everything, lunged across the deck of the cabin toward the chest. Not a sign of sand was around, where it waited clean and stolid in the shadows.

Abruptly, there was no deck to walk on.

It gave way underfoot and all around in a kind of splintering slow motion crumbling. It was like rotten linoleum. I made one savage grab for the guide line and missed. The steel bar banged against my helmet.

I spun forward and down, clawing at the darkness.

"I don't give a good goddamn how you bring him around," somebody said. "Just see to it!" I sat up, then lay back again and waited till my head stopped cracking.

"He's all right," Mike said.

I opened my eyes. I was stretched out on the deck. The sky overhead was smoking with dark gray clouds, and the boat rocked and rolled and pitched. Spray shot up over the side, splattering across me like a lash.

"Clyde," Willy said. "You've got to give this up."

"I'm not giving anything up."

"Are you all right?" It was Sally. "Jack?" She was kneeling beside me. I sat up and leaned against the side, reached over and grabbed her. She came against me, and for the first time I realized I was out of the diving suit.

"I was afraid, Jack."

That was all she said, with her head buried against my shoulder. My head cracked and snapped inside. My eyes felt like they were going to leave their sockets. I felt like hell. My stomach was queasy and there was a bad taste in my mouth.

A shadow fell across me. I looked up. Sally clung to me. Somebody was standing there in the diving dress. It was my old man, grinning, with that gold tooth gleaming through the face plate on the helmet.

"Jack," Mike kept saying. "Jack?"

Clyde came in close and grabbed the front of my shirt.

"What did you see?"

"Mike? How'd I get back here?"

"We pulled you in." He looked soberly at me. There was excitement in his eyes, too.

"It's down there," I said. "I saw the chest, Mike. It's under the poop deck, by an old bookcase. I went for it, but something happened."

"You almost didn't come up. That's what happened."

"Why can't he go down, now?" Clyde said.

"I'll go down," my old man said.

"Jack can't," Sally said. "Can he, Mike?"

"No."

"Clyde," Willy said. He stepped up to Clyde and faced him. "You got to let this go. There's a bad storm coming up. We haven't got a chance."

I interrupted then, and told Mike all about what was down there. Clyde began to act as if he'd lost his head. He kept pushing my old man toward the rail, telling him to hurry.

Mike said, "It's not wise, Holland."

"I'll go down," my old man said. "The hell with it."

I pulled myself to my feet. Mike explained that I'd been out cold over an hour and a half. Ever since I'd tumbled through the hole in the deck. They had caught the sudden, heavy drag on the line and had begun hauling in immediately. But the line was caught. It took all three of them. Clyde was too nervous to help. I'd been out, when they finally brought me back over the side.

My old man was already standing on the ladder. The wild, angry pitching of the boat was bad.

"Send a net down," he said. Then he pointed to the face plate on his helmet. He looked across at Clyde and something came into his eyes. "I'm going to get that chest. So remember our bargain."

"Get going," Clyde snapped.

He waved the gun around, rushed up to the rail, and snarled into my old man's face.

"You better get it, hear? Because if you don't, by Christ, you'll get this." He stuck the gun in my old man's face.

"I'll warn you for the last time," Mike said. "There's a storm coming up, and it's going to be bad. No telling what'll happen down there."

"Close this face plate."

Mike reached down and shut the plate on the helmet. My old man grabbed the guide line, went on down the ladder cumbersomely, and dropped.

We waited.

I thought about him going down and down along the line. He would land right there on top of the poop deck, by the sand. I could almost follow his movements. With any luck at all, he would be done in no time.

"I should have gone down."

"You couldn't," Sally said.

I saw she'd been crying. Her eyes were red, and she clung to me tightly.

"It took so long for them to bring you up," she said. "Mike didn't know what was wrong. He said they'd have to bring you up in stages on the chance you weren't dead already. Because, he said, if they brought you right on up, you'd probably die anyway."

"It was terrific," I said, remembering.

"It must have been awful."

"It was beautiful. I never saw anything like it."

Mike looked at me and cursed, then turned his back.

"See if you can find out what Holland's doing," Clyde said. I began to keep my eyes on him now. He was wound up tight. No telling what he'd do.

Mike was taking care of the lines with both hands.

"He's all right. Just signaled. He's on the bottom."

I told Mike about the current down there, and how we could never blast the wreck.

"I thought as much."

I tried to get next to Mike, so I could talk to him without Clyde overhearing, but the man was wise. He was so shot full of adrenalin he couldn't stand still. He missed nothing. His eyes were danger signals.

"We're going to have bad weather," Mike said. "He shouldn't be down there. Nobody should."

I didn't say anything.

"Take a look at that sky."

The clouds were mammoth black and gray and seething white, piling up, sailing with the boiling winds. The white sun blasted between the clouds, shooting brilliant rays down into the Gulf.

The Gulf was white-capped. You could feel the new lifting surge of the deck.

We waited for what seemed a long time. Nothing happened. Whenever Mike asked on the line how my old man was, he got the same answer: "Okay."

The only thing was, my old man kept asking for more and more line. Then, finally, Mike couldn't give him any more, because there was none left. So we waited, and all the time it got a little worse with the way Clyde acted.

Willy leaned against the side of the cabin. A steady rising wind was coming up. Willy stood there with his shoulders hunched. He looked like a man waiting for a bus on a windy, rain-swept corner.

"There's the signal," Mike said. "He wants us to bring up the net."

Clyde wouldn't drop his gun, now. But he jumped toward the side like a wild man. I went over and Mike and I heaved on the line. It wouldn't come.

"We'll have to use the winch," Mike said.

We rigged the winch, started the engine, and the line began coming up. It seemed endless. My heart hammered, and not alone for that chest, but because whatever was supposed to happen would now begin to happen.

You could see that in Clyde's eyes. The wind ripped still stronger across the decks.

The net came up. We slung it aboard. He had sent up a pile of junk. There was the wheel off an old cannon, an old shell-encrusted iron kettle with three legs, some hunks of broken iron chain, two solidly rusted musket barrels, and an iron spittoon.

Mike stayed with the lines.

Clyde went off his head, then. He cursed and swore, and called Sam Holland every name in the book.

Right then the sky burst wide open with lightning and thunder. It bellowed and rolled. The boat began to pitch like crazy.

"He's signaling," Mike said. "Something's happened down there!"

I went over by the rail.

"I can't get an answer," Mike said. "He must be caught up, somehow."

Sun still gleamed through the clouds on one side of the sky. But on the other, it was ripping wide open.

"We're going to catch it," Mike said. He struggled with the lines. "Come on. Give it everything you've got."

We got on the lines and pulled and hauled back across the deck, with the lines stretched out over the side. Then I heard Willy yelling in the wind. The words were carried away. Clyde ran up to the rail with that big double-bladed ax in his hand. He turned to us, with the brim of his hat blowing down flat against the side of his face. His eyes were wide.

"Stand clear," he said. "We can never get it now."

I dropped the lines and headed for the rail. The boat lifted high on the port side. I sprawled backward, as I tried to climb the heaving deck.

Clyde swung the ax. Once. Twice. Three times the huge double-bitted ax blade arched and gleamed and struck. Mike slumped back on the deck, holding two severed lines in his hands.

The life-line and the air-hose had been chopped neatly in two.

Clyde rushed against the rail, looking down into the roiling water.

I got up off my knees, and came across the deck at him. He was hanging over, watching down there.

Willy yelled something.

I grabbed Clyde's shoulder. As he came around, I nailed him hard in the face with my fist and grabbed the ax, twisting it from his hands. He cringed back, going for his gun. I swung the ax with the helve flat out. It caught him across the side of the head. He went flat out on the deck.

"Take care of Willy," I told Mike.

Piled on the deck beside the rail were several diver's weights. I grabbed one of these in each hand.

Sally screamed as I went over the rail.

Something had snapped inside my head. All I could think was, *You've got to do something.*

I struck the water and started down right next to the guide line. I managed to hook onto the line, twisted my legs around it. I let the weights carry me down into the darkening water. My head ached. I popped my ears, and came up short on the sand bank. It was not as it was before. Even down here, you could feel the swelling surge of the storm overhead.

I held to the weights, realizing my old man must have moved the guide line. Then I saw the bulk of the diving suit. There were two cut lines, trailing out along the sands, down toward the wreck. Then they came curling up again, and on the end of them was my old man in the diving suit.

He was clear up on the side of the sand bank, far above the wreck. I couldn't figure it. I dropped the weights and swam hard and came down over him where the water swirled around him. He dragged just above the sand, on his back. As I reached him, he turned over very slowly, and limply.

I saw his face in the face plate of the helmet.

I grabbed the suit, and looked in there. His eyes stared out at me. His mouth was open. His eyes shone in there. I saw the blind-wild, savage, choking contortions of his face. He was fighting for air. There was no water in the suit. I knew the air supply had been cut off somewhere down there by the wreck. He still wasn't out, still conscious, floating and dragging on the sands, staring wildly out at me. I grabbed for the shark knife on his suit, but it was gone.

Then you could hear the fantastic rumble.

It came up from over there where the hulk was.

Clouds of sand abruptly furled and smoked into the sea like an explosion. It rumbled and cracked and thumped through the water. The wreck was falling apart. You could see the big old stump of mast teeter and fall crashing amidships, down there. The big poop lifted and then the huge old ship crumbled with a thunderous, continuous underwater roar.

Something snagged at my feet.

I looked down, and saw my old man's face through the face plate. He stared angry-eyed out at nothing, his mouth spread wide in a big yell that nobody would ever hear.

He was snatched away. I saw the gleam of that gold tooth. He spun away through the water, torn sharply down after the vanishing, smoking wreck. The lines were caught somewhere inside the ship. They yanked him brutally, twisting, leaving a trail of seething bubbles. Then he was gone.

There was nothing there but the sand bank, and spreading clouds of fine sand.

I fought for the surface. My head was cracking with pain. The water was rapidly darkening. I burst onto the surface not far from the boat.

They called to me. I saw Sally on the rail.

Behind the boat, lightning ripped the skies, and rain slashed down, whipped like shot across my face.

Mike threw a line. I got it and they dragged me over to the boat. Gasping, I made it to the ladder, came up, and stood there on the deck.

"It's all gone," I said. "It went down."

Clyde was laid out on the deck almost where I'd left him. I leaned there, still fighting for breath. Sally came over and said things I couldn't hear.

I stared at Clyde. He was bound hand and foot. Willy was sitting on a box; he was tied up, too. Mike smacked me on the shoulder.

"You got to help me haul in the anchor, or I'll have to cut it clear."

We staggered up onto the bow. All I could think was the crazy way my old man had looked as he vanished off there into the darkness.

We leaned on the line. We hauled and hauled. It was like we were lifting a ton, I was so beat. We kept hauling.

Sally shouted something. She pointed down toward the water. We kept hauling on the line. The anchor ripped the wood, coming up over the side. It just hung there.

"Look," Sally said. "On the anchor!"

It was the big old chest.

It was secured with chain to one of the flukes on the anchor. Water streamed from it, hanging there, slamming against the, side of the boat. It was crusted with barnacles, just like the bulk down there had been.

Mike let out a yell. We laid on the line. I wasn't tired now. We fought and pulled and got it up on the rail and it crashed over on the deck.

It burst wide open.

The stuff poured out. Old dirty-looking coins of every description. Black ones. And some with golden highlights. Strewn among the coins were cut stones, and they looked bright and new.

It rolled and spread across the deck. Mike knelt down in the mess, and mangled it with his hands. He acted like a kid.

"Your father," Sally said. "He fixed it that way, so we'd be sure to get it."

I held her real tight. The boat rolled and pitched. The bow lifted violently and I had to hang on to the rail. Mike just knelt over there in all that mess of loot. He kept feeling around in it with his gnarled old hands.

And I knew a lot of things.

I knew how good it was to be back up here with Sally. How fine it was that those two, Clyde and Willy, were done with. I knew there would be plenty of explaining to the law, once we got back in port.

"Don't you see what he did?" Sally said.

"Sure," I said. "I see."

Because I sure as hell did see. That was another of the things I knew. My old man was gone for good. Right to the last he had been what he'd always been. A son of a bitch. A bastard. Because he didn't fix that chest to the anchor for anybody but himself. A crazy last scheme to win. He had lost.

But he was gone, now. And I had learned something, too.

I kissed Sally. It was good, full of all the promise I'd ever wanted. Then I looked over her shoulder into the slanting gray waves, with the lash of the rain, and the white sheets of lightning.

He had been some guy, all right. That was for sure.

THE END

If I Can Tell All of This Straight and True

BY GEORGE TUTTLE

In her essay "Notes on Gil Brewer," Verlaine Brewer, Gil's wife, writes: "Gil Brewer decided to become a writer at the age of nine, while watching his father type stories for the early pulp magazines." This would have been towards the end of his father, Gilbert Thomas Brewer's brief pulp career. He started in the late 1920s. Philsp.com, Phil Stephensen-Payne's magazine index website, lists his first story as "The Enemy's Man" which appeared in the August 16, 1928 issue of *War Stories*. He, like his son, published under the Gil Brewer by-line. He was Gilbert Thomas Brewer. The son was Gilbert John Brewer (the family called him Bud).

Not much is known about Gil's father. The October 11, 1926 issue of *Time* magazine writes about Gilbert T's work in archaeology. It introduces him with the line: "Late in August, digger Gilbert T. Brewer returned from a trip down the Mississippi Valley, to Mexico City and South America via Panama, with extensive evidence of Norse expeditions having penetrated this continent thoroughly in pre-Columbus days." The article went on to briefly talk about his discoveries.

A reference to Gilbert T's being in Panama can also be found in the Ancestry.com database in the New York Passenger Lists, 1820-1957. On March 17, 1925, he arrived in New York on a passenger ship called Panama. The port of departure was Cristobal, Canal Zone. It gives his age as 27 and his address as 55 Scotland Rd, Canandaigua, NY. It also cites his date and place of birth: May 12th 1898, Hoboken, NJ.

Gilbert T's efforts in archaeology and a dig in Point Bluff, New York, are mentioned in two articles by David R. Robinson for the *Crooked Lake Review*: "The 1938-1939 excavation by many persons was carried out under the direction of a newspaper reporter from Canandaigua, New York, Mr. Gilbert T. Brewer." Gilbert T. was a staff reporter for the *Daily Messenger* of Canandaigua, New York. He also worked on the radio in Rochester, New York. But as a writer, he is best remembered for an appearance in *Zeppelin*

Stories and a tale entitled: "The Gorilla of the Gas Bags." It is one of the most sought after pulp stories from one of the rarest pulp magazines. There is no available plot synopsis, but the cover image of a Gorilla dangling from a zeppelin is a memorable one.

There is no complete index of Gilbert T's fiction. Most of his stories are aviation fiction. The last known published work is the 1942 reprint of the short story "Spy Cloud" in the fall issue of *Wings*. It is quite possible he was not paid for this reprint and was not aware of its publication. The story was originally published in 1931 and it was not an uncommon practice in the pulps for all rights to be sold at the initial purchase. By the 1940s, Gilbert T. writing career was pretty much in the past: the pulps, the *Daily Messenger*, the radio work. He eventually took a job at the Samson Naval Training Base in Rochester, NY.

Googling the full name, Gilbert Thomas Brewer, reveals a site entitled "Ontario Co. News Articles" from USGenNet and a reprint of Gilbert T's marriage notice from 1922. The notice is 16 sentences in length. It starts: "The marriage of Gilbert Thomas Brewer, of Geneva and Miss Ruth W. Olschewske, took place at the Presbyterian Church last evening at 6 o'clock." Gilbert T. and Ruth were married on February 16, 1922, and Gilbert John was born on November 20, 1922 in Canandaigua, NY. He was the first of four children (Diana, David, and Nancy). Gil seems to be the only one of the four old enough to be aware of his father's pulp career.

Searching the Ancestry.com database, one can retrieve Gilbert John's Army enlistment record: "Enlistment Date: 8 Mar 1943; Civil Occupation: Laundry Machine Operator or Receiving or Shipping Checker (Receiving and shipping clerk.); Education: 3 years of high school." Gil Brewer served three years of service during World War II, the last year in Marseilles, France. After his discharge, he joined his family in St. Petersburg, Florida. Gilbert T. and Ruth, along with her father, John Olschewski, moved their families to St. Petersburg while Gil was in the Army. Gilbert T. started working at the Bay Pine Hospital in St. Petersburg, but after about a year, he had a mental breakdown and spent the remainder of his life in the VA hospital in Murfreesboro, Tennessee. Gilbert T. Brewer died on July 19, 1967 and was interned on July 21 at the Stones River National Battlefield in Murfreesboro.

In Verlaine Brewer's essay in the section entitled "Background," there is a series of memorable points about Gil and his father:

> Gil and his father were close. Not so, Gil and his mother. Mrs. Brewer had no understanding of writers, even though Gil's father was also a writer. The home life was not happy—especially since the father, like son, was addicted to alcohol. His father later had a mental breakdown,

was committed to a VA hospital, where he finally died. A tragic waste of a wonderful man.

Note: Gil worshipped his father: and worried through life that he'd end the same way.

These observations by Verlaine give Gil's life a noir backdrop. It is the starting point of her superbly written essay on Gil's life. He met Verlaine in 1947. She had moved to Florida from New York after a car accident. Marvin Lee, her then husband, and she were separated and he was living in St. Petersburg. Dorrie Lee, Verlaine's daughter-in-law explains:

She was in a car accident coming home from playing in a nightclub band and was seriously injured. When she recovered, Marvin went back to Nyack, NY, to get her and the two children, along with her widowed mother, and brought them to Florida. She met Gil soon after that. Marvin divorced her and raised the teenage children. They all remained cordial for the sake of the children and grandchildren.

Gil and Verlaine married in 1950 in South Carolina. Verlaine was a constant in Gil's life. She stuck by him and believed in him. Their mutual interest in writing had drawn them together. Verlaine was also a talented musician and artist. Verlaine's father was noted political cartoonist, illustrator William C Morris.

Gil's initial focus was serious literature, but he turned to popular fiction as he searched for a way to make a living. His first sale was to the pulp magazine *Detective Tales*. Shortly after that he was contacted by literary agent Joseph T. Shaw. Shaw saw great promise in Gil and wanted to represent him. It is unclear how Shaw became aware of Gil, but it seems logical that Harry Steeger or someone from *Detective Tales* might have been responsible. Under Shaw's direction, Gil started expanding on that first short story, "With This Gun," which appeared in the March 1951 issue, and created the novel, *Satan's Rib*. Gold Medal Books bought *Satan's Rib* and published it under the title *Satan Is a Woman* (1951). In the 1950s, title changes were common in paperback publishing. Most of Gil's books were subject to title changes, for example *The Screamer* became *And the Girl Screamed* (1956) and *The Screaming Lullaby* became *Wild to Possess* (1959).

Gil Brewer is one of the Gold Medal Boys, the second major school in hardboiled fiction. It includes writers Charles Williams, John D. MacDonald, David Goodis, Wade Miller, Lionel White, Harry Whittington, Day Keene, Bruno Fischer, H. Vernor Dixon, Benjamin Appel, Elliott Chaze, Clifton Adams, John McPartland, Peter Rabe, Vin Packard, and Robert Colby, and later, in the 1960s, Jim Thompson, Dan J.

Marlowe, Malcolm Braly, and Donald Hamilton. These writers brought a darker brand of hardboiled fiction to the forefront. It was hardboiled fiction that didn't rely on detectives to solve crimes. It wasn't that Gold Medal didn't have its share of private eyes—Richard Prather's Shell Scott is one of the biggest selling private eye series of all times. It was just that Gold Medal pushed a hardboiled alternative to detective fiction upon the masses. Its books were immensely successful. It fueled a paperback original boom and encouraged other publishers to get involved. Dell had its respected First Edition line, and Lion Books was one of the most cutting edge publishers of originals with the early crime novels of Jim Thompson. But none of the other publishers were as successful as Gold Medal. They had several million sellers at a time when million sellers were rare. Amongst the million sellers is Gil Brewer's *13 French Street*. (1951).

The Gold Medal Boys is the second major school. The first major school is the Black Mask Boys. *Black Mask*, a pulp fiction magazine, started the whole hardboiled genre with writers Carroll John Daly and Dashiell Hammett, and then advanced the genre with Erle Stanley Gardner, Raymond Chandler and Horace McCoy. Joseph T. Shaw, the same Shaw who managed Brewer's early career, became *Black Mask's* editor in 1926 and created one of the most distinctive magazines in pulp history. After Shaw's departure in 1936, *Black Mask* began to fade in prominence.

Paperbacks started appearing in the 1930s. In Britain, the Penguin line appeared in 1935, and in the United States, it was 1939 with Pocket Books. The early paperback houses published almost exclusively reprints, and were at the beck and call of hardcover publishers. Their initial presence did very little to change fiction markets in general or hardboiled fiction, specifically. Fawcett Publications changed everything.

Fawcett Publications did three things. In 1945, Fawcett signed a contract to distribute Penguin's stateside counterpart, New American Library or NAL. Their skill at newsstand distribution contributed greatly to the success of NAL's Signet line. It made Fawcett a major force and fueled paperback revolution. Second, Fawcett discovered Mickey Spillane. Fawcett's Circulation Director, Roscoe Fawcett, took Spillane's first novel, *I, the Jury* to NAL and offered to distribute it. In the words of Spillane: "He went to New American Library, which was Signet Books, and he said 'if you print this book I'll distribute it.' Now they can get distribution, so it's a win-win thing for them, but they have to get it published in hardback, so they go to Dutton and say if you print this, we'll do the paperback, so now it's win-win-win." Fawcett asked NAL for an initial printing of one million copies. This book quickly became the biggest selling mystery ever. Third, Fawcett debuted, in 1949, Gold Medal Books, the first line of paperback originals. As paperback originals rose into prominence, the pulps faded. It wasn't the only reason why pulps magazine died, but it was a major factor. Paperbacks became a dominate market for hardboiled fiction.

Richard A. Carroll, Gold Medal's Executive Editor and later, Editor-in-Chief, is often cited as the one responsible for the Gold Medal approach to fiction. He had a background as a Hollywood story editor and was not your typical paperback editor. Literary agent Donald MacCampbell stated of Carroll: "He was one of the first editors in the popular categories to accept anti hero lead characters."

By August 1951, it was obvious to all that Gold Medal was a success. A *Newsweek* magazine article, from the August 20th issue, reported that Gold Medal had total sales around 29,000,000 for their first 78 titles. Much of its success was attributed to unknowns. Gil Brewer was one of those unknowns. In 1956, Alice Payne Hackett's *60 Years of Best Sellers* reported that *13 French Street* had sales of 1,200,365. It was Gold Medal's eighth biggest seller at that time.

Joseph Shaw had a plan for Gil. According to Verlaine Brewer, he had prepared "a program of certain publications he wished Gil to slant for." But shortly after announcing this plan, Joseph T. Shaw was dead. Brewer's *Flight into Darkness* (1952) was the last thing he read before he died. Brewer explains in a note he wrote in 1962:

Joe finished reading it, went to lunch after sending it to GM (Dick Carroll, now also dead—1959) and returned early and died coming up in the elevator, of a heart attack—on the way to his office. J.T. Shaw was the very best—a gentleman, a fine editor, an excellent agent—and a "come hell or high water" friend. To my knowledge, he was one of the very last men of heart in the publishing and editorial world who understood, sympathized with, and believed in what an honest writer could do no matter how long it took—if the real talent was there.

In his first year, 1951, Brewer published three short stories in *Detective Tales* and three novels with Gold Medal Books. He also did a novelization of a Day Keene novella for the Australian paperback house Phantom Books. Keene and Brewer were friends and both part of a group of St. Petersburg, writers that included Harry Whittington, Talmage Powell, Jonathan Craig, Robert Turner and others.

From 1952 to 1954, Brewer generated four more Gold Medal novels. He took a break from short fiction and only returned to it when he changed literary agents. After Shaw's death, Brewer went through a couple of literary agents. At one point, he had the same agent as Day Keene and Harry Whittington. Then, he settled on the Scott Meredith Literary Agency. Meredith was the main supplier of crime short stories. From 1954 to the end of his career, short fiction was a key component of his output as it was with many of Scott Meredith's clients.

His string of Gold Medal titles ended in 1955. *The Squeeze* was rejected by Gold Medal and published by Ace Books. From 1955 to 1962, Brewer started diversifying and publishing with different publishers: Avon, Crest, Mystery House, Monarch, Berkley, and Lancer. Though he did three Gold Medal titles during this period, it wasn't his only book market.

Then Brewer stopped writing. Verlaine explained it: "In the 1960s, he suffered a mental breakdown. There was no writing for almost four years; hardly any drinking, but other frightening developments. He seemed unaware of his condition, or actions." Verlaine eventually had Gil institutionalized, but after a minimal stay, he was back. It took time for him to fully recover, but eventually he returned to writing. He did one last novel for Gold Medal, *The Hungry One* (1966), and then two novels for Banner, *The Tease* and *Sin for Me*, both in 1967. After that, he wrote his books in batches (like the *It Takes a Thief* TV tie-ins), under pseudonyms (Elaine Evans, Mark Bailey, and Luke Morgann), or ghosting for others (Ellery Queen, Hal Ellson, Al Conroy, and Harry Arvay). There was a very limited market for noir, and he had to take what assignments Scott Meredith could find for him. It was hard for most noir writers. The era of the noir thriller had passed. He published very little after 1977 and died in 1983. Renewed interest in noir only started to blossom again in 1984 with Black Lizard Books.

Brewer liked Scott Meredith as an agent, but he had a special fondness for Joseph T. Shaw. About Shaw, Brewer said, "He believed in my work; what I wanted to do, that is."

And what did Brewer want to do? What was his vision? The answer might be found in the opening passage of Gil's novel *A Killer Is Loose* (1954). The book begins:

> If I can tell all of this straight and true, and get Ralph Angers down here the way he really was, then I'll be happy. It's not going to be easy. There was nothing simple about Angers, except maybe the Godlike way he had of doing things. He was some guy, all right. In the news lately, you've read of men doing some of these things, like Angers. They were all red-hot under the same cold star when the wires snapped and Death became a pygmy.

Of course, most of Gil's character are not as Godlike as Ralph Angers. They are usually more human, filled with self-doubt. But this could be Gil's vision: "tell all of this straight and true."

But it is never easy to find the true vision of a writer. He is part of a process. In academia, they tend to simplify the process. They don't dwell on the editors, the agents, and all of those people who make a living out of publishing. Dwelling on these people make it seem more like a commercial rather than an artistic venture. But publishing is a commercial venture, and publishing is not about what is good or bad. Instead, it's about what is marketable. This is true with all published literature and is particularly true with popular fiction.

In the case of crime novels, the publishers who worked with Brewer liked nice tight plots and were are not partial to loose ends. They wanted an ending that will leave the readers satisfied and eager to buy another title from the same paperback line. These were mass market publishers and not publishers whose main focus was artistic vision. Story endings may sometimes have seemed dishonest. There was pressure on editors and writers to give the mass market what it wanted.

By 1965, *13 French Street* had total sales of 1,333,417 according to Alice Payne Hackett's *70 Years of Best Sellers*. This figure would not include a 1967 Gold Medal edition and various foreign language sales like the recent 2007 J'ai lu edition. Other popular successes for Gil were *The Brat* and *Little Tramp*. Both were published in 1957. *The Brat* was released by Gold Medal and *Little Tramp* by Fawcett's other line Crest. According to *Publishers Weekly, Little Tramp* was one of Crest's biggest sellers in 1957.

There is a discrepancy between what was popular and what is thought of as his best books. Though it is hard to get two people to agree on what is Gil's best, they will rarely cite his most popular titles. One title that *is* commonly cited as his best novel is *The Red Scarf.* The novel was rejected by Gold Medal and purchased by Mercury Mystery Book-Magazine in February 1955 for $400.00. It would have sold for five times that amount if Gold Medal had accepted it. Commercial success does not always translate into critical success.

As the 1950s and 1960s faded into the past, it was the authors who developed series characters (the Travis McGees and the Matt Helms), who became the names of the genre. Brewer's stand-alone noir thrillers were a key ingredient of Gold Medal's early success and the paperback original boom of the 1950s, but by 1955 with the mushrooming sales of Richard Prather's Shell Scott, and the start of two popular series—Edward S. Aaron's Sam Durell and Stephen Marlowe's Chester Drum—the tide had turned to detective and spy fiction. Gil tried his hand at more traditional private eye types—*Wild* (1958) featured private eye Lee Baron and *The Bitch* (also, 1958) offered the private detective team, Sam and Tate Morgan—but the traditional hardboiled detective never seemed to hold his interest. His fate and career was tied to noir.

More is known about Gilbert John Brewer than his father, Gilbert T.

There are several biographical pieces published. Besides Verlaine's article, there is also Bill Pronzini's "Forgotten Writers: Gil Brewer," which originally appeared in *Mystery Scene* magazine. A couple of newspaper pieces also exist – "Gil Brewer – Profile of an Author: Writing Is His Work and His Hobby" by Marianne Kelsey (*St. Petersburg Independent,* April 14, 1967) and "Gil Brewer Writes to Live and Lives to Write" by Richard Hill (*Tallahassee Floridian,* July 20, 1969). There is a critical biographical piece by Tim Dayton entitled "Gil Brewer" for *Dictionary of Literary Biography.* Of these articles, Verlaine Brewer's piece seems the most "straight and true." Pronzini's article is very good, but he purposely focuses on the negatives in Gil's life. Verlaine's piece is more balanced and probably more accurately captures the real person. Gil's life wasn't all darkness. Dorrie Lee, Verlaine's daughter-in-law offers some insight:

> Gil was a very interesting family member. He loved to come to dinner and attended all of the band concerts our two children were involved with. He also painted, played the organ and trumpet, and of course, read everything. He could talk with anyone about any subject and everyone always enjoyed having him around. That is, when he would venture out from his home. He kept the place dark and very, very cold. He and Verlaine, who was also a writer, but mainly an artist and musician, had a loving marriage. Of course, his bouts with alcoholism took their toll, but she hung in there with him through it all.

Not everything in Gil Brewer's life was noir. He had Verlaine.

Clarkston, GA
July 2007

Stark HouJe PreJJ